1001

ᴛhe Qaraq,

Book One

of

The Reincarnation Chronicles

by
Stephen Weinstock

A Qaraq Book.

Excerpts from ARABIAN NIGHTS, translated by Zack Zipes, translation
copyright © 1991 by Jack Zipes. Used by permission of Dutton Signet, a
division of Penguin Group (USA) LLC.

The translation of the Ronsard poem in Chapter 24 is by Andrew Lang,
from Ballads and Lyrics of Old France, Longman's Pocket Library, 1907.

Author Photograph: Scott Allen
Cover Art: Gabriel Weinstock

Qaraq Books
17 Sommer Ave.
Glen Ridge, NJ 07028

DEDICATION

To Sarah,
not Sahara, Silvie Saintonge, or any other incarnation,
just Sarah, my soul mate.

THE WORLDS MOST FULLY REVEALED IN BOOK ONE

THE SASSANID INCARNATIONS

Uzmeth, 140-year-old Sassanid Queen	Ooma
Dinzadeh, slave of Uzmeth	Diana
Ba'ash, slave and favorite of Uzmeth	Bax
Shah Zabar, Sassanid Prince	Zack
Ardryashir, slave to Uzmeth	Amar
Sharzad, daughter of Sassanid vizier	Sahara
Homma, an Indian elephant in Baghdad	Ooma

THE RED ISLE INCARNATIONS

Oumkratania, Queen of the Red Isle	Ooma
Roukh, ally of the Queens of the Red Isle	Bax
Sahnra, Goddess of the Red Isle	Sahara
Zanaj, the thief on the beach	Naji
(Zananzi, African trader	Naji)
Ambanari, God of the Red Isle	Amar
Khajy, Queen of the Red Isle	Cachay
D'aulai, Queen of the Red Isle	Diana
Zancq, son of priestess of the Red Isle	Zack
Vaalat, xalaphon, Instrument of the Red Isle	Verle

THE GEOLOGICAL INCARNATIONS

Vaalbara, primal landmass	Sahara
Seed-bearing plant, Carboniferous Period	Bax
Clumsy seed-bearing plant, Carboniferous Period	Porcy
Plant fossilized into a vein of coal	Porcy
Gondwanan at settling of South Pole	Amar
D'n-Gwn, Gondwanan chosen by Licgh Nuo	Diana
Ice Mountain, end of Gondwanaland	Ooma
Sea Bird, end of Gondwanaland	Verle

THE THIRTY YEARS WAR INCARNATIONS

Dike, The Zyp, Low Countries	Zack
Army camp follower, 30 Years War	Diana
Deserting soldier, 30 Years War	Amar
Sondre, refugee in 30 Years War	Sahara
Nils, six-year-old boy in 30 Years War	Naji
The Idea, Donne's room-as-the-universe	Naji

THE DRAGONFLY INCARNATIONS

Egg	Naji
Nymph-body	Sahara
Chitin Armor	Amar
Right Eye	Diana
Left Eye	Ooma
Front Wings	Zack
Back Wings	Porcy
Brain	Verle
Oversoul	Cachay
Animal Fossil, fused with Dragonfly fossil	Bax

ALL WORLDS REVEALED
IN *BOOK ONE*

10 - Dragonfly
9 - The Red Isle
8 - Gondwanaland/pre-Stone Age
7 - Persia/Mideast
6 - 30 Years War/Donne Idea
5 - Borzu + North-South Winds
4 - Story collection or Interlife tales
3 - China, The Seven Palaces
2 - 1500s France or Suburb
1* - Tree or Atom tale
Plus: 15 - 'lives within present lifetime' stories

* 1-10, 15 = number of lifetime stories appearing in Book One

ق

The Tale of Scheherazade and Shahryar

Once there was a mighty King of the Banu Sasan named Shahryar, who ruled with generosity and fairness. Shahryar expressed a strong desire to see his younger brother Shah Zaman, who ruled far away in Samarkand. After Shah Zaman made the long journey, Shahryar invited his brother on a hunt, but Shah Zaman declined, preferring to sit by the palace windows that overlooked the garden. As he rested he saw Shahryar's wife enter the garden through a secret door with twenty slave girls. To his shock he watched as the Queen and the slaves stripped off their clothes by the fountain, revealing that they were ten women and ten men. Then Shahryar's wife called out and a huge man named Sa'eed jumped down from the trees. He tossed the Queen to the ground and mounted her, as the male slaves enjoyed the girls. They satisfied themselves until sunset and then left through the secret door, except for Sa'eed, who climbed the tree and leapt over the palace wall.

When Shahryar returned from the hunt his brother Shah Zaman told him all that had transpired. Furious, Shahryar demanded that his brother prove his damning statements. So in a few days the King and his brother pretended to go hunting, but instead hid themselves in view of the garden. Once again Shahryar's wife and the slaves were joined by Sa'eed and satisfied their lusts for hours in the garden.

Despondent, Shahryar and his brother renounced their kingdoms and went off in search of someone suffering the same misfortune. Soon they met a woman enslaved by a jinnee, who coerced them to lay with her while the jinnee slept. She claimed that in revenge for her treatment by the jinnee she had lain with five hundred and seventy men. Marveling that a powerful jinnee suffered an even greater misfortune than his own, Shahryar vowed to never stay married long enough to be betrayed again.

Saying farewell to his brother, Shahryar returned to his kingdom, ordered his vizier to execute his wife, and slew all his concubines and their male slaves with his own sword. As he had vowed, during the next three years the King married a maiden every night and commanded his vizier to kill her the next morning. The people raised a great outcry against the King and parents fled with their daughters until there was not a single virgin left in the city. Fearing for his life, the vizier searched all over, becoming more and more distressed.

The vizier had two daughters, Scheherazade and Dunyazade. It was said that the older one, Scheherazade, had collected a thousand books and had read all the stories, histories, poems, philosophy and science contained within them. When Scheherazade saw her father's distress and learned of his plight, she asked, "How long will this slaughter of women last? Give me in marriage to Shahryar, that I may rescue the virgin daughters." The vizier refused, but Scheherazade insisted stubbornly until her father approached the King. The King, who had held Scheherazade exempt from his bloody practice, warned that the minister would have to kill his daughter the next day.

When Scheherazade heard that the King agreed to marry her she rejoiced. She planned with her sister Dunyazade to divert the King from his evil deed. That night, as the King prepared to penetrate Scheherazade, she began to cry. When the King asked her what was wrong, Scheherazade begged to see her sister for the last time. Dunyazade was allowed to sit at the foot of the couch while the King took his bride's maidenhead. Later, she asked Scheherazade to tell a marvelous story. Pleased with the idea, the King granted permission and Scheherazade, rejoicing inside, began her tale. When dawn arrived, she broke off in the middle and asked the King to spare her life so that she could finish the next night. Eager to hear the end of the story, the King agreed. The following night Dunyazade sat at the foot of the nuptial bed and after the lovemaking requested the end of the story. When dawn approached the King granted Scheherazade another night to continue her storytelling. In this way Scheherazade prolonged her life for a thousand and one nights.

During that time Scheherazade gave the King three sons and told him many stories full of moral lessons of admonition. Finally, she pleaded for her life for the sake of the children. Weeping, the King told her that he had pardoned her even before their first child had been born. He had never stopped blaming himself for his past actions and praised Scheherazade for rescuing the women of his kingdom. He brought his viziers and emirs together to prepare for an elaborate wedding, and the people rejoiced at the celebrations. Shahryar's brother Shah Zaman came from Samarkand and asked to be wed to Dunyazade as part of the festivities. In due time Shahryar summoned chroniclers to write down all that had happened. That is the origin of The Stories of the Thousand and One Nights.

PART ONE

1

—◦◦◦—

Sahara Fleming reacted with a start. She opened her eyes and saw the familiar fountain in the patio of her house. She must have drifted off. An hour ago Sahara had been studying her Arabic text of *The Thousand and One Nights*; now she bent down to pick up the heavy volume of *Alf Layla wa Layla* and replaced it on her legs. Hadn't she barely opened the book to the first words, 'A long time ago there was a mighty King'? Or had she read further into the Scheherazade story, the frame tale of the Arabian Nights? Why had her mind flooded with images? A talking baby? What a dream! She thought back to it.

Momma! It's me! I'm here!
What? Who is it? Where are you?
I'm in you. We're together now.
Inside me? Is it really you?
Yes! Aren't you happy, Momma?
Of course, my darling. I'm sorry, I'm so tired. I was falling asleep.
I know. Half-asleep, half-awake. It's the best time to reach you.
Have you been here all the time?

No, no. I just got here. Didn't you feel it?

Yes! The jolt woke me up. But I'm not awake, am I? Where are we?

Silly, Momma, we're inside your mind. Where else would we be?

Heavens, how would I know, sweetheart? Where have you been all this time?

I've been very busy. There's so much work to do!

What are you talking about?

Everyone's together again. In the same place! I'm the last one to arrive.

Who's everyone?

The qaraq, Momma! It's been centuries since we've all met.

Centuries? This is all very strange. Please help me understand, baby.

Poor Momma. They said you wouldn't remember anything. I didn't believe it. You have the best memory of all of us. You've had it since the Oldest World. I'll show you!

What are you doing to me? What am I seeing? It looks like an elephant.

You're funny, Momma. That's you! You and Vieldra. She gave you Retention.

Of memories? Wait, what's this? Some sort of glyphs?

The zojy, Momma! You foretold them.

Slow down, baby. What's this? *This* looks familiar. Medieval scribes? Arabic?

The stories, Momma! It's the qaraq putting together the Nights.

The Thousand and One Nights? How do you know about that? How do you know I study the origins of the Nights?

I know everything. I haven't been born yet. I haven't forgotten everything like you have. Don't worry, Momma, you'll know everything again. Look!

Is that Vieldra again? With me? She's saying goodbye? Where am I going?

Away! Forever! You figure out everything. Yay, Momma!

What do I figure out?

If I knew, do you think I'd be inside you, coming back for more?

You don't want to be born? Don't say that! Not after what I've just been through.

I'm sorry, Momma. I know it's been hard. But it's going to be all right. It's going to be great! We're all here and we're going to remember everything and make new stories and we're going to get the zojy and the Nights back on track because everything is possible. I can't wait to be born!

I can't wait either. You're … incredible! I love you, baby. Can I see you?

Here I am, Momma. Look!

Sahara had looked in her minds' eye again and saw a dark, womblike space, but she could not see her child. She called out but she no longer heard the voice. She examined the dark place more closely, searching, yearning, and felt drawn into it. With the child's strange words still echoing in her mind, she entered into a place of deep memory, a place between waking and sleeping, between life and death, or death and rebirth. She saw the zojy in front of her, or were they Arabic letters? She saw an elephant figure, but it was a decoration on a palace wall. Then a strange scene unfolded in front of the mother, like something out of a story from *The Thousand and One Nights*.

The dark space was now a room, a tiny, hidden room, an alcove. It was cramped and uncomfortable to her body. There was someone next to her in the alcove, obscured by the murky gloom. In front of her was a slat of light, a spyhole into a larger room. She knew it was important for her to look into the room, but she was afraid. Then the other person thrust her face up to the viewing hole. She gazed upon a hideous sight, and the entire memory coursed through her mind.

The Tale of Sharzad and Dinzadeh in the Alcove

Through the viewing slat I saw the unfortunate Purzai lying motionless on a bloodstained bed, the naked figure of Ardryashir astride her. The old Queen watched from a plush bench, sucking on a fingernail. Purzai was one of the last women left in the kingdom.

In one quick gesture, Ardryashir drew the curved blade from her throat.

I wrenched my head away. Crammed in beside me in the alcove, the Queen's slave Dinzadeh gripped my hair, forcing me to witness the terrible scene.

"You see, Sharzad!" she hissed in my ear. "You believe me now? It is Queen Uzmeth who wills this desecration." Dinzadeh had brought countless young women into the harem. Each one had disappeared. "Uzmeth is mad. She has lived over one hundred and forty years. She has preserved her body with wild, unspeakable practices."

"Forcing her lover to ravish helpless virgins?" I asked. "Watching him kill them?"

"This is why I brought you, Sharzad, to see for yourself."

"You risked my life! The Queen is inches away from us." I shook off Dinzadeh's grip on my hair. "How dare you! You are the slave. My father was the vizier."

4

"Yes, *was*. You are kept safely in the palace only by the good graces of Shahanshah Bahram IV and the Sassanid court. I am here to warn you, Sharzad."

"You are the handmaiden to the devil. Why would I trust you?"

"I hate obliging Uzmeth. How could any woman watch her sisters violated like this? You must believe that much of me. But I am afraid, Sharzad. The old Queen is more deranged than ever. Come away from your books and help me!"

I considered Dinzadeh's request. Ever since my father the vizier had died I had locked myself away in the palace libraries, pouring over histories, reading the ancient collections of myths from Hind and Alexandria, memorizing the local Persian tales. I was not expected to participate in the activities of the harem, and with all the chaos of the court around me, I enjoyed the peace and solitude.

My thoughts were disturbed by a noise from Uzmeth's room. With bitter words, Ardryashir commanded slaves to remove Purzai's mutilated body.

"He is the one you must seek, Sharzad," Dinzadeh whispered. "Ardryashir is the way to the Queen."

"Ardryashir is Uzmeth's demon lover. How could I get near him without suffering the same fate as every woman in Persia? You have put me in a terrible position, slave."

"Forgive me, but you are the only way out. You are the only female left in the palace who is neither slave, wife, nor child." Dinzadeh looked me deeply in the eye. "I know our situations have prevented us from being close. But by joining forces we can defeat this enemy, we can save the rest of the empire's children. I have the key to Uzmeth's secrets, and you have some secret knowledge – I know you do – some knowledge you have found in all your books."

Dinzadeh's words stirred within me an inner strength, a courage, to rescue this poor land. But what power did I have to do so, what ability? I could recall story after story from my readings, recount captivating lifetimes that reached back into times before memory. What good was this ability to defeat Queen Uzmeth, to win over Ardryashir, to save my people?

A vision of a higher power came into the mind of Sharzad, as it came into Sahara's mind. It was a power that had always initiated the important experiences of her soul. She saw a primordial being from the Oldest World give her this power, the gift of accessing memories of the deep past. At the moment of this empowering vision, Sharzad wondered if she had received this gift or if it was someone else, and Sahara wondered if Sharzad had received this gift or if it was herself. Was she Sharzad? Was she still dreaming? Everything was as obscure and ominous as the darkened alcove.

Suddenly Ardryashir shouted at Queen Uzmeth. My vision shattered, as did my inner resolve to save the land. I confronted Dinzadeh. "What am I to do? Must I risk my life for the slim chance to save others?"

Dinzadeh looked away from me and through the slat at Ardryashir. "Take the risk or not. Either way you are in peril. There are no more victims for me to procure from the land." She looked back at me. "You are next."

ق

Sahara had concocted some parallel version of the Scheherazade tale in her mind. Unconsciously, she stroked the large volume resting on her legs. As she thought through images from her fantasy she recognized the plight of the virgins and their daily demise from the ancient tale, as well as Scheherazade's dire need to rescue the land from further danger. But there were many differences. From her Middle Eastern studies, Sahara knew that in an early, Persian version of the tale, Scheherazade's sister Dunyazade appeared as a slave, like Dinzadeh in Sahara's rendition. But who was this ancient Queen Uzmeth? Who was her lover, Ardryashir? Why the depraved murders?

Most of all, Sahara Fleming wondered why the tale had seemed so vivid and real to her, more than a dream, as if she herself had hunched down in that dark alcove. Her head was still spinning from the experience; she clutched the book to her belly and bent over to breathe.

It was starting again. The stories, the visions – they were coming back.

2

The Tale of Sahnra and the Thief on the Beach

I am the new of the old.

I am this age's daughter of the keeper of the Vessel of the sacred Sound.

I am Sahnra, Goddess, unfledged fury, Protectress of the numinous Instrument. I have crossed the sea to savage the thief, to take back what is mine, to unpollute the Great Vessel. I followed him to an island halfway between our Red Isle and the mainland. The skeleton crew who had brought him there fled at my approach, tossing the Vessel out of their boat. The thief shouted curses at the crew fading into the horizon, all the while running up and down the beach, frantically searching for the holy article. Once he retrieved it, the profaner collapsed in the sand and seawater, clutching It to his breast.

As I hovered quietly over his form, this transgressor appeared as innocent as a sleeping child. Ready to strike, I moved in, but my anger washed away like the waves on the beach. If I am the new Daughter, and not the Mother, why did I feel nurturance and warmth in the pit of my center?

When I lifted the sleeping man in my arms, he awoke, struggling to hold onto the Vessel. The slime of sandy salt water made it easy for him to slip from my grasp.

I released my hair.

The power of my sand-red hair is legendary among the people of the Red Isle. It has the physical strength of the heartiest of fibers and the quickness and agility of a springing mountain cat. To be enwrapped in my red coils is to lay your soul bare to me. I can look into your memories, deep into your childhood, and further.

I uncoiled one of the longer tresses and wrapped it around the man's arms. As he continued to squirm I spiraled three curls to his face, winding them around his ears, behind his neck, and through his disheveled hair. Only then did he stare up at me in wonder.

"I am the Goddess Sahnra. You have profaned my temple and corrupted the Vessel contained within."

"It was already corrupt, your temple already desecrated. My only wish was –"

A razor sharp coil lashed him. "How dare you speak thus! You are a common thief."

"I take back what is rightfully mine! I am no –"

Again I stung his face. "Goddess! You will call me Goddess!"

The thief winced in pain. "Goddess – I intend no blasphemy. Your worshippers have done enough of that."

His insolence would not cease! My followers adhered strictly to the ancient rituals and ablutions. Yes, I was a new incarnation of the Protectress, but I knew that the sacred rites had existed as far back as Queen Oumkratania's reign on the Red Isle.

"What accusation are you leveling against my people?" I spun a tress tighter around his neck. "For your indignities you deserve death, but if you are lying your death will be gruesome and torturous."

"Just kill me and be done. Goddess."

"If you do not wish to tell me what you have to say, I will find out myself. I can probe into your mind." Enlacing his entire body with my hair, I tugged him closer to me, unleashed my probing energies, and searched deep within him. As he whimpered in anguish, I saw a flash of bronze, a haughty woman looking down, and a ship with fluttering sails. With each image I plucked from his mind, a new shot of agony pierced through him.

"Goddess, I swear to you I am an innocent!"

"Then speak your accusations or I will wrest them from your mind and whittle your life down to nothing." Once more I looked inside him, this time as deeply as I could. I was surprised by an image of myself cuddling a young child. I felt I had been with this child many, many times. Was it really me? Impossible!

"Goddess! Stop! I will tell you everything!"

"If you wish peace, show me one difficult truth from your tale."

"Very well, Goddess. It will expose a layer of dark rot among your people. You are only among them now because your predecessor was vilely destroyed. Behold."

I curled my hair around his head and looked into his memory. Clearly as the feel of sand on my skin I saw the great Instrument hanging proudly in its shrine. An incredibly tall man approached it, carrying an enormous mallet. Next to him stood a beautiful figure whom I recognized as the previous Goddess. As the man prepared himself, a dark female figure emerged behind the Goddess. She held a curved blade above the Goddess, ready to strike. The memory was completely vivid and real to me. I knew it was the truth.

As the man struck the Instrument with the mallet, the blade pierced the Goddess. The flooding Sound of the sacred Vessel drowned out her scream of shock and horror.

The entire moment ripped through me.

ق

Sahara Fleming woke up, gasping for air. Where was she? Persia? The Red Isle? In her panic, she tried to breathe, tried to recognize something in the dark. Then she saw the dim nighttime light coming in through the familiar curtains.

She was at home, in her bedroom, in Glenclaire, New Jersey. It was April, 1999.

Sahara switched on the light to ease her panic.

Her husband, Amar Rash, shifted in the bed next to her. "Jesus, Sahr, what's going on? You all right?"

She took several deep breaths. Her hand unconsciously went to her hair; a finger curled the reddish blond tangle.

Amar squinted in the light. "Another nightmare?"

Sahara did not answer.

"Sahr, you've got to talk about this. You haven't said a word in days."

Sahara exhaled loudly, threw back the covers, and got out of bed. As she fumbled for her slippers, she felt her husband watching her, sensed his anger rising. Amar Rash was a man used to making quick, confident decisions – he did not take well to this uncertainty.

"Sahr, just tell me you're okay. What am I supposed to do? Do you think it's a good idea to visit my family, to go away for a while? Would that be better?"

Sahara cocooned her slender frame in an oversized bathrobe.

"Sahara!" He pounded his fist on the nightstand. "Damn it!"

As Sahara rushed out of the room, Amar Rash picked up a book and hurled it against the wall.

3

Sahara had stopped speaking to her husband two weeks before, at the end of March. Night after night he had pushed her to say something, but now things had reached an impasse. Either they sank into a deep silence before sleep, or Amar stalked off to sleep in the den, to punish Sahara with solitude, or Sahara fled the bedroom herself. A day did not go by without her on the verge of leaving home. Fearing his potential violence, she kept him at a distance with her silence.

"It's not working, Sahr," Amar said, after dinner the next night. "I'm tired of getting mad – I know you're tired of it, too, that's the whole point, right?" Amar waited till Sahara took the plates into the kitchen, and then he brought in the rest of the dinner things. He stood behind her at the sink, longing to wrap himself around her.

But the kitchen was sensitive territory to them. This is where the terrible thing had happened two weeks ago. Amar placed the dishes on the counter next to the sink.

"Your terms, Sahr, whatever you want to talk about – what's wrong with me, the bad dreams, you name it." He walked out of the kitchen – he would let her think about it.

Sahara agonized over Amar's magnanimous invitation while she did the dishes. She invented extra chores so she could procrastinate the choice she knew was inevitable now. She was not ready to discuss all the issues with Amar: that was still too dangerous. There must be another way to break the ice.

Sahara found him on the couch in the living room, neutral territory. As simply as possible she said, "I'd like to tell you a story."

"Is this one of your dreams?" Amar asked.

"I just want to tell you a story."

"Like a fairy tale? 'There was a king who had two sons, one in the prime of manhood' – that sort of thing?"

"You're making it hard. You wanted me to talk, I'm talking. My terms."

"Sorry. I was just curious. Is it about us?"

"After what happened, you're lucky I'm even here."

"Fine," he bristled, "tell me a story."

Sahara sensed his anger and sat in the armchair farthest from the couch. "It came to me this morning, while I was outside trying to meditate." Sahara remembered the cool April air, the early spring sun on the patio, a perfect environment for meditation. But her mind was too uneasy and wandered from reverie to reverie. "Maybe it was the breeze rippling the water in the fountain, or the mix of cool and warm air, that brought on the story."

Amar gave her one of those looks that had made her fall in love with him. A deep, piercing gaze, a fascinated excitement, at what she was about to reveal.

She took a breath, closed her eyes, and began.

14

The Tale of the Two Winds

Consider the North and South winds, coming at each other from their respective Arctic and equatorial corners. The cold Northern air loves to rush down and invade the hot air at the equator and push it upward into the atmosphere. The hot Southern air rises above it all and then gets pulled northward. As the North wind heats up down at the equator, the South wind cools its breezes in the Arctic. The cold North wind becomes the hot South wind and visa versa.

Safe! This madman continues to pursue me, trying to throw me out with icy blows. He is a demon! As soon as I settle back here he shoves me away; where else am I to go but his frigid place, but then he comes stalking me up there. I vow never to leave my beloved desert again, hugging the waist of the world. But it is no use: I confront him, I get sand kicked in my face, and my stubbornness only perpetuates the hot and cold cycle.

After a while, who is really who? As the South wind, if I am a fiery redhead, do I become a deeply quiet blonde when I reach the Arctic Circle? When that cold-blooded killer moves south into my territory, does he also take up my overheated temper?

I was blowing along the top of a dune, praying for an end to these perpetual mood swings. I felt that nagging pressure creep up from behind – his familiar approach. I calmed my sirocco forces. Is it so bad, this relentless visitation, this dependable harassment? After all, he gives more attention to me than to the ice mountains up north.

He huffed up pillars of sand that made strange shapes in the sky. An image swirled about me of an errant, unfaithful husband who abandons his family. As my nemesis edged toward me, there came a more complex image: a second husband,

15

faithful to his wife, who comes to comfort the abandoned wife of the first husband. But the comforting can only go so far. They are trapped, yet manage to create something out of a disastrous situation.

A huge welling of emotion came over me from this unforeseen image. Did I want such a relationship with the North wind? There he was, two dunes away. It was time to fight, or to vanish up into the sky. It dawned on me that I had no interest in another fight, even if the outcome was remaining happily where I was in the hot desert.

I wanted to get away altogether! I felt a great longing to search the world, a deep need that had been buried under miles of sand. If I did not escape this imprisoning fate and set out for places unknown, my soul would shrivel up and die. As the North wind swept down, I let the pressure of the cold air push me high into the sky as I had done countless times before. I rose gleefully, not looking back at the northern violator with his chilling eye. Instead, I gazed down at the vast planet, a playground for seeking.

I wheeled away to the east. Letting go of any air pulling me North I formed a new, freer wind. I reached the coast by nightfall, slept in the grasses, and in the morning, moved out to sea.

ق

Amar Rash sat on the edge of the couch, listening intently to the end of his wife's story. His anger had washed away, and in its place came an old comforting emotion. A mix of Indian and Persian descent, Amar had grown up hearing ancient legends at bedtime. His mother Udeni loved the story cycles of India and the Near East. Sahara's curious tale triggered a deep nostalgia in Amar, as well as a curious wonder.

16

"Who are you?" Amar stood up with the impulse to embrace his wife. "That was fantastic – where does it come from?"

As Amar approached her, Sahara instinctually rose from the chair and moved toward the stairs at the other side of the living room. "I don't know. I don't recognize any source."

Amar also did not remember any such tale from his childhood. He knew that if Sahara, a scholar of ancient mythology, could not place the story, then it must have a different kind of origin. "Is it like a dream, like your inner thoughts?" Amar's face wrinkled. "Is this about our crummy relationship right now? Are you the South wind? Are you leaving me?"

"I can't do this now, Amar." Sahara escaped up the stairs to the bedroom, leaving her husband alone. Hurt by her departure, Amar struggled to hold down his anger, resisted the urge to follow her upstairs.

All he wanted was another story.

Sahara Fleming had broken her silence with the tale of the two Winds, but she went no further. Discussing the relevance of her visions to their marital problems meant risking Amar's volatile anger. She communicated only essentials: dinnertime, phone messages, a dental appointment. Amar tolerated this standoff tensely. Knowing what he had done, and sensing her fear, he had no choice but to accept her attitude.

The best defense against lingering terror is to keep busy with trivial absurdities. After a life on four continents as a free spirit, Sahara's change to suburban housewife in Glenclaire, New Jersey had been encumbering. But now she threw herself into the unending details of daily life to mask the pain deep within her. Dry cleaning meant searching for a misplaced ticket. Groceries meant finding fresh tarragon only at the fourth store. Cooking meant sponging up every spill before moving on to the next task. All were blessings.

Thank God it was April. She cherished hikes in the Glenclaire hills even though sometimes the quiet brought on troubled thoughts. She took her orange tabby cat, Sherry, for walks on Glenedge Boulevard. This enterprise was slow, with

Sherry raiding neighbors' shrubs, backtracking, darting forward a few yards.

One morning her neighbor called to her. "Another marathon with Sherry?"

Sahara had liked Zack Goodkin instantly when she moved in next door. She had had trepidations about giving up the cultural richness of New York City. Although white, she had grown up in places like Morocco and Egypt. She and Amar had chosen Glenclaire for its diverse population. Zack, an African-American with mixed parentage and a collector of artifacts from Asia and the Middle East, had eased these concerns when they first met. It was a lucky sign that by coincidence Amar had known Zack as a child in New York.

Zack's easy going manner was a relief to her current state of mind. "Got caffeine?" He pulled several shopping bags out of the trunk of his car. "I can dump these Javanese tree frogs in a quick minute if you do." Sahara pulled Sherry out of Zack's rock garden and motioned toward her house. Five minutes later she was brewing a fresh pot of coffee.

"So when's your next party?" Zack asked. "Maybe I'll get invited this time."

"I'm never inviting you to anything. It's more fun when you crash it." Sahara grinned at the memory of Zack and his boyfriend Jeffrey showing up the night of a party with several bottles of Amontillado, wearing graduation caps and gowns.

"We thought it was Sherry Hour," Zack joked, petting the cat.

"You still seeing Jeffrey?"

"No, that one's over. He couldn't handle the burbs. But it's cool." Zack ran his hand over his shaved head. "Did I mention he's an asshole?"

"There's got to be a zillion guys out there just waiting for you."

"Just looking for one good man now. Or so my therapist says."

"You have a therapist?"

"Doesn't everyone? She's above that New Age shop on Abbey Street."

Sahara had considered therapy but was afraid to broach the subject with Amar. And confusion and shame made it difficult to reveal her need to Zack. She tried humor.

"You have a therapist for love advice? I'm not good enough? Who is this gem?"

"Listen, Dr. Machiyoko is incredible. She had me yapping and sobbing and healing from Day One." Zack looked straight into Sahara's eyes. Could he tell she was interested for herself? As she looked back at him, a strange sense of recognition came over her.

The next day Sahara went downtown to Abbey Street. She entered the building between The Crystal Charm and Forever Young shops and found a small waiting area outside the office of Dr. Diana Machiyoko. She sat down, adjusted the shawl that enveloped her, played with a strand of hair, and ran through what she would say. As she summoned her courage, the office door opened. A head with straight bangs poked out.

"Sahara? I am Dr. Machiyoko. Please come in. I've been expecting you."

The therapist ushered Sahara into a lovely room, tastefully decorated with Shoji screens. On a table by the door was a simple, exquisite arrangement of flowers.

"How do you know my name? I didn't even call."

"I use a lot of intuitive techniques." Dr. Machiyoko gestured Sahara to a futon couch, and sat down opposite in a stylish gray armchair. "You could say that I'm psychic." She crossed her legs and leaned forward. "And Zack Goodkin told me you were coming." The therapist's serious expression dissolved into a girlish smile. "How can I help you?"

Sahara looked over at Dr. Machiyoko's innocent face, framed by a pageboy haircut, and questioned how much she should tell her. She decided not to plunge into her tale of marital woe, but to test the waters with her more curious problem.

"I've been having some very strange dreams lately. Visions, fantasies that come over me. They bring on very powerful feelings."

"What kinds of feelings?"

"Hard to describe. That's part of their power. The emotions seem so intimate and intense and yet distant and faraway. The vividness is disturbing."

"Disturbing. Is it just because of the sensation, or something else? In your life?"

Dr. Machiyoko was already honing in. Sahara chose her next words carefully. "I moved here two years ago. With my husband, for his career. I was working on a doctorate, but it's been ... difficult to continue." Sahara's throat tightened. "Right now we're barely speaking. The other night I told him one of the visions. It felt like a safer way to talk to him. But now he wants to hear more and it's too –. It's hard to discuss this."

"Let's take it slow," Dr. Machiyoko said. "Tell me about your husband."

Sahara was grateful that the therapist allowed her to back off. "Amar and I met in 1995 at the University of Chicago. I was a grad student at the Oriental Institute and he was in the School of Business. God, it's only four years ago but it feels like another lifetime."

"Let's start with that lifetime then. Tell me how you and Amar met. Close your eyes, make yourself comfortable, and let the tale unfold as if it were one of your visions."

21

Dr. Machiyoko's invitation to tell the story was so genuine that Sahara could not resist. She relaxed back on the futon and let her first encounter with Amar fill her mind.

The Tale of Common Ground

The first time I met Amar Rash was at The Common Ground Cafe. There were hardly any seats and a handsome young man came over to ask if he could share my table. He was East Indian, or perhaps Middle Eastern, with well-groomed hair and dark, compelling eyes. After a few minutes he asked me what language I was reading. He was impressed that a non-Iranian was reading Farsi and I explained that I was doing a doctorate in the Near Eastern Language program. His curiosity about me was charming, but I had work to do; I had decided not to let relationships get in the way of my research. At the same time I felt a familiar feeling of this man being off limits. How could I feel this way about a total stranger? I excused myself and left the cafe.

Over the next weeks I caught a few glimpses of the stranger on campus. Because my childhood had been spent in Morocco, India, and Egypt, I had an affinity for men from those societies. I felt a tingling attraction every time I saw his tall, majestic bearing. Once I ran into him at the bookstore. He greeted me as the honorary Persian with the sunshine hair, and gallantly introduced himself as Amar Rash, an MBA student from India and 56th St. and Lex. When I declined his flirtatious invitation to coffee, he declared that we would meet again with an authoritative wave of his hand. I was taken by his assurance.

I spent most of my time at a study carrel in a corner of the Near Eastern Language stacks in the library. One day I was searching for a book, intently looking at numbers on the spines. When I found my book, I slid it off the shelf, just as someone was pulling a book from the same spot on the other side. I bent forward and peered through the opening where the books had been. I recognized a pair of deep-set eyes. A moment later Amar Rash appeared at my side.

"I've always wanted to kiss a beautiful stranger in the stacks of a library."

"Stranger? I can't get rid of you," I teased.

Amar wasted no time and moved in for the kill. After an explosive foray of kisses we stumbled over to my desk in the hidden alcove. Our hands raced over our bodies. Nearly the same height, we were a perfect fit. But soon a library worker passed by with a creaky book cart and disturbed our passion. We escaped to The Common Ground Cafe.

"So what were you doing, stalking me in the stacks?" I asked him.

Amar laughed. "Honestly, I wasn't. What were you doing?"

"I asked you first."

"Fine. I can't tell you."

I was taken aback by this answer.

"Your turn," he said. "What are you researching?"

"*The Thousand and One Nights.* I'm writing a thesis on its origins."

"Hence the Farsi? The Persian origin of the Thousand and One Tales?"

"If there ever were that many. The whole thousand-and-one thing may have been Western overkill once the Nights hit Europe. The original versions may have been much more contained."

Amar looked at me intensely. "I love this. Just don't forget the Indian sources."

"Of course not, they're at the heart of things." I stroked his leg. "Aren't they?"

I was a goner. A few more flings in the library stacks left us frustrated for more. I coaxed Amar into asking me to a poetry reading of Rumi and some contemporary Persian poets. At the reading, the Rumi poems were full of images targeted for us, such as love as a messenger of mystery. Later at dinner, we laughed at our knowing looks and blushes during the reading.

Amar asked me, "How did you get into all this Arab lit anyway?"

"I was literally born and named in the Sahara. In Morocco. My family traveled a lot, a bunch of hippies. My sister died shortly after our time in North Africa. Later I became attracted to Arabic culture as a search for my roots."

"I'm sorry about your sister," he said, with genuine sympathy. "But if you traveled a lot, did you experience other cultures beside the desert?"

"The desert squeezed out any affinity in me for cold and wet. Though I don't mind Chicago now." I squeezed his hand. "And when I lived in London, I loved the blossoming ethnic scene, the new books and restaurants from India and Arab countries."

"When were you in London?" Amar asked curiously.

"Let's see ... 1979 to '82."

"Jesus, we were there at the same time. Where did you live?"

"Russell Square, by the British Museum."

"We lived about five minutes from each other! How old were you?"

"Ten, eleven."

"I was fourteen. Good thing we didn't meet. I would have gotten you into trouble."

We continued exploring our history on the couch in Amar's tidy bachelor apartment. He opened a bottle of very good wine, a passion he cultivated despite a student budget.

"You still haven't told me why you were stalking me that first day in the stacks."

"I didn't think you'd believe me," he said.

I tucked my legs under me, and leaned back magisterially. "Try me."

"Honestly, I was looking for a copy of the *Panchatartra*."

"The Indian folk-tale cycle?"

"Actually, the cycle within that cycle, the *Vetalapanchavinsati*."

"The King and the Vampire collection. I'm impressed. But you knew I was interested in Persian and Indian stories. Why not just tell me what you were doing?"

"You know how things happen in threes in many tales? Especially things denied until the third time? I got this urge to try out a little fairy tale logic on you."

"But I asked you seventeen times! You have the soul of an Arab trickster."

"Try a Persian Jew."

He told me more about his Indian, Persian, and Jewish background, a perfect match to my own roots and my research. Before the wine took over our brains and bodies, Amar asked me about my passion for The Arabian Nights.

"It's so vast," I said. "There is no book like it; there is no single, true version of it: every version changes it, adds stories, rewrites stories. It's been a living, breathing organism for over a thousand years."

"I love it when you talk about living breathing organisms." Amar continued to stroke long lines on my arms. "Go on."

25

"Today it's still alive. There's new scholarship, new structural approaches. It's a hot field."

"I love it when you talk about hot fields."

"And," I purred, "the tales are sensual, full of rich decoration, sumptuous food, and freewheeling, rampant sex." I gave into the inevitable and pulled Amar onto me. As we made love, finally free of clothes, everything about my life felt right. I had found an exotic lover, a soul mate connected to everything I loved. Pure physical joy overcame me.

Then something amazing happened. As soon as our breathing slowed to normal, there was a profound Silence. I've felt these moments a few times in my life, when time seems to come to a stop. At the end of a powerful piece of music there is that reverberating Silence. On a midday bus, you nod off for a few seconds, and when you awake you have a fresh burst of awareness. The ocean shore has similar breaks in sound, every four or five waves, when the whoosh of water stops for a moment of awed Silence.

As I lay next to Amar, that heightened moment of Silence was filled with feelings of rightness and love: "This is it, this is where my life is going, this is my man."

5

Sahara finished her story and opened her eyes. She was unsettled by Dr. Machiyoko, who was no longer sitting in the gray armchair. The therapist had brought a stool over to the futon and was sitting at Sahara's feet, peering intently at her new client.

"The origins of your relationship sound perfectly romantic. What happened?"

"Amar asked me to marry him. He finished school, received a position at Bruckner Associates in the World Trade Center, and we moved to New York. I was left with setting up our apartment. Then we moved here because so many clients and colleagues lived in the suburbs. Between moving, decorating, and entertaining, I haven't touched my thesis."

"So you resent being kept from your work? Is this the source of your troubles?"

"It's part of it. But ... there's also ... a month ago ..." Sahara could not continue.

Dr. Machiyoko returned to the gray armchair. "Why are you having these visions?"

"Maybe to get my personal needs back into my life. The fantastical stories force me back to the Nights, to my research. When I broke my silence with Amar, my first instinct was to tell him a story, to force *him* to deal with my work, not just his."

"These stories are very important to you. It's crucial you let them out. Tell more of them to Amar. These stories are a key to your marriage. And much more."

When the session ended Sahara questioned why Dr. Machiyoko had put emphasis on the stories. Wasn't her marriage the big crisis? But it had been her choice to start with the visions, to test the therapist. She decided Dr. Machiyoko had passed the test.

Sahara did not tell Amar she had seen a therapist, but that night she was more open with him. After dinner they settled into the living room couch and she told him the story of the Goddess Sahnra and the theft of the sacred Vessel. Amar was spellbound.

"What's the Red Isle?" he asked. "I don't recognize it from any legends I know."

"The wrestling on the beach is like the Greek Proteus myth," she said, "but that's it."

The long, enwrapping hair of the Goddess reminded Amar of his wife's gorgeous light red tresses; he had allowed himself to get wrapped up in them many times. And yet he did not see himself as the thief. "I love these stories. Will you tell me another?"

Sahara played nervously with her hair. The other story was Sharzad witnessing Ardryashir's violence against the women of Sassanid Persia. It was a reference to Scheherazade, and the King who would murder her if she did not tell him part of a story every night. Too close for comfort.

"Don't be greedy," she said. "Scheherazade's husband only got a bit of story each night."

"Don't play this game. If you're not going to talk to me in a normal way, at least tell me what you're going through. You've been overrun by these things, right?"

"No, not overrun," she half-lied, "I just can't predict when my mind is hit by an image. And it's incredibly vivid. I go somewhere when it happens. It's like I've lived in that world."

"One more story? Don't punish me. What's it going to take to redeem myself?"

"Amar, don't, I can't do this yet –"

"So I have to wait till you're ready to stoop to tell me a fucking story."

"This is the problem, I tell you too much and you fly off again."

"No, dammit, you tell me too *little* and I fly off. And I don't 'fly off' – you piss me off."

Amar was up from the couch now, pacing. Sahara felt a need to leave the room.

"Okay, tell me something about the story you just told. It was the nightmare, right?"

"Yes. I woke up when the knife struck the Goddess. Satisfied?"

"Don't mock me. I want to help, believe it or not. What else bothered you?"

"The thief. He feels like .. a child to me. I'm afraid of what I'm going to do to him."

"Because you're strangling him? Who is the child?" Sahara did not answer. "Don't do this! You need help!" He was dangerously close now. "*I need help!*"

Amar's words sent a stab of heat up her spine. When had he said that before? Her head spun. She felt she was entering his brain. She heard a name: *Ambanari*. She saw whirling sand. Blinding sun. "Amar ... I'm having one ... " Amar

29

watched as his wife's eyes rolled upward. He grabbed her as she fell and helped her down on the couch.

"Sahr, Sahr! Speak to me," he said.

In a strange voice, lower than her own, proud and forceful, Sahara spoke.

The Tale of the Boukh and the Desert Sky Battle

What is my sister Sahnra thinking? I have to recover the precious objects before the desert engulfs them. By now the vast region known as Sauhra, named after its Goddess-creator, has become pure, powerful desert. Sands keep emerging from under tree after grass after water hole, and keep shifting relentlessly with an unsettled force. Within minutes of dropping an object in any one place, it would disappear along with any other landmarks that might identify its position.

What was lost? My sister has been keeper of the Vessels over the centuries, and she can identify each and every one. As a child-God, I used to sneak into her forbidden sanctuary; if caught, they would put poor boy Ambanari into a freezing spell or send bad boy Ambanari among mortals for a moon or two. The punishments did not stop my pranks as the adult-God Ambanari. But I do not know the latest collection of holy relics in the sanctuary, and this inability makes finding the lost pieces difficult.

I need help.

I will call upon our ancient friend, the roukh, legendary bird that terrifies voyagers in the Indian and South Pacific seas. It is demonized for its enormous size and over-protectiveness

30

of its young. It is said that the huge winged creature comes from our Red Isle, and is commonly known as the elephant bird. Rumors are rusted truths: the roukh does spend many a happy hour with us on the island but in actuality comes up from further south; and the elephant bird, native to our shores, cannot fly to save its long neck. The roukh, on the other hand, not only can fly, but also can lift an elephant in its talons – elephant, not elephant bird – and fly away with ease.

Along with his enormous strength, the roukh has impeccable eyesight at great distances. To spot a buried bronze object in the vast sand sea of Sauhra from a giddy height is impossible; for a roukh it is but a challenge. For my roukh, the one who has been devoted to me since I was young God Ambanari of the Red Isle, this challenge was accepted with glee and excitement. Making preparations, I tied two small samples of bronze, one burnished, one bright, around the roukh's legs. The roukh soared for days above the Sauhra looking for any sign of a bronze object below.

I dare not let the roukh too far out of my sight, for fear that if it sees an object the shifting sand might cover it up in the next moment. I enjoy taking the form of various atmospheric phenomena – snowclouds, lightning, hail – and so I have transformed into a patch of clouds high above Sauhra. Since clouds are a rare occurrence in the desert sky, the roukh can find me immediately if it sights anything.

I wait for days. Not wanting my clouds to evaporate, I constantly moisten them with my God-sized sweat. The likelihood of rain increases. I laugh because my sister inhabits the soul of the desert and I take delight in sprinkling her with a little shower.

I hear a familiar shriek in the distance. The roukh has spotted bronze. I drive the stormclouds forward to reach the screaming bird. He clutches an object in his right talon.

Suddenly a sheet of sand whirls up against him and he vanishes from sight. I pull and push my clouds over to the site of the enormous sandstorm. It is my sister Sahnra, transforming the powerful strands of her hair into a driving sandstorm and attempting to whip the Instrument from the roukh's claw.

As I arrive at the scene of the storm I glimpse the roukh almost beaten down to earth by the sandstorm. I squeeze and wring the clouds until a violent rain begins to fall into the swirling sands. It is Sahnra's sand against Ambanari's rain; I blow, I shoot lightning, and the razor-sharp airborne sand grows thick with moisture and falls to the desert floor. The roukh shakes himself off and once again rises to the sky.

I have instructed the giant winged creature to fly due south to the Red Isle. For some reason, my sister blocks the path of the roukh with a vicious funnel of sand. The roukh gets caught up in this atmospheric whirlpool, as do I. I toss lightning; it accidentally ricochets around the maelstrom and hits the roukh. The roukh lashes out instinctively with a claw; my clouds are scattered everywhere. My clever sister has confused things; did she learn this tactic from me? Have I ever staged a mock fight to confuse her?

I am confused. Why would Sahnra wish to destroy one of her sacred Instruments? Is it purely to spite my effort to recover it? To vindicate her malevolence against the original thief of the Instrumentarium? But her reactions are so counterproductive, so destructive to her own best intentions! I vow never to overreact in such a way myself.

Sahnra whips the clouds and the sand and the roukh in greater violent circles. With an intuitive flash I pull back as hard as I can and then release all of my resistance. My half of the clouds flies off with the greatest of force away from Sahnra's area, like the shooting of an enormous slingshot. The roukh shoots away farther than anything else, and immediately takes control of its flight with monstrous grace. The noble bird clutches its right talon close to its body and heads northeast with unimaginable speed. It has saved the precious Vessel!

I gather my clouds around me and face Sahnra. Similarly, she turns to face me in a sea of cloud. I am prepared to behold the face of a monster, but it is only my forlorn sister. She reminds me of someone else, in the dim past – a mother, a lover, a spouse? – whom I kept at a similar distance. We hover unmoving and glare at each other with an exhausted anger, remaining this way for hours, for days, before either of us speaks. Even after we speak, we continue this face-off in the sky for centuries.

ق

Sahara fell into a light sleep after she finished the tale. Amar sat with her, fetched cool cloths to place on her warm forehead, rubbed her hands gently.

As he tended to his wife, Amar thought about the story that Sahara had just half muttered, half intoned in a low, male voice. He felt a truly bizarre sensation that the voice she had used was his. How could this be? Why did he feel a kindred spirit to this Ambanari, the brother-God-Wind-force?

Sahara stirred and opened her eyes. Her face tightened when she looked at him. He needed to reassure her.

He squeezed her hand gently. "You okay? That was a little scary." Amar picked up a glass of water and propped up her head to drink as he spoke. "You had another vision. Do you remember? I think it was about the same world, the Red Isle."

"But it was the desert. I remember bits. I'll remember more later."

"These experiences really take a lot out of you. Are you sure it's –"

33

"I don't have much choice. I can't exactly fend them off."

"I mean are you sure it's safe ... for the baby?"

Sahara sat up, placed the water glass down, and took Amar's hand. She placed it on her belly and looked him in the eyes. "The baby's just fine."

6

─────⟆∿∿⟆─────

Sahara next saw Dr. Machiyoko the third week in April. She was grateful the therapist did not sit on the stool at the foot of the couch, but in the gray armchair.

"How are you, Sahara?" When Sahara began to describe recent events with her husband, the therapist interrupted. "No, Sahara, how are you feeling?"

"I'm not sure I understand what you mean."

"How many months along are you?" Dr. Machiyoko asked in a matter of fact tone.

Sahara had not told anyone except Amar about her pregnancy. "I'm in my fourth month. The baby's fine. How did you know?"

"Didn't I tell you I'm psychic?" Dr. Machiyoko laughed. "I feel the baby's presence very strongly. This tiny soul exerts a power over you." Dr. Machiyoko crossed her legs and twisted one around the other tightly. "Sahara, tell me about last New Year's."

Again Sahara was taken aback by the therapist's hidden knowledge, then she remembered: "Did Zack tell you about the party?"

"He might have mentioned it. I sense a connection with the baby."

Sahara was not ready to talk about the dire consequences of the 1999 New Year's party so she started with the celebration. "Life was going well for us, at least for Amar. He loved working at the World Trade Center, and he made a killing in the market that year. By the time the party was over we were very happy, very drunk, and a little too wild."

"You got pregnant and you weren't expecting that."

Sahara's throat constricted. Why was this so difficult?

Dr. Machiyoko saw her patient's inner struggle. "Sahara, do you want this child?"

"Absolutely. No question."

"So what's the problem?"

Amar's the problem, Sahara thought. But she was unable to say more.

"Let's get back to the visions. I hope they'll release your anxiety. Tell me one of your stories." Dr. Machiyoko pulled the stool over to the futon couch. What is this all about, Sahara wondered? Having her therapist so near was at once disturbing and oddly comforting. She told the therapist the two Red Isle stories. The therapist made no comments, but asked excitedly for another story, so Sahara told the tale of the Two Winds.

Dr. Machiyoko finally spoke: "The desert sky fight reminds me of the dueling winds."

"Aren't they connected because they all come out of my imagination?" Sahara asked. "Like dreams, where everyday life gets transformed into symbols?"

"The common links can be seen as symbols of your crisis: the desert as a battlefield (the Sauhra, or Sahara: you); a child-thief (the baby) stealing your life away."

"The sacred objects – my study of ancient literature – being stolen from me."

"This explains a lot, but I think there's more going on. Are there any more images?"

"A really important one, which I haven't told Amar yet. It feels too close to home."

Sahara recounted the Sharzad tale, with Dr. Machiyoko writing furiously on the stool. The therapist continued writing after Sahara finished. Finally, she looked up as if surprised Sahara was still there. "This is quite ... rich ... and fascinating," Dr. Machiyoko started, deep in her own thoughts. Suddenly she rose from the stool. "Time's up. Go to Crystal Charm, in a few days. Have Ann-Marie recommend some meditation music. Try to relax."

How bizarre, Sahara thought. Just when Sahara had gotten to her most telling vision, Dr. Machiyoko was recommending meditation tapes. Nonetheless, she set up another appointment and a few days later went to Crystal Charm. When she got home, she noticed that there was an extra, unmarked cassette in the bag. Curious, she prepared a space to meditate, and turned on the tape machine.

An unfamiliar female voice recounted a story.

At dinner Sahara told her husband about the extra tape. Should she tell him about Dr. Machiyoko? Because of the connection between Ardryashir's violent actions and Amar's anger, Sahara had avoided sharing the Sharzad tale with him. The new story was about the vile Queen Uzmeth, told through the eyes of her slave, Dinzadeh. With it, she could more safely prepare him for the Sharzad tale.

"This story is set in Sassanid Persia, the last great empire to battle the Romans and succumb to the Muslims. We're in the reign of Bahram IV, end of the 4th Century A.D."

"How the hell do you know all that?" Amar asked.

"I did my homework – this is my field, in case you forgot. The Sasans first developed the Thousand Nights framing device. The first line of the Scheherazade text contains the phrase 'of the Banu Sasan in the lands of India and China.' Some believe the Scheherazade character was modeled after an historical Sassanid Queen."

"So Bahram IV was the king who married and killed a virgin every night?"

"Not in this tale. It's different, more complicated." Noticing Amar's interest, Sahara let go of her fears. They moved to the living room to listen to the tape.

The Tale of Uzmeth and Dinzadeh

Who is the source of the evil over the land? You are, Uzmeth, you who have seen better days. Days of the early Empire: you have told me tales of the old Shahanshahs, the first Bahrams, the great Shahpur. And you have cursed the tainting of the fire cult, the prohibition of animal sacrifice, the meddling of the Romans, the spinelessness of the Zoroastrian Muved leaders. You determined to live on to fight for the old ways, you went deeper into the occult knowledge of Ahura Mazda, and you discovered a secret.

Whereupon came the orgies, the rites of concupiscence. Your worship moved from the hearth to the bed. You used your position at court to set up a system of procurement, a network of harlotry. In your ascendance you had dozens at your beck and cue, you'd wag one finger and a secret chain of command would spread through the tunnels under the palace. You'd suck on one long fingernail and three nubile couples would appear in your midst. And after a time, the secret you had discovered paid off: the wall of debauchery you erected around you preserved your youth. Your sex slaves spent themselves to death, but you thrived, for you alone bore the secret of how to employ those excesses.

You pulled yourself out of the schemes of the court, petty to you in those years of initial discovery and experiment. Why care for the banalities of politics when the secret of eternal youth bloomed in your palm? And so you lost your voice at court. You had only your secret network, and that dwindled. Threatened and powerless, you turned desperate, you chose to sow chaos at court. You used your lover Ardryashir to abduct fresh victims outside the palace gates for the orgiastic ritual. You turned your network for procurement into a web of derangement. The orgies became more insistent, less ritualized. Dangerous.

The day Ardryashir burst into my father's shop and carried me off to the palace I made no struggle. I did not grimace when I first beheld your face, did not flinch when you inspected my stripped body. From that first night I was brought to your feet, oh vile Queen Uzmeth, you recognized my talents. When I shied from the lust feasts, preferring to take it all in rather than have it take me, you goaded me to contribute. Somehow I convinced Ardryashir to bring me with him on his next marketplace rampage, and I brought back more new 'contributions' than he did. From then on I gathered more bodies than ever. I drummed up a zealous passion in all of them, and I sparked the orgies with a new fire without inserting a finger myself. You marveled at my skill, exempted me from the orgies, put me in charge of procurement and inducement of the Sasan youth. I have tried to justify my zeal by raising the quality of life for those I have brought inside the walls.

How could I have foreseen the dementing of your mind, tormented Uzmeth? After all those years of physical preservation and perfection, who could have predicted the toll on your psyche? Who could ever have distinguished between a lust-crazed anarch and an insane sadist? Who would not drown in your sea of chaos? How I have yearned for advice, navigating the treacherous waters over the years. How I have felt the void of a parental figure, someone for me to ask for help. But I have been the helper, the adviser, the parent to the abused youth.

Yet I have moments of sensing a need that has been with me from deep in my past, a feeling that someone has been lost to me. But there is no someone for me. And now I have failed all the others. I have failed to staunch Uzmeth's poison, failed to stem Ardryashir's transformation into a monster.

I turn to the only one who might help.

You, Sharzad.

7

"That's it?" Amar asked when the tape was over. "Who is Sharzad?"

"The vizier's daughter."

"I don't understand. How do you know?"

Sahara felt a knot in her stomach as she prepared to tell the Sharzad tale. "In the Scheherazade story, two sisters, Scheherazade and Dunyazade, help each other overcome the murderous King. In an old Persian version, Dunyazade was not Scheherazade's sister but a slave – that must be Dinzadeh. Sharzad must be a prototype for Scheherazade – the vizier's daughter.

"There's no murderous King here. You're taking a leap because of your research."

"Oh, great. Now you're doubting my abilities to interpret my research?" She could not stop herself. "It's bad enough you've prevented me from doing my work."

"I've prevented you from nothing. If you're so concerned about your work time, why in hell do you want a baby now? You'll have no time left at all."

"If I'm relegated to domestic duties in this marriage, I might as well start a family. Let me raise a child while I'm in indentured servitude!" Sahara was angry now. It was the first time she had allowed herself such expression to her husband.

"All right, let's take a breath." Amar wanted to avoid a serious fight. "I'm sorry I doubted your theory before. You're the expert. I just wondered why you were so certain about Sharzad – she hardly figures in this story."

Sahara was beyond caution now. "I received my own story, with Dinzadeh and Sharzad. About a month ago."

"A month ago? Why haven't you told me?"

"Frankly, I was afraid of your reaction."

"Tell me the story."

"Now I'm your little slave girl; if I don't obey you'll cut off my head?"

Amar smiled. "Don't give me any ideas."

Sahara let out a deep sigh. "Your wish is my command, O mighty King." As plainly as possible, she described the sordid scene with Uzmeth watching Ardryashir kill Purzai.

When she finished Sahara asked, "Do you see what frightens me?"

Amar shook his head yes. "Go back to the Scheherazade tale for a minute. The Queen in that story cuckolds the King by having orgies behind his back. When he discovers them, he kills her, the entire harem, and starts in on a virgin a night. In your version, the Queen is still alive when the murders start. And who exactly is the King?"

"Historically, it's Bahram IV, but Uzmeth seems to have nothing to do with him. She's lived through so many Shahs she's a free agent. But how did Uzmeth's orgiastic, 'life-giving' rituals turn into violent murders of the kingdom's young women? There's something between the two stories."

"And how did you get a hold of this tape? It so clearly relates to your tale."

Sahara felt emboldened by Amar's calm inquisitiveness. "I guess it's confessional day. I got it at a store my therapist recommended."

Amar sat up. "Therapist? Since when do – don't tell me – all month, right?"

"I had to do something, Amar. Zack recommended Dr. Machiyoko."

"Zack! What have you been –"

"Don't worry. He has no idea why I'm going. Anyway, I think you might like her."

"Me? Let me absorb the fact that *you've* been seeing her – behind my back."

"Amar, Dr. Machiyoko wants us to think beyond our problems now."

"If you're thinking what I think you are, forget it. I'm not going to any therapist. There's nothing wrong with me. I'm not the one having hallucinations. I'm not the one refusing to speak, telling lies, not budging about anything. Don't drag me to your shrink."

With a swipe of his hand, he left the room.

"What a schmuck. No wonder you've been so blue, baby." Porcelain Honeywell reached her short arm toward the coffee on Sahara's patio table. It was an overcast but warm morning at the start of May. Porcy, as she was called, had been the couple's realtor when they bought their Glenclaire house and remained in close contact. Sahara had unloaded everything on Porcy: the pregnancy, the tensions with Amar, and her bizarre visions. Porcy was quite interested in the fantasies, since she used to work as a psychic.

Porcelain Honeywell was a short, squat woman who alternately appeared voluptuous and thickset. Her coloring suggested a mix of African-American and Latin heritage. Since Porcy did not know her biological parents, she did not pigeonhole people into ethnic or racial types. She considered herself a blend of all peoples.

"I welcome all people to Glenclaire. As a realtor, I want as varied a community as possible. But I should have barred the gates to that husband of yours. When you two were house hunting, I just didn't like him." Porcy took another gulp of coffee. "You want to know why, I'll tell you. You've told a lot of stories this morning. It's my turn."

The Tale of the Glenclaire Realtor

We all have those times when we meet someone and instantly like them, without much to go on. There are also those times when we dislike someone immediately, for no apparent reason. We can even despise them, get knots in our stomach, and feel an urgency to get away from them. Who knows why this happens? It's one of those mysterious, unconscious puzzles buried deep in our psyches.

We don't like admitting these irrational negative responses since most of us think of ourselves as logical and sociable creatures. As a realtor I like the feeling of building a community by bringing people to Glenclaire. I love people. Just not Amar Rash.

Two years ago I started out as a realtor. Ooma Qadir, Amar's young intern and a native of Glenclaire, gave him one of my business cards. She was quick to please her boss, she knew he was househunting, and so she got my name from her parents' dogwalker. At my first meeting with Amar I saw he had an overbearing pride in his financial conquests on Wall Street. If I hadn't needed clients, I would have referred him to another realtor. I disliked him so intensely that I questioned what could be going on underneath it.

But then I met you, his beautiful wife, Sahara Fleming. The name itself won me over. At least Amar had good taste. Out of my inexplicable emotions, I decided: I would sell a wonderful house to you, Sahara, but torment Amar as much as possible in the process.

My first showdown was at Amar's office in the World Trade Center. He insisted that I come into New York for financial briefings when it was completely unnecessary. I had to put a stop to it. Ooma showed me Amar's schedule and I would call him with "urgent' messages during his most important meetings. I showed up and got him babbling on about his dream house when his bosses were in earshot. Finally, I sent a posse of realtors to pop up every fifteen minutes and hound him. That ended the office visits.

Once the two of you started looking on weekends, I launched my next offensive. Amar was looking for the elegant, showy kind of house that would impress visiting clients. Struggling with the move to the suburbs, you wanted an oasis, something exotic or quirky or eccentric. I suggested that you each look separately, find a dream house, and then share your ideas. This gave me better opportunity to please you and torment Amar.

I borrowed the most broken down jalopies when I showed Amar houses, but drove you around in a comfortable BMW. I brought you to an expensive restaurant for lunch, but took Amar to a dilapidated falafel stand and made him pay. I showed him what he wanted, but I also cajoled him into liking the area and browbeat him into financial realities.

Then the inevitable happened: I got to know Amar, and began to understand what you saw in your swaggering stockbroker. One Saturday I took him up into the Glenclaire hills to admire the view of the New York skyline. As he gingerly picked at the greasy pork sandwich I had packed for him, he questioned me.

"How'd you ever get into this business?"

"I got some vocational training in it. At a mental institution."

Amar laughed. "What prevents me from murdering you up on this secluded cliff?"

"Your wife," I said, and not missing a beat: "Do you adore her?"

Amar looked out at the view and made a sweeping gesture that took in a hundred Jersey communities, the city and its environs, and the ocean beyond. "Vastly."

With that gesture, I thought: maybe I should stop torturing the guy.

Soon after I got a call from Zack Goodkin, one of my first clients and the son of an old friend. Zack told me the house next door to his was going on the market soon and that I should jump on it. This house fit Amar's bill: columns, hedges, long driveway and lawn. If you remember, I took you to see it first, with some advice:

"Listen, honey, this house isn't your mug of tea. Here's how to think about it. Give Amar the outside of the house. It can appear as stately as any mansion he wants. And slowly, you take over the inside. Make it as tie-dyed and funky and bamboo as you want."

You were silent on the drive over. As we walked through the house, you said finally, "You're right, Porcy, I won't have much choice here. I'll just have to add some touches."

At that moment we went through a set of French doors that led outside. There, we found an exquisite Mediterranean patio, complete with a babbling fountain at its center. The floor was laid with Spanish terra cotta tile, and the walls were laced with intricate, filigree designs. Crawling vines, potted trees, and fragrant flowers were everywhere.

"I love it!" Sahara cried out.

It was left to Amar to negotiate the deal. Near to the closing on the house, I went to Amar's office to have him sign some papers, but Ooma told me that he was at his grandfather Ardra's jewelry store in the Diamond District. As she took me there Ooma explained that Amar was trying to reconcile Ardra with his father Solomon. In a dark back room of the store we found Amar sitting with Ardra, a kindly, alert, aged Indian man, and Solomon, a very properly dressed man in his 50's whose eyes were fixed on the floor.

There was a palpable tension in the air, which Ardra dispelled by asking me details about the house in a thick Indian accent. When I mentioned that I had received a tip from Zack Goodkin the old man's face lit up. He explained that as a child Zack was often in his store and helped out by strolling baby Amar around the neighborhood.

When Amar confirmed this coincidence he looked directly at me, perhaps the first time we had shared such a glance. I experienced a jolt of recognition, like the psychic flashes I get when reading someone's palm or chakras. I received an image of someone sharing a story; was it Zack telling the baby Amar? Zack telling someone else, much earlier in time? And then, with Amar still gazing my way, I saw in my mind's eye the image of a black salamander. Why did this man have such a strange effect on me?

I left with the papers, refreshed by a new perspective on Amar. I was touched by his desire to heal his family's situation and bemused by our intimate moment of eye contact. I was moved and – Hallelujah! – you two moved into a new home. I was also surprised to discover that Zack and Amar had a child-hood connection. It was the first clue that there were connections between the people I knew in Glenclaire. I was here to help people, that much I already knew, but I sensed that it was going to be at a deeper level than selling them houses. Amar forced me to this realization by having to deal with his unpleasantness only to discover that there was more to him. Thanks to him, I realized I was bringing people to Glenclaire for some purpose.

ق

"So spill, girlfriend," Porcy continued, "what's up between Amar's father and grandpa?"

"I don't know much," Sahara answered, "and frankly, Amar didn't tell me half of your househunting saga. I know he and Zack knew each other as kids, but that's all."

"I guess you're the storyteller in the family, kiddo. Maybe I'll pay Zack a friendly realtor's social call. I'd like more juice on my little group of Glenclaireans."

"Porcy, go easy on the gossip with Zack. He's got this tie with Amar, and – "

"I won't say a word, babe. Except to share a Red Isle story or two."

After Porcy left, Sahara was haunted by the idea of people coming together in Glenclaire for some higher purpose. Hadn't she heard that somewhere else recently? Something about a strange group coming together for the first time in centuries. Who had told her? What was the purpose?

Some very important work? In the Jersey suburbs?

8

Sahara did not receive any new visions from mid-April to mid-May. She considered that once she had started telling her stories to Amar and others, once she had released some of the silent pressure weighing on her, her unconscious mind eased up and stopped the visions. In the last two weeks she and Amar had somehow regained an equilibrium of courtesy, but neither had dared to go farther than that. She was a bit relieved that the dreams had stopped, but was anxious that a new image might pop up any day. She caught herself snapping out of daydreams, or starting awake right at the edge of falling asleep, fearing the dreamlike tales would descend upon her.

But she missed them, too.

One afternoon, as Sahara retrieved the mail, a plain manila envelope fell from the box. When she bent down to pick it up she noticed the envelope contained no markings, not even an address or postmark.

Someone had dropped off the package by hand.

She went inside to open the envelope. Who would have sent this? What could be inside? She pulled out several sheets of plain white paper covered with single-spaced typed lines. Sahara read the first few sentences:

Why are you putting up with it? Why did you let him do that to you? Should you have left? How much longer can you stand this?

Sahara felt a sickening shiver run up her spine. The words spoke directly to her, mimicked her own thoughts. She continued reading and a story began to unfold.

The Tale of the Demise of the Bed Isle

Zancq asked himself the same questions every day. His work was hard, but traveling from village to village gave him time to think back on his plight. (Why did they sneer at you, especially that awful Minister of Affairs?) Zancq was the youngest of Queen D'aulai's court. He had not known D'aulai or any of her lapdogs when they were lowly shoreline scavengers. They were in full power when he was born, and, growing up in the fortress sanctuary, he had envied the energy and force of those giving the commands. His mother, Jaya, a high priestess, keeper of the sacred Instrument, had put her son forward in court, a move readily accepted by the Queen. The dxylo-dxyla, the holy Instrument recovered by D'aulai and named after her in deference, was the foundation of the Queen's right and power. She dared not deny the priestess who protected the Vessel and gave it sanctity.

But Zancq's new status at court had been short-lived. (Why do they call you tadpole and urchin, mock your connection to mother?) He envied and followed the royals, hoping for

advancement, but already the Queen faced difficulties secur-
ing her reign; she was focused on quelling minor rebellions
and not on a young, minor court figure. The Minister of Affairs
was a drunken, boisterous man who barely believed in the jus-
tification of the Queen's mission to restore the ancient Goddess
cult, let alone the sanctity of the dxylo-dxyla. Feigning respect
for the Queen, he sought to mock Zancq – and the dxylo-dxyla
– by insisting that the young courtier travel on the mainland,
spreading the serene beauty of the Instrument to the unbelieving tribes there. Before Zancq knew it, he was supplied with a
boat, a reproduction of the bronze Instrument, and two temple
musicians.

How is dragging the dxylo-dxyla from town to town ever
going to advance you at court, Zancq asked himself as he
trudged on the dusty road to the next village. He would not
return with tribute from strangers: there would be no proof
of his success to impress those at home. His mother had
given him simple instructions: encourage newcomers to the
Instrument to try their own hands at fashioning and playing
similar kinds of music. So at each village, Zancq invoked and
praised Queen D'aulai, and Queen Oumkratania, thought to
be the original Goddess who gave the Instrument to the people, and then let the musicians demonstrate the dxylo-dxyla's
charms. The rest happened naturally.

The two temple musicians sat facing each other across the
bronze bars, raised their mallets and began to swing deftly on
each side, interlocking their complex rhythms at great speed,
until the hollow resonators underneath the bars filled the village with a shimmering, indescribable sound. And always,
small children ran to the front of the crowd to get the closest
look at the wondrous actions of the musicians, and folk came
out from every corner of the village to hear the strange new
music. Everyone who listened and watched was in awe and

delight. Always the villagers listened and celebrated deep into the night, begged them to stay longer, fondled and worshipped the dxylo-dxyla. Zancq stayed until he saw the first replicas of the Instrument being attempted by children or adults; as soon as the imitative process had begun, he left.

Despite the foolproof success of his first visits to the mainland, despite the smiles and squeals of delight from every man, woman, and child, when he returned to the court Zancq made known that he resented his job. He begged the Minister to send someone else in his stead. He told the Queen that the Instrument was beloved by all who heard it, and that because of that her glory was reaching people all along the coastline. He argued that to proliferate the Queen's fame further inland, he needed a team of travelers. He would oversee them at court, perhaps head a Ministry of Exportation.

But it was no use; things were getting out of control on the Red Isle. Two figures had emerged calling themselves God-Protectors of the Instrument. Queen D'aulai retaliated by claiming she was the direct descendant of Oumkratania, the ancient Goddess figure who had begun the rites of the Instrument. The brother and sister God-Protectors accused Queen D'aulai of deceiving the people, and raised an army to take back the Instrument and oust the Queen. The Queen's Minister responded by demanding that all courtiers and soldiers defend the fortress and suppress the rebellion. As far as Zancq's proposal to expand his travel team was concerned, the Minister found such an undertaking inadvisable.

'The Minister found such an undertaking inadvisable.' The words sounded familiar to Sahara. She thought they might come from the Scheherazade tale of *The Thousand and One Nights*. Were the two God-Protectors the same as Sahnra and her brother Ambanari, from the other Red Isle story? The

Instrument was now called the dxylo-dxyla, a musical instrument. And who was this Queen D'aulai?

Sahara went back to reading the story.

Worse for Zancq, his mother Jaya was suspected of siding with the enemy. Indeed, the priestess had looked at Zancq's sojourn to the continent as a purer form of worship of the Instrument, and had secretly doubted the Queen's true nature. When Queen D'aulai declared herself the only true Goddess of the dxylo-dxyla, Jaya knew this to be severe untruth and could no longer mask her distrust.

We need to get as far away from here as possible, Zancq told himself and his mother: return to the mainland with one of your musicians. Civil war had broken out, staining the island truly red. During a catastrophic battle on the inland plateau, when an earthquake created by the two enemy Gods swallowed the Queen's troops whole, Zancq and his tiny crew quickly and quietly set sail for the shoreline.

On this trip they traveled further up the coast until they found themselves following the trade routes that eventually led to the West country. Jaya herself took over for the second musician, but the long days on the road wearied her. Zancq knew that he would have to learn to play the Instrument himself. His concern for his mother, the frustrations at performing the fast rhythms, and the knowledge that nothing he accomplished could save him at court, made his days dragging the dxylo-dxyla from village to village bleak and torturous. He lacked the drive and energy to whip up excitement as they entered a village. If his mother was asleep or resting away from the crowd, Zancq skipped the invocation to Oumkratania and played halfheartedly, barely keeping up with the musician.

Nonetheless, people everywhere continued to delight in the music, the joggling rhythms, the flying mallets, and the metallic shimmer of the sound. Zancq passed through some villages he had visited on his first trip, and observed that the locals had fashioned a bevy of imitation dxylo-dxylas, usually made of wood and not bronze, and were creating their own spirited syncopations. The music was joyful and infectious.

After a time, Jaya became too ill to continue the arduous travel, and wished to see her beloved homeland. Zancq thought to himself: you're going home to bury her. His musician partner, fed up with Zancq's lackluster playing, agreed to turn back. Within weeks the trio found themselves in sight of the shores of the Red Isle.

From a mile away they saw ominous columns of smoke.

They docked the boat near the Queen's new fortress, next to where Jaya had presided in the sanctuary of the Instrument. The shore was littered with bodies, burnt, slashed, and torn apart as if by wild beasts. What had once been a quiet fishing community was now an open graveyard. Zancq and the musician fashioned a makeshift stretcher out of thatch from a ruined cottage and carried Jaya toward the fortress. Along the way they saw a pyre of animal-like figures with savage, yellow-eyes. There were also signs of natural disasters. A ferocious monsoon had ripped through the coast, strewing huts and other shelters everywhere. Several fissures had gashed the countryside; thunder strikes had caused massive fires and destruction.

The Gods had retaliated.

Zancq thanked the great God Ambanari, brother of Sahnra, that his mother was barely conscious when they arrived at her shrine, so that she would not witness her ravaged acolytes, the cracked temple pillars, and the stolen or destroyed musical instruments. The sacred Instrument itself lay on the floor, its frame shattered, bars strewn everywhere.

Zancq said farewell to the musician, who pleaded to go off to his home village in search of his own people. They had laid Zancq's mother in the berth that had housed the Instrument before its demise; the space was virtually untouched and would serve as a bed for his mother's last comforts, as well as her final resting place.

Zancq stayed up the long, feverish night at his mother's side. In the morning, she looked up for one last time at the brilliant blue of the sky. In his extreme emotional state he thought he had seen her stare like this once before. Was it someone else? He felt a deep sense of gratitude to her and a debt that he could never repay. When her spirit was released to the skies above the island, Zancq wept uncontrollably. He covered her with holy robes and blessed her with the Goddess prayer before leaving the temple.

Zancq took a quicker route back to his boat, avoiding the blood-spattered shoreline by walking through the ruined fortress. A perverse attraction caused him to pass through the Queen's central courtyard. As he suspected, he encountered one of the worst atrocities – and one of the most satisfying. On the royal dais were the Queen, the Minister of Affairs, and several of the other highest officers of the land, spitted on skewers driven through their torsos. A dozen half-mad citizens staggered about the platform, guarding their captives.

At one end two larger than life bodies rotated on their spits. Though he recognized all the other victims from his days at court, Zancq did not know this pair.

"Halt! Come no further unless you wish to be roasted on the fire as well," one of the desperate guards barked at Zancq. "Name your business."

"I offer no battle," he said, "I only wish to know the names of these last two," gaining courage as he thought of his salvation, "so I may sing the praises of your great deeds."

The distressed guard came closer to Zancq, who inched backward. "You have rightly chosen the greatest of our deeds," the guard said, "for these are the divinities who dared oppose the Queen. They are deities no longer, for the great Queen showed us by her sacrifice the key to the Gods' vulnerability. They could raise hurricanes and thunderclouds, but they could not escape the bite of the roasting spit."

"Sahnra. Ambanari," Zancq gasped. He slowly backed out of the chamber: "The world must hear of the sacrifice ... the beginning of ... freedom." Zancq turned and ran.

The dxylo-dxyla would never appear on the Red Isle again. Zancq returned to the mainland with his Instrument, battered and worn from its years of travel along the coast, up through the trade routes, far into the West. Zancq's work was his means of survival: each village would know of his coming, and greet him and feed him and celebrate the coming of the dxylo-dxyla. In many of the villages new to him, his work was already done; when he arrived the townspeople had already heard of the tricky rhythms of the mallets, and had begun to make music. Talking drums, pitched turtle shells, xylophones, balafons, and war toms proliferated everywhere.

Zancq sat one day along a riverbank, enjoying the water on his bare feet as he watched local women work their rice for that day's dinner. He had seen famine throughout the continent, but had never known a tribe to give up its musical instruments for the sake of a grain of rice. He had seen further war and bloodshed, but he had never heard an army without its drums to send them into battle. He had seen disaster and unrest and sadness, but music and rhythm had accompanied every one of these hardships. People would never give up their pleasure or their expression or their love of the sound. It was what helped Zancq survive; it was what helped the world survive.

As he watched the women pound the rice in wooden mortars he laughed to himself. You really missed out on that court position, old friend. Stuck here peddling this old bone board to these poor natives. What a pathetic life you've led. Zancq knew he was the only one who had escaped the terrible fate of his homeland, a fate caught up in the very Instrument he still lugged around the mainland. On the Red Isle it had become a symbol of power and greed and eventual devastation, and here, in these Godforsaken places, the Instrument, Rhythm, and Music itself was a thing of happiness and survival. It had nothing to do with power or glory.

The pounding of the rice mortars gradually changed to an organized sound; Zancq smiled at the familiar interlocking rhythms that emerged as the women listened closely to each other and went from unison motif to a new complex rhythm when one of them shifted their rhythm over a beat. Zancq marveled at the sound, splashed his foot to the beat, and felt his heart swell.

ق

Sahara finished the story with a great mix of emotions. She was moved by the growth of Zancq's appreciation and compassion, but why had she received a story centered on him? She was horrified by the downfall of the Red Isle, but she wanted to know the true causes of this devastation. She recognized the brother and sister deities, but tried to relate their demise with Sahnra's struggles with the thief and Ambanari's battle with his sister.

She sat for over an hour, trying to piece it together. And there was the biggest but simplest of questions: who had sent her this package? She did not notice the approaching sunset or the room growing dark.

Until she heard Amar unlock the front door.

"Who could this be from? You got the tape after you saw that therapist."

"Dr. Machiyoko's out of town, so she would've mailed it, but there's no postmark."

Amar was pacing the living room. "Who else knows about your Red Isle tales?"

Sahara thought before she spoke. "I might have told Porcy about them."

"Lord help me! That pudgy little doughnut drives me nuts. She's prying in our life?"

Amar stopped his pacing and plopped down in the arm-chair. "I feel like I'm connected to all this somehow. Ambanari's the brother of the Goddess Sahnra, right?"

"Yes. You feel connected to him?"

"He's like a kindred spirit. Chasing his sister to protect the precious Instrument, only to wind up roasted on the grill back home. Sounds like one of my good days lately."

"So you agree with my sequence: the thief on the beach warns the Goddess about the decline of her Red Isle cult; she hides the Instrument in the desert –"

"– and her brother takes it back. Then a new Queen, worse than ever, takes over, and the deities, the court, and the people tear each other apart."

This was going better; at dinner, a bottle from Amar's collection of wines helped. "What decayed the Red Isle's court?"

"I'm still trying to guess who sent the package. Someone in Glenclaire is aware of the connections between the three Red Isle stories."

"Okay, try to hear this. Porcy feels she's involved with a group of Glenclaireans that are connected by some deeper purpose. Because of the linked tales, she may be right."

"And her idea is valid because ... she read your palm?"

"That woman holds a lot of truth, wise guy. She told me about your family." Amar shot her a look. Sahara had thought this was safer territory than perhaps it was. "She told me she met your father Sol and grandfather Ardra. You've never told me about their falling out."

Sahara watched her husband sigh. She was grateful to see him vulnerable for the first time in weeks. "I never really wanted you mixed up in it. You were my fresh start."

"Tell the fresh start about your grandfather. What's Ardra like?"

"Like a man who got his way on pure perseverance and charm. But unforgiving if you crossed him. Like when my father disobeyed him."

"When was that? What did Sol do? Tell me a story for a change."

"My grandfather comes from a family of jewelers in India," Amar began.

"Really? How wonderful!"

"They didn't make horse saddles lined with gold and jewels. It's tough, not exotic."

59

"Sorry, I'll shut up," Sahara said, lying back on the couch. "I'm all ears."

The Tale of Ardra and Solomon Bash

My grandfather Ardra Rash struggles hard when he immigrates to New York and makes his way into Manhattan's Diamond District. The years of hard work lead him to adopt a value with single-minded purpose: never mix business and pleasure. He determines to instill this principle in his three sons, especially the eldest, Solomon.

Sol has a healthy and normal childhood except for one fact. He is completely oblivious to the little details of life. Perhaps he inherited Ardra's sense of entitlement to anything he wants. If he wants something, he does whatever it takes to get it, but along the way, taking out the garbage, mailing a letter, remembering to eat lunch are all forgotten. Sol Rash is like a toddler walking shakily through a room, ignoring anything in his way. It drives his parents and brothers crazy. His mother Rita is a devout Jew and the family observes the rituals strictly. To neglect a candle-lighting, miss synagogue, or forget it is Passover and eat a hoagie – Sol's transgressions are sacrilege to Rita.

Somehow Sol gets by, perhaps because the important things – studying, friends, work goals – are given the full force of his energy. But his flaw comes in touch with Ardra's primary principle once Sol is in college. He meets Udeni Udenta in his junior year. Having never known such an infatuation, his grades slip, his friends stop calling, and by senior year, he loses sight of any plan for his future. It is the mid-60s, so the culture can support such a laissez-faire attitude.

But not Ardra and Rita Rash. Both parents become puffing adders of concern as Sol nears graduation, and as his chances of graduation lessen. Over winter break Ardra sits the lad down and reinforces his moral precept. Business before pleasure. Take care of your work life first. Secure the nest before you fill it. But Sol proposes to Udeni. Infuriated, Ardra threatens to disown him. The wedding takes place, Udeni becomes pregnant and they graduate, without prospects.

Having no prospects was as popular as the Beatles in 1967, the year of my birth. Ardra insists that Sol work in the family business until he gets sorted out. At first there is a quiet but tense stalemate between father and son. As a baby, I am a sore reminder of Sol's disobedience to Ardra. Sol and Udeni are still passionately in love, it is the Summer of Love, then Woodstock – Ardra and Rita are often left babysitting. As a result, the ice is broken, and my grandparents bond with me before my parents. I chew on diamond necklaces as a luxury pacifier, eat samosas and drink tea before I can speak.

As the 70's begin, it is clear that Sol is hopeless in the business: details are neglected, sales are not closed, and receipts are lost. Too often my grandparents have to arrange ad hoc sitters, including the adolescent Zack. Economic times get tougher, Ardra can no longer tolerate Sol's actions, and he fires him. Sol refuses help from Udeni's family in Detroit, and various relatives invite us to India. We are banished to Delhi.

My father is broken by the move to Delhi, but also becomes a new man forged in the fire of hard times. Now his focus is on survival, on saving his family, and on proving to Ardra that he can make the right choices. His goal is to return to the United States a richer man than his father. He works every hour, but neglects his relatives, and so after a few years, he wears out his welcome. Fortunately, he has made enough money to move us to London by the late 70's, where he lands work in the oil business.

But tragedy strikes: my mother is murdered on the street in a robbery. We are devastated. Sol leaves me with Ardra and Rita in New York for a time while he consoles with the Udenta clan in Detroit. His grief bonds him to the family and he stays on, finding even better work at the Ford Motor Company. He meets his goal to reenter the United States better off than his father.

But Sol feels like he has achieved his goal at the cost of his beloved wife. He has come full circle, now adopting his father's maxim – do not mix business with family. And so, as I grow up, my father's control over my choices is stifling. And yet, I welcome both my father and grandfather's business advice. I determine to make a killing in the market to avoid my father's struggle. I delay college to experience some hands-on work at his side. In 1988, the year before I start college at Michigan State, I use my saved money to revisit England and India, and travel to many places in-between.

One of the stops along the way is a caravan ride in the Syrian Desert. On the third day, at twilight, as we approach the next oasis, the caravan passes a man, kneeling over a tiny watering pool. He is quite old, but there is a luminous glow shimmering off of his body. He is poised to drink from the pool, but he remains still, staring deeply into the shallow water – at his reflection or something beyond it? As an immediate answer to my question, I have a flash of familiarity. I have not seen this man at this pool before and I myself have not knelt at a pool like it. It is more that I sense that this man has been here before, has seen his reflection before, and has seen others watching him, others reflected back at him as if he was looking into their eyes and not a pool of water.

And then the caravan passes him by. I laugh at myself, pull myself out of my deep, interior moment. I have been traveling too long, it is time to stop wandering and get back on my chosen path. I make my stay short with my Delhi relatives (there is still tension), and come home to college. You know the rest: graduate school at University of Chicago School of Business, meeting you, making a killing on Wall Street.

It all seems so easy and straightforward: getting married in no way interferes with my success in business. And both are a source of pride to Ardra and my father. This is the leverage that enables me to convince my father to come to New York and speak with Ardra. So using the business end of the stick to effect a healing in the family is also no problem. Single-handedly I dispel the belief that mixing family and work is a curse.

When Ardra first hears that my father is coming to reunite with him after all those years, he is so touched that his blood pressure plummets and he passes out. He realizes it is time to rethink his will, since he might not have long to live. But when my father arrives, the subject of the will becomes a long, protracted negotiation. My father haggles about this clause or that stick of furniture, often placing me in the middle.

And so my family (especially with my mother gone) has become about nit-picking details to me. Perhaps I cannot ignore these worthless details until my grandfather dies, but until then, the failure of the reconciliation has me seeing eye to eye with the family curse.

ق

"And with our marriage in shambles, I have to agree with Ardra and Sol's rule against mixing family and work," Amar continued. "I was right not to want children yet."

"Ah! This is why you finally opened up about your family," Sahara said. "That's why I was honored with a story. You set me up for a moral about not wanting a child."

"I want a child! You never understood that!" Sahara flinched at Amar's shouts, but then saw that he was not angry but impassioned. "I want children with you, but at the right time. I'm doing well in the market, but there's talk of a correction in the near future. No one knows what might happen when the year 2000 comes. There's even a 'Y2K' theory that when the world's computers shift from 1999 to 2000, all the banks will crash. We can't be too careful."

"We *can* be too careful, Amar. Listen to yourself. You're resisting your own family with all this banking paranoia. You're mixing work with family the way Ardra feared."

"No, I'm only postponing raising a family because of work. All I asked of you was to wait a little bit more, to settle into the house, to let me make my mark. I begged you!"

Sahara stopped herself before reacting. This was the dispute that had sparked everything, that had led to the worst night of their marriage, the night they had not been able to confront yet. She looked into her husband's eyes. "I'm sorry. I'm sorry for –"

"It doesn't matter. It's too late, we're having this baby."

"I'm having this baby. You haven't decided yet."

"What's that supposed to mean?"

"You don't want this child right now, that's all I know."

"I want to protect our child, by making sure we're ready."

"Then get ready. Let's heal this mess we're in. Come to therapy with me."

"You've slowed my career with this baby. I'm not wasting more time with therapy!"

Sahara did not risk Amar's anger any further that night, or in the following weeks. She had greater challenges ahead of her.

10

Ooma Qadir was the hardest working intern that the offices of Bruckner Associates had ever seen. She had started working during the summers before and after her senior year in high school, and the firm hired her part-time when she entered Glenclaire State University. Ooma was uncomplaining about doing the most menial task, and had a passion for work. Amar had recognized Ooma's drive early on and snatched her up as his assistant. He wondered if her work ethic derived from her upbringing in a fairly strict Islamic household. 'There's a girl in no hurry to breed,' he said about her lately, with a cutting edge.

Ooma had been fascinated with Amar's household ever since she had helped Porcy find him a house in Glenclaire. She had offered her services at Amar's New Year's party that year to get a closer look inside the house. It had been an intense night: she had made a drunken spectacle of herself, and had to be driven home early by good neighbor Zack.

In Ooma's murky memory of that night, she had a sense that something magical was going on in that house. For this reason, she had kept a closer eye on her boss, and perhaps not for this reason alone: Amar was good-looking, he was kind to Ooma, and like her, he had Persian roots. She had had a strict moral upbringing, so she would never cross a line with the boss; nonetheless she kept her thick, dark hair and tight-fitting clothes in immaculate condition for the office.

During the spring, Ooma noticed that Amar was having difficult moods. She did not say anything because her boss never took his feelings out on her. But lately he stayed late each night. There was always too much work to do, but during the third week of May there was nothing unusual; Amar was staying late for some other reason. Ooma said nothing until the night Amar asked her to stay late and she found him at his desk staring out into space.

"And we're working ourselves to death at ten o'clock because ...?"

"Sorry, sorry," Amar said, snapping to. "Do you need to get home?"

"I'm fine, as long we really need to be here."

"Let's get out of here." Amar offered Ooma a ride back to Glenclaire. In the car, his silence got to her. She asked him what the matter was.

"Stuff at home?" she pried. Amar was resistant to speaking at first; he knew better than to talk to a young, attractive girl about his unhappy love life. But when he mentioned Sahara's strange stories, Ooma caught her breath. There is something magical going on!

Amar felt awkward sharing such odd confidences, but Ooma urged him to tell the tales of Sharzad, Dinzadeh, and Queen Uzmeth. Before they knew it Amar pulled his car in front of Ooma's house, kept the motor running, and continued the Sassanid story. Ooma listened with rapt attention; she chewed on a nail as she watched Amar. And then, at a moment when Amar mentioned Queen Uzmeth placing a finger in her mouth, the two became aware of Ooma's similar pose. They gazed deeply into each other's eyes.

"Oh my God," Ooma said, lowering her finger. "I just got this flash, about the – " Ooma closed her eyes, and a string of images entered her head: alabaster pillars, a line of muscle-bound serving men, a hand stroking her leg under splendid and expensive cloth. She reopened her eyes, gazed once more at Amar, and said:

"I know how Queen Uzmeth lived a hundred and fifty years." And she began a story.

The Tale of Uzmeth's First Orgy

Why did I bring her back to Ctesiphon, this dirty one, this Dnund, perfect name for her, wallowing in the mud outside the walls of the old palace in Hecatomphylos, unable to enter, but insisting – always insisting this one! – insisting that she belonged there, that she had to return the star lamp: do you take a shine to the lamp, mistress? she joked, and I was taken by the lamp in the shape of a star – how was I to know that I would find the secret of the lamp, that I would discover the hidden catch on the central compartment, that I would find the writing inside, and Dnund would marvel at the discovery, it is meant for you, mistress, it is your salvation, it will be our secret this is why I have returned, Dnund babbled, filthy mendicant, and she explained her attraction to Hecatomphylos, what it took for her to arrive at the ancient Parthian capital, and the awful foreboding she felt as she approached the palace, a horror from a past life, a crime she needed to revisit, to purify her immortal soul; hearing that I was taken in, it wasn't the lamp or the hidden writing, it was her intense belief, she said she knew the secrets of the fire cult, she knew Ahura Mazda intimately – this was definitely one of her crazed delusions – but still, she was in touch with something I sought, for why had I gone to Hecatomphylos in the first place, if not to find some archaic clue from our Parthian ancestors and like them we will be soon gone I thought, looking up to the battered walls of the palace at Hecatomphylos: is our Sassanid palace at Ctesiphon in any better situation, the Romans breathing down its walls, Ctesiphon saved at the last second by the death of the Roman Emperor, three Bahrams come and gone since my birth five decades ago, the third King barely seated on his weak throne when he was doomed: in a moment he was no longer Shahanshah, Kings of Kings, how desperate a title, hoping for the ultimate when it might last only overnight; and this is like all our lives, especially mine, the young Princess betrothed to one Shahanshah Bahram, only to be Queen for a moment, only by luck kept on afterward, for forty years living in the shadows of the court, but how long will it last, I could be out in the mud, Dnund-like, at any moment and so I brought her back to Ctesiphon with me, a kind of talisman to remind me of my imminent demise, a talisman who contains a secret to longer life, hidden inside her own central compartment, the key to the writing on the star lamp – did she lead me to believe that she had this knowledge, or did I merely wish it? and so I have taken her in, and bathed her, and clothed her, but at first I did not give her food, I denied her nourishment to show her that I had not been taken in completely, I starved her how was I to know that her starvation nourished her soul, fed the very part of her that I wanted, the visionary part, the part of her I saw into at Hecatomphylos: in her straw-floored cell Dnund intoned, muttered arcane chants, her head snapping up violently with intention; I sent for the Muveds to interpret her words but they sniggered, thought her mad, me deranged, I sent them away having learned nothing so I fed Dnund, renewed her strength, then intoxicated her, poured powerful drafts down her throat and the visions returned; this time I sent scribes to write down every word, every groan and belch, and secretly showed them to the most brilliant viziers, who scratched their heads and whispered about me behind pillars, so I sent them away, sobered up Dnund, smothered her with oils, fetched eunuchs to massage and pommel her, abandoned all tricks and sat with her myself, questioning her, berating her, praising her, letting her drift into trance, neither of us sleeping for days and nights; when the visions returned I kept her sharp and focused, stuck my fingers in her ears if she drifted off, shoved them down her throat if she sickened, created a tight bond between us.

And she revealed it to me, the secret.

I will never reveal the secret to another soul, certainly not the words that accompany the secret, the words emblazoned on the star lamp, unreadable to anyone but a Parthian, or perhaps an ancient Sumerian, but which formed on the lips of Dnund as she savaged me with her secret directives, insisted on audacious actions – insisted, always insisted with a fierceness – actions which were not secret but secretive, monstrous, calumnious, actions which would incite vicious gossip at court, force me underground, give me outsider status, but which would be worth any disgrace and so at the full moon, with the pretext of an arcane fire cult practice, Dnund's commands were met: ten males and ten females gathered and, as Dnund watched over the proceedings with great fervor, the group began to fondle and copulate, at first in pairs and then willy-nilly, in an ever-changing roiling sea of bodies; only at this moment was I, the eleventh female, to climb atop the seething mount of lust, lay back in full, naked vulnerability, and await the eleventh male, whom I was to let enter me regardless of his manner and appearance, in full trust of the situation I bucked and bobbed atop the twenty bodies, and the eleventh male appeared and approached me; I almost faltered, almost ceased the orgy, almost let my pride overtake my need, for there in front of me was an innocent lad, barely into his teens, obese and flabby, whose organ was barely visible under the folds of fat hanging about his groin, who was in no way fit to satisfy a hungry, worldly Queen like myself I knew this was the test, I lay back and gave into vulnerability, gullibility, and humility, I recited the magic words Dnund had whispered to me, I concentrated with all my might on the ethereal secret she had shared with me, then suddenly I felt the hardness enter me, never mind the fleshy softness all around it, this boy could go to lengths with the best of them, never mind his massiveness, he was light as a feather, held aloft by the males to offset his weight, and never mind his youth, for he ploughed me with the seasoned skill of an old farmhand, enhanced by my open, accepting state of mind and I gasped for air and my eyes shot open again and the youth and I reached a delicious climax and as we moaned and groaned the other males and females pulled us apart and enfolded us into their swarm and other males entered me and I was not sure whether I needed to continue my state of acceptance or whether I could stop at any time but no matter because I did not wish to stop and the more we embraced and passed each other back and forth the more I wanted even after I was well spent and could not take anymore but still the males kept on past my exhaustion and energy and well-being until I could no longer stand it and lost consciousness.

In the morning I felt refreshed, like years had lifted off of me. I looked in the mirror and saw that I appeared no older than the age of the boy.

I had discovered the key to everlasting youth.

ق

11

―◦◦◦―

"What happened then?" Porcelain Honeywell demanded. Sahara had just repeated Uzmeth's story to her, and told the real estate agent about Amar's late night working with Ooma. "Not that I would believe everything Amar told you." They were sitting outside on Sahara's patio, next to the bubbling fountain. Porcy wore a purple poncho over her stocky frame despite the warm spring air.

"Oh, he's telling the truth," Sahara smiled. "He confessed everything about Ooma to me to show his honesty and his genuine interest in the stories."

"But did he shag her in the back seat after the story? After hearing about an orgy? Honey, shall I get the divorce papers? How are you dealing with this?"

Sahara took a sip of coffee and looked at the fountain. "It has its benefits. Amar was quite turned on by her story and ... let's say he brought his work home with him."

"Very nice. You guys have needed a little extracurricular."

"But Porcy, I was much more disturbed about Ooma receiving the story in the first place. It's weird enough that I experience these things. Now someone else is!"

"Amazing, isn't it? And couldn't happen to a nicer girl."

"How can you be so matter-of-fact? She dreamed up the same evil Queen as me!"

"But what did I tell you? Am I the voice of the people or what? This is another one of those connections, like between me and Amar and Zack when you found your house."

"This isn't about real estate, Porcy, this is about mental hallucinations of Fourth Century Persia."

"It's about people in Glenclaire connecting in a mysterious way. We're coming out of the woodwork. Even my Bax."

"Bax." Sahara reminded herself of the young man Porcy brought to her New Year's party. "The guy Amar caught heavy petting with Ooma?"

"Ooma again! See, another interesting connection: dark-braided Middle Eastern cutie meets fair-haired Colorado cowboy."

"He's been living with you for a couple years, right? You devil."

"You think that big hunk would go for a little brown dumpling like me? He must be eight feet tall. No, I find him odd jobs, help him figure out his life. Bit of a messed up pup. We do psychic readings, I Ching, Tarot. That's how he received his story."

"Excuse me?"

"We were doing a reading and he drew the Ten of Swords. That card shows a man lying with ten swords in his back. He was upset."

"I'm upset! You're telling me someone else is having visions out of the blue?"

"Out of the image on the card. We explored it and he began recounting an entire tale. With Queen Uzmeth. Orgies and everything."

"You're freaking me out! *Another* Persian tale?"

"Yep. Beautiful maidens, high-breasted virgins, the whole schmear."

"Porcy, what is going on?" Sahara vaguely recalled a voice telling her about all this.

Porcy gave Sahara a gentle smile of understanding, which contrasted her previous jocularity. "Don't worry, sweetie. It's going to be all right. Try to believe me: we're part of an amazing thing, people with amazing abilities, right here in the burbs."

Sahara felt overwhelmed, but attempted to calm herself. "So Bax told you a story?"

"I helped fill in a bit. He's a man of few words. His tale is about a slave named Ba'ash. Dinzadeh procured him for the palace orgies and he became Uzmeth's favorite. He replaced Ardryashir as the Queen's lover. That's when his troubles began."

The Tale of the Nighttime Stalker

Shah Zabar. Don't like him. Sniffs around too much. New lord at court. Ruled small kingdom. Outskirts of Empire. Overrun. Hordes from East. Shah Zabar escapes. Hiding out here in Ctesiphon. Safe haven. Brought his new bride. Like her. Everyone likes her. Even the women. Even Dinzadeh. Precious beauty.

But don't like Shah Zabar. He's wary of whole court. Unsafe haven. Allies into enemies. Hoards his bride. Grab her up otherwise. Private orgy. Away from Uzmeth. Or with. No matter. Uzmeth treats me well. Despite Dinzadeh's warnings.

What would Uzmeth do to me? I am silver to her. Cast Ardryashir from her bed. For me. Me, the older man. Age means all to her. The ageless one. Thrives on youth. So why take me as lover? As old as Dinzadeh. Oldest member of orgy. Also biggest member of orgy. Hugest member in orgy. Long in years, but longer in bed.

I have spiced up the rites. Added the surprise factor. Threw in curves. Uzmeth never knows when. Taking advantage of her. Of sharing her bed. Good night kiss. Then four girls appear. Under the sheepskins. Two males. Behind the curtain. A couple in the closet. Already coupled. Hundred and fifty year old juices flowing. That's why. Not just my hugeness. (That doesn't hurt.) My tricks, too. That's why I'm silver.

That's why Ardryashir is out. Furious, but out. He was once silver. Once betrothed to Uzmeth. Once adored. Imbued with great powers. Used by her to sow chaos. Shake up things in Ctseiphon. Ardryashir was master of devastation. Slip into marketplace as if invisible. Leave trail of chaos behind him. Hens with necks twisted. Purses filched, moved to another's pocket. Accusations hurled. Knives drawn. Merchandise scattered. No one knew the real source of trouble.

Fear and suspicion spread to the court. Romans peck at us from the outside. But court chews itself from the inside. All thanks to Ardryashir. Started with an innocent poisoning. Then a couple found slashed. Confusion spread. Uzmeth's protection. While true dangers lurk her ways are no threat. What's an orgy next to a strangling?

But the strangled hens have come home to roost. Infiltrated Uzmeth's orgy harem. Assassin in our midst. Chaos scheme backfired. Fox in the coop. Three girls dead already. Many more close calls. None of it at Uzmeth's request. So can't be Ardryashir. Her assassins work elsewhere. Ctesiphon truly unsafe haven. All are scared.

Shah Zabar fears for his bride. Still, I don't trust him. Maybe he's the killer. Protect his own. By despoiling others. Jealous of harem. His bride number one. Stake his place at court. Don't mess with me. The look in his eye. Wild and worried.

Who else could it be? A courtier offended by the rites? Punishing the girls? Possibly. An assassin ordered by Shahanshah Bahram? Clean up the coop. Possibly. But the Romans are the real threat to Shahanshah. Why waste his time?

My coins are on Shah Zabar.

Uzmeth agrees. Especially now. After last night. Out on the rampart. Feeling the breeze. She loves the North wind. Cooling off the desert. Stood there with her eyes closed. Taking it in.

Then a hand on her shoulder. Felt like a lover. Thought it was me. Or...? Hand over her mouth. Knife to her throat. Quick cut. Killer away. Uzmeth dropped. I found her. Blood still warm. But clotted. Opened her eyes. Looked at me and smiled. Bring me wet cloth she hissed. Wipe this filth off.

Uzmeth was on her feet in the hour. Orgies not only lengthen her life. She never gets sick. Heals wounds instantly. Never dies. Invulnerable.

I suspected Dinzadeh then. Freedom her goal. Rid of the mistress. But she knows mistress cannot die. Better than anyone. Seems even to know Uzmeth's secret. Secret, inner practice during orgy. While naked and vulnerable. Brings invulnerability. How could Dinzadeh know? Acts as if she taught Uzmeth. Impossible. Uzmeth tells no one.

Uzmeth does not suspect Dinzadeh. If so, suspects everyone. Dinzadeh too obedient. And now fresh murders. Orgy boys this time. Why would Dinzadeh? Brought us all in from outside. Saved us. Protects us. Why destroy her foundlings?

Down to Shah Zabar. Steer clear. Keep him away. Ardryashir and I patrol at night. Hounds after the fox. Ardryashir first. While I warm up the bed. Then my shift after Uzmeth satisfied. (But never sated!)

Palace peaceful at night. Moonlight over the orgy slave quarters. Sleeping beauties. Hover over the girls longer than boy quarters. Make sure they're safe. Everyone in their beds. Everyone warm. Might need to warm one up. (Ardryashir does it.) Like tonight. Just for a minute. (Does Ardryashir miss Uzmeth's bed?) Climb in with one girl. (He jests with me about it.) Lovely soft sleepy moans. (He encourages me.) Safe in my arms. Warm. Moves into me. My robe. My strength. My –

The boys! Lingering here. Too long for my own good. Pull away. My robe. Dash to the boys' quarters. Hear a sound. Where? What? Movement at other end. Run down the beds. Wait! This bed. Streak of wet. Shiny. Moonlit. Black red. Bloody boy! Victim. On my watch!

The movement again. Someone there. Definitely. Truth time. Pull on my knife. Caught in my robe. Fool! Fucking, lingering, fool!

Knife out. Out. Come out. I hiss. Come out, Shah Zabar. Deathly quiet. Hiding coward. Show yourself. Weakling. Skulking. Coward!

The taunts work. The killer appears. You! No! Why? Not possible!

I raise my knife. Step forward. How can this be? Too strange. And on my watch. A huge, strange shame of responsibility. Wasn't there. Drop the knife. Shake my head. Why you? Cannot look at you. Turn away. All gone wrong. Head in my hands. Try to make sense.

Quick stab. Knife. In my back. Of course. Lost my mind. Too shocked. Lost my head. Cry out. Boys awake. Killer gone.

Lost my life.

ق

Sahara snapped out of her intense concentration. At her feet she saw Dr. Diana Machiyoko seated on the stool. Sahara had just finished reconstructing Bax's story as Porcy had described it. She was tired, halfway through her pregnancy and feeling alternately pumped with energy and wiped out. Although Dr. Machiyoko had been back in town since the middle of May, their recent sessions had only served as catch up. Every time Sahara brought up her marriage, Dr. Machiyoko asked for another story.

The therapist returned to her armchair, deep in thought. Sahara finally broke the silence. "I'm not just disturbed by Ooma and Bax having visions. These are pretty creepy stories, especially the stalking killer."

"Yes, I can see how it's overwhelming. But let's look at this tale for a moment. How do you feel about Ba'ash's murder?"

"It's disturbing, of course. I don't like Uzmeth. Do you think she's the killer?"

"Why would she kill her own slaves? She needs them for her orgies."

"But we also know that at some point she was killing off the kingdom's young women, and that must've depleted her ranks."

"Why do you think she did that?"

"I've been trying to figure that out. First off, Uzmeth's meeting with Dnund and her first orgy came a hundred years before Dinzadeh warned Sharzad about the killings. If we're to trust Ooma's story. And we know Ardryashir created mayhem outside the harem to aid Uzmeth when he was her favorite. But afterward, Ba'ash replaced Ardryashir as her favorite. I think that the chaos Ardryashir created, followed by the crumbling of the harem, the murder of Ba'ash, and the attempt on her own life – all of this unhinged Uzmeth's mind. So she devastated the country's female population, the most insane act of all."

"Excellent!" Dr. Machiyoko grinned. "Do you see what you're doing?"

"I'm just trying to make sense of things."

"Yes, by making connections. Each of these tales came from a different source. One came to you, another was on a tape, another came to Ooma when she was with your husband, and another came from Bax, via Porcy. That frightens you, and yet you're taking each story at its word, looking at the inner connections between them."

"So I take them seriously, I believe them. Does that mean I'm crazy?"

"Not at all." Dr. Machiyoko was getting animated. "When you have one of these images, what does it feel like? A fantasy? Your imagination going over the top?"

"It might start like that, but once it starts unfolding, it's very real, bizarrely real."

Dr. Machiyoko crossed and uncrossed her legs. "Could these stories be real?"

"Don't I have them because of Amar? Because of my vulnerable state?"

"Partly. But why are Ooma and Bax receiving stories?" The therapist leaned in toward Sahara. "Their tales are just as vivid and tangible as yours, and the connections between them all give an even greater reality to them."

"Am I supposed to be having an epiphany right now?"

"No, it is my turn to reveal something. A theory. I just want to put you into a receptive place to hear it. I don't think these are stories, at least not make-believe stories."

"Then what are they?" Sahara asked.

"Past life recalls."

12

Sahara felt a chill up her spine. "Past lives?"

Dr. Machiyoko nodded. "Many things trigger past life recalls. Usually fleeting, like *déjà vu*s. But emotional stress or trauma can bring on fuller, more intense regressions to our past lives."

"You're saying that I've actually *lived* these experiences, that I *was* these people? What about Bax and Ooma? I hardly know them but I lived in Persia with them?" Dr. Machiyoko's suggestion was too much to take in. She had barely absorbed that other people were having visions, connected to hers. But reincarnation?

"Nothing's certain, Sahara. We should focus on the possibility *you're* having memories."

"So who was I? What was I dealing with?"

"Exactly the right questions. Take these Persian stories for example."

"I must be Sharzad. Does that mean I was the actual Scheherazade of history?"

"That's more in your realm of expertise," the therapist answered, "I wouldn't know how Sharzad is related to Scheherazade."

"But this is unbelievable! If I actually lived the life of the historical person who became Scheherazade, then I have access to some incredible information for my research."

"And how incredible it is that in this lifetime you have chosen to study her."

"It makes me want to learn more. But I can't just jump back into my research. I'm trapped with Amar, his false promises, his anger. Doctor, if I wasn't nuts before, I am now. One minute I'm freaked out about seeing past lives, the next I'm ecstatic, and now I'm ready to slit my wrists."

"Okay, let's take a moment." Dr. Machiyoko leaned forward and said quietly, "It's going to be all right. This is a gift you have, an amazing gift. You'll find your way."

Sahara nodded acknowledgement. "Thanks. I just need to use it." She took a deep breath. "I haven't even told you my latest story. Do you want to hear it?"

Dr. Machiyoko looked at the clock. It was well past time to stop. "Absolutely."

The Tale of the Supercontinent

On Monday I woke up and had a strange feeling, not just a sleepy, half-conscious feeling, but also a sense that objects around me were at once miles away and so close that they were part of my skin. The sensation retreated to the back of my mind as I began my daily tasks. Amar and I said very little at breakfast and after he had gone, I cleared the dishes, wiped down the counter, and filled the sink with water to rinse the plates.

I stood at the sink watching the warm water rise. An oily residue from the eggs and butter created swirling liquid masses. I became mesmerized. The oily masses took on shape and forms, objects emerging in the liquid: animals, faces, and then countries and continents. I recognized Africa, Australia, South America, India. The shapes flowed around one another like a miniature continental drift, but with no realistic direction or orientation.

I turned off the faucet. The submerged dishes were like tectonic plates holding the movement of water in slow check. Gradually, the shapes slowed down their movements and came together to form one vast supercontinent in the center of the sink. My strange, large-scale sense of space returned, and for a moment I felt like I was looking at the Earth, not as a graphic map, but a true replica of an ancient planet. Then it seemed that I was resting on the surface, part of the Earth's crust. I transformed into a chunk of the planet.

Am I dead? I cannot move. I stare up into space and I see the familiar Spirits of the air, the Energies, the nuclear Forces, flying and racing through the sky. I know their motions, I know that space, I am below all that, in the place they look down on, the place of the fiery planet.

I am not dead. I am resting, this is certain, and I am certainly glad of it, the peaceful, non-exertion is a glorious boon to me, for I feel I have been constantly changing. I am embedded in something that does not allow motion and that orients me toward the sky. The planet is no longer fiery but warm and cooling, strong and solid. I let myself sink comfortably into it. The Spirits above me seem like creatures of the past, floating in the land of the dead.

I burst out laughing. I was about to submerge my hands into the supercontinental waters of the sink when I stopped, uneasy about breaking the spell I had created. I went out to do the shopping early. On Abbey Street, I went to the cheese shop for a wedge of Camembert and picked up a pound of

Sumatra beans at To a Tea. It had begun to rain and small pools of water were forming on the sidewalk and street. In one puddle oil and gas from the cars was swirling around in the rainwater. My mind focused on the shape forming in the liquid and I saw a familiar outline: the supercontinent rotating on the waters.

Why can't I move? I need the rest, but how long will I be planted here? I cannot move to look around, but gradually I learn that I can be aware of all the areas around me. There are stray tendrils of flame left over from the burning and cooling of the planet. Time flows on and I sense the ground forming for miles and miles on every side.

The land. The land is what holds me, comforts me, replenishes me. I sense huge fields of liquid rising and lowering at the edges of the new land, giving definition to it. Still I do not move. Unknowable amounts of time crawl on. I send out my sensors and see how far my awareness extends. I become aware of a huge landmass, but I cannot gain my bearings, for the drifting of the earth confounds me at every turn.

I heighten my powers of concentration and sense a vast coastline rimming me like an immense halo. It stretches down toward the south; the southern lands seem endless and majestic. I feel a great pride in my homeland.

A car drove through the puddle and sprayed me with the oily water. I had no idea how long I had been staring at it. I drove to the supermarket, threw a pound of shrimp and some root vegetables into the basket. On the way home I bought some Indian cumin at the spice shop, looked at cabinets in a furniture store. At home I put away the groceries, looked up a recipe, cleaned up a mess after I dropped a mug of tea.

Fed up with these banalities, I did some online research and learned that scientists think the continents may have been drifting, forming supercontinents, breaking apart, and re-forming new ones for billions of years. I saw one configuration where Siberia was southern and Antarctica was northern. The descriptions of the forming and movement of the landmasses matched the essence of my reveries. There is physical evidence for the most recent ones, hundreds of millions of years old, which have names like Rodinia, Pangaea, and Gondwana. But since their formation was cyclical, theoretically there were earlier supercontinents. I felt a tingle reading about Ur, and a recognition looking at the name Vaalbara, which was smaller than Australia, but the single landmass on the planet over three billion years ago. Was my fantasy about these early supercontinents?

The fading afternoon light played tricks on the computer screen. As shadowy patterns formed on the screen, I stared at Antarctica in its various positions, resisting its final resting place at the South Pole for millions and millions of years. Dusk approached. I forgot about dinner. I was lost once more in the swirling images.

Over the billennia I learn to move freely around the landmass. I stretch out to the coastlines, rise above to the mountaintops, and dive below the valleys and the nearby sea floors to touch bottom on the Earth's mantle. I travel swiftly, but I remain grounded in the beloved earth, wearing myself out until I collapse back on the surface.

I look across the land, pleased to see that the huger volcanoes and fiery chasms have subsided, and that they have left wispy flumes of smoke rising from the land. I perceive these smoky curls as beautiful tresses waving in the wind above my lands; I pretend I am stroking them myself. As figurehead of my vast homeland, I proudly display myself to the Spirits in the sky above.

I imagine their admiration at my accomplishment over hundreds of epochs. I have turned the old, harsh, evolving land into a new, but familiar, friend. I have learned loyalty to a native land. If I were to leave this corner of the world, if my motherland were to break off from the rest of the landmass, I would seek to return here to my foundation, I would rekindle my allegiance, I would feel a familial bond to all those who inhabit or honor this land.

It was dark. I ran to the kitchen to make dinner. I had little hope of it being ready before Amar got home. I chopped the vegetables, ends of turnips and carrots flying onto the floor; I threw them in the oven as I whipped up a spicy shrimp recipe on top of the stove. I was about to look in the refrigerator for some sort of dessert concoction when I noticed the flashing light on the answering machine. When had the phone rang?

The message was from Amar. He was working late in the office. Again.

I ate dinner alone. I desperately wanted to tell Amar my story. I wondered if Ooma Qadir was telling Amar another of *her* stories. I wanted out of this unhealthy marriage, but I needed my man. I should have left Amar after his first danger-ous threat, but something kept me with him, some magical, uncontrollable force.

"You blabbed this to Dr. Machiyoko?" Zack Goodkin poured Sahara another cup of mint tea. They sat in Zack's living room, cluttered with ceramics, wall hangings, paintings, colorful throw pillows, painted wooden frogs, Asian statuary, goblets. After her session with the therapist had left her more confused than ever about past lives, Glenclaireans with stories, and what to do about her marriage, Sahara sought refuge at Zack's house. She told him about the supercontinent story from the therapy session, Bax's Persian tale from Porcy, and Ooma's tale from Amar.

"Dr. Machiyoko thinks the force linking me to Amar is rooted in our past lives."

"I've been to India a number of times with my trading biz, and they eat past life stuff for breakfast. But a supercontinent in your last life? Believing you were Scheherazade's cousin-in-law is hard enough. But a Goddess on some mythical, red island?"

"Or the South wind? I know it's a huge stretch. But it feels totally real. I really watched a murder hidden in an alcove, I was really on a beach holding that little thief –"

" – and on the dawn of the fourth day you really took your leave of the king," Zack mocked. "You must be nuts, except that there's other loonies in town. Ooma, Bax, Porcy –"

"Porcy just told me Bax's story. She didn't have one of her own."

Zack cleared their mugs and replaced them with a bottle of wine and two glasses. Sahara saw the look of concern on his face. "Zack, what is it?"

Pouring the wine, Zack said, "Sorry to break this to you, in your vulnerable state. But guess what? Porcy told me a tale! And it relates to yours."

13

———

"Please tell me you're joking," Sahara said. "Your realtor shares visions with you?"

"She's more than my realtor actually," Zack said, "she's an old friend of my mother's."

"Who's next in the Glenclaire Visionary Society? How did the story come to her?"

"She was meditating in a tiny niche in her apartment. She began to feel closed in, like the small space was pushing against her. Fighting off the initial panic, she focused until she got a clear sense of a location. She saw a piece of land, forming, changing, moving."

"What's that got to do with her small space?"

"I'll try to explain. Here's the story."

The Tale of the Bituminous Coal Deposit

It took six feet of our compact plant matter to produce a bed of bituminous coal one foot thick.

Although our root systems contained many yards of matter in all directions, when it came time to hunker down in the swamp and get squeezed into coal, we lost touch with our roots. We detached, left only with the foot long body of our plant stem and branches.

The compaction process was a real headache. Millennia of boulders, shale deposits, and discarded caves jammed down on our reed-thin backsides: for a puny foot long weed to bear it was asking too much. And if a six foot bundle of *compacted* plants went into a foot of coal, imagine how many feet of poor, innocent plant life went into compacting the bundle in the first place. A single foot long plant was mashed down to a fifth of an inch of the black stuff. We'd be lucky if half of our body was still there in the finished product.

It makes me sick to think about it. All that pushing and shoving, getting whapped by someone trying to swing his branch out of the way. The broken joints, the bent over forms, the splatters of green ooze. Pounded into each other, we moved from bruising to death, then transcended death to become new matter, transformed from new matter into a dense, new, atramentous world.

I tried to fight it. I hid at first, watching my comrades from a corner of the swamp. But rocks descended upon me and I joined my fellow victims. Perhaps in banding together we would show a new force, but we played right into the hands of the coal-makers; they wanted us all in the same space, to make their comminution easier. There was no place to hide, no space to crawl into. I fought back even harder. We would not be crushed!

But when there was no room to move, when we knew that every available space was going to be filled, when we could not breathe because three, four, seven plants inhabited the same molecular territory. Panic struck. A frenzy of impossible motion erupted from our mashed selves. Screams of terror shot beyond our deaths. The tighter we grew, the more immobile in our inkiness, the more electrically charged we were with fright.

Sooner or millions of years later, we had to accept our fate. Most of us chose to remember the ordeal as a purifying experience: the space had been cleared, all the extraneous bodies and loiterers had been cleared out of the garden. Rather than panic that there was no room left at all, we chose to feel that a new space had been created, a new room to inhabit, visit, relish. We were prepared for something unique.

This kind of thinking pissed me off. I had found something to fight for, and now my former allies were rolling over like lumps of coal. As best I could, I pulled myself into a tighter bundle, doubled myself over to avoid the sheepish looks all around me. An image popped in and out of my head: a bedridden child, feeling above the world, weary of the souls around him. Very strange and distant. Why did it seem familiar?

As I achieved isolating myself from the lumpish fools crushing in on me, a new sensation shot through my black marrow, a tingling, an electric throb, a dull spark. I looked up and saw that everyone was on fire with the same sensation, a glow on our vein of coal.

Was this our reward for the millennia of suffering? It felt too good to be true, but in that moment of exhilaration, I felt a much larger purpose to our being imprisoned as we were, a purpose that went beyond our shelf of coal, out to the land around us, to a destination unknown but worthy of our struggle. We were no longer stuck, no longer immobile; we were moving, drawn toward some greater end-of-the-earth mission. At the same time I also felt an at-homeness, a settling down, a satisfaction with exactly where I was. I could no longer be disgruntled because I had found the perfect place to be.

ق

"Porcy's bed of coal is like your supercontinent forming," Zack said. "There's definitely a connection."

"It's still creeping me out that you two were chatting about past life visions. It feels like the whole town knew a secret before me."

Zack did not answer right away. He drained his wine glass. "I'm not surprised Ooma is having these visions. Remember I drove her home on New Year's, after she almost passed out from drinking? She's a susceptible thing."

"Thanks to Ooma, Dr. Machiyoko thinks I should tell Amar about the past life theory. Since he's searched Ooma out to reveal stories to him, I should act on his need to explore them in a deeper way, bring him closer to me. As she put it, I should 'honorably escort him for one whole day' into the workings of my feelings."

"Bizarre, but sage. Would you rather Amar not talk to Ooma at all? Even if it meant losing some stories related to your past lives?"

Sahara had no answer. The baby kicked. "Zack."

"What? You're thanking me for that insightful question?"

"I need a nap."

14

~oJo~

Later that week, Sahara and Amar received another mysterious, unmarked package. Inside, it contained a typed script
of a dialogue between two personages, Queen Uzmeth (clearly
placing its location in Sassanid Persia), and Shah Zabar.

The Tale of Shah Zabar and the Mystery Killer

Queen Uzmeth: How is it possible? I refuse to believe he is
responsible. You lie!
Shah Zabar: Forgive me, noble Queen. I have only your
safety and good will in mind. You must believe me.
Uzmeth: Why? You are ruler of a kingdom out in the
middle of nowhere, overrun by savage tribes. But no matter,
you are the honored guest of Shahanshah Bahram.

Zabar: Noble Queen. Uzmeth. Times are fragile. The palace rests on shaky ground. Murders within. Nightly shadows stalking the halls, often striking.

Uzmeth: You may be an honored guest, but you are tedious.

Zabar: The intensity of life at Ctesiphon has plagued me. And my own Queen. I have awakened from more than one nightmare. In one I had a vision of your death –

Uzmeth: Impossible.

Zabar: In dreams everything is possible. I heard your wails. And I was responsible. I do not know why, but I woke with the feeling that I had already let you down, that I was beholden to you.

Uzmeth: So you came to reveal the identity of the killer who has been stalking my harem? And you expect me to believe you because of some preposterous dream?

Zabar: The whole court has been threatened by this murderer. You have lost many young men and women. Innocent residents like Sharzad have been stalked through the hallways; even your slave Dinzadeh has been tormented.

Uzmeth: What has Dinzadeh told you? Out with it, if you wish my trust!

Zabar: My young bride sought out Dinzadeh for protection and comfort. She saw how your slave was taking care of the other slaves and protecting them from this killer.

Uzmeth: Dinzadeh was flattered by someone other than a slave seeking her aid.

Zabar: She took my bride under her wing.

Uzmeth: She took her to bed!

Zabar: What!

Uzmeth: I know many things, Shah Zabar. Now I know you have come to me not because of a useless dream, but because you have lost your love to my slave. Do you search for new love? Do you know what I have to offer?

Zabar: I seek love no more. I have given my heart and it has failed me. I have been a compassionate ruler and what did it gain me? I have been a caring lover and what has it brought me? Centuries of loving kindness and understanding could not serve me in the least. Do not mock me with love!

Uzmeth: Quell your anger, Zabar. Your fury will not return your bride to your arms.

Zabar: Yes. That is also what he said. He whose name I have shared with you. Risked my life to tell you. The killer.

Uzmeth: You sought love advice from a killer?

Zabar: By chance. I was aware of my wife's dalliance with Dinzadeh, but petrified to confront her. My tiny entourage has been so fragile since seeking asylum at Ctesiphon. But I was hagridden by the thought of the two of them slithering over each other's bodies. I needed help. I was drawn to him like a fly to rotting fruit. He offered to kill her right away! I was thunderstruck. I had to hold him back, I could not bear to see my beautiful bride disappear.

Uzmeth: But she was cuckolding you. With a woman. A slave!

Zabar: I loved her! Love fed my obsession. The would-be assassin argued that especially since love fired me, I must act on my love. If it was not returned, my ardor must transform to another physical outlet.

Uzmeth: Violence.

Zabar: Could the instinct toward violence be so close to the thrills of love? The killer confessed to me that he had known love and had been wronged in love. He wept at my feet over this love. He had been cast out, belittled, and left with the same obsession as I. Inside his heart the seed of violence had been planted. It grew bigger each night he lay alone in bed. His whole body shook with anger and despair.

Uzmeth: All from love.

Zabar: From obsession. Did I know when my love stopped and possession took hold? It felt like I had been born with blood on my soul. But I could not stay away from my advisor; I followed him through the halls, through his night watch; we were bonded, we felt each other's pain. He convinced me that she must die and that I alone should do the deed. It was the only way for me to drive out the demon-love-blood in my soul. He urged me on. I was terrified. He told me of his killings. He killed before me, in front of my eyes. I broke off from him, but returned. Again and again he had me witness his love-driven, demon-led killings. I begged him to stop, but I was fascinated, pained, tempted.

Uzmeth: I understand, Zabar. I believe you. I recognize this killer now. I see the truth. Tell me the end. Will you kill her?

Zabar: I have, Queen. Her body is still warm. She lies in Dinzadeh's room. I wished to inform you before Dinzadeh did. I simply did not wish that –

Uzmeth: That I would suspect you, the obvious murderer of your bride, of being the killer of young men and women in my harem. Especially since the murder took place in the room of my chief slave. You wish protection.

Zabar: You read my soul, noble Queen.

Uzmeth: It is a fair trade. The killer's name for the protection of your good name. Easily done. Your bride's death was simply another in the string of gruesome deeds occurring within these walls. Of course, I cannot guarantee you ultimate protection from anyone else at court. But the court has gladly turned a blind eye, ever since the murders became contained within my domain. They suspect it is all part of my strange practice.

But consider one thing, Shah Zabar. Do not show anything but grief for your bride. If you show any sign of anger or jealousy toward Dinzadeh, you will be suspected. And if you touch one lock of Dinzadeh's hair, I will annihilate you. She is mine. Understood?

Zabar: Yes. But what will become of the killer?

Uzmeth: All your talk of the killer's advice, his true thoughts: you have inspired me.

Zabar: Surely you must kill him?

Uzmeth: Not necessarily. Do not fret, Zabar. He will never suspect your betrayal.

Zabar: But won't he continue to kill if he lives?

Uzmeth: That's the delicious part. I know just how to deal with him.

ق

Once Sahara had reviewed the latest stories with Amar, they began discussing the script. "Who the hell is Shah Zabar?" Amar asked.

In answer, Sahara quoted from the Scheherazade story: " 'As soon as the vizier drew near *Shah Zaman's* court...' Maybe Shah Zabar is similar to Shah Zaman."

"The King's brother," Amar said, "who was also cuckolded by his Queen."

"He hacked her to pieces for it," Sahara added. "According to some versions, Shah Zaman also murdered wife after wife. The brothers were bonded in blood."

"The way Shah Zabar and the mystery killer are. So the stalking killer isn't Zabar."

"But how did we go from Uzmeth knowing the secret of youth with her bloodless orgies, to murdering virgins?" Sahara wanted more help piecing things together, but she needed to approach a tricky subject with her husband. "Amar, aren't you amazed that the stories come from different people and have all these connections? Dr. Machiyoko has a theory about the stories."

"Does it clear up all their confusions?"

"She thinks they're past lives."

Amar had heard plenty about reincarnation and karma during his childhood in India. But he had never firmly believed in it after the family moved away from New Delhi. "You're saying your Persian story is your past life as Sharzad?"

"Who is a historical version of Scheherazade. Isn't that amazing, given my work?"

"Isn't it just as plausible that you had that vision because of your work on the Nights, that it's all rolling around in your head?"

"I've considered that." She was disappointed in his reaction. "What about all these strange tapes and packages? Why do those stories mysteriously relate to mine?"

"They're bizarre, but that doesn't make them about past lives. Someone who knows the stories is messing with us. That nut Porcy could be up to something."

"Someone could be playing with us, or there might be a special connection going on. I just don't know. What I do know is that when I receive one of these visions, I have a powerful certainty that *it has happened before*. How do you explain that?"

Amar felt a new seriousness from his wife. "I don't know. I'm not having the visions."

"Do you believe what I'm saying?" Sahara asked, with an intense focus.

"I want to believe you. But you're asking me to take quite a leap of faith here."

"Same leap I'm taking. I'm not sure what it means, but the past life theory makes a certain sense to me."

"All right, I'll assume this theory makes a certain sense. What does that do for us?"

"It makes us see ourselves more vividly in the tales. Wouldn't that help us see what's going on, what's going wrong with us?"

"How?" He was making her do all the work.

"Let's go back to the Red Isle stories. Remember my recall about Sahnra and her brother Ambanari, fighting in the desert skies?"

"Yes, you scared me half to death, I thought you'd lose the baby."

Sahara was taken aback. "You were worried about the baby?"

"God yes. Sahr, I didn't want this baby, but I'm not looking to kill it!"

"I'm sorry, love, don't get mad, I'm just happy to hear it."

They both took a breath. "Okay," he said, "Ambanari – I felt a kindred spirit."

"Right. I think you were Ambanari in a past life."

"I was a God who flew in the clouds. With a mythical roukh. Protector of mallet instruments."

"I know, it's far-fetched. I don't have a clue what that sacred Instrument business is all about. But we know it had some great power. It was a matter of life and death for that culture. As Sahnra, I murdered a poor, mortal thief over it."

Amar grimaced. "Murdered the thief? You never told me."

"I don't know what I did to him. The vision ended, but I felt inside that I might have."

"The tales don't always add up. We don't know why Sahnra buried the Instrument. One minute they're battling over it, the next they're both cooked on a spit because of it."

"That's my point, Amar, if we were the brother and sister Gods, if these were our past lives together, the Instrument took its toll on our relationship. We were fierce warriors at times, enemies at times, allies at times, martyrs at times."

"In other words, we've been through the mill together, and here we are doing it again."

Sahara sat back on the couch and twirled a lock of hair. "You're catching on."

"We already know we're going through the mill, what big revelation is that?"

"Isn't it breathtaking to think of the scope of what we've been through?" At least they weren't fighting about it. At least she had brought up the subject. Sahara rested on her laurels.

15

Up until a few months before, Sahara and Amar's favorite restaurant in Glenclaire had been Roy's Cafe. It was run by the friendly Fitzgerald family, who had cashed in on a menu that was a perfect compromise between a typical pricey establishment in Glenclaire and a Jersey diner. Every Friday Amar would walk to Roy's from the train station and meet Sahara to celebrate the end of the work week. Since their feuding began they had not gone a single time. But things had lightened up a bit since their initial talk about past lives. Sahara was heartened that Amar had suggested they meet there that Friday.

He was late. Sahara had been hopeful that with their new ease Amar would stop staying late at work, but he had missed dinner twice that week. Sitting alone at Roy's was awkward. Even though the line to get in was increasing, Sahara did not want to give up the table. She had made fun of her neighbors who had followed the fad of cellular phones, but now she wished she had one to call Amar. She desperately wanted a glass of wine, but she could not have one. It was June, the last weeks of her second trimester, and she did not want to jeopardize how healthy she was feeling.

When Amar walked in an hour late, Sahara was furious. She feared his own anger if she confronted him, so she kept silent. Amar was full of good cheer. He shrugged off his lateness and appeased his wife with flattery. "You look beautiful. You're definitely showing, and it looks good on you. Rounds out that gorgeous face."

"Let's order," Sahara said.

Amar picked up his menu, determined to lighten the mood. "Good day?" Sahara merely grunted. "I had a great day. Got a lot accomplished. They're putting on a lot of pressure to get all our systems together in time for the millennium change. Thank God for Ooma: she is a wonder. As soon as you ask for something – it's done."

"I'll bet," Sahara said, against her better judgment.

Amar showed no reaction. "She's a good kid and a hard worker. Fascinated by you." He reached across the table and squeezed her hand. "But who wouldn't be?"

Suddenly Sahara realized that Amar was leading somewhere, his good spirits a set-up for something. After they ordered he revealed that on the train home, Ooma had told him a new story. She had received the tale when a taste in her mouth, a flavor, a sensation, had brought her into the fantasy. On the train she had poured forth a torrent of words.

The Tale of Oumkratania, First Queen of the Bed Isle

I have everything.
Rose-water mango palmfruit the vanilla orchids blended to open up my senses enter my body bathe me in delicious

feeling like a licking breeze teasing my naked skin. A little dog walks by sniffs at me licks my elbow whose dog is this is she hungry plentiful food here for man woman animal bird lizard alike. Plentiful roasted meats succulent fruits all my courtiers lie full and drunk about the palace breathing in the layered scents lightly fingering each other's skin calling for yet another song from the lutenists. Bulbuls fly freely in and out of the courtyard the pet monkey of the Minister clambers up the palms and there is that dog again is that the Minster's too it is into everything someone tie it up I won't have it loose like that in my court. My courtiers always calm me down with such flare-ups it is not important my Queen do not trouble yourself your Graciousness the ones more intimate with me will even lay hands on me massage my neck rub my back with the rose-water stroke my loins or poke their tongues in there to distract me.

Sweet manipulations what cares have I another quat slice gets placed in my mouth I do love the juices running down the little rivulets at the corners of my lips I can call a servant to come and clean up the trails of juice with a damp cloth or if it's a muscled helot I ask him to remove the wet stains with any part of his body that pleases me for I can command anyone in my queendom and get anything on the Red Isle. I, Queen Oumkratania, rule my people strongly and capably and in return I receive anything I want not in a barbaric manner but peaceably and willingly for the queendom flourishes as long as the Queen flourishes.

So why is that ridiculous dog still running loose running in circles everyone except me laughing and finding her so entertaining how pathetic and now it's coming over here cocking its head as if to ask me what's wrong lying down in the exact pose I am in it mocks me the court giggles and attempts to ward off my anger it's just an innocent little thing our Queen.

But it is strange how well it mimics me how well it seems to know my mood how funny not laughable but funny strange it looks at me so familiarly and I see it as a most familiar thing how long has it been at court isn't it new no it seems like it's been here as long as I as old as – I see something old ancient no timeless no I see myself reflected in its calm eyes an old dog with no new tricks I am this dog this dog was – the great Queen who has rose-water springs flowing throughout her palace who has countless musicians so that there is always music flowing who provides the most plentiful table to her courtiers and her loving people the great Queen Oumkratania is no greater than this little mocking dog.

I have nothing.

"Amar, how much have you told Ooma of my tales?"

Amar took several sips of wine before speaking. "Bits and pieces. Enough that she knew her story was connected to others. That it was worth telling me."

Sahara was seething. He had been an hour late, thoughtlessly offered her some wine, and admitted he was sharing stories behind her back. Amar saw her distress.

"What is it? You're mad because Ooma has some inside information?" Sahara was saved from answering by the food arriving, but Amar continued. "I get it, you think she made up her story. Why? To kiss the ground in front of me? To get in my pants? Do you really think a college kid with a strict Muslim upbringing would do that?"

Sahara attacked her Nicoise salad with a vengeance. Amar continued Ooma's tale.

Leave me take this vile animal from my sight no more merriment close the gates dismiss the court send the Minister to my rooms for quiet and most dreadful counsel.

102

What have I to live for tell me wise counselor what good is all this pleasure and entertainment if I feel no greater than a dog lying at my own feet tell me sharp advisor what use have I for the unlimited power over my people the surrounding islands and the mainland if I feel that I have no power over this desolate feeling that has invaded my soul?

"What would you wish, your Majestic?"

I wish for nothing on this earth, for I have everything possible from the red earth of our shores what more could I wish for how greedy of me to seek more from others what else could make me unfeel this terrible malaise?

"Perhaps the dog reminds you of our limited animal life. While the tall giraffa roams the central grasslands, the thick alephont stomps the mainland ground, all we have is the slithering crocodilus and my pet monkey. Shall I introduce a new beast to the island?"

No no no great Minister what care have I for new animals or riches or even rare plant life which our isle has in abundance what thing could make me contented even if it were a thing from the nearby shores it would just be another thing that someone else has smelled before tasted before captured before me.

"Then the Queen wishes for something never before seen? A novelty?"

Novelty perhaps but not if it were just a passing fancy born from the mind of a crowd pleaser or skinlicking courtier only if it were the true new thing unimagined from any imagination at court a thing so new that all would marvel at court and in the field all would travel for miles to see to hear to touch this Thing this holy treasure.

"It would transform the Queen from a great presence in this life to a Queen to be remembered for lifetimes to come."

Glory.

The Thing would immortalize my name It would live on after I have gone after a new Queen took my place her newness lessened by the glory of Oumkratania the coming Queens could not surpass my glory unless they basked in Its light in Its sound in whatever It contained that surpassed marvel prayer dedication faith glory glory glory.

I wish for Glory my Minister. Bring me that Thing that will bring me Glory.

In between bites, Amar said, "We were wondering about the corruption in the Red Isle court. Why the thief stole the objects, why Sahnra buried them – both to protect the Instrument from the court and Queens – and why the nation ended up in a horrible war. Oumkratania was their ancient Queen, the seed. Her personal need for glory started the corruption."

"Maybe." Sahara tossed her fork onto the empty plate.

"What is wrong with you? You're the one fascinated with all the links. Here's Ooma, completely on her own, getting a vision that fills in a gap from other stories. It's amazing."

Sahara had had enough. "You listen to my tales but refuse to believe there's anything to them. But as soon as some hot new thing opens her mouth, it's 'amazing' to you. How the fuck you think I feel about that?"

Sahara had raised her voice enough to attract the attention of the table next to theirs.

"Oh, come on!" Amar said. "I think Ooma's story is amazing when I think of *yours*! You two barely know one another and you receive stories that relate to each other. Aren't you glad I'm taking things seriously? I might even entertain that past life theory."

"Big of you. It would've been nice for you to see me and be more interested in what I might have to say before telling me how interesting or amazing your co-worker is."

Amar breathed. "Forgive me, love." He asked for dessert menus. "Want to hear the end?"

And so the Minister brought me the marvel of the ages, an Instrument of the largest dimensions that made a truly wonderful sound the true Sound of the Ages that the people never tired of and revered and worshipped and craved and it was too much for them the One Sound that was played for its Sound was gigantic like the roar of a God and yet it was of this earth and the Queen proclaimed that it was from the red earth of her queendom that she had created it for her people to march out into war with it strapped on their back she had created it for her court to sound out at the ceremonies of greatest pomp she had created it for her priestesses and acolytes to protect and bathe in healing oils which when watered down became healing fluids for the sick and lame and the Queen was loved and praised and venerated for her Great Creation and when she died she was buried below the ground upon which the Instrument rested and the Queen's name was remembered whenever one thought of or laid eyes on or heard the marvelous Instrument.

And the Instrument was the Great Gong, the Gong Ageng, the bronze Soul of the World, the Marker of Time, the Maker of Endlessness.

ق

They discussed the story over Hot Fudge Sundaes. Despite her foul mood Sahara was eager to process the new information. She realized that at first the Instrument had been a gong and later was replaced by a xylophone such as the dxylo-dxyla. Later Queens must have needed to claim new instruments as their own invention. What she did not understand yet was how the corruption had got so out of control in later times.

105

As his cappuccino arrived, Amar asked, "So do you mind if I tells things to Ooma?"

"Of course I mind. But at least I have one consolation. If the tale she told you is her past life, then she was Oumkratania – one slimy individual."

"Why is that a consolation? That's terrible!"

Sahara sipped her tea. "Zack was sure right when he asked if I'd rather Ooma keep away from you, or continue her stories."

"You told Zack about us? Behind my back? He's an old friend. How dare you! Who else have you told? That therapist. Porcy, for God's sake? Everyone!"

"So what? What if they know about our problems? You need to deal with all of it, you need to deal with what's wrong with us. You need to be in therapy with me!"

"Not again!"

"Not again!" Sahara mocked Amar's officious tone. "We both need it. We both can work on this past life idea. We can piece this out together, get to the bottom of it all."

"But I don't know if I believe in –"

"I don't know either. It's crazy!" She raised her voice. "But you're as wrapped up in it as I am. You just won't commit to the idea. Like with the baby, you won't commit!"

"Okay, stop." Amar saw they were being watched. He snapped for the check. "I said I was committed, I stopped hounding you about the baby."

"That's not enough. You have to be totally *for* your child."

"You know, look who's talking. You've blabbed about your past lives all over town, but who have you told that your pregnant?"

Sahara was struck. "Lots of ... people ... Dr. Machiyoko ..."

"That it? Porcy? Zack? Don't tell me who's not committed to our child," he gloated.

Amar had pushed too hard. He was right. She had not told Porcy or Zack about the baby in terms of what had happened with Amar. That was too shameful to talk about. But she wanted this baby. She put her face in her hands and began to cry.

"I can't do this alone, Amar." She paused between tears. "I need you. I've been afraid to tell anyone because I've felt ... alone ... like it really wasn't going to happen, like it could not happen if I didn't know you were there to help me."

Amar was silenced. Sahara looked up and implored her husband. "Come with me to see Dr. Machiyoko. Help me. I beg you. It will be good. For us. For the baby."

Amar rose from the table, helped Sahara up, and embraced her. As they left the restaurant the owners looked relieved as they said goodbye. Outside, Amar gently brushed away his wife's tears.

"All right, love. I'll go."

16

When Sahara and Amar arrived at Diana Machiyoko's office, the therapist was speaking quietly with an old man with gray-brown skin and salt-and-pepper dreadlocks. Sahara sensed that the stooped man had been a tall, dignified figure in his youth.

"The vizier's charge, Mademoiselle." He handed the therapist a slip of paper.

Dr. Machiyoko opened the paper, then smiled. "Thank you, Verle."

The old man nodded and disappeared. "The vizier's charge?" Sahara questioned. Ignoring Sahara's question, Dr. Machiyoko welcomed the couple inside her office. The window blinds darkened the space and let in glints of warm June sunshine.

"Sahara, take my chair. Amar, please, lie down and relax yourself."

"I beg your pardon?" he said.

Sahara moved to the armchair. Dr. Machiyoko went to her stool at the foot of the couch. "Forgive my bluntness. I'd like to take you back to a lifetime. Using hypnosis."

Amar sat gingerly on the futon, but did not lie down.

"Are you interested in the connections that have surfaced between the stories?" Dr. Machiyoko asked. When Amar nodded, she said, "The two of you are in crisis right now. But you've received a wonderful gift. These connections, the stories themselves: they are keys to understanding and healing your situation."

Amar continued to sit on the couch. "Where are you taking me ... back to?"

"The last story I heard from Sahara was about Shah Zabar revealing the killer to Uzmeth. I'd like to find out who done it."

"You think I know?" Amar said, a hint of affront in his voice.

"I think you do," she said.

"How would you know that I —"

"She's psychic," Sahara said, not entirely joking.

"Everyone's a psychic," Amar said.

"Except you," the therapist said. "I've been wondering why you haven't received any recalls. I believe you have past life stories inside you. I think you're fascinated by all the stories because you're tied to everything. Wouldn't you like to find out?"

Amar slowly lay down on the couch.

The therapist gave him a series of commands to relax deeply, open up his mind to receive, and travel back to the palace at Ctesiphon. It took a short while for Amar to respond, but to his wife's astonishment, he began to speak in a harsher, but weary voice.

Ardryashir's Tale

"Who are you?" the therapist prompted.

– Ardryashir. Uzmeth's slave. And no one's.

"Where are you?"

– It is dark. I am standing over a body. I have a knife in my hand.

"Whose body is it?"

– Ba'ash. The scoundrel who shared Uzmeth's bed.

"You've killed him?"

– Bad enough he was devious. Sneaking maidens into Uzmeth's bed. Outside of the orgy rituals. But now he's taking the younger ones at night. While on guard.

"Weren't you doing the same thing? And encouraging him?"

– So I told him. To bring him out. Now he's caught. Going the way of others.

"Others?"

– I have killed many.

"He's the killer!" Sahara exclaimed. "Amar!"

"No," Dr. Machiyoko corrected. "Ardryashir is the killer. We don't know the connection to your husband yet. Not for sure." She continued her questioning. "Ardryashir. How do you feel about killing all of the people?"

– I mourn them, but I do not regret. They are her tainted ones.

"Tainted?"

– Uzmeth has lost her way. She used me to sow unrest for years. I chipped away at dependable life outside the palace walls, in the market, down the water wells, at court and in the harem: intrigues, humiliations, backstabbing, self-hatred. Now everyone and everything is poisoned and Uzmeth is drawn into madness. Already she slights the rituals.

"And Ba'ash? Was he tainted? What do you think as you look upon him?"

– Musth. Musth. The word echoes in my ears. I do not know why. I do not know the word. Yet it is familiar. Is it Lust? Ba'ash is betrayed by cycles of lust surrounding him, chasing him. He lets his life fall apart because of it.

"What does this mean to you?"

– I have let my own life fall apart. I no longer truly serve Uzmeth. Vengeance brings no clarity.

"You are confused?"

– Lost. Hurt.

"Hurt? What has hurt you?"

– Love's betrayal. Stings from the dim past. Uzmeth abandons me.

"And so you kill?"

– I swipe them away.

"How will this be resolved? Take us forward in time."

– A secret room. Uzmeth's. Not for the rituals. She threatens me with horrible punishments for attempting to kill her. For killing Ba'ash, depleting her harem. But she wishes to bestow forgiveness.

"Forgiveness? For your horrible crimes?"

– I jump at the chance! Uzmeth favors me again!

"At what price?"

– She wants to rebuild the harem. She wants me to continue fomenting instability, not just at court, but also throughout the land. Her plan is insane.

"What is it?"

– Dinzadeh captures virgins from outside the palace. One at a time, she promises them to me. As Uzmeth watches, I marry a maiden, ravish her, and destroy her that same night.

"And you agree?"

– I am her slave. She can destroy me otherwise. Viciously. And...

"What?"

– She loves me. Again.

"But you say she is mad. Is her love true? Where does this madness lead?"

– I am a carnal killing machine. Week after week, some-times night after night. For a year. Maybe two or three. It is a painful blur. I become lost in the host of innocent faces.

"Do you remember anyone?"

– Toward the end. Proud Purzai. Pleading for all her sis-ters. Anger swells up in me as Uzmeth watches. I feel a thou-sand eyes upon me. I erupt into a rage after.

"What happens?"

– Nothing. Dinzadeh runs out of virgins. The land is dry. We all wait. Dinzadeh scours villages. She is stalling. Wants it to end. Delaying something.

"What?"

– Dinzadeh has to turn to the court. To Sharzad, the vizier's daughter. Both her parents dead. Sharzad is sustained by the whim of Shahanshah Bahram. But his power is crumbling. My charge was to bring down the Empire, not so it is vulner-able to the Romans, but unstable on its feet. To distract the court away from Uzmeth's depravities.

"So what happens to Sharzad?"

– Dinzadeh offers her to me. Uzmeth is overjoyed. It has been a long time since the last victim. Bring on the mating!

"As Uzmeth watches. And then?"

– We finish. It is time to kill Sharzad. Uzmeth raises her evil finger for me to strike. The nightmare is about to recur.

Dr. Machiyoko looked over at Sahara, then back to Amar. "Go on."

– Before I do anything...

"You're smiling!"

– Before Uzmeth can intervene...

"What is it?"

– Sharzad tells us a story.

ق

17

⸻◠◡◠⸻

"The birth of Scheherazade," Sahara intoned in a low, awe-struck whisper. "That's the most fascinating variation on how Scheherazade began telling her stories. And now I know why Queen Uzmeth went from happy little orgies to the slaughter of the virgins."

Shaking off the hypnosis state, Amar said, "Yeah, because I had a wounded heart and decapitated her harem, Uzmeth punished me by continuing my role as killer."

"I'm proud of you." Sahara cozied up to her husband on the futon.

"Because I left no virgin standing?"

"No, because you had your first recall. And you owned up to it, acknowledged the roots of violence in your soul. You were like the killer, the demon who hounds the first tales that Scheherazade tells the King. In those tales a victim must tell the demon a story or die, just as the King threatens Scheherazade's life unless he hears a new tale."

Sahara felt encouraged to bring up the darkest moment from their past few months. "And just as Sahnra, in my tale, threatened to annihilate the thief unless he told me his story.

And now, in our present lifetime, you yourself love my stories, even though you've threatened –"

"You make a very important point, Sahara," Dr. Machiyoko said.

"Excuse me, I'm not finished," Sahara said.

"Let's listen to Dr. Machiyoko," Amar said, happy to change the subject. "If I'm the King, then she's the Queen of therapists in our circle."

"Not even Minister of Affairs, but I hope this place is suitable quarters for the palace." Dr. Machiyoko moved over to the couch. "If you'll switch places, I'd like to try another unusual tact. Since we're seeing such unusual connections, I'd like to share one of my recalls."

"One of yours?" Sahara asked, frustrated by the therapist's interruption.

"I practice self-hypnosis on a regular basis. To relax, to explore past lives –"

"You have these recalls on purpose?" Amar asked.

"It's all part of therapy. These images tell us what's going on at the subconscious level, what our deepest issues are."

"But if you say they're part of the subconscious, why believe they're past lives?"

"Because of some of my experiences. I know you're struggling with the belief, Amar, so maybe my recall will help convince you. It takes place on the Red Isle."

"We received another mystery story about the Red Isle," he said.

"Don't tell me. Let's see if there's any connection with mine."

"What's your story about? Who's in it?"

Dr. Machiyoko stretched out on the futon. "The two of you, who else?"

The Tale of Queen D'aulai's False Reign

"You go get it!" the brother God, Ambanari said. "You're the one who lost it. I was trying to bring it back here. For your beloved people who hate you right now."

"Trying to bring it back here?" Sahnra spat back. "Crushed to dust by that oversized birdbrain? That was extremely helpful."

"You weren't exactly helpful – raising a sandstorm, a rainstorm, and a cyclone!"

"I was protecting the relics! Guarding them from further harm."

"Guarding them? You had them covered up with mountains of desert sand."

"The holy Instruments have been pilfered twice now. My Sauhra was a safe hiding place. Until your rock-head swooped in."

Ambanari took a breath before his next attack, and spoke calmly. "Sister, if you mean to help your people out of the predicament they are in now, if you wish to be cherished again, if you want to save this land, why would you want to keep the Gong Ageng and the Aula-aula as far away as possible?"

"There are treacherous men about. I already dealt with one who would have stolen the Instruments. Another made copies of them and sold them to those outside our land. I had to block his path."

"With an entire desert? Thousands of people had their homes destroyed by your desert, people who had never heard of the Instruments. Your worshippers think you're moody, vengeful, forgetful, unpredictable, and insane."

"Queen D'aulai has poisoned my name. Thrown me out of my own sanctuary."

"What are you going to do?" Ambanari demanded. The queendom is on the verge of ruin, the Aula-aula, the only original relic, is locked up in the Queen's palace. She's even changed its name to sound like hers, Dylo-daula or something. I say storm the gates. Turn into a monsoon."

"Curse D'aulai," Sahnra said. She is no Queen, just a fishergirl. Has the Red Isle ever had a true Queen? Oumkratania? Her legacy was corrupted."

"You didn't want to hear about the corruption when that poor thief first told you. He paid the price for telling the truth. What you did was inhumane."

"Maybe I overreact. But your vendettas last centuries. Some day you'll kill me."

"If the people don't do it first." Ambanari looked sharply at his sister. "We are not invulnerable. Take back the Instrument before it's too late."

"Then help me."

"You made the mess, you clean it up."

"Where is the Instrument?"

"D'aulai's home village. Where she found the –"

"Ha! Some poor fisherman found it in his net. Brought it home for a little good luck."

"And D'aulai stole it out of his hut in the night," Ambanari said. "Yes, I've heard that tale. But another tale says she was washed up on the beach herself, as good as dead. She had a vision of a heavenly world, where each soul must look back on his life as if it was a dream. The vision helped her recover her senses, and in that very moment she recovered the Instrument from the sand."

"It is her so-called pious side that brought madness to the island," Sahnra said. "D'aulai used the Holy Relic for her own glory, and raised a fever in the population that is out of control."

"But there have been true miracles. The Aula-aula washed up on shore, returned after my roukh lost it. Quite a favor to us. Take It back, sister."

"Take It back from hundreds of overzealous villagers, who rip apart anyone who dares approach the sacred Instrument?"

"I've heard they're like mad apes with yellow eyes, ferocious and obscene."

Sahnra said, "How am I to get at the blessed Relic with such an unholy guard?"

"It is said that as a child Queen D'aulai was the most obedient soul, honoring parents, relatives, neighbors alike. Her obedience led her into subservience, enslavement, and her prepious destitution. And her breaking with Obedience led her to great power. The Oath of Disobedience. The Queen has thousands of enslaved, obedient followers. Imagine this myth spread throughout the population: to truly obey the Queen's purpose, throw off the chains of Obedience. Thousands would forsake the law, until dissident resembled zealot."

"That would ruin her power," Sahnra said. "Her radiance must be extinguished. Her little rebellious eruption against obedience must be quelled. She has become overzealous."

"At the expense of everything truly sacred."

"After all our arguing and fighting, I see your way, brother. I have listened to you, and you will give no assistance? The loss of the Instruments may be on my shoulders, but the Red Isle faces even graver problems now. Are you so little concerned?"

"I am weary, sister. The people, the Queens, the Instruments have slipped through our fingers too many times. But I will help you. I will whisper the virtue of Disobedience throughout the air. I will be a wind of change. Once the Queen's fortress cracks and you have the Aula-aula, I will wind further up into the atmosphere and join the clouds."

"Perhaps I will join you there, brother. Later. For now, we are agreed."

ق

"So did I astound you with any information connected to your new Red Isle story?"

"Afraid not," Amar answered, "Ooma told me that Queen Oumkratania started the whole Instrument thing because of her need for glory. The Gods in your tale are clueless about Oumkratania's motives."

"But now we know how the war started," Sahara said, "though we don't know about the corruption at the time of the thieves, or who returned the Aula-aula to the Red Isle."

"There's something I don't understand," Amar said. You told us your recall of Ambanari and Sahnra talking together. Which means the two of us, right?" Amar looked pointedly at the therapist. "How is that possible? How do you know of our conversation?"

"My guess is that one of Queen D'aulai's spies was listening in," Dr. Machiyoko answered. "So I know about your conversation for one simple reason. I was Queen D'aulai. I unleashed untold devastation upon you."

Sahara had difficulty imagining the delicate therapist being a bloodthirsty murderer.

"Sahara, any of us may have done unspeakable acts of violence in a past life. You may have to reconsider your opinion of the violence in Amar's soul. We have only touched the surface of why Ardryashir was driven to such murderous intent. And we have no idea where that lifetime fits in terms of his soul's long journey to the present time."

Sahara thought: she told us her story to ease my anxiety about the tensions at home. She's discounting their seriousness because I haven't discussed everything that led to that terrible night in the kitchen. I have to confront what happened with Amar!

"Doctor, even if our souls were capable of violence in a past life, I have been a victim of Amar's violence in *this* life. That is why I came to you, not just to tell stories."

Sahara saw Amar's good spirits wither into a tense look of warning. Dr. Machiyoko sat on the edge of the couch. "I'm sorry but we are almost out of time. Let's wait –"

"But I'm ready! Amar is here. It's been weeks leading up to this point. I am not shrugging off the killer lurking in his soul because of your story about an evil Queen. That's ridiculous! This man insisted I get an abortion! He wanted me to kill my child!"

18

—⁓—

"That's water under the bridge," Amar said. "I didn't want a baby at first, but now we're having it and that's that."

"You *refused* this child, you pushed for an abortion, and when I resisted –"

"You did what you wanted to, regardless of how I felt!"

"This sounds like a crucial conversation," Dr. Machiyoko said. "You both need to hear what the other one is saying. We should pick this up next time."

"What, you're both out to shut me up? You're leaving me with this murderer?"

"I may have been a killer in one so-called past life, but in another I was your brother Ambanari, who supported you through crisis after crisis."

"Yes, by battling me in the sky, and begrudgingly helping me in a war that destroyed us, which you would've escaped by flying off to the clouds."

"The sky connection is interesting in those tales," Dr. Machiyoko offered. "Ambanari and Sahnra could have been reborn as the North and South winds."

"Still locked in struggle," Amar said, "stuck in an endless cycle of hot and cold."

"Until I, the South wind, flew off to the East African coast," Sahara muttered. "To escape."

"Which, I'm afraid, you have to do now," the therapist said. "My eight o'clock's here."

Sahara had wanted the session to help them, to heal them, and she was glad Amar had found some benefit. But she was feeling angry and manipulated. Amar asked why Sahara was ungrateful for the work that had just happened. But she could not express what was bothering her to Amar. She had worked so hard to get him to therapy that she dared not ruin it now.

At home, Amar suggested they go for a walk. It was getting dark, the June twilight bringing on a warm wind, the darkening sky hinting at a storm. Amar did most of the talking. As they walked down Glenedge Boulevard, she began to feel flushed and queasy. They approached an intersection, and Sahara felt sharp pangs in her abdomen. She doubled over and pain overtook her.

Amar led her to a bench at the bus stop. Sahara could not move or talk. Desperate, Amar got up, ready to rush home to call for help. Why hadn't he bought one of those new cell phones?

"I'll be back, Sahr. Hang in there. I'll be right back!"

Sahara looked up to see her husband running away from her. The wind whipped hair into her face. The pain was unbearable. She focused on the swirling wind, hoping to escape the pain.

The Tale of the Escape Wind

Was he far behind? Did he see where she went? Did he even go after her?

She had ridden off on an Escape wind, an armlet of the main branch, a Wind of Change. She was no longer the South wind, but rode this wind that blew dissent and invention throughout the world, in whatever direction it wished. She loved exploring and searching the world as she had never done before. The searching felt so natural to her, as if the desire for it had arisen from the depths of her soul, where it had been buried for eons.

The Escape wind is a predictably unpredictable force, the chaotic breeze that picks up the air from the flutter of a Japanese butterfly's wings and sends it halfway around the world to create an Atlantic hurricane. It is the pollen-bearing air that births giant oaks. It is the malevolent sprite that carries airborne germs into the nostrils of healthy mammals.

But the Escape wind also exhales the golden breath of inspiration, which spreads enlightenment from place to place. It is the friend of traders who share their knowledge and culture with those they meet. And every so often there is that miraculous and mysterious coalescing of ideas that suddenly turns into a nation's or a school's or an individual's Golden Age. It is usually short-lived in its purest and most potent form: Fifth Century Athens, the Spanish Caliphate, the Beatles' eight good years. There is always a Golden Age going on somewhere in the world, perhaps only one at any wind-given time. The pixilated Escape winds flow like the mellifluous, golden Hyblaean honey of Sicily. No one knows where the golden breath will end up next.

A new stab of pain jolted Sahara from her phantasy. The wind blew fiercely. Was she having a recall of life as the wind, or was it pure escapist fantasy? Where was Amar?

Darkness was settling into the sky. One of the town gas lamps illuminated a tree ten yards from the bus stop bench.

Under the strange, irrational logic of pain, Sahara felt the glowing tree was comforting, knew she had to go to the tree to be protected. The tree had some great powerful meaning in her life. She struggled to her feet, and inched over to the tree, bent halfway over, clutching her womb. When she reached the tree, her arms shot forward to grasp it, hanging on to its solid trunk with a will to live, to save her child.

Newspaper and litter blew in whirlpools all around her. To Sahara, the wind sent a protective circle around the tree. A sudden gust of air thrust a single page of paper flat against the tree, right next to her face. Sinking further into her frenzied logic, Sahara saw the page as a sign; she reached out to grasp its important message:

A THING OF THE PAST
SUPPORT GROUP FOR PAST LIFE EXPLORATION

TUESDAYS, 7 PM
UNITARIAN CHURCH, GLENCLAIRE
Elvira Young, Facilitator

Bring An Open Mind

Why had this paper flown into her hands? She clutched the page tightly. A past life group? In Glenclaire? Sahara's mind drifted away again, the thought of past life exploration superseding the pain. The sound of the wind engulfed her, surrounded her, shielded her.

Was he there? Does the wind bear him after me?
The Escape winds of Change also shift power from one direction to the next. Before 1000 B.C. the powers of the world lay in the East, the Mideast, the fertile crescents of

123

civilization. Then the winds blew the power to the West, to Greece and Rome. Before this shift, women had ruled, matriarchies abounded with their wisdom and their Goddesses. After, patriarchies supplanted them with their armies, their courts, their demagogues, and their women as Furies.

At the fulcrum of this shift, the bearish North wind came after the sultry South wind. He drove her into the armlets of the Escape wind, which continued onward to new lands, stretched out over the centuries, and settled into the 1500's, the Age of Exploration. It was the wind that pushed the ships forward on their journeys, scattered the growing Diasporas to the Four Winds, and allowed the great Islamic power centers to be blown away.

Throughout, did the North wind pursue her, grab her, lift her up, carry her?

Sahara could barely perceive what was happening to her. She was being handled, lifted, carried, whisked away. She felt she was hurling out of control, speeding, lights flashing. She clutched onto something: the flyer? herself? a hand? She hung on for dear life. A new voice came into her mind. It was the Other, the voice of the North wind –

– chasing her, riding this insane wind, she must not escape, how dare she think she can leave her place. I will not stay to rot in a sweltering desert. I will not become the desert wind. My place is up North, and now I waste my breath trying to catch her on this out of control stormwind. I hang onto to every fiber of air, like a drowning man clutching a plank on a raging sea.

I am not meant for this heat. I am the North wind, icy, cutting, bleak. One frozen lash of my arctic air and that's it: a quick end. I am almost on her now. I extend my frigid fingers out to her tailwinds. You are a coward, escaping thus, I accuse. Why doesn't she fight?

Instead, she tosses images back at me, images she claims to be inside her memory, that remind her of the folly of truly understanding cowardice: daily travelers who risk injury to their bodies: are they heroes or cowardly in their unthinking dependency on the daily journey? And those that do not dare the journey but stay safely at home, perhaps they are not the cowards but the true adventurers, exploring the inner landscape of the self, the most treacherous quest of all.

The voice supplanted the pain and somehow was a familiar comfort to her. She felt her harried form jostled and turned, poked and manipulated.

Then the South Wind, now part of the Escape wind, invites me to come along – audacious!

– dares me to leave our Arctic-equator treadmill and seek my own Golden Age. As I halt, shocked at her presumption, she whips ahead, off to the East, down to the coast.

I am more furious than ever! I am overheating! I would have destroyed her had I the chance, but no matter. There will be others. I wheel away into the atmosphere and head North to cool down, to temper my wrath, to smolder and plan revenges.

ق

The images of heat and rage merged with the distress in Sahara's body. Panic and confusion wracked her mind. Just as she could take no more, everything went dark.

END OF PART ONE

PART TWO

19

In the hospital, a groggy, medicated Sahara was not aware of the terrible testing she had gone through at the bus stop, or the danger to her pregnancy. Shock protected her from further pain. Instead, she had an unexpected optimism that she had reached an accord with Amar. In her daze, she literally saw a light at the end of the tunnel.

The Tale of the Ascension to the Fourth Level of Heaven

It had been lifetimes since I'd just stopped. The end of the previous universe had been full of conspiracy, betrayal, vengeance, cataclysm – and that was just the final week! The blinding light of this new universe was a welcome change, but with it came further intensity. I embraced the newness of it all, loved pioneering the first energy systems, the creation of the Spirit Force that emanates out of me now. Then I clung to a slowly moving landmass on a new planet, a pretext for establishing a bond. I let my lives last billions of years. Shedding my reputation as an innovator, I remained a happy little microbe, sloshing in the primordial oceans and running a nice cookshop while everyone else evolved. I needed the rest.

So here I found true peace. There was nothing on Terram like these cooling waters. This was no oceanic body of water, with all the pushing and fighting, the millioned colonies spewing on the waves. This interlife was a relief. I was in my Heaven of blessed relief.

There are six levels of the Spirit world that lie between Terram and its lunar orbit. I started in the second level, just up from the mother planet. All was dark, frightening if not for the refreshing liquid surrounding me, entering my spirit body. The liquid was water only in my imagination, like the mud I felt I was rolling in, the slime that oozed through my transparent veins. As I took stock of my surroundings I realized the water was a gaseous matter that was sifting in and out of me. The mud had a weighted feeling, though nothing here had any real weight. The slime was a luminiferous substance that coated my ethereal shape. I breathed out the Heavenly gases, sending them down to the earth, for the living to inhale and boost their spiritual make-up. Even the fish, those new pioneers of the oceans, took in eight out of nine parts oxygen in their water, some of it mixed with Spirit breath.

I discovered that the weightless weight I felt on me was malleable. I could transport myself through the second level. The luminiferous fluid in my veins made me yearn for a new form. I had had lives in the dark waters of Terram, other lives of light in the young universe. Dark or light, which would it be? I had loved both, grown weary of both. Why not just stay here in the coolness for an eternity, shed all that brilliance of being?

When all was said and done, the second level was not a particularly attractive location, especially for deep contemplation and soul searching. How long could I really last in mindless bliss? Perhaps forever, If I was truly selfless, but being only second level I knew I was not ready for that sort of mindlessness. Who was? I remembered a child wise beyond his years, a vague memory of a trip with him to a suburb where he thought he had lived a past life. Staying here would be like a peaceful suburb, which drives you crazy with boredom and desire. I was ready to move on.

I noticed a faint light seeping in from above. As I craned my ghostly neck to see, my form inched along toward the light. I realized to my delight that I was no longer swimming. My intent to move on had mobilized the substance beneath me, changing it from liquid to solid. I was moving on top of it, planting myself into its substantialness with legs of desire. I crawled, I walked on knees, I shuffled along!

The way toward the light became steeper. I was aware of a vector proceeding uphill, though there was no road or hill visible. As I climbed I was newly aware of my weariness, and paused to rest many times. My path toward the faint light became an alternation of motion and rest, between the desire to discover what waited at the height and the need to remain right where I was. Perhaps this process was my reason for being in this Heaven. My initial reaction to this was one of panic: am I stuck here forever, to climb and cling, rise and fall, move and rest?

Working myself into a froth would not help. Once I relaxed, my journey became a game. I rested as if I was never going to move, then bolted forward. I plumped myself up with Spirit air and Heaven blood, and then collapsed on the indiscernible path. Angelic beings must observe my progress, I thought, and my playful stopping-and-starting was for their entertainment as well as my own. I forgot about my destination and fully enjoyed my teasing game. I had achieved a wonderful balance between my three points of query: dark, light and rest.

Then I was in a new area, which was considerably brighter. I had made it to the next level! A peaceful feeling of happiness permeated my unearthly senses. I was in a splendid garden containing species I had never seen. The largest plants had thick stems with an earthen color and a hardened texture. The stems reached into the sky, sprouting a lattice network of long branches. Each branch contained smaller and smaller branches that sported lovely growths that would detach and flutter to the ground. Throughout the garden gentle breezes tickled this foliage and carried the sound of quiet bells and the smell of soft perfume. The whole effect teased me into a mood of playfulness and relaxation.

I found the most delicious glade of the large plantings to recuperate after my recent journey and many previous lifetimes. There I hid, perfectly content with its balance of dark from the shade, light from this new level, and glorious rest. To say I slept for an eternity would be false, since I would frequently awake for a moment to breathe in the perfumed ether or feel the tickle of a leaf falling on my brow.

Thereupon, the King commanded ...

Mixed in with the strange images of the hospital room around her – breathing machines that looked like tentacled monsters, fleeting images from the Arabian Nights, recent past life recalls, the dream of a Heaven above – Sahara knew that Amar was there.

... various nobles and lords of the realm...

He was there, her King, pressuring doctors, pacing the room, returning to the bed to hold her hand. Each time Sahara felt Amar's comforting presence, she drifted back....

I began to distinguish a new sensation after a long time. I would awake upon feeling this new thrill and it would vanish. I decided that the next time I was awakened by this tingle I would feign sleep and try to discover the source of the pleasure. Soon enough it came, a gentle pressure on my lower regions, a slight liquidy touch, though on occasion with a harder stroke. I felt waves of pleasure roll through me until the passion reached an indescribable peak. I could no longer pretend I was sleeping.

My eyes opened and to my delight I saw a translucent creature, like myself but with a beauty that outshone any moon or star I had ever seen. The being was entwined around me, though which part of him ended and which part of me began I could not say. His angelic breath played up and down my form, his enlaced arms and legs caressed and dandled me. I gasped with surprise as two feathery forms emerged from my companion's back. The protrusions were as transparent as the rest of him, but with a muscularity and strength. As our spirit bodies rocked in a delightful rhythm, his back extensions unfurled and pulsed up and down. His entire figure began to buck furiously and I clutched him more tightly. Our enmeshed shapes began to elevate from the ground and we slowly rose through the trees. The branches lightly whipped my surface; the leaves brushed my glowing pleasure centers. I returned these new sensations with strokes of my own, delivering my partner hugs and grabs and bites. I felt ten times ten ecstasies, and then times ten. We soared upward, beyond the canopy of the trees, reaching a new level of Spirit atmosphere, a new altitude, and a heightened and final climax.

My angelic lover gently returned us to the top of the canopy of trees, where we marveled at each other's forms. He pointed upward to the next level, and there I saw many winged creatures, frolicking and gliding through the celestial sphere. The light was even more pure and enticing. I yearned to be among those beings; I desired the next level of light.

It became clear that I had been partnered with this winged fellow not just for angelic love. He spoke to me of the six levels of Heaven and their relative worth. He enjoined me to speak of my past lives, though he seemed to know everything about them. As we spoke, I had two revelations: first, I was losing patience with rest and contemplation, and second, I had chosen the light over the dark. It seemed obvious once I stated it to my lover-mentor, but I had been holding on to the power and pleasure of my darker experiences over several life-times. It was time to embrace the light, and the image of the winged community up in the distant air drove me to action.

I begged my companion to fly me up there, just for a taste, but he warned me that I required much more training and work on my soul. I expressed my great pioneering spirit to him, implored him to give me a chance to jump into something fresh and new. He admitted that I had recovered enough to assume the challenge of a new life, and one of an evolved nature on Terram, but again warned that I was no match for the intense air of the next level.

I knew my angel was not a perfect being. He had reached a certain spirit level and was in training for the next. I was his charge, and occasionally he would return from a short trip with further instructions, or criticisms of how he had handled a recent discussion with me. Although I enjoyed our trysts, he initiated lovemaking with a desperate need. In short, he was no angel.

I decided I would parcel out my sexual favors, driving my partner to new lusts. I requested small trips up into the higher air in exchange for love. My winged lover agreed begrudgingly. Finally I abstained for a drawn-out period that drove my partner mad with desire. I was careful not to beg for anything, but simply showed a lust and need that brought my lover to a passion I had never seen. He sprouted his wings as we heated up and we ascended. I wrapped myself around him tightly, pampered him with every pleasure stroke I had learned, and teasingly stopped and started my courtesies, just like the game I had played with myself as I had walked up the path from second to third level. He was aflame. I whispered love thoughts in his ear, until my main theme became "Fly me higher!" He pumped his wings harder and harder and ascended the heights. I was to arrive at the next level! Soon I would don my own wings and swirl the air in all its purity.

No sooner did I have this thought than a strange burning took me by surprise. My insides, coated with the breath of passion, turned black with fire and smoke and I writhed as much in pain as in pleasure. My companion snapped out of his sexual reverie and rushed me down to the level below. It was too late: I had not been ready to withstand the ether of the next level and it consumed me. As my form disintegrated with the fires of my desire, my partner looked me in the eye. He did not reveal remorse or terror, but simply a pleasant smile, as if to assure me that I was getting what I wanted after all. I would leave this Heaven and return to Terram, where I would find a new life as a more evolved being on the verge of discovery. There I could experience the transition from water to land to air in a safer, natural way, and then continue my journey toward the next Heaven.

20

Sahara awoke the next morning at home, in the arms of her husband. It was the weekend after their therapy session, and her hospitalization, and they were able to sleep in. Sahara had had a close bout with high blood pressure, and the doctors had feared a case of eclampsia, given her extreme abdominal pains. Once they had sedated her and lowered her blood pressure, they were amazed to discover that the baby was stronger than ever, and that its heartbeat and stress level had been virtually unaffected. Although a mystery, the couple was grateful that the baby was safe.

"I was terrified," Amar said. "You clutched me in the ambulance like a life preserver."

"You did rescue me, didn't you?"

"Yes, but I don't know if I would have made it if I hadn't run into Zack. He was nearby in his car almost as soon as I started running home."

"How did he know, and respond so fast?" she wondered.

"Just lucky." Amar pulled her close to him, as if she might slip away at any moment.

Sahara's doctor ordered a strong dose of rest. Amar took time off from work and joined his wife in bed. It had been months since they had shared such simple intimacy. He brought her flowers regularly, and they cooed and soothed their hurt feelings.

Although they were careful not to probe what had been touched on in therapy, Sahara was hopeful. Some level of tension had been released. Moreover, Sahara had received that remarkable vision of Heaven. Recalling past lives begged the question of an afterlife: here was the first evidence of the soul's journey between lifetimes! And now paradise was briefly spilling over into their present life: Amar eased her sore body with loving touches, and Sahara assuaged his soul with a new story.

The Tale of Shaell and Arand's Ultimate Happiness

All my life in The Suburb I have aimed to please. As a child, good little Shaell was taught to entertain guests at parties with charming stories. At the local school I got good grades to please my teachers. And to please my parents, their beautiful Shaell was very careful choosing friends, especially boyfriends, knowing that whoever rang my doorbell might be my future spouse.

All it took was one to transgress the acceptable limits. Fondling his way to my heart and blouse buttons, Arand Offmore liberated me for the first of two crucial times in my life. How perfect: at once I could please someone and instantly get some pleasure out of it. The pleasure I visibly and audibly gave him greatly outweighed those small tsks and glances of displeasure from others. I gobbled up my youth with an earthy lust, and yet I was no wanton. Part of pleasing was caring and sensitivity, and so my lover was carefully wrapped in a loving, loyal relationship.

And so I wed Arand Offmore, in our town simply known as The Suburb, at the church equidistant from our family houses. There was a lovely touch to this match. I had never expected any rewards other than my own ecstasies in lovemaking. Arand, a do-gooder with a huge generosity, had no great need to satisfy a craving for himself. What we two, Arand and Shaell Offmore, gave to each other was surprising, enormous, embarrassing, breathtaking, and wondrous.

Sahara and Amar passed the month of June as if Spring did not wish to leave. Sahara read aloud from *The Thousand and One Nights*, particularly its sauciest passages. When Amar could stand no more of his wife's literary teases, he asked if her body was too tender for love. In response she climbed on top him, exposed her spreading belly, and commanded him to rise. The thief probed inside the magical cave; the vizier entered the waiting city; the poet inscribed his name on the unfurled scroll; the explorer penetrated the mists of the hidden valley. As Sahara entwined her fingers through her long reddish-golden hair, she admitted the patron into her theater of delights.

Her eye caught the roses on the nightstand and new images came through her.

After the first dozen bouquets from Arand came new books, blouses and skirts, tickets to concerts. Arand made a game of it: one week I would receive a pouch of sandalwood incense, a pair of sunglasses, new shoes, and vouchers to gamble at a casino in the City, then the next week, the gifts arrived in reverse order: gambling chits, shoes, glasses, incense. My gratitude shifted from politeness to delight, but then to queru-lous suspicion. "Is there a trick?" or "What does he want of me?" A ravenous pleaser like myself cannot accept gifts with-out the juices of reciprocation flowing.

I took the challenge of Arand's generosity to our marital bed. And to the soft maroon chair in the west corner of the living room, on top of the dining table, against the kitchen sink, and sunk into the thickly piled basement carpet. I ambushed Arand as he stepped through the front door from work, with barrages of kisses, ferocious unfastening of coats and ties, knee-banging lowerings of pleated pants. Every gift was met with a long night of physical paradise. Neither Arand nor I had a sense of who was giving and who was returning the favor. The roller coaster of gratitude ran out of control. Years passed before there was any sign of marital passion subsiding.

Late in our marriage, well after college graduations of the children, Arand was transferred at his job. Ironically, only a few years stood before retirement and so, loyal to our house and town, we decided to bear out a separation for the remain-ing time.

At first, the gifts came by mail: new mixing bowls, a pearl-inlayed jewelry box, gift certificates to a local spa. Despite the onset of age and flight delays, I traveled to Arand to bestow my thanks in Arand's steamy one-bedroom bungalow of love. As always my instincts were confirmed by Arand's utter delight, this time not just during my pleasing embraces, but also in my very appearance at his door.

Arand responded in kind. Gifts came not only by mail, but also by messenger, by telegram, or through various friends, neighbors, and store clerks. And presents just magically appeared. I would wake to find a new nightgown next to me in bed. I would open the refrigerator to discover a basket of cheeses and tropical fruits. I would start the car and hear a new recording of my favorite violinist.

I had more and more trouble reciprocating. Travel became costly and prohibitive. Requests for volunteer work and luncheon dates inundated me, and to my secret shame I jumped at any chance to cover my loneliness and pining with activity. In the year before Arand's retirement, my sexual desire ceased. I was mortified. I made countless excuses and apologies when my visits to Arand slacked off. When he found time to visit me, I apologized for endless meetings and activities. Delighted I was busying myself, Arand visited less and dug in at work for the home stretch.

As his presence diminished, I noticed something mundane about the gifts. In the clear light of maturity and solitude, I observed that the extravagance of the gifts only served to mask a clockwork regularity to Arand's generosity. So simple and blinding was this realization that it laid me low for weeks. I did not try to reach out to Arand, nor shrink from him, nor even exert any strategy of gratitude, asexual or otherwise. It made no difference.

Arand continued to be generous, to a virtue. I eased my concern by realizing that like myself, Arand simply acted generously because he derived pleasure from it. In considering the gifts that went out to colleagues, friends, and postal workers, I saw that it was simply Arand's nature to act this way. And then, the realization hit me. I had been too busy to please, too bound to reciprocate, too distant to understand. From a distance, I finally saw that Arand neither sought, needed, nor expected reciprocation. He simply loved me, even now, when I was unable to please him.

Amar wondered if he had been Arand Offmore in a past life. How many of Sahara's other recalls had involved him? If he had been Ambanari, how had she recalled the desert battle from his perspective? Sahara assumed that she had channeled that lifetime through him, just as she had received the North wind's story when clutching onto him. Sahara was concerned that Amar felt alienated because he was not receiving stories on his own, especially since he was aware of people in Glenclaire who were. But Amar did not seem to be disturbed by this fact. In fact, each day he affirmed their well-being in some way.

"I know the name of our boy."

Sahara was surprised. "You've thought of a name? It's a boy?"

"They had to do tests at the hospital. They asked me if I wanted to know the sex."

"And you were going to tell me ... when?"

"Don't be mad."

"I'm not." Sahara took Amar's hands. "You were actually thinking about a name."

"For our boy." Amar squeezed her hands. "Naji."

"What does it mean?"

"Distinguished. Intelligent. And: rescued from danger."

"He *was* rescued from danger. Naji Rash. I love it. I love you."

He placed his hand on Sahara's belly and rubbed. "Finish the story."

Arand's retirement was a quadruple celebration for us. First, with my new realization, I relaxed my fears of what to expect when we were reunited: I simply enjoyed the continuous presence of my man once more. Second, the transfer position had indeed been worth it: the company actually encouraged an older employee with a higher salary to retire through lavish severance and bonuses. We experienced such a windfall that, after a reasonable period of time back in his longtime nest in The Suburb, Arand surprised me with travel arrangements for a cruise around the world. Third: the new discovery of our unconditional love, and my emotional relaxation because of it, brought back my sexual appetite. I found myself launching surprise love attacks on Arand, with or without gift in hand. The fourth and ultimate happiness was in understanding that I had found the perfect match for myself.

21

⸺◦◦◦⸺

Since Amar had taken time off from work, by the end of the third week of June he was swamped at the office. He made sure he did not stay into the night, and returned home each evening with take-out food that he and Sahara shared in bed.

When Ooma Qadir expressed her concern over Amar's absence, he explained recent events to her. She delighted in the theory that the unfolding stories were past life memories. Ooma was convinced of it immediately, showing a certainty that beguiled Amar. How could she be so hooked on the belief, with so little evidence, he questioned.

"I love to believe in things, even if they don't make sense or are contradictory."

"But you're only eighteen, you're so young," Amar said.

"But I'm not stupid. You know I graduated high school a year early. I'm interning for you, aren't I, on Wall Street? I'm serious about what I believe in."

"Is your family behind this ... faith?"

"I'm first generation Iranian-American. Mom and Dad are good Moslems but not fundamentalists. I love Sufi poetry, sing in a Sufi choir thanks to them. But I'm your average American girl. Junk food through high school, ate anything that's not halal behind my parent's back. They believe in a girl getting an education, have no problem with me seeking a career. I want to be good to my family, but I want to be part of this world, want to be hip, successful. How do you do that and praise Allah with Mom and Dad, too? And Moslems aren't exactly popular in this country."

Amar shifted in his desk chair, sizing up his assistant, whose deep-set black eyes were at once hypnotic and innocent. "Do you have siblings?"

Ooma pulled a lollipop from her purse. "My brother Ali's back in Teheran. I have a little sister, too. She's Daddy's girl right now."

"Were you ever like your little sister?"

"Sure. The good daughter of the sultan. Veil down to here. Loved the whole thing."

"That's the true believer part, right? What was that like?"

Ooma rolled the lollipop around in her mouth. "All right. I'll tell you a story."

The Tale of the Faithful Young Moslem and her Secret Book

I'm seven. My parents are throwing a big party, ten, twenty friends from the Persian community in Glenclaire. Mom's in the Prophet's Seventh Heaven, cooking up a storm, preparing the house, and I help with the pastries, sneak sugar and dates on the side. My Dad has taught me several ghazal lyrics: Sufi love songs that are directed toward the mystical and divine, which I don't totally understand, they're kind of racy if you're in the know, but he's coached me well, he's proud of me. He's in the Seventh Heaven, too. He lets me learn the things that only boys learn, he's not that strict but he feels I must respect the spiritual ideas of the culture.

Even before I recite anything, I feel proud of my smart dad, proud of my beautiful culture, proud of myself. The words he teaches me remind me of the secret book I keep in my room, in my closet, that no one knows about except me, partly because I took it when it didn't belong to me. I found it on a bench outside the Glenclaire Library, where all the homeless people sit, but no one was around that morning and there was a book, and it was beautiful, special, and it was in Arabic! I learned Farsi from my family, and some Arabic from the poetry and prayers. I knew the book was meant for me: who would leave a Moslem holy book lying around? Whoever did deserved to lose it, and I felt a weird satisfaction that I was cleaning up from some careless person's loss.

I snuck the book home, and it became my secret, sacred, prized possession. I hid it in my closet, where I go with my flashlight and look at the pictures and try to read the words from the little Arabic I know. Mostly I held it close and dreamed about where it came from and what it means, and images came sometimes, of ancient, mystical libraries full of such books, with benches all around for magical people to sit and read, and secret dark corners where the books are stored. When I thought of these dark places and held the book on my belly I felt a tingly, holy, liquidy feeling inside of me.

It is not right to feel too much of such things, but I feel that way before the party, special, excited, pretty. I have a new blue dress that my mother begs me to take off until the party – how can I help in the kitchen with the dress on, it will get dirty – I relent but can't wait to put it back on.

The dark blue of evening finally arrives. My big brother Ali and I greet all the guests at the front door. We are beautiful, everyone is charmed, dinner is delicious. I have never heard such serious and animated talk, don't understand much of it, but recognize some people are angry with the U.S.A. and some with Iran. I do not like the sound of hateful words against people.

After dinner, the guests get comfortable around our living room with tea and date cakes. I stand in the center in my blue dress: what a beautiful child, they say, just like Nuzhet ez Zeman some old guy says, and Dad explains that she was a Princess from the Arabian Nights who stood in all her beauty, reciting wisdom to the court. I recite my poems, taking breaths, emphasizing words, making gestures with my hands as my dad taught me. The guests love me, clap loudly, the men question me about the poems, and then exclaim: what an intelligent and beautiful child.

My father beams in delight. I am in the Seventh Heaven, which lies in America.

Even the ones with hatred in their voices for other people have only love in their eyes now, and I love Islam and Allah, and Mom and Dad, and all my friends, and our town in America. I have faith that we can all live together in the Seventh Heaven, the one the Prophet traveled to in his vision, his Mi'raj, but this will not be a mirage for me, it will be real.

That happened right before the Gulf War. It was harder for us after that, but I still had faith, Dad's love for America was infectious, and I wanted to be a good Moslem and a good American, and even later in high school, when I was a better American than a Moslem, I never lost my faith, my love, or my optimism that everything will work out.

I still live with my parents, I still have faith. I know Islam will thrive and America will thrive, and I want to thrive, to do well, and to do something to fight the hatred, to bring people together. I think the terrible struggle between the West and the Mideast will lead to a better awareness of the two sides, just as the Crusades, as cruel as it was, brought so many Arabic ideas to Europe. There will be a new harmony in the future.

ق

"That's where my faith comes from," Ooma finished, "it goes back to my childhood, my family traditions, and a little cult I started in my bedroom closet. I love my beliefs, so when you talk about past lives, I'm all there." She took a lick of her lollipop.

"I'm glad you're happy," Amar said.

As they returned to their tasks, Amar thought he should check in with Sahara. He wondered how she might react knowing he was spending his time talking to Ooma. She might be upset and that would not be healthy for either her or the baby.

"Ooma," he said, calling over to her at a nearby desk, "let's keep our little talks to ourselves. Okay?"

Ooma looked quizzical for a second, and then gave Amar a sweet, little smile.

"Sure, boss."

22

That same night Sahara and Amar went to bed early. Lying next to him, she felt her husband was slightly distant. Intuitively, she took a chance and voiced her thoughts.

"How's that Ooma?" she started, tenderly nuzzling into his arm.

Amar put his arm around his wife. "She's fine. Useful as ever."

"Told you any new stories?"

Amar did not want to get into this, but he did not want to lie either. "No. She's just told me about growing up Muslim. She believes in Islam in a new way, a new kind of faith."

"You like that about her?"

"She fits with our interests, Sahr, the Mideast, Arabic studies, the Nights, the stories."

"The recalls, you mean? The past lives?"

"If that's what they are." Amar wanted to get away from Ooma. "Had any today?"

Sahara nestled down in the bed. "About you." She liked these moments when she had him, when she tamed this unpredictable beast. "Arand spoke to me."

"Arand? The husband in your suburb story?"

"Yes. I wanted to wallow in the bliss of that place. I visualized our house in The Suburb, Arand and Shaell's house. And then he spoke to me."

"You received *my* suburb story, as the husband, without me here?

"Yes. It's about a whole delivery of gifts he has brought forth, set up like a camp of boxes, crates, bales, loads."

"Mr. Generous. Has anything changed?" He kissed her cheek. "Let's hear it."

The Tale of the Thirty-Seventh Birtheve Surprise

I sit in the living room, waiting for the carrier to pull up. It's Shaell's birtheve, her thirty-seventh, and I'm doing something special. Twenty-two, fifty, seventy-six, those are the 'big' birtheves in The Suburb, but poor thirty-seven, stuck in limbo between late youth and middle years, is a time ripe for depression or hollowness. It needs to be filled.

There isn't a week that I don't think about giving something to Shaell. I don't fool myself into believing that the giving of objects replaces genuine warmth and caring. It just makes me feel good in some very quiet, assured place in my soul. Since half of gift giving is the surprise, I work just as hard on the unpredictable timing and delivery of the present as I do on the thing itself. For weeks I have been modest in my generosities as if I was gradually pulling out of my habit. I was just preparing for today's surprise.

After lunch the carrier pulls up to the curb. I sign a form and watch the lawn fill with boxes. A second vehicle arrives, driven by two crusty Cityzens with an attitude against Burbans. Most of their load is containers that are devilish to open, with those awful sheaths and straps. They finish unloading as the third and fourth carriers arrive.

Shaell is away for the afternoon: I presented her with a chit for a skin and hair spa this morning, as if that were going to be my sole birtheve present. By the time she arrives home, she is unable to drive the vehicle anywhere near the house, and can only see the upper story since the delivered goods block every inch of the downstairs. She attempts to walk up the sidewalk to the front door but finds herself in a maze of my devising, which leads her on a path directly into my arms.

"Thirty-seven more," I greet her, the birtheve catch phrase barely off my tongue before Shaell's mouth meets mine. She is shocked and delighted and teases me for my trickery and excess. She is so eager to show her gratitude that it takes some doing to convince her that she should open everything first.

And so she does: a new set of burbain sheets and blankets for the bedroom; three distinct bouquets of wildflowers picked from a large monadnock located in the Plains outlying The Suburb; twelve rolls of decorative wallpapers with a pattern of sable roundels interlocking with sheafs of grain and feathery plumes; a free-standing candle-lamp that releases smoke in the shape of the Offmore insignia; all manner of products from the cetiver plant: fragrant perfumes, body oils, bath beads, woven doormats; six casks of frozen shellusks from the Bataveur littorals, accompanied by three vats of delicious dipping sauces; fifteen boites of sweet endbrains of the konnovie bird, a delicacy among the younger generation of Cityzens, not for everyone, but one of Shaell's recent cravings; a fourteen-pass Commuter plassticket, good until next Chillester; an octelian necklace, all eight strands emblazoned with jeweled puckstones, matching earrings, and a contrasting bracelet made of beige rainbeads; a set of three fur-lined dildos, small, medium, and large, an apology for the next long business trip I will be taking (she is extremely touched by this gift but stood looking at them for a moment and then told me that the three of them reminded her of something she could not remember); a lifetime supply of Oaken Bits, Shaell's favorite breakfast food; a pet yurid, the common variety without the epipubic bones, inside its own subterrarium, whom she immediately christened Foster; eleven bags of yurid food (on sale at eleven for seven); and a miniature yurid parcourse complete with flaming wheel and headstand; twelve hundred cases of Igmidian Plantlife, the miracle growth used for garden, kitchen, and cosmetic purposes; a signed copy of "Figments" by the Astron-Aburbanian writer Farough Manleaif; two chthithoprint screens of underwater life between Suburb and City (11 X 6.5); eight dozen squirrel-driven ankle belts, for –

ق

"Sahr! Enough!" Amar held his wife in his arms, drawing her back from the trancelike litany. "The gift list got away from you," he said. "You lost control."

"YOU lost control," Sahara said, reaching for a glass of water on the nightstand. "I hadn't even finished – that was just one birthday, imagine the rest, the regular presents, the other birthdays, the surprise appearances of gifts in later years...."

"Where'd we get all the money?" Amar said, quizzically.

Sahara finished drinking and put down the glass. She had to be patient with his questioning. The recalls might be the salvation of their relationship. She tried a new tact.

151

"In Islamic literature, like *The Thousand and One Nights*, there's no such thing as fiction. Fiction means lies, untruths, a sin. So the stories use narrators: I heard this from so and so who got it from so and so. It's a way of verifying the tale as truth, a recounting of a real thing."

"So Arand spoke to you and that makes the tale a truth? From your lips to Allah? Because you're an Arabic student I'm supposed to believe in past lives?"

Amar had crossed a line, Sahara thought. Arabic 'student' instead of 'scholar' or even 'Ph.D. candidate,' the very thing her husband was preventing her from pursuing. That verbal slight alone was worth turning over and pretending to go to sleep. Then there was the tone of disrespect for Islam. And the discounting of her recalls, her gift.

"So," she began patiently, "you'd rather believe in your new, Persian helper?"

"Oh-ho!" Amar exclaimed, rolling over to Sahara and pushing his hips against her. "You're the only Arabic expert for me."

"Convince me."

"Ooma's a kid." Amar continued moving his hips. "But I can probe your depths."

Sahara began to respond to Amar's movements, but wasn't ready to drop the discussion. "You don't really believe in me. You like my stories, they're fun, you're interested in them for yourself. But these stories are keeping us together right now. I hope we're on the mend. I hope the recalls will help. The Suburb lifetime was over-the-top bliss. Maybe we're being given a vision of bliss, the ideal state of our relationship in the past, the simple bliss that we're always trying to recapture."

"So let's recapture it right now. Even if it's a vision or a dream."

"I think it was a past life," Sahara said simply. "Have some more faith."

"I do. I have faith in you. In us. A new kind of faith." He pulled her on top of him.

A new kind of faith, Sahara thought. Isn't that what he had said about Ooma?

23

Zack Goodkin was nine years older than Amar: Zack was twelve when he baby-sat toddler Amar, and the two became surrogate baby and older brother. After Zack graduated high school the two rarely crossed paths, although Amar had been in touch with Zack's mother, Cachay Goodkin, while they were both graduate students in Chicago.

One Wednesday in late June Amar saw Zack come out of his house for the morning paper. Amar was on his way to the train.

"How's it going, little brother?" Zack asked.

"You haven't called me that in years," Amar replied. "Good thing, too. Big brother."

Zack smiled at Amar's light tone. He had seemed burdened recently. "Sahara better?"

"She's much stronger. Thanks for asking."

"The hospital scared the bejesus out of me," Zack said. "Baby's fine?"

"Naji's fine, too."

"Naji, is it? Nice name. When is the little bundle of pleasure happening?"

"Beginning of October."

"Amazing. Birth and rebirths, all in one handy wife."

"So you've heard the past life theory." Amar was glad his old friend was there, but he had yet to talk to him about the stories. It had bothered him that Sahara had shared things with Zack, but maybe it would be good to talk things through with a friend.

"Pretty crazy, those stories," Zack said. "Storm clouds fighting, mystery killers in harems."

"You know that one? I'm in the doghouse, because I'm not convinced they're past lives." Amar wanted to know where Zack stood on the issue. "Can you blame me?"

"How can we have been inanimate objects in past lives? Like clouds, or coal?"

"They're organic matter, I suppose. But, it's a stretch. And places like the Red Isle."

"Or the roukh," Zack continued. "Right out of the Arabian Nights. You must wonder if it's just Sahara's background feeding her these things. And the mystery packages?"

Zack had always been a sponge soaking up people's words and ideas. Was that was why he was so familiar with recent events? Amar was curious about Zack's knowledge. He looked at his watch: he had to leave immediately to make the 7:12 train. But he could wait for the 7:56....

"Yeah, it's crazy," Amar said. "Just last night Sahara's watching a cooking show or walking the cat or something and boom, she's in Western France, early 1600's."

"Cardinal Richelieu," Zack said. "Religious persecutions, local wars, lovely times."

"Very good. I'm impressed."

"I deal in antiquities. I know my shit. So what's the story?"

"I came home early from work the other day, a rare event. Sahara had all kinds of things cooking on the stove, or I should

155

say overcooking. I discovered her in the pantry closet, sitting on a stool, one hand holding a sheaf of pasta, the other a handful of dried wildflowers. God knows where she was. I didn't dare disturb her, but her breathing seemed fine so I went to rescue dinner. When she came around she had a story to tell."

The Tale of the Marriage of Silvie Saintonge

I've had it with Aquitaine. Over and over, the girls babble on about their 'knights' as if a thousand of the lumbering men of this village could equal even one knight. They could search and search our ancient land of the Santons, from the Loire to the peaks of Spain, and never find this chivalrous love. And this land, now renamed Saintonge, my own family name, has shrunk and split from its neighboring territories. I tell my silly, daydreaming friends, we are no longer part of Aquitaine. Let La Reine Eleanor go. Don't chase a dream.

Saintonge. A Christian version of the pagan Santons, neither saint nor angel. If I could dream like the other girls I would heal the sick, help the poor. I would enter the abbey.

I was, inside L'Abbaye, ready to seek asylum from the babbling girls, from the wars throughout the dukedoms, from the world of men. So fortunate to have such a large and beautiful convent in my hometown of Saintes. I could almost believe in my dream of sainthood, myself, Sylvie Saintonge, Saint Sylvie. I could believe in the higher power of my Lord looking down on me.

But I exited the abbey that day, as I do every week after my faithful visit. This time I would not return. My mind was

made up. I would never attain sainthood. I would not find
the hero of my dreams, as my friends fantasized. Why should I
search for some lofty ideal? I would simply choose a husband
and make him my true love. The Lord says we should love
everyone; I should be able to love anyone fully and truly.

I settled down with Guilaum, the blacksmith of our village
outside of Saintes. He was a good man, a rare mix of gentle
husband and brute, banging away at his anvil by day, sitting
by the fire with his pipe by night. We had known each other
since childhood and during those years I teased him relentlessly to see him blush. As we grew to marriageable age,
I soon found teasing an unnecessary preliminary to earthier
pursuits. If I called, Guilaum came; if he desired me, I gave in
easily. I did not feel a deep love and reconsidered the abbey
as a tempting alternative to Guilaum's affections. But I saw in
him a dependable man, even an ambitious one, and a potential
father.

My heart opened to Guilaum. I was soon rewarded with
nights of passion. While my friends gossiped about their ideal
lovers fizzling out too early in bed I kept silent about my
Guilaum. He was an embarrassment of riches: tender, sensitive to my desires, and completely infatuated with me. Our
nights spilled over into days; more than once we tumbled in
the oily earth behind the smithy. This was preferable to waiting for a knight.

My best friend Chantal was less fortunate. She had bargained for Aquitaine, burned herself out on intense trysts, and
waited years to marry, while Guilaum and I produced three
fine boys. By the time our eldest was stoking the fires for his
Papa, and I became Guilaum's best salesperson for his new
lock-and-key trade, Chantal had foresworn love.

And then the new baker moved to the village. He was
escaping the brutal death of his wife in the crossfire of another

battle sparked by Richelieu. This sad man baked his way into all our hearts with his amazing delicacies. Chantal befriended him to ease his entry into town life. Soon they discovered why each had suffered their paths of love: so that they could find each other, vulnerable, unencumbered, shivering with need.

The wedding coincided with our youngest's tenth birthday, and two finer cakes had never been devoured in the village. The new couple's love deepened and spread onto our own marriage. Chantal and I had long, quiet talks in the morning. She spoke litanies about her deep, mutual love. I could speak of Guilaum's love for me, but I for him? In the midst of wars throughout the land, the children and I were safe, our house was warm, our bellies full. Wasn't this enough?

Five years after Chantal's wedding, our whole family was working in the prosperous locksmith trade. We purchased the neighboring house, enlarged the smithy, and made room for our eldest's new wife and baby. I expanded the kitchen to include a separate mudroom as an entrance, a receptacle for the filthy clothes and boots of my hard workers.

I was even able to afford some special fabric from Paris, with a pattern of sable roundels interlocking with sheaves of grain and feathery plumes. As I worked with my new fabric, I could actually convince myself I was not in a lonely French village, but living in the place I dreamed of, or having a memory of such a place. It was a good time, the highlight of my marriage to Guilaum.

In the winter of that year, Chantal's husband contracted a vicious fever and died.

Between everyone in our family, we made sure Chantal was looked after, ate her meals, got out of bed every day. For months our talks ceased; love was too painful to discuss. When we resumed our chats, it was not as it used to be. There was a palpable tension between us. One morning a sound like the house settling shot in from the curtained-off mudroom. I flinched. Why was this unease so bitter between us? I chose to confront Chantal and this unspoken torture.

Chantal warmed her hands on her mug of tea for a full minute before answering. "Sylvie, I am not angry at you, but you still have Guilaum. You have been together for years. I am now alone and childless with only a brief memory of love."

"You know how terrible I feel for your loss. I am not so foolish as to pretend to understand your grief for a moment. But must it come between us?"

"I can't help it," she answered. "I see the simple love between you and Guilaum, the work you share, the children. How can your love not bring me further grief?"

"Love! All my life I have heard nothing but this fantasy of love. Does it really exist? Does it only cause pain?"

"How can you say this? I was ecstatic in love, just like in the stories and songs. Do you deny it for yourself? Don't you love Guilaum?"

I felt a surge of panic from the directness of Chantal's question. Did I love Guilaum? I never allowed myself to think of such things, I had grown tired of this subject long ago. But the pleading look in my friend's eyes demanded an answer.

"I am very content. Guilaum is a good man, a good husband, and a wonderful father. I chose to be with him for these reasons. Not for love."

Chantal stared at me through her grief. "I am glad you are content, Sylvie," Chantal said. "That would not be enough for me. Not after what I've felt."

"But is it not better to live a full, contented life than to search for an ideal that may not exist? Or – forgive me, Chantal – to find an ideal and lose your way when it is gone?"

My questions hit Chantal hard. She glared at me, then put her mug down and stood to leave. As she walked through the curtain into the outside room, I heard her gasp. The outside door closed. Only then did I rise to see why she had gasped.

In the outer room Guilaum stood silent. He had heard everything I had said.

Sahara wept at the end of her story, Amar told Zack. We tried to understand why it affected her so deeply. Was I Guilaum, was she afraid of hurting me, of losing me? I didn't dare question whether the tale was truly a reflection of her love for me, or lack of it.

We were amazed that a new world had opened to her. Why France, a more recent time in history? And this puzzler: Silvie Saintonge stared at a wallpaper pattern of grain and plumes. One of Arand Offmore's gifts in The Suburb was wallpaper with grain and plumes. Silvie thought she was having a memory of a place with this wallpaper. Did Silvie have a *déjà vu* of a lifetime in The Suburb; was Sahara recalling her soul in a previous lifetime recalling her soul in a previous lifetime?

ق

"Wow, I can almost buy it as a past life," Zack said. "At least I've heard of the city of Saintes. But The Suburb – what is that?"

"Could be Glenclaire, via Sahr's imagination, a place we had an ideal marriage."

"Speaking of imagination," Zack said, "the bit about Sahara crying over losing you – that's pretty far-fetched. I'd have left you months ago."

"Eat shit and die." It had been a while since Amar had joked about his marriage.

"Can you wait a sec? I just remembered I have something for you."

160

Before Amar could answer, Zack rushed into his house. He returned quickly with a piece of crumpled paper. He handed it to Amar, who smoothed it out, and read:

A THING OF THE PAST
SUPPORT GROUP FOR PAST LIFE EXPLORATION

TUESDAYS, 7 PM
UNITARIAN CHURCH, GLENCLAIRE
Elvira Young, Facilitator

Bring An Open Mind

24

Amar stared at the flyer in wonder.

"Where the hell did this come from?"

"Sahara had this in her hand when we picked her up in my car," Zack explained. "She must have dropped it in the back seat. I thought you might be interested."

"I thought you didn't believe in this crap."

"I don't," Zack said, hesitantly. "Anyway, it's Sahara's, she should have it back."

"I'll take it under advisement," Amar said, stuffing the paper in his briefcase. "Got to get my train."

"Right, pass GO, make a beeline for the train line, and proceed straight to the palace." Zack held onto Amar's sleeve. "Sure you don't want to hear another story?"

"Don't tell me *you're* having these things, too?"

"Maybe it's mine, or it might be someone else's," Zack said playfully. "It's a companion tale to the French story, about Silvie Saintonge's husband, Guilaum."

"So it's my story?" He looked at his watch. "I'll take the 8:23. Just tell me."

The Locksmith's Tale

Guilaum Coursoit sat huddled over his fourth wine cup at the tavern. His friends had gone home long ago. They were sick of his pathetic prattle by now. Sylvie this, Silvie that – why would anyone listen for more than five minutes?

She was a good wife, a simple beauty, an unmatched lover in their first days. Back then, his friend Pascal had advised him to pay a poet to write her a love poem. Guilaum could not read the words scrawled on the paper, so Guilaum had to pay another man to help him memorize the poem. The man had the nerve to tell him that the poem was not an original, but the work of someone named Ronsard, and that his style was out of favor at court. Guilaum should have taken the haughty comments as a sign of warning, but what did he care about floweriness or an extra syllable here and there? He was in love. Guilaum still remembered a passage from the poem:

> If you have pity, child, give o'er;
> Give back the heart you stole from me,
> Pirate, setting so little store
> On this your captive from Love's sea,
> Holding his misery for gain,
> And making pleasure of his pain.

When Silvie first heard the poem she flung herself into Guilaum's arms. Why shouldn't he have thought she was in love? Three boys from their bed play, from Guilaum's lust and her desire. Never a sour note. Complete faith, support, and respect.

But no love. There never had been. Now he could say she truly stole his heart, made pleasure of his pain. Curse the woman!

Guilaum drained his cup and considered leaving. To go where? Off a cliff, it would be less painful. He called for another cup. The barkeep gave him a critical stare.

He had been so grateful at first. Silvie Saintonge loves me! Years of taunts and insults as a child: he assumed she hated him. She wants me! She wishes to be my wife!

Silvie had told Chantal she married him, but not for love. Guilaum had stood in his own mudroom, frozen by the overheard statement, colder than if he were exposed to the frigid elements outside. What had he done, or not done? He had worked hard to sustain a good life. He had refused her nothing. She had wanted the mud room, the house next door, even that fabric. She had been pleased with the gifts, had looked at me as if looking into my soul. Why wasn't it enough? Or was it not about generosity, this love?

He thought of his locksmith trade and how he had built it up. It had been her cousin who introduced Guilaum to a master clockmaker who had trained him in the new lever tumbler design. Guilaum produced many of these locks and Silvie sold them around the village and countryside. Guilaum preferred the dark, enclosed space of his smithy to being out in the open air of the village. He was uncomfortable asking for work, but Sylvie thrived on it.

Guilaum hated that they fed off the wars in France in those times, but the truth was that no one felt secure. Any week a royal army or renegade pack might march into town and ransack a few homes, in the name of the King or any power-hungry duke. The new locks gave people a small answer to their fears. How could a soldier get past this new lock, they thought, so please give me an extra key. Safety is what they all wanted. Why shouldn't he, their local smith, help fill this need?

Yet Guilaum's marriage was no longer safe. His locks will be his safety, both in the monies they provide, and in the comfort they give. He will forge each tumbler with a precision unsurpassed in the region. Guilaum envisioned a new cabinet on the wall of the smithy, where he could store and organize every size and shape of lock and key needed for every possible door. It would be his own well-run kingdom, a land of perfect order. Already the locksmith business was so prosperous Guilaum had been able to hand over the horse–shodding trade to his eldest son. Now he could put all his efforts into his new controlled kingdom.

But it was Silvie who had brought in most of the business. Damn the woman! He needed her. He loved her. Could he keep up their partnership? He must focus on the locks, the keys, and the needs of the villagers. She was just doing a job for him, serving the needs of his kingdom of locks and keys. Was not this a woman's place, to serve? Love was not the issue here.

Guilaum finished the cup of wine. His head sank on the table. The barkeep shook him by the shoulder. It was time to lock up. Pushed around by his own locks! Guilaum stumbled to the door and made his way home. He had been sleeping on a palette of straw in the smithy, but his determination to get on with his life led him to his bedchamber. He considered mounting Silvie in her sleep, and then collapsed on top of the blankets.

Guilaum dreamed he was in his smithy, standing by the forge, looking across at his new cabinet. Every lock was perfectly in place next to its key. In one space hung a key but no lock. Guilaum held the missing lock in his hand. He stepped toward the cabinet to replace the lock but after a few steps he was prevented by a metal collar of his own design around his neck, attached to a chain fastened to the stone wall. He pulled on the chain, strode forward with all his might. His neck bulged, his back tensed. The chain shattered into a hundred separate links and Guilaum flew across the space. He reached out to gain his balance and the lock in his hand jammed into the cabinet, landing perfectly in its place.

Guilaum awoke in a sweat. It was bright morning. Silvie was no longer in bed. Next door he could hear his son's anvil already chiming in rhythm. His head throbbing, Guilaum forced himself up. He poured a bucket of water over his head and got dressed.

Silvie was out of the house, no doubt collecting fees or knocking on new, lockless doors. She had left out his morning bread on the table. Guilaum chewed on it. It was time for him to take some initiative in finding customers, even if it meant exposing himself to the discomfort of the outdoors. He walked out the door, locking it as he left. Silvie had never asked the village cabinetmaker if he needed a lock on his shop. Guilaum headed in that direction, ready to barter.

ق

"So what do you think?" Zack asked when he was through. "Not an ideal marriage at all, but they've got something going, right?"

"Soul mates aren't always perfectly in love," Amar responded, worried by the tale. "I can relate to this guy. He loves his wife, and she's giving him grief. It definitely feels like another rocky patch in our past relationships."

Zack made a noise like a penalty buzzer in a game show. "Sorry, not the correct answer. This isn't your story at all. I did not hear it from your wife, nor did I conjure it up."

"Where did it come from?"

"My mother."

"Cachay?"

"We were traveling in France, the one time she visited me over there, through the Saintonge area, on the way home from the town of Cognac, to be exact. And she's spouting off all kinds of information about the Santons, and Richelieu, and the town of Saintes. She has no idea how she knows this stuff, except perhaps it's the cognac talking, but it keeps coming out of her. At dinner that night she launches into this story."

"So you're saying she was Guilaum," Amar said quietly.

"If it's a bona fide past life, it would be my mother's, not yours; you were never married to Sahara in France at that time."

"Sahara married your mother? I don't know if I can handle that."

"You don't have to handle it, you don't have to believe it, you don't even have to believe Sahara was married to *you* in a past life. As I have ably demonstrated, you can be convinced a story is about your past life when that's not even close to the truth. Does that debunk whether you and Sahara are soul mates? Does it diminish the fascination of Sahara's stories, of my mother's story? I don't think so."

Unexpectedly, Zack embraced Amar and whispered in his ear. "What am I trying to say? Relax, little brother. Don't get too caught up in all this. Give Sahara all the support you can." Zack released his friend. "Better catch your train."

"Shit! I'll never get a parking place now!"

As Amar got in his car to drive to the station, Zack called after him:

"Don't forget to give Sahara that flyer!"

25

―⁊⁊⁊―

Amar Rash felt more relaxed in those first days of July, but Sahara was another story. Amar would come home to find his wife, his Queen, asleep on the couch, and think how peaceful she was. But Sahara was entering her third trimester just as the summer was entering its first heat wave; as the mercury rose to the top of the thermometer Sahara sank to the bottom of the couch.

On July 4 Amar threw a small party for colleagues. She was grateful he had it catered; it was hard enough for her to do the meet and greet. It was odd to have a gathering on a Tuesday, and something nagged her about it. What was significant about Tuesday? Why did she suspect it had to do with her collapse against the tree?

Later that week a storm cooled things off and Sahara gathered enough strength to go shopping. Afterward, she told herself the baby needed a huge ice cream cone. After downing the refreshing treat, she returned to her car in the parking lot next to the Unitarian Church. An elderly black man came out of the church and walked toward the lot. As he got nearer, Sahara saw something familiar about his salt-and-pepper dreadlocks.

"Excuse me, Miss, most sorry to bother you." Although stooped, the man must have been over six feet tall. His face was chiseled like rock in a sea wind. Sahara recognized him as the man at Dr. Machiyoko's doorway before the session with Amar.

"We want you to have this." The aged fellow placed a surprisingly firm hand on Sahara's arm and handed her the flyer about the past life support group.

"There was nothing this last Tuesday, because of Independence Day," the man said. A look of ancient knowing flashed across his craggy face, and then his gaze turned downward, shy, awkward. "But we're counting on you for next Tuesday."

Tuesday! This is what she was trying to remember! It was the flyer from the night at the tree. She had dropped it in Zack's car. How could she have forgotten such a thing? She looked up from the flyer to speak to the old man.

He was gone.

After Sahara unpacked the groceries at home, she lay down to rest and look at the flyer. She noticed tightly packed handwriting that filled the reverse side of the paper.

The Message of Verlin Walker

You're probably wondering about the old geezer who shoved this thing at you. Busy at the church, otherwise would have stayed to tell all in person. The name's Verlin Walker. Pushing ninety, give or take a decade. Been around, but I'll only waste your time on my most current activities: WHO IS VERLE WALKER?

He's a rare fool that only till recently got his head straight on to figure out what he was doing with his life. (It's never too late.)

Verle showed up in Glenclaire ten years ago convinced he was ready for a new lease on life, and proceeded to bung it up good. Thought he'd go about secretly doing his thing, but that got him nowhere fast. He needed to connect, that was the ticket. He had to come out from hiding and face the race again.

Verle was homeless by choice. Like the great Islamic kings he had read about on a journey to Mecca during one of his past lives in this life, Verle knew that being rich was a damnation and being poor a blessing. Then this confused, emptied man found the Unitarian Church, not for its spiritual offerings, but for gainful employment. The church building, an Arts and Crafts style wooden affair from the early 20th Century, was blessed with wisteria plantings and delicate rounded beams and windows everywhere. Much too much for an old soul like Verlin to handle, but too much for the full-time handyman. So Verle was hired as an extra pair of hands, resident custodian for events past six o'clock or for odd-hour deliveries. All in exchange for an attic retreat that he could call home.

Verle became aware of all the meetings, groups, and clubs needing this and that at the church, and began reaching out and re-connecting to humanity. An enterprising Glenclairean, who volunteered in the soup kitchen, asked if she could host a group in Verle's attic home. When she told him it was a group for past lives Verle said yes, helped get the group going, and brought in an expert he knew from the church. He joined the group himself, puzzling out the links between present and past life. Amazing things started to happen. Occasionally someone recalled a fantastical past life, making love to the magnetic forces of the cosmos, say, and it triggered a memory in Verle of a lifetime in a universe previous to the universe previous to this one! Then members of the group discovered they had lived past lives with others in the group, even with others in Glenclaire.

Now that some of those curious connections have fallen onto your doorstep, aren't you dying to join us? I found out the hard way that I needed to connect to others to climb out of the burrow I'd dug. You need to share your past life stories, puzzle things out with us, solve the mysteries of our total identity, not just individual entities, but tooootal identity.

Tuesday! (Wednesday works, too, but we have parking competition with the Ethics committee.) Please come! Thank you!

ق

Sahara was touched by Verlin Walker's charming missive-confessional. She did not understand how this group had found her, but she welcomed the idea of exploring the strange new events in her life with a group of kindred spirits.

What should she tell Amar about the group? Should he go with her? Or should she go alone at first? And not tell him? Did he see the flyer that night? The last time Sahara had withheld information from her husband was when she delayed telling him she was pregnant. That led to disaster. But she had needed time to think on her own, just as she did now. She should discuss this with Dr. Machiyoko. That was the answer!

26

That same day Amar took Ooma Qadir to lunch.

It was the end of Ooma's second year working for Amar, and since she had worked so many late nights recently, Amar wanted to reward her. Also, Ooma was so convinced of the veracity of past lives and Zack so skeptical, that they stood for the back and forth going on in Amar's mind. He wanted to hear more from Ooma.

"I can't stop thinking about my two memories," she said, over a plank of sushi. "But if they're past lives, I'm a little disturbed. In both I'm a creepy Queen. Uzmeth holds orgies, and then watches her lover kill virgins. Yucch! Oumkratania has everything she wants, but fakes some sacred artifact so everyone will honor her." Ooma dipped a piece of sushi into her sauce bowl. "I'm a good girl, boss. I still live with my parents, I work my butt off, and I'm a practicing Muslim. Why are my past lives so wretched? How did I get so good?"

Amar hesitated with his next comment. With his chopsticks, Amar cut two rolls in four pieces with a single stroke. "Sahara and I are going through the same thing. Most of our stories have come in pairs: husband and wife in The Suburb

– the only happy one – fighting brother and sister on the Red Isle, hopelessly entangled North and South wind –"

" – and Ardryashir and Sharzad, my murderous lover and the woman who defies him. You could be working through something, moving toward the happiest lifetimes."

"Depending on the 'birth order' of the lifetimes. In another order, we might have started out deliriously happy, then descended into a hell of nastiness. And here we are."

"Told you it's disturbing," Ooma said. "And confusing: I don't know *what* to make of my newest one. Don't even think it's mine."

"How do you people do it? When? What happened?"

Ooma lowered her head like a child: "You won't get mad?"

"Why would I be mad?"

"It was with Bax."

Amar felt a flush of heat in his chest. "You're your own woman, Ooma. I have no right to tell you who to hang out with."

"Unless it's at your house. At a party."

"You were seriously drunk. I was worried what the boy might do to you."

"Thanks, Dad."

He dismissed her jibe with a wave of a chopstick. "So what happened?"

"We ran into each other at Rock-It Records. He's seen me there before. We walked around for a while, sat on a bench in the park, held hands. Then my palms got sweaty. The sweaty places began to feel more intense, and my mind started attaching something to these little islands of sensation. Before I knew it, I could access another world through the weird perceptions. I had the thought that if I let go of Bax's hand I would lose touch with this world. I realized that the other reality was connected to him."

"What was the world?"

"China. Centuries ago sometime, when men had many wives. It was a story about a lord constructing a system where his seven wives gave him seven pleasures in seven palaces, built of seven different materials. Like a folk tale. I was having a recall set in China! I didn't want to let go of Bax' hand."

"And Bax just sat there? He wasn't worried about you?"

"I began to talk to him. The words came very simply, slowly, like the way he talks. I didn't think it was my perceptions, but his, coming to me through our hands. I'll tell you."

The Tale of the Seven Chinese Palaces

Find the perfect scheme. Little Deng She teases me: you will not stop with the diamond palace. But I will. Seven is enough. But then – find the perfect scheme.

Variety is the father of pleasure. Intense joy in satiation turns sour. Rare little tastes annoy. The perfect balance of quantity, excellence, surprise.

First experiment this week. Goes well. All four wives compliant in changing palaces each day. Third wife a bit confused. Adorable when she and second wife turn up together in alabaster palace. Most enjoyable night. Keep surprises.

Four too predictable. Five better. One of the eunuchs knows local beauty. Enthusiastic recommendation. So: fifth wife. Why not six, or seven, same number as palaces?

Tidy scheme. Seven palaces, seven wives. Each day wives rotate to different palace. Covers one week. Love Deng She's idea: Each new week first wife starts at different palace. All

174

other wives shift over accordingly. (Third wife baffled.) Covers seven weeks.

Second wife makes problem clear. Can't be expected to provide any pleasure each night (she has enough trouble with massage). Perhaps Deng She can find answer. But too busy now with ailing seventh wife.

It will work! Each palace devoted to single pleasure. Seven will be enough. Every seven weeks pleasures rotate: covers seven times seven weeks. Almost a full year!

Fourth wife seen behind screen with eunuch! Not a eunuch? Not enough pleasure for wives?

Pleasures must rotate through the palaces in reverse direction of wives. Order of palaces always the same?

If seventh wife died, and Deng She tended to her, what might be Deng She's fate as new seventh wife? Why did I not see her beauty before? Beautiful, rounded bottom. She is frightened. Much blood on the first night. Still, I am pleased.

So tedious! Must spy on fourth wife and 'eunuch' now. More unrest besides this? Ask Deng She for help? Too young and unspoiled still. Perhaps fifth wife.

First wife getting on my nerves. Can't she learn a new song? Make music palace include other throat pleasures. Rotate order of palaces after all? Or is it this: no matter how intricate the whole weave, if one thread sticks out, the effect is ruined.

News of lost sister Oolon. Separated at birth. Hidden away from deadly enemies. Each of us. Different place in provinces. No complaints from me. Seven palaces! All comforts. Like I spent past life here. In happy exile. Floating, above world. Recommend to all. Sit out. Keep your distance. But now exile is over. Oolon will return here.

Discover fourth wife and false eunuch's trysting place. Fifth wife and I know all their meetings now. Funny how they have their own rotation scheme. For now we just watch.

Deng She has convinced me: rotate the palaces at will. So smart ever since we were children. Her beauty grows each day. Palace rotation occurs at my will when I sense sameness growing on wives. Third wife will have to be guided by the hand.

When will Oolon arrive? How will wives treat her? Delicate. At least sixth wife is overjoyed by prospect. Make her Oolon's welcomer.

When fifth wife knows the eunuch is at it with fourth wife she runs to me. Practically undressed as we reach our spy hole. Muffle her sighs with my hand from behind. Four of us enter Heaven together: how has such betrayal led to such paradise?

How announce new rotation of palaces? All wives help in choice? An orgy?

Sister Oolon arrives at last. So familiar yet we've never met. Bond of siblings.

Fourth wife pregnant. Oolon very curious about all the palaces, the rotations, and now this occurrence. Perhaps for the best that fifth wife and I cease. Shame.

All is well. I can be happy to the end of days. The perfect scheme. Surrounded by brilliant Deng She, noble sister Oolon, beautiful wives. Fourth wife's baby is but a little matter, I tell Oolon. She presses me for other complaints. But all is well. All is perfection.

ق

"So you think that was Bax's lifetime?" Amar asked.

"When I asked him if he recognized anything about it, he just said 'Mebbe' in that quiet, man-from-Colorado voice of his."

"I'll tell Sahara about it. Maybe she, or Dr. Machiyoko, can shed some light on it."

Ooma finished her last piece of sushi. "Dr. Machiyoko?"

Amar had crossed the line into sharing his marital issues with Ooma. "Therapist. We're seeing her tomorrow."

"You guys are in therapy? I didn't know."

"Since all this started, the stories, Sahara being pregnant." How much should he say? He wanted to tell Ooma, but he held back.

"Having a baby must make it intense. You'll work it all out," Ooma said, genuinely. "Or your kid'll be raised by a raging God and Goddess. So when is therapy tomorrow?"

"Five o'clock," Amar said. "I was going to duck out a tad early."

"Boss. The McClellan meeting?"

"Shit! I totally forgot."

"Have me run the meeting. I've been here two years."

"Sorry, way too important for a trial run. What am I going to do?"

"For starters, have me put your therapy sessions into the schedule. Then give me a raise."

27

When Amar told Sahara that he would have to miss their therapy session, she was more relieved than annoyed. Sahara missed her one-on-one time with Dr. Machiyoko, and hoped the therapist would clarify what to tell Amar about the past life group. Amar's doubts bothered Sahara, tempted her to question the veracity of the recalls. He still enjoyed hearing new stories and, to Sahara's discomfort, had brought home a Chinese tale from Ooma. Aroused by the images of sensual pleasure in the seven palaces, he took Sahara to bed before dinner was on the table. At this point in the pregnancy, sex was extremely difficult for her, unwanted and uncomfortable. She had lain there wondering whether Amar was making love to her, to Ooma, or to Deng She.

He was simply too much for her right now.

Dr. Machiyoko expressed concern that Amar was not present at the session to discuss Sahara's issues. But with the mention of the name Deng She, Dr. Machiyoko's mind seemed to go somewhere else. Moving the stool to the foot of the couch, she insisted Sahara recount the Chinese tale. Afterward, the therapist looked troubled: she was convinced that she had lived in the Chinese provinces as Deng She, that the lord's name was Xa, and that his sister Oolon had sought to rival and humiliate her in unspeakable ways. Pain filled the therapist's face as she closed her eyes and let the memories pour forth.

The Tale of the Corruption of the Seven Palaces

How had it come to this? You feel the ultimate humiliation lying next to her, all eyes on you, especially Xa. You are ready to leap up in fury, to quit that place forever.

Can you, Deng She? You've enjoyed nothing but a life of luxury. The Great Wall is hundreds of li to the east but what you lack from being in the provinces you've gained from the opulence surrounding you. But for you the seven palaces are a tedium. The variety is for Xa alone: the fifth moon brings Deng She to the alabaster palace for a night of throat pleasures. You see the rotation pattern all too clearly, since you designed it. You are tired of his favorite positions, the predictable physical rhythms, the known vintages.

You try to remember the pleasures in their original form: the oils of the hot baths you loved as a child, the silky noodles fed to you and you to Xa, the horseplay with real horses. Think back to those times, so far back that it is like visiting a past life. The innocent play becomes so expanded that you imagine yourself romping in the cosmos. But then a troubling figure comes into your memory, someone despoiling that world.

As it is in the Heavens, so on Earth: it is *she* who brings it all to ruin, not in the past, but the passing present. The sister Oolon: archrival, equal but opposite beauty, usurper of the palace protocols. Once, each wife was mistress of her own palace for one day. It was part of Xa's continued pleasure to be denied in the diamond palace of cockfighting one night, only to have sweet revenge on that wife, discovered in the rice wine orgy at the porcelain palace the next night, or just to return to the diamond palace the next night to find a different and completely obliging lover. But once the sister, Onerous Oolon as she was called in secret, took charge, the spree was over.

You considered suicide but Oolon beat you to it, dramatizing each of her demands and schemes with a knife to her breast. If only Xa had been a bit too slow to intervene. You considered escape, but besides having no ally to lead you out of the mountains, Oolon posted new guards at the palaces, and not for your protection.

Finally, you retreated into the very routines that entrapped you, embraced the planned unpredictability with mute, reserved abandon. Your overzealousness at pleasure making resulted in your current state of satiation. Your success at pleasing your lord, her brother, targeted you as Oolon's archrival. So she staged the final act of her evil drama, her ruination of the seven palaces, the seven pleasures, and the seven wives, leaving you, the seventh wife, in this state of humiliation, degradation, and naked shame.

ق

Dr. Machiyoko's eyes shot open. "So sorry! I completely took over your session."

It was the second time the therapist had done so, Sahara noted with curiosity. "Are you all right?" she asked.

"I'm great. This one will allay your husband's doubts about past lives."

"Because it connects to the story Ooma told him?"

"About Bax! And I didn't plan this one," Dr. Machiyoko said. "These connections are amazing. You have to tell Amar, urge him to return to therapy, rekindle his sense of wonder. Invite him to the past life support group."

"How do you know about the group?" Sahara asked pointedly.

"I'm psychic, remember?" She grinned. "Isn't that what you wanted to talk about?"

How *did* she know about it, Sahara wondered. "I'm confused. One minute I want to invite Amar, the next I'm scared he'll come. I don't even want to tell him it's happening."

"He has his doubts, you have yours. You must share these feelings with him."

"No way! When I finally told him I was pregnant, I went back and forth so many times about the abortion that it drove him nuts. He hates hemming and hawing. He's the master of quick decisions, makes them every second at the World Trade Center."

"You have to do what's comfortable for you. But I think Amar would be interested."

"He'll certainly want to know what Oolon did to sabotage the seven palaces."

"If he was truly skeptical he wouldn't care. With wondering comes faith."

"I can't get him to see that." In surprise, Sahara thought: I don't *want* him to see that.

Dr. Machiyoko uncrossed her legs and leaned forward. "Sahara: you're going to the meeting, right?" Sahara nodded. "So go. With or without Amar. It's Step One for you, and that's a step toward Amar seeing."

"Seeing what?"

"Anything is possible." Dr. Machiyoko crossed her legs. "Everything is possible."

28

The following Tuesday Sahara left the house before Amar came home. She had told him that Porcy wanted a girls' night out, and prayed he didn't check it out. Parking the car a few blocks from the church, she approached the meeting slowly and cautiously, curious but full of foreboding. It was not even close to seven o'clock, so she walked down toward the Glen near the train station. Without realizing it, she made a bee-line to the tree. She placed a hand gently on the trunk, half-expecting to launch into a recall. She smiled: I am going to this meeting to have more recalls, I don't need a tree. I don't need a meeting either. New doubts seized her. Why had they come after her?

There was a warm, delicious summer wind, but Sahara felt a chill remembering the wind on the night she had taken ill. She looked at her watch for the fifth time in ten minutes, put her back against the tree, and gazed down at the stream running through the Glen. The railroad tracks that ran into New York City paralleled the stream; steep banks rose up from the stream, separating the town and station from the dark swath of the Glen that spread out below. Sahara tried to imagine the Glen a hundred years ago, when it was the central social area of the town. It would have been full of people sitting by the stream, strolling the paths, and listening to a band in the gazebo.

Sahara's fantasy was interrupted by a slap against the tree. The wind had blown a piece of paper flat against the bark. She looked at it in disbelief. The flyer! Instinctively, she looked around for someone who had planted the paper while she was in reverie. No one. Leaving the flyer, she pushed herself off the tree and headed for the church. Enough daydreaming. They're coming after me again, whoever the hell they are. It's time.

When she arrived at the Unitarian church, the round lines of the Arts and Crafts style architecture, the dark wood shingles and hanging vines calmed her nerves. It looked like a storybook house. Waiting for Sahara in the lobby was the old man with the gray dreadlocks, Verlin Walker. Sahara was surprised at how familiar and comforting his warm smile was.

"I knew you'd come!" He shook her hand with a strong grip. "We're expecting you. And you're expecting, too." He indicated Sahara's belly and laughed at his little joke.

"Who's we?" Sahara was unsure what else to say.

"I'll show you. I must do a few things and then I'll be right up." He walked her to a set of back stairs off a commons area. "Keep walking till you run out of stairs."

Sahara went up about three flights when she heard a voice. At the top of the stairs the voice seemed fainter. She stepped down a number of steps until the voice came louder again, some trick of the building's acoustics. Maybe she would eavesdrop a little, get herself acclimated, before she entered the room. Listening closely, she thought she recognized the voice. At first she could only make out snatches, phrases, but after her ears adjusted Sahara was surprised by what she heard.

The Tale of the Doomed Tree

... the mills are desperate ... survival ... new people moving to Glenclaire ... from the City ... want houses ... trees. Will they bring down the mills ... save the stream from enslavement ... return the Glen to its natural state ... you will not live to see these things come to pass ... if the mills will devour more trees, or if the town will come to its senses and protect its trees in the Glen.

How could you be so unlucky? How could you let them take you? And what can you do, you helpless being? All you have is your branches, soon to be chopped off, your leaves, soon to be ground up, your seeds, soon to be scattered use-lessly –

Seeds! Not useless! That's what you must do! Scatter more seeds than you ever have. Wait for strong winds and let go of all your spores, your flying offspring, your future. Don't reach out to the hill, the farms, the fields, you can drop them right here in the Glen. Do not be passive: act against your oppressors! Bring down a rain of seeds in a double wedding of spores and earth. Make the Glen dense with saplings. Let them make paper out of you, bind you in their books, set them aside unread. You will have a true legacy.

And let your offspring grow in the sun and rain, let them take over mill space, let them see the future you never will know, that you can only guess. Let them see the city dwellers invade the mill town, let them see boats take the city workers down the stream to work. No, boats will be too large for the waters; there will be ships made of earth, of metals, that bear wheels like carts. So let your descendants see the metal carts transport the folk to and from the city every day, in a new work force that will make mills seem puny and unprosperous, that will dismantle the mills. Let the trees of your lineage see the town grow, break away from other towns, become its own force, and gain the ability to make its own decisions. Let them see the young and strong town look at its namesake, its Glen, and choose to use it for sport and raucous activity, to almost ruin it, as they had with the mills, with one pleasure-seeking building after another: an amusement park, an amphitheater, a skate park. Finally, let the next generation of trees see the good people mend their ways, choose to leave the Glen for simple ambling and quietude, and trust that the trees will protect the land if the town protects the trees, if it keeps the Glen forever green.

You were once a seed, a twirling pod with a soul, looking for a home in the earth. You grew up in the Glen and now face the danger of the mill's saws. But you will hurl your seed up the banks of the Glen to sprout on the ground overlooking the stream. And that tree will grow new branches, spread new seeds, and generate new trees. It is like the cycle of seasons that has passed through your branches over the years, the cycles of wet and dry spells that have challenged the running waters of the Glen, the cycles of people who come and go in the town, building up one facility and then tearing it down for a new one. It is even larger than the Glen, than the town, than the lands around, something familiar to you with your canopy up in the sky, facing the sun, something beyond the sun, beyond the stars: a cycle that builds up and then destroys the entire cosmos, and then starts all over again.

Forever. Forever anew. Forever green.

ق

"Lovely stuff, huh?"

Verlin Walker startled Sahara. Engrossed in the voice, she had not noticed the old man approaching on the stairs, listening along with her.

"His misfortune seems much greater than ours," Verlin said quietly to himself. Looking up at her, he said, "At the beginning, when I was not a part of the group, I would sit out here and listen. Until I realized I should be inside the room with the rest of them."

"I didn't want to interrupt."

"Perfectly fine, my friend, I wouldn't jump right in there either." A warm smile lit up his ashen-brown face. "You'll be fine. Shall we?"

"Yes, please," she said, standing, "Verlaine?"

"Verlin, but call me Verle." He opened the door and stuck his head in. "Ms. Sahara Fleming," he announced, mock-elegantly.

Sahara entered the room. There was a small circle of chairs in the central space of an attic room. A simple sleeping area occupied one end of the room, and a dining area with kitchenette the other. There were only three people seated in the chairs: one was a white-haired woman wearing a colorful, floral shawl. Sahara recognized the other two.

It was Zack and Porcy.

29

"I knew I recognized that voice!" Sahara said, entering the room.

"It's about time," Zack said, coming out of his reverie slowly.

"Honey child!" Porcy said, getting up to greet Sahara with a big hug.

"Glad you're here," Zack said, "If I had to write out another story I'd die."

"It was you who left the packages?" Sahara asked. "Why didn't you just invite me?"

"Don't trust that husband of yours," Porcy replied, "thought he might muck it up."

"What about the tape?" Sahara asked. "Was that you, too?"

Porcy and Zack looked over at Verle. "Me and Miss Elvira recorded it right here."

"I'm Elvi, facilitator of the group. That was my voice on the tape." Despite her flowing white hair, Elvira Young did not seem old to Sahara, though she would have been hard pressed to guess her age. She had an attractive dignity, with a subtle sparkle in her eye. Elvi shook hands with Sahara and ushered her to a chair. "I apologize for our trickery. Normally I believe in open honesty. Without that we couldn't run this group."

"But some of us can't resist a little puzzle," Verle said. "Sweet mystery of life."

"It worked," Sahara said. "So who put the flyer in the tree?"

"I planted that," Zack confessed, "right before I picked you up that night. Lucky I was there when you got sick. Didn't plan on being a rescue operation."

"I'm grateful for that," Sahara said. "What about the flyer in the tree tonight?"

"Tonight? Same tree?" Zack asked. "That's pretty weird. The other day I was going by it and a horrible tension took hold of me. I sat down on the bench and images filled my head, of early days in Glenclaire as a tree! That's what I was sharing when you came. I didn't know if it was real or not, so I did a little research."

Zack explained that Glenclaire was a community that broke off from New Ark, now Newark, New Jersey. Founded on lands purchased from the Lenape Indians, farmland miles up the hill from New Ark, Glenclaire formed when settlers remained at the watering places along its central ravine, the Glen. Zack placed the time of his tree in the first half of the 19th Century, when industrial mills flourished and cleared many trees for their purposes. Zack found correspondences between later historical changes and the tree's 'prophecies:' the metal ships carting people to the city (the railroad), city enterprises making the millwork seem puny (mills supplanted by urban growth and suburban commuters), and specific recreation buildings from Glenclaire's past. The tree had lived and died in Glenclaire.

"Not before hurling its seed up the bank," Sahara said, "where our tree now stands. So you were the parent tree in a past life?"

Zack groaned. "*I* don't know! I doubt any of us were *trees*. These images in my head could've been suggested by my living in Glenclaire."

"Zack, baby," Porcy said, "you didn't know all this town history before your weird vibe by the tree. Did you know we might get a skate park in the Glen?"

"That would involve teenagers? I don't think so."

"And did you know – I do, because realtors know this kind of stuff – that one of the town mottos for preservation of the Glen was 'forever green'?" Zack shook his head. "So how does that stuff get in your head? Did the tree tell you? That's as weird as past lives."

Even if Zack was as skeptical as Amar, and Porcy as argumentative, Sahara was grateful her two friends were in the group. "I still want to know how the group's flyer hit the tree before I came here tonight, just as Zack was telling his story of the tree!"

Elvi spoke with a calm grace. "It is these coincidences and mysteries that have brought us together as a group, believers and doubters as one, trying to puzzle it all out."

Sahara said, "I'm glad that some of the mysteries had a simple explanation: you guys were messing with me. The clues are overwhelming sometimes."

"I know, sweetie," Porcy empathized. "I was given clues, too. This group came together because of them. If I hadn't passed out on Verle's bed, we wouldn't all be here."

"The History of the Group, According to Miss Porcelain," Verle said. "Lay it on us."

The Tale of the Vision in the Attic

We mustn't forget a single contact, or so goes my realtor's creed. My first clues came from settling people in

Glenclaire and remembering unusual connections between them, like learning about Zack and Amar as children. We mustn't forget our past either: I had a difficult childhood but people helped me through it. This made me reach out to those less fortunate. I volunteered at the Unitarian Church's blood drives, toy donations, and food services for the homeless. That's how I met Verle and received the ultimate clue.

I was working the soup kitchen a few times a month. Since Verle was the caretaker, I bugged him every time I needed a mop, a hand with a heavy box of food cans, or even some company as I stirred the soup pots. We developed a mutual understanding and respect. We didn't sense any special bond, but we could count on each other's help.

One extremely hot July evening a year ago, I skipped dinner before coming to the church. The kitchen had retained much of the day's heat and was oppressive. I felt light-headed from the heat and steam and asked Verle if there was a place to lie down. He held onto me as we slowly climbed the three flights of stairs to his attic room. Everything was spinning. He practically carried me up the last steps. I didn't realize the old coot was so strong.

The moment I walked in here, my head stopped spinning. Instead, an odd, magnified perception took hold of me. The room began to glow. Verle led me to the bed at one end of the room, and propped my head up on some pillows. I could see the eating area at the other end, and along the sides were niches under the gables of the slanted roof. Here were photographs, flowers, incense holders and Verle's personal shrine. The center of the space was open, with an old Persian rug covering most of the floor.

I stared at the carpet and let my eye wander around the repeating motifs throughout the design. Every motif, border design, flower or other shape that appeared in the top half of the rug was repeated in exact mirror image in the bottom half of the rug. Similarly, every visual image in the left side of the rug was reflected on the right side. I looked at every piece, every upside-down or inside-out part of the rug, fascinated by the pattern.

And then a very strange thing happened: faces emerged out of the floral design. Bodies floated up from the borders and arabesques. I looked out into the attic space and saw more faces and bodies, many human, some not. They materialized from the gable niches, above the shrine. One by one, they slowly moved forward into the space! They were blurry, but I thought I recognized Sahara, her husband, Zack, his mother, others I didn't know. They formed a circle in the center of the room, just as we sit today.

Are these the people I've gathered to Glenclaire, I wondered? What have they come to tell me? Without words, I asked them, one by one: what are we meant to do?

And then new faces and creatures rose up from the rug: a flower transformed into a dragonfly; a woman with a veil drifted upward; a lost soul floated in-between the borders of neighboring universes. Each figure joined the circle above the carpet, lining up behind one of the original people, forming larger and larger outer circles.

Who were they? Why did they align to someone I recognized from the present day? What was their connection?

After many of these rug beings merged into the circle, they began whirling, forming a vortex into which countless more were drawn. Then they spun off into the air, or melted back into the floor, and the spinning whirlpool began to slow down. About a dozen of the original faces came to a halt. The new circle they created above the rug contained two gaps, one filled by a woman I would meet soon, Elvi, the other by the real face of Verle.

191

I described my entire vision and he was impressed by what I had discovered in his attic space. Over the next weeks we continued to talk about what the circle of faces meant. Then Verle introduced me to Elvira Young, whom I had seen at services in the church. She had offered some spiritual workshops, including one on past life regression. When I told Elvi about the beings lined up behind our faces in the circle, she said it was a vision of a group of souls bringing its past lives into consciousness.

It did not take much to convince Elvi to be facilitator of a group, or to convince Verle to hold the meetings in his loft space. It was this sacred space, this higher ground, this lofty pavilion that launched and honored the beginning of our work. For me, it was as if I began a new lifetime, looking back to the past and piecing together the clues in the present.

ق

Porcy finished with a benedictory statement: "Thank you, Verle, for offering the space, so I didn't have to beat you into submission. Thank you, Elvi, for making our circle complete. And thanks for being here, Zack and Sahara. We have four good people."

"Five." Verle acknowledged Porcy's work in gathering the group. "Counting you."

30

"Porcy, you've given me an idea," Elvi said. "Since Sahara has just joined us, we should give her a taste of the early life-within-a-life exercise."

"I just did that," Porcy asked. "How about my childhood visions, or when I met Bax."

"Let's give someone else a turn," the facilitator responded. "Sahara, you're no novice to past life recall, but this is different. The idea is that within our present day lifetime, we have many separate experiences, some of which seem very foreign to where we are today. Like when people say about a previous job or old relationship: 'But that was in another lifetime'."

"Right," Sahara said, "I get it."

"To warm up to being regressed, some hypnotherapists like to bring a person back to an early childhood experience. Same idea here: a time in your life that feels like another lifetime, an early life-within-a-life. Let's give her an example."

Verle said, "At my age, I've had more lives within lives than some of you have had reincarnations. Allow me to go."

"Excellent. Sahara, you observe this week. We're just thrilled you're here."

And so Verle began.

The Tale of the Ugliest Bride in New Orleans

I was born in 1906, so I've hurdled over ninety. I'm not too bad to look at for an old soul, but it wasn't always like that. This is the story of how I got uglified.

I grew up in the South, pretty backwoods at that. I was a determined little fellow and managed to get myself a bit of schooling and a lot of work. But I couldn't wait to hit the big cities. I was naive back then, very different. Same initials, different guy. Call him Mr. V.

The first place Mr. V. got to was New Orleans. He walked for hours, taking in the bright colors of the houses, the music floating out of every alley. It tickled him endlessly.

One day Mr. V. was strolling by a church when he heard the most intoxicating music he had ever heard. Delicate strains of the church organ twisted around a solid beat coming from tubas and trombones, all spiced up with banjos and tambourines and the like. There was a crowd of people milling about and he wondered what the big occasion was. He inched his way into the onlookers and asked a pretty little girl what was going on. He always had his eye out for a pretty girl, because he was a good-looking boy himself.

"Why it's the wedding of the year," the girl replied, not without a bit of a twinkle. "Madame Penelope has finally found herself a mate and she's sparing no expense."

"Who's Madame Penelope?"

"Why you're a green little thing ain't ya? She's the most important and powerful Madame in town. Owns and runs three fancy houses that all the gentleman attend. And," she leaned closer for the next bit of information and whispered, "she's a most powerful *manbo* of the old religion."

"Vodou?" Mr. V. whispered back, enjoying the touch of her ear on his lips.

"A most ancient form, with juju so strong it can melt the hair off your head."

"She must be something."

"Quite something." The girl ceased her intimate whispering and stood on her toes for a better view. "This will be a big day."

"Come on then!" Mr. V. grabbed the girl's hand and began making his way through the crowd. He pushed and pulled, twice losing her hand. They came in sight of the church pews, then inched along the side toward the altar. Once they were close enough for a good view, he asked, "Why is a Vodou Queen getting married in a church?"

"She embraces all religion. She wanted a solemn Christian service because the day is so important to her. Tonight there'll be another ritual—"

Before the girl could explain, the beautiful music stopped, and the magnificent organ played solo, a solemn entrance music. From the other side near the altar, the groom stepped up: a bearded dwarf wearing a topcoat of greens, purples and oranges. The sight was so shocking to our backwoods boy that he could barely stifle a laugh.

From a door in the center of the nave, away from the crowd, six small monkeys ran in, tossing magnolias wildly in the air. Following the monkeys, four gigantic men appeared with shaved heads, tuxedo trousers and suspenders, but no shirts, holding the long poles of an elegant litter draped with

195

green, purple, and orange curtains. The giants carried the litter into the church aisle and proceeded to the altar.

The spectacle was so bizarre that young Mr. V. knew not whether to gasp or howl with laughter. The girl poked him in the ribs to remind him of the solemnity of the occasion.

The organ came to a climactic fanfare and ceased. The curtains on the litter were whisked back by the bearers, who then receded into the shadows. Slowly and genteelly, Madame Penelope stepped from the litter and climbed the steps to the altar. Her veil covered her face and body, obscuring her figure from the congregation.

The ceremony itself was traditional, although the monkeys did make an occasional tumble over the top of the litter. When it came time to kiss the bride, two of the bald giants stepped up to the dwarf groom and hoisted him up to the level of Madame Penelope's face. Two others approached her and, with a dramatic gesture, lifted the floor length veil. To his amazement, this is what Mr. V. saw:

Madame Penelope was the ugliest creature he had ever seen. She had elaborately colored and teased hair, which rose up in purple and silver wisps from random points in her skull; her forehead sagged over one continuous eyebrow; tiny red beady eyes protruded from dark, hollow sockets. Her nose resembled a medium-sized eggplant, her skin the graying craters of the moon; her cheeks jowled down like horse testicles, loose and swaying; the few tusk-like brown teeth poked out from her purple-stained lips at odd and various angles; her neck was nearly a foot long, and her grizzled chin only slightly less. This monstrosity of a head was precariously balanced atop mountainous shoulders; her breasts were wildly uneven, the right one voluminously draped to her navel, the left as small and flat as a pecan. Her one attractive feature, a tiny and fragile waist, was upstaged by hips the width of a small rowboat and knock-kneed, fla-mingo-like legs.

Mr. V. watched the dwarf positioned for a kiss. No longer able to hold his emotions, Mr. V. screamed.

Madame Penelope lurched back at the sound and swung around in its direction. As she caught sight of the perpetra-tor, her horrifying visage locked onto his. Then, the entire experience, the monkeys, the giants, the dwarf, the crowd, and Madame Penelope's staring face all conspired to unleash from the poor boy the greatest howl of uncontrollable laughter. As much as he tried to stifle himself, Mr. V. shrieked with more piercing guffaws.

Madame Penelope let only eleven seconds of this affront pass. Then, without a glance toward those gathered, she raised her puffy arms in a gesture of incantation. She repeated a sim-ple phrase in a strange language seven times, each time raising her rasping nasal voice to greater volumes. The girl backed away from Mr. V. in great fear. On the seventh time, the laugh-ter came to an abrupt halt. The boy's hands flew to his throat. Madame Penelope extended her shaking hand at him.

"I curse you scoundrel! You have ruined the one beauti-ful day of my life, so I ruin any beauty you will ever know." A hot wind blew against the boy's face. The preacher's pul-pit began to shake. Smoke billowed from the crucifix. Five babies wailed.

Somehow the foolish young man was able to uproot his feet and run from Madame Penelope. He crashed into the crowd, which parted from fear of catching the curse. He ran into the street, and kept running until he was a mile from the church.

And what was Madame Penelope's curse? The ancient eye for an eye, but in this case involving many more body parts. When he reached his twenties, Mr. V. first noticed a large wart form on his nose, then the whole nose transformed into the shape of a root vegetable. Then his skin cracked, his hair fell out, his eyes crossed. Over the years, he got uglier and uglier. (After the description of Madame Penelope, why beat a rotting horse?)

Until he was fifty, Mr. V knew no love, no more pretty girls, no kindness from strangers, only horrified stares and vicious laughs. He took night jobs, jobs working underground; he even robbed a few places, hid out while his looks worsened, changed his name to Verlin Walker. The life of crime didn't stick, but the name did. He never forgot the music that lured him to his fate in the church, never heard it again, but he listened and played music all his life – that was his source of beauty in this life.

He tried various doctors and healers, spent years methodically trying to fix each deformity and blemish, sought out Vodou healers, magic potions, and cult shamans. Finally, he learned of a lasting remedy from an ancient Vodou *manbo* who recognized the curse, knew the story, which was infamous in New Orleans for years, and laughed her head off remembering it. The cure was to receive an act of genuine love from a woman. At first he thought to find a kindly nun or teacher who would supply the love. But it had to be a *desirous* love, a carnal love.

For years, Mr. V. searched for a woman who would not only show him compassion, but desire. But how was this possible? Who would even look at him for more than a second, let alone for an hour, and with desire in her heart? After thirty years with the curse, Mr. V. finally met a woman who found it in her heart and loins to bed him, for one night.

Mr. V.'s face and body slowly returned to its original form, gracefully aging in the process. But the damage had been done: he mourned at the grave of his lost beauty, his lost youth and middle age. He mourned over and over, losing track of what was present and what past. Even after his looks returned, after thirty years of feeling shamed, hiding from people, and never knowing love, Mr. V. stopped searching for love and kept his distance from humanity.

ق

Verle had caught everyone by surprise. What had started out as farce ended in the utmost sadness. Sahara felt a great empathy toward this man.

"The letter you wrote me, Verle, I understand now why you did things in secret –"

Verle cut her off. "That was a private note, Madame."

Sahara saw a grave look of concern in Verle's eyes: his secrets involved people in the room! "What I mean to say, Mr. V., is there's no more need to keep your distance."

"Who cares if those potions had no effect: your search paid off," Porcy chimed in. Someone loved you. Who was the woman? I'm dying to hear that story."

With the same look of concern, Verle answered, "Another time. Another story about another early life within my life." Then he smiled, "Told you I had a shipload of them."

"The facilitator says it's late." Elvi asked Sahara, "The exercise was clear?"

Sahara nodded and the meeting ended. On her way home, Sahara was brimming with thoughts. Zack had a memory as *the tree*! Her *neighbor* was having recalls, too! Elvira Young, with her white hair, seemed otherworldly. What secrets could sweet old Verle want to keep from the group?

Speaking of secrets, what am I going to say to Amar?

31

"Lamaze Without Husbands?" Amar questioned. "You expect me to believe that?"

"Why would you even care?" Sahara said. "You're busy working late with Ooma."

"We've been through that already. You're withholding something, like when you didn't tell me you were pregnant."

"We've been through that, too. I did tell you! I just needed time to think."

"To decide without talking to me, you mean. You went from Pro-Choice to Pro-Life behind my back."

He was going too far. "I am Pro-Choice. But my choice was to have the baby."

"Enough. Just tell me the truth. Where have you been the last two Tuesdays?"

"You tell me the truth. Did Ooma tell you a new recall?"

"Yes, she did. Now tell me. I know it wasn't Lamaze Without Husbands."

"How would you know?"

"I checked at the church."

"You checked up on me? I don't believe it."

"Believe it."

"It's a past life group, okay? Porcy and Zack were there."

"Zack? Why didn't you tell me? Sahara, this is a betrayal." They looked at each other in silence for a moment. "All right: I'll tell you Ooma's recall if you tell me yours."

"Fine," Sahara conceded. "You first."

They had not argued for weeks. Both were glad to settle the argument without much damage. Calming himself, Amar got his briefcase and took out a set of pages. "Ooma was concerned about the Chinese story she had received through Bax, about the lord Xa, the seven palaces, and his sister Oolon. You told me Dr. Machiyoko's story of the seventh wife Deng She."

"You told Ooma about that?"

"Yes. We wanted to know how Oolon had caused the palaces' downfall. So Ooma did some journaling about it, and her pen just took over."

"You mean automatic writing?"

"She didn't go into details about the process. But it's in writing, I can read it to you."

"She showed you her personal journal?"

"Down girl. She xeroxed the pages. She's a secretary, remember? She wanted me to share it with you, to get your input."

Sahara felt better about Ooma to hear it, but only said, "Let's have it."

The Tale of Oolon's Revenge in the Seven Palaces

I have grown weary of secrets.

I am the Queen of Secrets, of having them of keeping them of being kept from them and now I happily expose all for I wish to have no more secrets I want everything told I want to know everything what she is up to who is hiding what under his belt and who is more beautiful: Deng She or myself – Oolon, onerous Oolon.

I am not onerous though the world has me so since I was a child keeping my true identity a secret my brother and his grand scheme a secret the schemes of the wives and eunuchs and babies a secret his true love a secret his Deng She who lies next to me dark beautiful with her cropped hair why did she cut it hateable act making her skin and cheeks and face more beautiful than ever I will destroy her all this has made me Onerous Oolon.

Where is he! This is his day his contest his choice either he has Deng She and I die by sword never to plague him again or he has me as whatever he wishes sister lover procurer of a new crop of bearers of pleasures and he agreed to the tanta-lizing contest I devised he was caught he was on fire but he is not here yet and here she and I lie naked staring at each other not staring at the eunuchs especially the false ones I will expose all of them no longer in their palatial safehouses safe from their past politics disguised as eunuchs hiding their jour-ney to the safe west a new life for them now a new identity

just like me as a girl precious Oolon protected from the warlords who would wipe out our entire family protect her erase her identity growing up as a disgusting peasant I must have known it was false in my bones I sensed that I was falsely imprisoned on the farm such a strong feeling like remember-ing a past life where I escaped to a city I rebelled I hated every minute of my secret disguise knee deep in the paddy clearing out the oxen stalls why me but I did not know who I was until my thirteenth birthday glorious day you are beautiful noble born with noble parents kept safe all these years from murderers but they are gone now you may take your birthright I cried for it I knew it I was never so happy so proud and so angry a terrible secret to make a child live through death might have been better than all the indignity I suffered but I was alive I would come into my birthright

and so we traveled to the west the journey to the west without the monkey or the monk instead the secret invisible followers of the family but where are the rest gone no mother father aunts uncles but have faith you have a brother and we go to him now a brother the second beautiful terrible secret why was I not at least able to live with him while I suffered as a peasant and then I saw the palaces where he lived the fury mounted again why was I not here as a child with him my lady it would have been too dangerous they cowered why did he have opulence and I the pigs and the mud it was the best way the safest my lady I will remember this fury they will pay these so called followers

and so I watched every move and understood my brother's secret grand plan the third terrible beautiful secret of the seven palaces the rotation of his delights I would have been in a fury at all his pleasure but I loved him my brother my only family my precious one and so I accepted this new life system of pleasure but not for me the followers said it would be inappropriate my lady I asked my loving brother for he loved me too if I could serve him by overseeing the palaces I would make it ever better for him I would serve his every pleasure and he loved me so he said yes and I oversaw the seven palaces and my first choice was to have all the followers who chose the pigs and mud for me murdered and so the palaces became my life my choice

but where is he where is my faithful brother faithful to my wishes could he have broken his faith but how could he pass up such a spectacle his two beauties naked on their slabs ala-baster and wood fair and dark luscious long and cropped hair my delicate breasts and those globes of hers I despise Deng She with the ruddier complexion I've worked so hard at my creamy skin after all those years in the wet muck I will not be denied my natural beauty for his pleasure to serve up pleas-ures those wives those unfaithful wives

at first they seemed so innocent and compliant the third wife in the silver palace with a suggestive dance and I would only suggest at first and he liked my suggestions as well as her suggestiveness no I wasn't competitive they were his wives I was his sister at long last the sister of the seven palaces and then I would ask him my brother so that I may serve you bet-ter are you satisfied was the dance suggestive enough and at first he would smile and nod all is well but slowly I would gain his trust no she had done better before no I did not wish she had played that song so much and then it was the first wife who did not please him anymore then she would never please him I would not stand for such lack of service faith excel-lence and I did away with the first wife oh so quietly at first a quiet little poison oh so secret the fourth terrible secret of the imperfect beautiful wives

I was the Queen of Secrets but now without the first wife the rotation scheme was marred now my brother you should share the secrets of your scheme with me so I could correct and he did for he loved me but no I was not in competition they were the wives and must be the perfect wives so who is perfect my brother who is your favorite so hard to judge then who is your least favorite and so the second wife left us again in secret and of course the rotation was adjusted now five wives having to double up on pleasures or be ready to appear in two possible palaces it became harder but they should have to work for it if I had to work in the paddy for years without my brother you can work a little harder to please my brother but the third wife could not keep up and I had her killed as a show for the other wives no more secrets they needed to know what their pleasure was worth and yes my sweet brother I will find new wives but this takes time these are the best wives neh?

though I saw they were becoming unhappy and there were whispers and lies kept from me and I discovered the fifth terrible secret how can she have let herself become pregnant we have things for this and more lies whispers and why is the eunuch Zhou Dong always with Deng She I hired him personally and then I discovered the sixth secret the fourth wife with the first false eunuch and then the fifth there have been too many brats born these three years and I know they are not all from your seed yes we have false eunuchs and false wives it is time to choose who is worthy I cannot deny your pleasures but let it be with one wife who is the favorite you love you trust who services you who has no secrets

and he chose Deng She the seventh wife why did I not see all along that the last wife was the first and not the sixth wife who had been my one ally my secret assassin but then her murder was no secret only my fury but no more secrets let the fury out I do not trust this seventh wife first love who is this Zhou Dong who she talks with day and night you must be sure of her brother you must decide Deng She or Onerous Oolon who is more faithful who is more beautiful who is your true love let me stage a contest and you will choose

but he does not even appear though the naked contest was for him what can you lose I said what haven't I lost he shouted what more can you take from me he bellowed but he agreed quietly and sanely perhaps it was for show and he is gone back to the world of politics no longer safe out here in his world of seven palaces with no more secrets

I will have no more secrets so come my false eunuch the first eunuch I discovered pumping himself into the fourth wife I was a fury it was easy to have her killed after the first three but not the false eunuch helped me uncover the sixth terrible secret of the other false eunuchs but beautiful secret for me now exposing his secret for all the other eunuchs to see and expose my lascivious scheme the seventh beautiful secret my secret that I am ready for the false eunuch's hard falsehood and what he can do with it in me too much for any real man to turn away too much for the other false eunuchs in the watching crowd let me take it treasure it and I will see what other treasures rise up: the strong shaved brute rises up first he shall be in the alabaster palace for cockfighting and there: the red-haired red-pubed slender one he the gold palace for dramas and there: the one whose truth is carved like a Mongol sword the mosaic music throat pleasure oh deeper now and now seven false eunuchs exposed come to me let me see all stand before me naked as the day

what is happening! Zhou Dong un-strapping the olive-skinned whore Deng She where does he think but don't stop my loves let them go if she leaves so much the better I have all of them to myself: the short one already fondling himself in anticipation he'll be my fifth lover porcelain opium pleasures and there: with the long Uighric braid down his back my sixth consort silver rice-wine and this is my last great secret ready to release itself: golden skinned lion-maned diamond palace of dance my last secret at age fifteen I am of age I have my first bloodletting passion I am now Queen of the seven palaces I have bared all exposed all taken all enjoyed all pleasured all and all are mine.

ق

What Amar did not tell Sahara about that night with Ooma was that he had a sexual reaction to the story, an embarrassing reaction, a delightful reaction. Ooma saw it as she spoke of the naked contest between Deng She and Oolon and the sister's coupling with the false eunuchs. Ooma was discrete and kept her eyes away from Amar's physical response.

Nor did Amar share the conversations he and Ooma had afterward: the realizations that Ooma may have lived a lifetime with Bax as her brother Xa and Dr. Machiyoko as her rival Deng She, the wonder at such a pleasure-besotted lifetime, the light-hearted confession by Amar that his marriage lacked such pleasures lately, the aggravation he described concerning Sahara's suspicious nights out, and the subtle hints from the assistant that she could gather some information about activities at the Glenclaire Unitarian Church.

If only half of these intimate exchanges had occurred between the two of them, it would have been enough to turn the tide in Amar's marriage.

32

"That's Ooma's story. So why didn't you tell me about these two meetings?"

Playing with a lock of hair, Sahara sighed. "I was anxious about going in the first place, just by myself. With you, it would have been ... complicated."

"Why? You want me at therapy."

"Look how that's worked out," Sahara scolded. "I didn't want you going one week and not the next, doubting this person's past life, accepting that one's. Complicated!"

"All right, all right. So how was it?" Nervous about Amar's brooding anger, Sahara began detailing the first meeting at the church. She relaxed with his fascination with the tales. Once again her storytelling calmed the demon in their marriage. Amar marveled that his wife had discovered a new source of stories, as if in her research she had uncovered a missing volume of the Nights or the *Panchatartra*. And like her, Amar felt an immediate bond with Verle, and looked forward to more stories from him and the others.

"I'm surprised Zack buys into all this," he said.

"Zack's totally into it, despite his doubts. The second meeting was all about him."

"You're going to tell me everything. Right?"

And so Sahara described the second meeting.

When I arrived last Tuesday, Verle, Elvi, Porcy, and Zack were there again, but sitting in the circle with them was Dr. Machiyoko! The group had kept her involvement a secret. In fact, they had not told me everything about the mystery tape recording: Dr. Machiyoko had arranged with the owner of the Crystal Charm to slip it into my bag.

"I never do that kind of thing," Dr. Machiyoko apologized, "but once the group heard you had a Persian recall they insisted I share my lifetime with you somehow. After I hypnotized Amar they couldn't wait to hear about his life as Ardryashir."

Suddenly I understood many of Dr. Machiyoko's reactions during sessions, such as slipping into trance herself and telling a story. She was as interested in hearing and sharing recalls as she was in my therapy. "You told my recalls to the group?" I asked.

"And I passed on the stories you told me and Zack," Porcy said. "After I got the group going, how could I not try to piece them all together? I want us to share everything. I want to tell you about my childhood visions, my life-within-a- lifetime –"

"Thank you, Porcy," Elvi interrupted. "Let's show Sahara another early life exercise."

"I could talk about my previous life as a psychic healer."

"Let's give Zack a turn, Porcy," Elvi suggested gently. "Zack, tell us about that time you went to Porcy for a reading."

"My mother made me," Zack said. "Cachay was helping out Porcy, about six years ago, making sure she had enough work. I was visiting from Paris, where I lived then. I had been away from the States for a long time, and my career wasn't so hot in France."

Porcy scoffed. "If it weren't for me, you'd still be playing flute on the Left Bank, and I do mean on the bank of the river. You hadn't been home to see your Mama in years, which startled me because the first message I got from the reading was that this boy was brought up in a house of love. True love shone down on him from both parents."

"What kind of reading did you do?" Elvi asked.

"I just read his aura as soon as he walked in. We made this tight connection."

"You mean you lit into me," Zack said.

"Sweets, that's how I got your story out of you. But go ahead, you tell it."

The Tale of the Prodigal Son's Return from Paris

It was the 70s. Everyone was exploring. My parents were very tolerant and I was very free to try new music, drugs, and sex. I wouldn't buy into this psychic double-talk if it hadn't been for all the drugs and philosophy floating around. I got comfortable being gay real fast. Those were great years. And I was a good boy. My Dad died before I was in high school, and Mom had to work so hard after that. I felt I had to stay close. I went to Yale, close to my Mom in New Haven. The hardest thing was pulling away from her.

But my mother thought I should be on my own. We took a trip to India at the end of high school, and she saw how much I loved to travel, so Cachay gave me a trip to Europe for college graduation. Everywhere I went I sent her something special. The first thing was one of those Indian elephants with the glass and mirror decorations. I found it in an Indian import shop in London. As I continued traveling in Asia, Africa, and the Middle East in the early 80s, I developed this habit of sending gifts back to Mom and friends and boyfriends from every shop and marketplace. It became an obsession. Also a necessity – I needed money, so I started buying, selling, and trading objects for cash.

It started with little things, the elephant, a grass snake, wicker shakers from Mali, prayer rugs from Medina. Things got bigger. I'd buy a warehouse of ottomans in Turkey, a seven foot tall Buddha for a friend's garden, fourteen working fountains from Spain. The fountains did me in. I had nowhere to put them for a while. I knew I had to cut it out, settle down, and figure out what the hell I was doing.

I found a buyer in Paris, and an apartment with a courtyard. The landlord loved the one fountain I had kept, so I installed it, along with myself, in an apartment next to his son. The son became my lover. François was a beautiful Algerian musician, who was wild, tender, talented, and spiritual. He had quite a history, but we were both ready to settle down.

The other thing I did throughout my travels was play flute. I played solo on the walls of Dubrovnik, with gypsy bands in the cafes of Budapest, for temple dancers in Bhutan. I had played mostly jazz and bad Jethro Tull in college, but my travels opened up my playing to new scales and breathing techniques. François loved my style and got me gigs with his musician friends. I was determined to make a living at it, so I played everywhere: jazz bands, chamber orchestras, world fusion groups, theater, dance, and weddings.

211

"It was a waste of your time," Porcy interrupted. "When I 'lit into you,' it was because my reading told me you were talented, but your real success lay in your other career."

Zack's only response was, "May I go on?"

The import/export thing was my other career, which I had been doing with the gifts and trading for years. And I kept doing it on the side into the 90s in Paris. I got hip to the Internet in the early years, spent hours tracking down rare items and new, faraway dealers. As much as I loved to visit new places, now I could travel in my living room and do ten times as much work. I became a major supplier for places like Pier One.

It was hard to put down my flute. I was convinced if I put enough time into it, I would make it as a musician. It takes a lot to get me to budge. Unfortunately, it took a tragedy. When I was a kid, I went away to camp for a month one summer. When I came back, my Dad died. The house of love began to crumble. That history repeated itself now.

François found out he was sick. It took me months to have the guts to get tested, but by some miracle I was okay. His father and I took good care of François and he hung in there. Then one day I saw a relic on a Beirut website, a very small silver scroll-holder I had heard about for years. The date was around 10th Century Persia. No one knew what such a small scroll might have been used for. And no one had ever been able to open it to see what was inside, though there were theories about hidden buttons and secret catches.

There are two things about me and this business. One is that though I can unload bulk collections as good as the next big bwana, I live for the individual find. The other thing is that mishandling drives me crazy. I have nightmares of lost shipments and cracked vases. So I had to go to Beirut. I trusted no one to handle my baby. François was sick so I was determined to travel as fast as I could. It took a month to track it down and then I was on the plane back to Paris, my scroll holder in my lap.

I was too late. François' father thought he was holding onto life for my return, but he didn't make it. I was numb for weeks. Without François' energy, my music career was over. I became aware how shaky it had always been, and just gave up on it.

Then Cachay wrote that she was going to law school, and demanded my presence to help her rent out her New Jersey house so she could move to Chicago. I threw a few things in a suitcase and left my room in chaos. Seeing my Mom go off was harder than I thought. François' death made it feel like I was going to lose her, like I had lost him, like I had lost my dad. My mother made me see Porcy, who told me I was on the wrong track.

With Porcy's voice ringing in my ear I returned to Paris. The scroll-holder had vanished. This was the bombshell that exploded all the feelings inside me. A voice in my head told me I was nothing, I had lost everyone, I had lost the object closest to my heart. I had *zilch*. I had been speaking French for so long that I had forgotten the comic impact of this word. It gave me a creepy feeling of failure and indecision, of abandoning and being abandoned by people I loved. The word whispered in the next room, resonated over millennia. I sobbed uncontrollably for the first time since François had died.

For months I didn't touch the flute. Porcy was right, even though I wasn't quite ready to hear it. I was so furious with her meddling in cahoots with Cachay that I actually thought:

what will this damned whore do during my long absence from my mother's house? But economics forced me to do some trading. I found that looking for new things was some kind of consolation. I threw myself into it, and after a while knew it would be easier to work out of the States. Most of my port-of-entry work was in New York, and hoping from Paris that things would arrive safe had my skin crawling. Three months before Cachay finished at the University of Chicago, I moved to New York, set myself up before helping her move back to Glenclaire. It was a great comfort to have her back.

One weird thing happened in my session with Porcy that haunted me later. I had this very quiet feeling, like I blinked and a new version of the same reality sparked into place, the way a movie screen pops for a second when they change reels. I knew that my life was continuing, but sensed that a different life-path had opened up.

ق

Sahara continued describing the second meeting to Amar.

I was the first to speak after Zack finished. "I had a similar moment shortly after I met Amar. I felt my life switch tracks at that moment."

"Exactly," Zack said, "I can buy that. But past lives, lives as trees, or in mythical worlds like the Red Isle, or Heaven. I have trouble with that."

"You recalled a time in Heaven?" I asked.

"Sure, by automatic doodling," Zack joked. "I don't know if it was real."

"I had a vision in Heaven. It was in the Earth's atmosphere. I evolved from a swimming creature to a walking and flying creature."

"How did you know it was Heaven?"

"When a luminescent being with wings made love to me."

"Oh my," Porcy said.

"Come by anytime and tell me that one in private," Verle teased.

33

_~~_

Hanging on every word Sahara told him, Amar asked if she had shared her Heaven story at the second meeting. She replied that, instead, Zack had described a different version of Heaven, though strangely familiar to her. She recreated it for her husband.

The Tale of the Spirit and the Mer-Couple

Just calm down. Stay out of it. Look what's happened the last six, seven times. Nothing but trouble. Biting off way more than you can swallow. Just because others have it doesn't mean the world has to be turned upside-down to get it, too. Just take it easy. Relax, hover, float, look down but don't touch.

They've set you up with a nice view, over the ocean, blue and beautiful. For those that need rest and relaxation but can't stay away, they said, without even entering the first level, stay far below the stratoline, as if you were still in the world, but hover safely above, out of touch. Limbo. Just what the healer ordered. Think about your desires, your aggressions, and your assertive actions lately. Maybe it's time to unwind, to let someone else do the driving for a while. Fly above the ocean, watch the blue hallways of waves come and go, enjoy the vast, peaceful endlessness.

Who are you kidding, this is the ultimate boredom, nice for a minute and then – next! Let's have some action, some wild-life, maybe a dolphin or two? That's better, very sweet, all you have to do is dream up a dolphin and there's a whole school of them. Did you do that? Just by thinking it? We create our own reality. Didn't someone say that? Or rather think that. So what can you imagine behind all this blue?

How about an island, a huge, fantastical, paradise of an island, floating miraculously in the middle of the sea. And there you have it, Atlantis, newly civilized and governed, gor-geous mists drifting through its mountains. On its shores the Atlanteans in their pastel colored robes peacefully go about their business. It's a place for the Gods. Drift down to the water, just outside the harbor, alight on those rocks flanking the aquatic courtyard of the port. Settle in for a bit, enjoy the view, watch the boats, the workers, the fishermen.

But what is this? There is a glint of something on the rocks to the other side of the harbor, turquoise specks, some-thing low, hiding. There, slipping into the water, swimming away from the shore, a sea creature up to no good. Spying on the land people, darting in and out of rocks, hiding and watching. Follow her, she's heading out to those rocks a ways out. Climbing onto one of the rocks. Look at that fin! I've never seen such a dazzling mosaic of colors, and her hair, not just red, not just yellow, but a web of gold, ochre, crim-son, tangerine, with flecks of aquamarine throughout. What a beauty!

She lies back on the rock, her hair flowing down to luminous breasts, aglow with the reflection of the sun on her human skin. At the top of her thighs, between her legs, where the skin joins the multicolored scales of her long, slender fin, is a dark complex of textures, a mélange of skin, scale, hair, dark folds of labia and soft flesh.

Would I were alive again! Would that I could live in the sea in my next life, unfold my triton parts, wrap myself around her. I stare at her for hours as she suns herself, hover as close as I can get. But wait! Your mental powers, your imaginative abilities, you can will into being whatever you want. And so sweetest of fantasies turn into waking dreams. For her, too. The fin curls up on itself, the textured triangle where skin meets scale starts to twitch and tease. She places her human hands on her watery loins and lets the feelings take over.

Gently, gently, my mind works over her body. It grows dark around us, the sun sets. And then horrors! her male counterpart returns from the day's fishing, sees his mate writhing on the rock, and enjoys the reality I have engineered through my fantasy.

How dare he! How can you stand for it! Every ounce of peace and satisfaction you have gained since departing the world is gone. Fury! Rage! A dark, destructive thought rips forth and hurls itself on his pleasure-seeking form. As if a hundred sharp coral ripped through his loins, he is torn off the lovely she-creature and dashed against the rock, again and again. As he sinks down the rock he reaches for his love, but manages only to grab a pale-green sea plant. His body falls into the water and stains the moonlit waves.

What have you done? Is this your evolution as a soul? Is this why you were given the power of the mind over matter? Have you learned nothing from all your failures, all your attempts at power and innovation, all your aggressive tendencies?

You were never this way. In the deep past of your soul, you were a follower, a cipher, *zilch*, exiled from complacent suburbs for being too complacent. You tried to prove otherwise by charging forward into brash new worlds. Look where it's gotten you.

The Mer-creature leans over the rock, gazing into the water where her mate has departed, never to be seen again. Her tears splash the wet rocks, each tear bouncing into the sea. You see each one grow into a small shape, first a blob of shining jelly, then forming a small body. Her tears turn into the offspring she will never have with her mate. Her mind is filled with the sorrow of losing the bearer of the seed of her children. In her imagination she sees the loss of every possible child. You see her fantasy turn into reality, her tears turn into the lost children, each with its own little tail disappearing beneath the foam.

Your heart aches. You have no tears to shed so you just gaze down on her watery tears and suffer with her. Her suffering has ripped a terrible, ingrown thing from your soul, a driving thing stuck there for lifetimes, and replaced it with a truer feeling, not a fantasy.

You feel compassion.

It will do her no good, but she will survive. As dawn approaches, she swims back to the Atlantis shore and resumes her spying, transferring her rage into dark plots.

You have changed. You watch her by the shores and cheer her on. But your best wishes might mean the destruction of the paradise isle. You wish your sea beauty love and happiness and retreat. Best not to wish for anything else. You fly up to the stratoline and tuck yourself into some lower level of the Heavens. You are content to be gobbled up by the ethereal jaws and spat out into some quiet, subservient lifetime.

ق

At the meeting, Zack came out of the story. "At first this imaginative ditty just seemed weird. Then I thought: I saw Limbo, a life after death, a vision of where we go."

"Past life literature calls them interlives," Elvi said, "which we experience many ways."

"But the violence in the story disturbed me, it rang false with the afterlife idea, interlife, sorry. Why was I thinking about myself as willful, heterosexual, and murderous?"

"You were also flying, above an ocean, and had the ability to make your fantasies become reality," Dr. Machiyoko said. "These are symbols of your unconscious, crying out."

"Hold that thought, Doc. After the Mer-couple tale, I had the vision of the tree in the Glen, and that got me thinking. In the fantasy story, I'm dead. I become responsible for lots of mermaid seed scattering upon the water, then choose to enter a new, more passive life. But in the tree story, I am about to die, and take action by spreading my seeds around the Glen, so I can depart the world on a strong note. I've just taken my life to a new place, after Paris and François. I've climbed out of a place of death and taken action to start again."

"So what are you saying, Zack?" Elvi prompted.

"It's not real. It's my unconscious surfacing, like in a dream. It's not a past life."

"What about the sex? The murder?" Porcy asked. "I know that's all unconscious, Id stuff, but what's it got to do with you right now? Maybe it comes from a time when your soul was going through all that obnoxious stuff –"

220

" – which may be generally related to your soul's struggle with when to be passive and when to act, when to change your life, when to fight being *zilch*," Dr. Machiyoko argued."

"Here's another thought," Elvi offered. "There are similarities between the two tales, but with little twists. Such variations can be a sign of karma working itself out. Because you abused your powers, so to speak, in the interlife, you paid for it as the tree, by being destroyed by millers, who were abusing their forest. In the interlife you saw unborn seed scatter and disappear, and so as a tree you spread your seed to preserve life."

"How do we even know the interlife tale preceded the tree story?" Zack asked.

"Easy," Porcy said, "Atlantis came before Glenclaire."

"But thousands of years before," he replied. "Doesn't karma happen in the next life? And how do we know if there was an Atlantis, or if a tree can have a soul with karma?"

"See, I'm not the only doubting Thomas," Amar commented, as Sahara paused her account.

"So cozy up to your old naysayer friend. Come to the next meeting." When Amar hesitated, Sahara said, "You don't even want to come to therapy." If he didn't work on his anger, she thought, how could I trust him not to disrupt the sensitive process of the group?

"I'm very skeptical about Dr. Machiyoko," Amar said. "I'm not sure she should be in a group with her clients. I wouldn't want my privacy compromised."

"I felt that way at first. But those traditional boundaries are insignificant, given that we're among a group of people who may have lived a hundred lifetimes together, and who have the gift to be aware of them. We want to gather the evidence however we can. If you don't –"

"Then I don't belong in the group. Do you want to exclude me just because I'm the only one who can't recall a past life at will?"

Sahara took her husband's hand. "Is that what's bothering you? Verle hasn't shared any actual past life stories. You were able to under hypnosis – what difference does it make?"

Amar flung Sahara's hands away. "You've got all the answers. And always without my input. You share our stories without my consent. Join the group without me. Decide to have a baby without me."

"You're upset because you had no control over these things? You didn't want me to have a baby, and so now you don't want me to be in the group, is that it?"

"No. I'm just uncomfortable with you sharing intimate things with practical strangers."

"Amar, it's my life, too. You don't know things about my life that I've told the group."

"That makes me feel so much better," he said bitterly.

Sahara should have been nervous about her husband's mounting anger. For some reason – the solidarity of the group? the sure protection of having a story to tell? – she was calm, confident, and sympathetic to his anguish. She knew how Scheherazade must have felt.

"Would you like to hear what I told them?" she asked. "It's the story of my life."

34

Sahara continued her description of the second meeting to Amar.

After Zack's interlife story stirred up controversy, Elvi got the group back on track. I appreciated her quiet and simple way as facilitator, even though she put me in the hot seat.

"Sahara, it's time for you to tell us of an earlier life within your lifetime."

I hesitated, but not out of nervousness. It was difficult to choose one time since my family had moved to a new place every three years: born in Morocco, age three in India, six in Egypt, nine London, etc.

Elvi spoke calmly. "Just pick one meaningful time. What in your past defines you? If your sister approached the city you lived in, what would you show her?"

Oddly, Elvi's question triggered a memory about my sister. I began my story.

The Tale of the Three-Year Migration Pattern

I've been moving on my whole life. My family moved on from India to Egypt when my sister died in a tragic accident, placing undue stress on my parents. My father and I moved on from Egypt when my mother ran off with the son of a sheikh who had rejected his own family. When my father learned that my mother had died of an African virus, we moved away from London. We left Finland after I ran away from the cold, tried to reach Mecca and return to the desert, but only got as far as Greece, where I became seriously ill. I moved on from New Mexico when my father left for Berkeley with his new stepfamily, from Mexico when my father became ill, and from Berkeley when I realized we didn't need each other. Now I've moved on from Chicago and New York to follow my husband.

I don't know why we moved away from Morocco, my birth-place. My parents had been looking for peace and love for years, well before the Vietnam War and the hippies. By the time I was three years old in 1973, Morocco had become too crowded for them. Perhaps they were running away from the people who were running away from society.

SAHARA FLEMING's THREE-YEAR MIGRATION
PATTERN

1970   Born, Morocco

1973   New Delhi, India

1976   Cairo, Egypt

1979   London, England

1982   Helsinki, Finland

1985   Sante Fe, New Mexico, USA

1988   San Miguel de Allende, Mexico

1991   Berkeley, California, USA

1994   Chicago, Illinois, USA

1997   New York, New York; Glenclaire, New Jersey, USA

For me, growing up with outcasts and ex-pats made for a fascinating early childhood. As I got older I wished to know more about my roots in Morocco, especially since it had been the only place I had lived where both my mother and sister were alive. While at the University of Chicago I met a Professor Agib, who had known my mother in Egypt, where she had told him family stories. He shared with me this memory about my time in Morocco.

My sister and I had been part of a large group of children who played together all day and night, American kids, Moroccan, Spanish, Gypsy, hippie, African, as well as many free-spirited adults. I was socialized very early. Most nights we would all be out under the stars together. Some kids might dress up in fantastical garb – a sultan, a sorcerer, a Bedouin camping out in the desert. We would build a fire, someone would strum a guitar, and we'd watch the moon and stars come out. Then we would bray at the sky, howl like dogs, roar like big cats, or make up sounds of mystical creatures. Local dogs and cats joined in, occasionally a parent or two. Once we had had our fill, the main event occurred. One of the older children would begin a story from the Arabian Nights. I'm sure there were other folktales mixed in, but it is the way of The Nights to include any and all comers. The magical spell of the tale hushed us, held us, and prepared us for bed.

One night our last year there I cried out to tell the tale. The older children sniggered a bit, then indulged this two-and-a-half-year-old storyteller. To everyone's amazement I began a tale of a brother and sister who run away from home to go on the pilgrimage to Mecca. One gets very ill and loses the other along the way, but they eventually reunite. No one had ever heard this tale, so they didn't know how I could have. And yet I recited it with perfect confidence, including the names of many characters, as if in a trance. I wasn't able to tell the tale again or even recognize it when it was repeated on other nights.

I also described a vision while in my trance, according to my sister, who told my mother, who told Prof. Agib, who told me in Chicago. In the vision I saw a boy speaking to a group of people. Addressing them with a candid statement, he said that one day I would walk away from the whole group. While speaking, the boy used a strange word:

Qaraq.

By recounting this story from my childhood Prof. Agib lured me into researching the origins of the Nights as a search for my identity. He recognized the story I had told as part of the long historical cycle of King Omar – right out of The Nights! How had I known it? Prof. Agib and I explored this and other mysteries and we became close friends. Eventually, he revealed that he was the son of the sheikh who had run off with my mother.

When I asked if he knew what the word *qaraq* meant, he thought of two place names in the world: Qaraq, Jordan, and a town on the island of Koror, hundreds of miles off the Philippines coast. Looking up some etymological texts he discovered that the prefix *qara* meant *dark* in the old Turkish dialect of the Ottoman Empire. There were other roots (karak, kar, (e)ger) in other obscure languages (Oyrat, Tatar, Avestan) with other meanings (eyeball, bandit, to be awake). None of these were satisfactory explanations.

To this day I don't know the significance of the word, but I associate it with the search for my roots and my mysterious childhood recitation of an Arabian Nights tale. Maybe the day I learn its true meaning will be the day I stop moving from place to place.

ق

When I finished my account, Elvi spoke to the group.

"Of course there's a simple explanation for the word *qaraq*. The boy was speaking about a group of people. He was referring to this group. You are the qaraq."

35

Amar interrupted Sahara's description of the meeting. "*Karock*? Like karass, in Vonnegut? A special group meant to be together? Is it about past life groups?"

Sahara replied that Elvi had explained that the word meant an extraordinary group, but more than a past life support group. The group pressed Elvi for more information, questioned how she knew they were a qaraq, and wondered why Sahara might walk away from them. Elvi answered that some things should remain a mystery for the present time. Instead, she pointed out the parallel between the Arabian Nights story about a girl escaping to Mecca and the same fate Sahara suffered as a teenager. Elvi went further, Sahara told Amar, finishing her narration of the meeting of the *qaraq*.

"Sahara, your past life work is going to unearth all kinds of connections to *The Thousand and One Nights*. You've already discovered that you and Amar had lifetimes in Persia that were prototypes for Scheherazade and the King, worlds reflecting each other."

I agreed with her. "The Nights start out with the Scheherazade story, the tale of a monstrous King who threatens her life until she tells him a story. What's interesting is that the first few stories she tells – the Merchant and the Demon, the Fisherman and the Demon – are also stories where a demon threatens death and the victim is saved by telling tales."

"Meta-fiction in the Middle Ages," Zack said.

"Not really, but a sophisticated structure, the frame tale reflected by its inner stories."

"You and Amar are recycling this old yarn," Porcy said. "I mean, he's a challenge to you, yet your stories keep him at bay. In most of his past lives he's a scourge to you."

"Except for their idyllic soul mating in The Suburb," Zack pointed out. "Even there he showered gifts in excess, like a Sultan. The Scheherazade tale fits you both."

"So you've got them all hooked on the Nights," Amar said. "But the King in the Nights wasn't always bad; he started out good. He was screwed over by his wife."

"You're right," Sahara said. "Shahryar and his brother Shah Zaman 'each ruled with equity and fairness' before their troubles started."

"I hate that you're building me up as a monster. Or discussing things about your life I don't know. You never told me how your sister died in India."

"I don't like talking about it. I'm sorry, love, but this group is important to me. Maybe you *should* join."

"I thought we were working on us," he said, moodily. "For baby Naji."

"This is part of that work. I promise to share everything the group hears from now on."

It was well past midnight and they went to bed. Sahara cuddled with her husband. "I'll make it up to you. I've got a new story, in a world no one has recalled yet. See, being in the group gets my juices flowing."

They lay there, touching each other. They had reached a delicate impasse. Amar would not come closer to accepting the past life work and she would not give it up. His anger seemed to be quieted, but whatever progress they had made earlier in the summer was at a standstill. And now the sex had come to this, a little groping at pleasure. She had only stories to give him, so she kept her demon at bay by telling him the next one.

The Tale of the Wartime Hideout

I slammed the door quickly behind me. There was no bolt since a good portion of the door was in splinters. I put my back up against it and slid down to the floor.

For now I was safe. From the soldiers. From the war.

How did I know there were soldiers coming? Grandmama knew. She told me:

Sondre, you must find a secluded room in town. There will be many, for the people have fled. It is too late to leave now. It will not be safe on the road. If you don't meet soldiers, there will be bad people about, thieves and rascals. A young girl like you, Sondre, no longer a child, will be victim to their mischief.

I am old. The soldiers will pass me by. Perhaps they will be merciful and kill me swiftly. You are young.. You must survive. You will.

There will be strangers coming into the town looking for shelter. One stranger came to me, begging for some bread with a few useless coins. He knew cousin Berthe from her old village. He was on the run from soldiers who destroyed his home. He told me:

The war is a day away from everywhere. There is no fiefdom, no dukedom, no nation that is not involved. Time was when it was local, this family against that one, this church against that parish. Then it was a whole kingdom going after another, claiming their right to pray to their God, their army sweeping over their neighbor's barley fields.

Of course the victims needed allies, and got stronger against their enemies, and then the enemies needed allies to fight back the new coalitions. Now every King has taken a side, every noble has been conscripted, every border is bloodstained.

I have seen smoke rising from the village across the river. I have met destitute merchants on the road, having lost their home, a hand, an eye. I have seen the disease that travels with the armies, innocent victims of it wandering the roads. I have looked away from the soldiers who lop off their heads for sport, in the name of health and public safety.

I will give you some advice for the price of this bread. Advice for your daughter, or your daughter's daughter. Advice from an old minstrel I met on the road. He has traveled many lands and seen the war everywhere. He told me:

They say we are in the third decade of this war, but the war is older than I, and I am very old. When I was young my grandmama told me tales of the war, not battles of legend but real events of her childhood. The early days of the war were brave and ambitious: heroes went off in the morning and songs were sung of them that night.

I was one of the singers, the bringer of news from village to village, singing of this conflict and that rescue. As time went on, simple melodies could no longer hold all the complex events on the battlefield. I was asked for chronicles that looked back decades.

The war passed into its tenth decade, and I into my sixth. Peace treaties were written, torn up, rewritten. My voice could no longer sing all the songs. My brain could no longer remember all the words. I learned my letters, sold a song for a quill, a chronicle for a bottle of ink. Soon a scroll was no longer good enough, so I drank ale with bookbinders. They spoke to me passionately of the coming day when books would be *printed*, and not scritched onto parchment by a bird's tail feather.

Eventually everything became locked up safe in the covers of books and people forgot how long the war had gone on. Their bones knew it, their growling stomachs knew it, but with benumbed fear they thought the war was only three decades old.

And so I sing the one song I have left. It tells of a young girl who hears the soldiers marching toward her village. She hides in a dark, secluded parlor, surrounds herself with the things of the room, and learns every niche and corner of it. This room becomes her new world and she lives as if it is everywhere and everything she will experience.

So the old minstrel sang me his song, and I gave him a coin. I took to the road and came here, and I share the song with you as a warning. Wake up from your numbness. It is too late to fight the war, but not too late to save yourself. Tell your daughters and your daughters' daughters: run and hide, find a safe, secure room, and make it your new world.

And so I tell you, granddaughter, of the minstrel's song and the merchant's advice. Go now: give your grandmama a kiss. Stop your tears, for you must be brave and find a safe room. Behind the baker's there's a hidden alley where the homes lie underground. There are three wealthy homes with fine things, useless now, but you will be comfortable.

And so I embraced grandmama for the last time and set out for the bakery. I took all the stale bread I could hold.

Perhaps the soldiers will take what they want, and move on. And not take me. I searched the alley behind the bakery and went through a doorway hidden in the shadows. It led to the downstairs portion of a home. I crept along a dark hallway until I found the door to the room. I slammed the door quickly behind me, put my back up against it, and slid down to the floor. I was safe.

Inside the room were caches of nuts and brandies, odd pictures of animals, a globe, children's toys, wood for the fire, a sewing board. Enough to busy myself. In one corner was a book, an odd wondrous thing. I opened the pages and gazed at the figures drawn on them. These are words I might know or speak every day, but which I could never recognize written in the book. Who wrote this book? Who owned it? I put the book on my lap, flipped through the pages, and pretended I was reading.

I called my room the house of Sondre. I locked myself away in this trunk of a world, survived on a crust of bread each day, and pretended to write sad, compelling verses with my quill. I slept and dreamed to my heart's content. Happiness curled up from the base of my spine, an ancient secret feeling, the pleasure of escaping from the world. I ended my life while still living, content to eat and drink and sleep, but aware of making the choice.

The feeling went deep into my bones, like an animal contented to stay in her shaded grove with fruits and roots, a neverending stream of drinking and bathing water, and a soft, mossy bank where she sleeps all day and night and dreams only of her shaded grove with fruits and roots, a neverending stream of drinking and bathing water, and a soft, mossy bank where she sleeps all day and night and dreams only of her shaded grove....

ق

"Where did that story come from?"

Sahara opened her eyes and sat up in bed to answer her husband. She was so sleepy now. "I was having coffee at Zack's house this morning. He has a print of a Dutch Master and the room in the painting is just like that, cluttered with piles of things, a universe of *stuff*. I got lost in it, as if I stepped inside, and remembered holing up in the room, the complete isolation of it, the cozy nookiness of it. I was Sondre, that much is clear to me."

"And you told Zack all this?"

"No, husband," she said wearily. "You are the first to hear this tale."

"So you sat there for twenty minutes, lost in the painting, while Zack sipped his coffee, and when you snapped out of it, you said 'Thanks for the java' and that was that?" Sahara sighed for effect. "I just want to know how it works, recalling these things. Maybe I'm a skeptic, but I'm also curious. I don't get recalls, remember?"

"Okay. Sometimes it doesn't happen all at once. I looked at the painting and felt I was there. I remembered the war, the room hideout, maybe an object or two. That just took a few seconds. I glanced back at it occasionally to fill in a few more things. When I got home, I sat out on the patio, stared at the fountain, and meditated until the story came back. I don't know what happens next in the tale. Can I go to bed now?"

They turned out the lights and tentatively curled up next to each other. A few minutes later Amar spoke: "Sahr. I can't go to the meetings. I can't be part of the group. It would be a spectator sport for me. I'm not comfortable with that."

"Fine, love. Whatever you..." She was asleep.

36

During the last week of July the group convened again. Sahara, Zack, Verle, Dr. Machiyoko, and Elvi waited a few minutes for Porcy to arrive. Sahara related Amar's negative reactions to the group and his rejection of joining it. "What's a soul mate if not someone following you through lifetime after lifetime? He should participate in the discovery of what it all means."

"At the very least he should be continuing therapy," Dr. Machiyoko said, "but this is an excellent place to discover deep causes of problems. He should join the group."

"If he actually wants to," Verle said, sitting off in a corner of his attic loft.

"If *we* want him to! Let us enjoy our meetings without dealing with that man." It was Porcy, just arriving. "Sorry we're late."

A young man came in behind her, ducking his head as he passed through the door. Baxter Tenderheel stood at six-foot-six and had a strong, extremely handsome face. His natural musculature gave him the appearance of a football player.

"This is Bax, everyone. You may remember him from Sahara's New Year's party." Handshakes and greetings came from around the circle. Bax looked shyly at Porcy, who sat down and patted the chair next to her.

The group continued debating Amar's position in the group. Elvi observed that their heated reactions indicated unresolved past life history. Sahara agreed that she and Amar needed to resolve some of their issues before Naji was born. When the group pressed her, she confessed that when she chose to have the baby against Amar's wishes, he was extremely angry. She still could not bring herself to talk about the terrible incident in the kitchen, but she admitted to living in fear of Amar's temper. The group intensified their feelings: Amar must attend the group, he must stay away from the group, or Sahara must stay away from him. With no immediate resolution, Elvi tabled the argument.

"If I'd known we had to hash out new members, I'd have waited on Bax," Porcy said. "I'm hoping he'll be more than a guest."

Elvi asked Bax if he was interested in joining the group. His lowered head and disheveled clothes gave him the appearance of a little boy, a distinct contrast to his oversized, powerful build. "Don't really know," he said at last, with a little sniff. He looked up, hoping to see the answer on someone's face. His eyes rested on Sahara. "I guess."

"Just observe for today and see what you think," Elvi said gently, "We'll do our early life exercise. It's something you'd start with. Dr. Machiyoko, you're up."

The therapist was reluctant to take her turn. She uncurled her right leg from the chair and planted her feet on the ground, as if steadying herself. "I'm so used to listening. It's hard to shift." She curled her left leg back up on the chair. "I've been thinking about that word, qaraq, the name for this group. It reminded me how I got interested in group work, and how I got started as a therapist. It goes back to my childhood."

The Tale of the Romance in the Japanese Tea Garden

You can say that my parents had the Asian reticence to talking about themselves. You were told: Poppa worked as a government official back in Japan. Came to the States before the war. Met my mom, they married and had my brother and me. That's it. As a child I sensed there was something inside them they did not want to say.

I spent years getting it out of them. I felt like a detective sometimes. My dad was a wall of silence, so I started with Mom. As a small child I asked her, "When did you and Poppa meet?"

"In 1950, at the beautiful Botanical Garden in Golden Gate Park in San Francisco. Poppa had been a gardener and I worked for a florist. Poppa was embarrassed about being a gardener but after the war it was the only job he could get. Never say this to him," my mother cautioned. I could tell I was trespassing on delicate ground. A few years later my mother mentioned that my father proposed to her in 1955.

"Five years after you met? Why did he wait so long?"

She seemed caught off guard. She told me that my father was very shy.

I wasn't satisfied. Later in high school, I became interested in the Japanese Internment Camps. "Were you in a camp during the war?" I asked. My mother looked up from the Peruvian lilies she was arranging. Her expression told me that she had

238

been in one. "Was Poppa?" Again her stern face told me yes. "Did you meet Poppa in an internment camp?"

She put down her flowers and nodded. "I first saw him collecting stones for a rock garden. He would meditate there. I joined him a few times. It was an island of peace in all the sadness of the time."

"Why did it take so many years for you to marry?"

She hesitated, then picked up the lilies. "You must ask your father."

It took me years to get up the courage to talk to him about it. I came home from college one Christmas, and he asked me about my studies. My brother had not chosen an academic path, so my father had a quiet excitement about my interests.

"This psychology? Is this not a man's job?"

"Poppa, you know that's all changed. There have always been women shrinks. Freud's daughter Anna was one of the first."

He grunted. "You like it?"

"I love it." He gave a half smile. I took a deep breath. "I have to write up a family history for a class. I've heard so little from you and Momma. May I ask some questions?"

"For class? Yes. You may."

To my great surprise, my father opened up immediately. He was a different person: soft, thoughtful, even poetic.

He told me how he met Momma in the camps. Everyone was tossed together there. People from very different classes in Japan were sharing bunks, meals, and work together. One day he saw a beautiful woman across the mess hall. He looked forward to seeing her face every meal. By the time he approached her to speak, he already had the feeling inside like blossoming cherry petals. He was in love.

As it turned out my mother was from a peasant family in Japan. My father came from a courtly, bureaucratic family. In

Japan their paths would never have crossed. He got to know her, even asked her to a dance, but he could not pursue the relationship because of their difference. When the war ended he said goodbye.

So it was a great coincidence, a push from Heaven he mused, when they ran into each other. Things had loosened up since the war, so he felt freer to speak with her. The Japanese Teahouse in Golden Gate Park was a safe, appropriate place to meet. Although a tourist attraction, to my father it was a reminder of the old values within their new American world. It allowed him to see this lovely woman but held him to their class separation. In this light, they saw each other at the Teahouse practically every Sunday for five years.

"Five years!" I had long since stopped pretending to take notes. "Momma was either very crazy or very in love."

"Some of both, like day and night meeting at sunset."

"Poppa, I never knew you were such a poet," I said. He grunted. "But you got married. How did it happen?"

He told me that after five years my mother gave up on him. One Sunday he found a note pinned to the wooden railing next to where they always sat. Politely and demurely, my mother wrote him that she could not meet anymore.

"I was crushed," he said. "She knew I thought she was below me. I felt great misery. I did not know how to get her back. I would have done anything." My father stared ahead in silence for a whole minute. His silence and expression told me much. I saw a man who had been on the brink of suicide, and ashamed that he did not have the courage to go through with it.

I recognized his feeling without him speaking it, recognized the lure of suicide somewhere deep inside myself, the feeling of having those you love abandon you even though you know they love you. The feeling came from a dark sector of my soul. It scared me so I knew the memory must frighten Poppa. I pulled him out of the silence.

"Poppa, what did you do? How did you get Momma back?"

My father looked up from his reverie, and smiled a rare, vulnerable smile.

"As I sat there with my head down on the table, a young Japanese man came up to me and asked if I was all right. He wore a knit cap pulled over his ears and sunglasses, and had a sensitive look to him. I trusted him immediately and told him everything."

"Well man, do you love the woman?" his voice was soft, though he spoke directly.

"Yes. With all my heart."

"Then go speak with her."

"I do not even know where she lives. I have kept her that separate from me."

"Do you know where she works?"

"Yes – but I could never go there and plead."

"Then I shall go and find out what I can. Let us meet here again next Sunday."

My father told me that because of his desperation, he gladly put his fate into the hands of this stranger. The go-between reported back that my mother did not wish to speak with any-one. This tormented my father. The one ray of hope was that she requested that the young man return.

"She told me you knew her in the camps," the man in the cap said.

"Yes," my father answered. "But I was too proud to pursue her."

"Even in America? Anyone can be with anyone."

The two men continued like this for several months. One day, the man said:

241

"What would you have me do? You refuse to go to her properly. I cannot continue this or allow this. She is a decent, honest woman. I have a mind to woo her myself."

"No! You are right. I am not even worthy of her. Fool. Fool." My father pounded his fists against his head, then buried his face in his hands. "All I want to do is ask her to marry me. I have wanted to ask her since I first saw her. I wish she were my wife."

My father felt the touch of soft lips against his hair. He looked up. To his shock it was the young man. "Stop your crying." More kisses on his bruised hands. "She will be your wife." Off came the sunglasses and the hat. Long beautiful hair black as obsidian tumbled from the cap.

It was Momma.

"She tricked you!" I said. "No wonder she didn't tell me. She'd never shame you."

"But humble me she did. We were married that very day."

I stood up and embraced my father. "Thank you Poppa. It's a wonderful story."

When I told my mother, we had a nice chuckle. She told me that she apologized to him for the trick for weeks after, but that he loved her all the more for it. I didn't bring it up again. I respected their privacy. But I did notice that there was a new warmth between them. I had rarely heard them laugh together and now they joked all the time. It was lovely.

When my brother heard the story he pumped Poppa for more information about the camps, especially the rock garden my father had built. Poppa confessed that when he left the camp he took many of the stones with him, to remind him of the war. He put some in the Botanical Garden, gave one to Momma, and decorated our backyard with the rest.

My father's body grew weak one year, and my brother came to help out. As his plane approached the city, he felt a swelling of emotion. When he got to the house, he asked Poppa – very ceremonially – if he could have one of the stones, to carry it on. My father was very moved by the gesture and gave it to him with tears in his eyes.

This was all my doing. I persisted at getting the truth out of my parents. I got the story out of my father. It was crucial for him to unleash it. Afterwards, he and my mother became lighter in spirit. They released that tension and beautiful intimacy from their past. And there was an epiphany between my father and his son. I helped heal my family.

I was no longer the little detective or secret psychic from my childhood. My parents' healing was my first act of therapy. It affirmed my path to become a psychiatrist.

37

"So that's why I prefer listening to talking," Dr. Machiyoko concluded. "Listening to other people's stories goes all the way back to my childhood."

Sahara thought of the therapist listening intently on her stool at the foot of the couch. "You're just like Dunyazade, Scheherazade's little sister. She asked for a story every mid-night before the King could lop off Scheherazade's head. Dunyazade saved her sister's life, which led to a healing between Scheherazade and the King."

"A healer – I like this character," Dr. Machiyoko said.

"Bax is very special to me for the same reason," Porcy said. "He saved my life."

This was news. Everyone in the circle leaned forward.

"Bax had just moved to New York and was living on the streets. I was in the city late one night and was mugged at gunpoint. Bax appeared out of nowhere, all six-foot-six of him, and chased the mugger down the street."

"Our hero," Sahara said, and Bax lowered his head.

"What's more amazing is what I found out about him later. Bax was homeless, so I thanked him with a train ticket to come out to the soup kitchen at the church. When he showed up, I offered to put him up for a while. As I got to know him better, I discovered he had an intense fear of death. It was amazing he stood up to someone with a gun in their hand."

"Usually scared," Bax admitted shyly. "I hear a plane, think I'm gonna die. But if someone's in trouble, I jump."

"Bax, tracing a fear back to a trauma in a past life can release it," Elvi said. "Weren't you stabbed in the back in your Persian lifetime, as Ba'ash?"

"Back stabbing counts as traumatic experience," Zack said. "Except among theater professionals."

Porcy turned to Zack. "You were the one he thought killed him – Shahzaman."

"But it turned out to be Ardryashir," Zack said, "my good buddy Amar."

"But my Ba'ash recall didn't help," Bax said. "Still shaky."

"I think Bax has had a recent cycle of lives that went from bad to worse," Porcy said.

"We can take you back to those lives under hypnosis," Elvi said.

"Understood, ma'am," Bax said. "But no thanks."

"Of course, darlin, no one's gonna force you," Porcy said. "But you could share your journal. Bax has kept a journal for five years, ever since he ran away from home."

Verle saw Bax's fright. "He doesn't have to share it if he doesn't want to, Porcelain."

"Sooner or later he does," Zack said.

"That's not fair, I got a week's grace period," Sahara said.

"But you just made me expose my childhood," Dr. Machiyoko said.

"All right!" Bax stood up from his chair; his towering six-foot-six form silenced the group. He fumbled with his untidy shirttail and pulled a folded up spiral notebook from his back pocket. Then he sat back down. "I'll read it."

The Tale of the Journey to the East

1/10/94   Highway 80 heading West.

Out of there. Easier than I thought. The Last Supper. The short Xmas dinner. Probably miss Mom the most. The others? Too many sibs—won't even notice I'm gone. Not for a while. Until school catches up.

Fucking military school. All Dad's idea. Fucking Dad. Military mayhem. Launch them Lockheeds. Ride on, World Death. Yee haw! Won't have nothing to do with it. Killing machine. Engines of death. Missile *silos*: Colorado's chief crop is nukes.

Face it I'm scared. Wake up scared. Gonna die any second. Known that death tingle since forever. Like I can't make it past twenty if I tried.

Don't need no nuke-farming school to shorten my short life. Out of there. Sad though. Sorry if Mom misses me. Interstate of tears.

4/16/94   San Francisco Golden Gate Park.

Spending the night. Smoking. Fucking. Can't beat California girls. Beat off in the bushes every time one walks by. Asian chicks too. Nice. Not much of that in Colorado.

7/94

Nasty scene. Someone unloading some bad E. Julia and Frank almost down. It mighta been me. Mr. Death closing in on me in The Haight.

Heading for LA. Nice redhead in the train station. Last beauty in the Bay. Too old? Going the wrong way anyway.

5/01/96   May Day, British Columbia.

On the road again. LA a drag. Sunny California with an icicle heart. Hitch up to Seattle—nice times in the woods along the way. Seattle cool. Cappuccino at the Fotomat. Grunge on a stick. Rock on! All the Goth girls you can eat. Enough of black nails and metal skulls. Death thing getting to me again. Looking for something and it ain't here.

11/11/96   Hyde Park, Chicago.

Nice to be back in a city. Farms on the brain. Slaughterhouses. From sea to shining sea. Going vegan. If I don't kill it maybe it won't kill me. That death rattle again.

Saw the redhead on Quad. From San Francisco! Dream babe. Floating in and out of my life. Death antidote. Follow her next time.

Too much deep dish. Too many creepy comix. Shouldn't be in the city.

6/16/97   Outside Munising, Upper Peninsula Michigan.

Never seen so many guns. And I'm from Colorado! Me and my big mouth. Mr. B.S. Ann Arbor Radical. Death to death machine! Then come with us up north. The beautiful U.P. The militant extremists. Out in the woods with a million M-16s. Ah, nature!

How do I get outta here? Hot tip to another cell where I'm needed? Just sneak away? Pray they don't shoot me. Should've stayed in Ann Arbor. Pass for a junior. Lied my way right into those sororities. Magna cum. Now I'm fucked.

7/02/97

Gotta get outta here by the Fourth. They're planning a mean ass fireworks display. Finnish Fucking Liberation Army. Kalevala with a vengeance. My grunge goth black leather anarchist anti-government days. Prefer salad.

Go! Hit Canada, scoot over to Vermont and down. Call the cops on the way.

Independence Day.

3/98   Northhampton, Mass.

Too many close shaves. Is life so precious when it's fragile? Why is it so precious if it's so short? A dollar ninety-five is not more precious than a thousand bucks.

Mr. Wallow In It. Can't write another depressing poem. Fear bad enough. My dark shit'll kill anyone. Eyes blackened with the pencils of sleeplessness. Jesus Q.

Need to keep moving. Stay cool, away from people, away from action. Drift.

7/98   The Big Apple.

Not so dangerous here. Get lost in the crowd. Atoms, molecules. Bouncing off each other. Electron in an outer orbit. Solitude of uncertainty. Drift.

Get anything here. Serve it up. If I croak before twenty-one, is it worth it?

Journey to the East. San Francisco, Los Angeles, Seattle, Canada, Chicago, Ann Arbor, U.P., Vermont, Mass, NYC. 10 stops. Maybe one more. Where's it? What's it?

Redhead! Other end of subway car. Who's it? San Francisco, Chicago, now NYC. Where else have I seen her? Stay down in subway. Maybe see her again.

10/01/98
Drift.

ق

When Bax was done reading, Elvi commented, "You've been in and out of some dicey situations, but I sense that none of them are the source of your deep fear."

"No, ma'am," Bax said.

"Though gun running on the Fourth would set me on edge," Zack said.

"We've worked through his fears, with some success," Porcy said. "I've learned from Bax, too. Our bond shows me there's an infinite number of ways of finding a family. That helped me figure out why I was gathering people in Glenclaire, and what my vision here in Verle's loft meant."

"Bax, when you're ready to do a regression, tell us," Elvi stated. "For now, we should stop for the night."

"Hold on," Sahara said, "Bax, this red-haired woman you saw in California and Chicago and New York. What does she represent to you? Who do you think she is?"

"Oh, I know who she is." Sahara felt a chill up her spine as Bax looked directly at her.

"It's you."

38

All week Sahara wondered at the amazing serendipity of Bax seeing her during his travels across country. She contemplated how their past lives might link them, but she had no connection to his Persian or Chinese lives. At the New Year's party Bax had given her several long gazes, and she had returned them. She found him attractive but had never considered that her past life work might draw her to another man. She was too busy worrying about her husband and Ooma Qadir. And Bax had his eye on Ooma! Who was she in all this? One thing was clear: she would not tell Amar about Bax's attraction to her, and she prayed the group would be discrete. When she told Amar about the meeting, she barely mentioned the sad-eyed young man from Colorado.

At the next meeting no one mentioned Bax's infatuation with Sahara, the elephant in the room. It was now August and they were in the middle of a heat wave. Every degree of the church's heat had risen to Verle's attic, and it was not just the seven-month pregnant Sahara who was suffering. Verle promised he had a short recall to share.

"We've heard a lot of strange tales. It's a lot to take in someone's life in the 16th Century when they're sitting right across from you. But I'm about to tell my life as a sea gull. On Gondwanaland, the supercontinent that broke apart into our continents today.

"I had a recall like that," Sahara said, "except it was another landmass preceding Gondwanaland by millions or billions of years."

Verle winked at Sahara. "So I heard. Got me interested in the history of the planet, so I looked things up on the Church computer. Gondwana was one of two huge pieces that split from the supercontinent Pangaea about two hundred million years ago. Then it took a hundred and fifty million years to break apart into our four southern continents.

"Sahara, I also heard about your trick of seeing landmasses in oily water. So one hot night I stared at the sweat on my skin. These strange shapes emerged and the name Gondwanaland popped into my head. That's when I knew it was a big fake."

"Why?" Elvi asked.

"Cryptoamnesia. The theory that we're born a blank slate, without any *prior knowledge*, and that anything we have in our head we learn in this life. So: I hear Sahara's story as a landmass, I look up Gondwanaland, I space out staring at my arm, and – bingo – I've cooked up a recipe for a past life. I've tasted all the ingredients in this life, and my tongue puts them together to perceive as a past life."

"You know what's bizarre about this idea?" Zack asked. "The more connections we find – things one person says that are reflected in another's story – the more we believe that the connections are a kind of proof of purchase in past lives. But from what Verle is saying, the more connections, the more it proves cryptoamnesia, that we're creating so-called recalls by piecing together each others' stories."

"There's also the theory that past life regressions are derived from childhood incidents and traumas," Dr. Machiyoko explained. "Excessive grief seizes someone, and they work it out by believing the trauma happened in a past life."

"So it's all bunk then," Zack declared. "Great, let's go home. I'm sweating like a pig."

"I want to hear Verle's story!" Sahara said. "I don't care if it's scotch taped together with his Gondwanaland research and a traumatic bike accident when he was six."

"Real problem is," Verle said, "it's unfinished."

"Those of us with *faith*," Porcy said, "will find someone in the qaraq to finish it."

"Very well," Verle said, "but I'm kicking you all out when I'm done. Too damn hot."

The Tale of the Bird's Eye View

The bird – think of her as an ancient sea gull – flew higher and higher into the cold Southern sky. She wanted to get some distance from the impending choice she had to make, as her ancestors had always done. They had seen such rifts before, and had used their abilities of flight and distance to puzzle out the consequences. This split was relatively miniscule, but perhaps that was the tragedy: so small, so personal.

The birds have watched the land moving for generations, witnessed the continents breaking apart for years. Imprinting the coastline of a recently formed southeastern edge, hundreds of birds scoured the globe, examined every bend and zigzag of every shore, until they recognized the matching, reverse coastline of the landmass. In so doing the gulls tracked the northward wanderings of a future chunk of Asia. Elsewhere they saw the sleek whip-like tail of the piece that had first separated from Gondwana and found its home in the equatorial embrace of future South America. Not far behind, a chunk of Africa passed along the Atlantic highway to wander up to its place, the Indian subcontinent left its triangular bite mark on the diminishing supercontinent, Madagascar broke from India to stay south, and Arabia detached itself and jostled for a place between the African, Indian, and Asian chunks.

An epoch later Australia split, which left Antarctica and one remaining bit.

The gull had witnessed none of this first hand, for it had happened eons ago. But in her collective avian mind, she recognized the matching coastlines, the missing pieces of the supercontinental puzzle, the past and future lives of the continents. She climbed higher and higher, perusing the wide panorama. There are fish down there, and other things to eat, but views feed the soul, too. The final coastline catastrophe was still in the making, in an area that the bird had spent most of her time on the planet. She was faced with a terrible choice: of the two chunks of land about to break apart, where did her loyalties lie? Which was her true home? She let the winds lift her, as if a new view would solve her problem.

In the center of Gondwanaland had been a vast mountain, once all springtime lushness, more recently a frozen waste. The ice mountain was sleek in its sun glow, but shaky and nervous at its volcanic roots. Once omphalos of the Earth's most splendid landmass, then abandoned for the tropics, the mountain had suffered centuries and centuries of humiliation. At Australia's defection the poor mountain was no longer centerpiece of Gondwanaland, but was left standing precariously at the edge of the northern coast. Attempting iceberg suicide, the mountain threw staggering chunks of ice into the sea below. In a half-mad striptease of inverted shame, the mountain cried, "You took Africa, why not take this?" and jet-tisoned layers of rock and timberline. "You want Arabia, have this," and vomited a tonnage of snow-caked earth into the frigid sea.

The result of this sensual breakdown was a love child. Australia had left shallow waters in her wake, and the falling mountain chunks landed on a mysteriously green ocean bottom. The detritus crashed and mixed with Australia's remains and rose above the water level. And so a Baby mountain emerged at the foot of the North face of the Gondwanan mountain. At first, in its madness, the ice mountain thought its miniature twin mocked it and hurled more debris at the fledgling. This destructive intention only built up the new creation.

In time, the mountain saw its offspring for what it was. It was a crisp spring day and the parent huddled in exhaustion from the previous night's unleashing. As if in childlike imitation of its petulant Mother, or perhaps as a gesture of peace, Baby mountain tossed a landslide of rubble into the tiny channel that separated parent and child. The infant's spewings glided across the waters and nuzzled against the Gondwanan giant. A pause. An instant of recognition. Then a hail of tears from Mother mountain, a succession of landslides that filled the separating channel and connected Baby to Mother's breast.

It was 600,000 years before history, give or take an Ice Age. The bird had flown into a time of peace and love between giant and dwarf iceberg. But deep in its brain, a brain that had known the first propulsions in the ocean, the flight of dragon-flies, the death of dinosaurs, the bird knew that the peace and love would be short-lived. She recognized a familiar pattern of change, the death and rebirth of worlds, taking place below her eyes. At her distance in the sky, this knowledge was a comfort. She would have to choose on which rock to land, but she knew it was part of a much larger cycle of life.

She flew down again, ready to fish the waters between Mother and Baby mountain.

ق

39

Sahara repeated Verle's story to Amar after the meeting, and Amar told it to Ooma the next day after work. Immediately upon hearing it, Ooma had a recall of the Mother Mountain, which picked up where Verle's tale ended, like the matching outlines of continents.

The Tale of the Last Piece of Gondwanaland

How long have I shown loyalty to the lands around me, even as they drifted away? Do I continue my loyal pledge now that I am the proud figurehead of the new Antarctic, or do I let go, the last shard of Gondwanaland, left in my dotage with only the comfort of love? I should celebrate the coming of my Child as a rebirth of my majesty, a reminder of a deep memory of the celebration at the birth of princes and princesses. I do celebrate every day by throwing down ancient rocks for the

Child's nourishment, tossing a wall of scree so that Baby may sport a new inlet, jettisoning a shelf of ice for a peak atop the infant.

There is something special about my Child; she emanates an enchanted greenish glow. The gull who perches on her shores basks in the greenish tint, then flies to my side, alights on the giant fingers of my cliffs. We both gaze adoringly at the Child.

The bird's peaceful sessions atop the smaller iceberg were one day disturbed by unpredictable flurries of rock and ice coming from the Mother. Why? Overindulgent pampering? Jealous fits of barely suppressed rage? The bird was good at puzzles of the spatial sort; this was of the heart, impossible to piece together. The gull cared deeply for the two mountains. It was she who first noticed that, with each new hit of rock on the Baby's terrain, the connecting piece of ice, which secured Child to Mother, became less stable.

During a particularly embroiled argument, the Mother Mountain launched an enormous volume of ice from the highest peak. As it accelerated from the fall, one chunk smashed on a weak crack in the connecting ice and another crashed into the belly of the Baby mountain, forcing it backward. With a tremendous explosive snap, Baby ripped away from its Mother and pushed back into the sea.

The gull floats in midair, on the stillness between us. My Child is moving farther out to sea, a voyager cast about in the waves. It is not too late! Wake out of your shock! I spew more rocks. I can still bridge the gap between us, and repair what has happened. Reach out with your own earth, Child. Stop looking up at me. I did not mean to send you away, to divide us. It was my volatile nature: mountains have deep, rumbling insides.

But why do you not stir? You do not wish to return to me? You want freedom, of course, the independence of the Child, but no, you are the same as me, you are made of my flesh and rock, you must serve this land like me. You must remain true, like the birds, which have returned here for millennia. They have been loyal. The gull circles now, preparing to come back to me, to land on her true Mother, as you must, too.

The gull circled over the Mother Mountain, though it knew the mighty migrations of continents were at an end. This was the end of the world as it had been. The mountain would fall into the sea with grief, and the Baby would be the last landmass to drift with the tide. And so the gull swooped down to the south-facing slopes of the Child mountain, now a floating island, and alighted on a favorite point. Facing the mountain across the cold waters, she watched the Mother let loose final bursts of stone, then became still. The gull felt the Mother's icy stare.

What a humiliation that a bird showed me the sham of obedience, the travesty of loyalty. And my own Child, the planetary runaway, disappeared into the dim horizon of abandonment. I reject you, as well as all you continents who have left me. I will remain here, frozen unto you, controlling the level of your seas and shores. Birds, stay away from the South, or I will breed into you the inability to fly, trap you inside blubbery, confining bodies. And Baby mountain, no more Child of mine, island unto yourself, I curse you forever: go drift about the seas, find your resting place, attract the power lines of the planet into you – but one day you too will suffer betrayal, crumble, disappear below the waves.

As the newly created island drifted further from its Mother source, the sun beat down on ice and bird. In answer, the greenish tint under the iceberg glowed more brightly. Time passed. The sun grew stronger. Each time the bird made small forays for fish, it returned to an island that was less ice and more green. The continents found their resting places in the oceans; their last movements whirlpooled the waters between Africa and the Americas, created gulf streams and countercurrents, pulled the island into the center of the Atlantic.

Springs and summers came. The green tint became grass and vegetation. Insects came to life, drawing more birds. Mates fought for the gull's attentions. The island tripled in size. Underwater, its enormous mass reached out to all aquatic life and its roots entangled with vast gardens of seaweed, forming an anchor in the middle of the ocean.

Many generations of the bird's offspring were born on the island. A newly hatched chick looked out from its egg and felt the island below, solid, stable, unmoving.

The final journey of the island of Atlantis was over.

ق

"Atlantis!" Amar looked at Ooma as she finished her tale. "Of course – the final curse on the island, about its sinking into the sea. Does that mean Atlantis was real, if Verle remembers it, and you do – as a bird and a mountain?"

Ooma did not answer. They sat in a bar at the train station, where Amar had taken her to tell the story. Instead of touching her ginger ale, Ooma nibbled the end of a knuckle. Finally she said, "I feel a great sadness."

"You were the Mother Mountain. You lost your child."

"It's more than that. I was good, I was loyal, and it all fell apart. There's something else way down in there, the sadness turning to giving up, not caring, I don't know...." Ooma put

259

her head in her hands, but tears did not come, only a sinking into the feeling.

Amar lifted his hand to her head and stroked her hair. She moaned thankfully. He looked around the bar to see if he recognized anyone. Then he let his hand move to her shoulders and down her long braid of thick, dark hair. He could feel how much he had been holding back. Reached the base of her spine he continued to rub her body.

His touch awakened something deep inside her, surprising, tempting, and frightening. She sat up. "We're not going here, boss."

After a moment, he let go. "Sorry, sorry. It's this group. It's driving Sahr away from me. Things were getting better, but the group complicates things. It's messed up."

She had been right to rebuff him, but she hoped he had made a pass at her because he was attracted, not because he was distraught about his wife. She raised her voice. "Why is it messed up? The stories are the important thing. I have faith in their truth. You may not buy Atlantis or me as Mother Mountain, but it's real to me."

"It's real to you, it's real to Sahr, to everyone in that damn group! But not me!"

"Screw the group!" Ooma let her distress at Amar erupt in the noisy bar.

Surprised by her reaction, Amar appeased her. "But without Verle's tale, you wouldn't have had your recall. The group's work is important to us."

"Why don't we both join the group?"

"Sahara would probably quit if you joined."

Amar saw that Ooma was stunned. The passionate expression on her face was beautiful to him. Things were too complicated, too confusing and conflicted. He hated this indecision.

He threw some money down for the check. "Enough. Let's get out of here."

Ooma let her anger subside into rejection, and got up to go. Trying to joke, she said, "Just keep your hands to yourself. I'm a good Muslim girl."

Amar laughed. "And I'm a nice Jewish boy."

On the train home Amar resolved to do something positive for his marriage. His guilt made him tell Sahara about Ooma's recall and agree to go back to therapy.

At the next session Dr. Machiyoko observed that the couple was on the brink of going deeper in their work, but that they were both anxious about it. She chose to start the session on more neutral ground. Seated at the foot of the couch, the therapist listened to Ooma's tale about the crumbling of Gondwanaland.

Like Ooma, Dr. Machiyoko had recalled a lifetime on the Southern landmass in response to Verle's tale of the ice mountain. But the therapist's story occurred at the outset of the continental break-up, at a much earlier, warmer time.

Sahara and Amar listened in wonder to the new story.

40

The Tale of the Liegh Nuo

For generations there had been nothing but happy families. A happy child had nothing to do but grow up and start a new happy family. The land was green and endless, offering abundant produce and expansive playfields. No one remembered when the first families had arrived, but everyone felt a loyalty to their land.

D'n-Gwn stood in front of her home watching her young daughter play. The child beamed with delight as she tried to take hold of the stick. D'n-Gwn remembered playing Get-the-Stick herself as if it were only days before. Soon the others would be along, and the pack of little ones would waddle off to the playfield together. It was not D'n-Gwn's turn to watch them, so she had the day free. Sometimes she followed and watched her child from the seclusion of a bush. These private moments were precious to her.

The first fissure appeared one dawn after a surprisingly cold night. It split the playfield in half. The children were fascinated by the crevasse, the parents mortified. A new play-field was secured almost immediately. The families took turns doing a new job: the watch on the crevasse, so no young one would venture too close.

After the third fissure a meeting took place. Accustomed to happiness, the families were baffled by the recent disasters. They felt confident that there would always be new playfields and more produce to eat, but there was no way to prevent more rifts.

It was agreed that the Licgh Nuo should convene.

The Licgh Nuo had not met in D'n-Gwn's lifetime, even though she was a member of the council, a position she had inherited from her family. On the council were a few oldsters who had knowledge that had been handed down over the generations, just in case of a circumstance like this one. It was time to pass on the wisdom.

Licgh Nuo did not mean High Council; the term referred to a hibernation practice. The purpose of going into a deep sleep was to receive images, or Licgh, full of advice, warning, and prophecy. The Licgh Nuo was the light that needed to be shed on the current crisis. The Licgh Nuo determined who would be chosen to go into the sleep state. To enter the Licgh was a privilege and a special gift. To choose, the members would form a circle, try to enter into hibernation, and wait for it to be clear who had been chosen.

The oldsters led the group to a secluded grove of aspen trees in the nearby hills. Ominous and foreboding, the late afternoon shadows introduced an unseasonable chill to the air. Once everyone was on the ground, the waiting began. Darkness fell. Distant rumblings suggested new fissures were occurring. D'n-Gwn could not concentrate and looked around at the group. She fought madly to keep her eyes open. After much time she let herself drift off, but kept her eyelids half open with a quiet but fierce determination. D'n-Gwn could stare off like this forever. Eventually, she visualized something.

A vague patch of white formed in front of her, growing into an enormous shape. As it approached D'n-Gwn felt an accompanying shiver as the shape turned into a cold, white mountain of ice. Huge cascading floes of whiteness fell from its sides. She saw her own land, the hills surrounding her, transformed into icebergs. Large areas of white land broke off from the mountainous shores. These were the fissures of the future.

Her land was part of a monumental mass that had already traveled the seas, south to the Pole, then north and west, then back to the Pole. The fissures were the rifts between the polar lands and the rest of the mass pulling away again. The land of the families will rip in two, one part leaving, and one part remaining, to become a land of cutting ice.

D'n-Gwn awoke, her torso twisted, her head thrust back, vulnerable to the sights she had witnessed. All the others in the circle stared at her. After a few moments D'n-Gwn realized what had happened. She had seen the Licgh Nuo. She was the chosen.

The days that followed were as intense as the vision itself. Once she told all she had seen, it was clear that the families had to relocate. The fissures were separating the living areas from the playfields. Generations of complacent contentment had not prepared them for these decisions. Most families preferred to remain with their homes, so they found new areas for the playfields directly behind their current shelters.

D'n-Gwn was numb throughout much of the discussions since the Licgh Nuo had weakened her greatly. Grateful for her special gift, the families competed to help with her children's care while she rested. Visions visited D'n-Gwn as she lay in her hut: voyages through the stars, royal infants held aloft, strange creatures with three noses. When she regained her strength, the Licgh gave her a final vision. She saw what the families must do.

D'n-Gwn arose and went to find everyone. It was extremely quiet outside. She saw a new fissure directly in front of the dwellings. Panicked, D'n-Gwn ran near the edge of the crevasse, searching for the end of the divide. There was undamaged land a short way down the rift. She crossed over, feeling reassured when she reached the other side.

She heard shouts on the other side of the fissure, from where she had just come. She looked back and saw her family and others running toward her. They screamed for her to return to their side. The families had moved a safe distance behind the dwellings before the final chasms separated them from the old playfields. They had waited till the last moment to awaken D'n-Gwn, to allow her to rest. The time had come.

D'n-Gwn was heart-stricken. "A new vision told me to leave the dwellings, to stay near the playfields on this side. This land will not drift away. The other lands will break off and endlessly roam the seas, dividing into newer and newer realms. By remaining loyal to the area I stand on now, the families will be stable, secured to this spot by great forces."

But what of the cold and the ice? The other families? You must come!

"No. The ice will not come in our lifetimes, or in many lifetimes. This is your land. Those before you were connected to this land, even as it roamed the oceans. You must remain true. Come to me!" D'n-Gwn's children ran across the remaining land bridge into her embrace. Friends and believers closest to her followed. Angry that she had let them down as the chosen, the others ran back and returned with a furious, howling mob. More joined D'n-Gwn, but most chose to stay.

The happiness of the families disintegrated, just as the remaining land bridge collapsed into the earth.

The families on both sides of the divide heard a tremendous rushing sound. They all stepped back, fearing another fissure would pull them into the crevasse. Instead the opposing lands whooshed apart and great gushes of white water began to fill the chasm. In no time, in an eternity, an ocean roared up to separate the colonies.

D'n-Gwn carefully walked to the new shore. She looked out to the shrinking mob in the distance. She could still hear their screams above the waves, castigating her for leaving them without warning. For a horrible moment she felt the urge to throw herself into the sea, to swim back to the majority, or to dive underwater in hopes of finding some new family that would accept her.

She felt the brush of her little one's head against her body. Instinctively she reached down to protect her from the water. Can we play now, the innocent one asked? D'n-Gwn was thankful for the small family that had followed her. They would start over; they would renew their love for each other and the land.

"Yes, little one. You can play now."

ق

"This story ends just like Ooma and Verle's," Amar said, "with continents separating."

"Porcy and I had lives on continents, too," Sahara said, "which makes five of us."

"Six," Dr. Machiyoko corrected. "Zack's mer-people recall was in Atlantis, Ooma's ended with the creation of Atlantis. The links are extraordinary. So is the time frame. Verle told me that the South Pole didn't freeze until forty

266

million years ago. My lifetime could be at least sixty million years old."

"The civilization of Atlantis was supposed to have begun two hundred thousand years ago," Sahara said. "So the qaraq is connected over vast amounts of time."

"How is that possible?" Amar doubted.

The therapist answered. "There's the cryptoamnesia theory that would say that Sahara's initial landmass recall triggered everyone else's stories in association."

"Meaning they're all imagined," he said.

"Maybe. But I think this group not only has special powers of recall, but also has been together at special times in history. For these recalls, we've gone through some kind of planetary separation anxiety. Collectively, we must all have ancient memories of the ground under us shifting, wandering, and re-forming. That's heavy duty karma."

"The only ones I know in the group concerned about separation," Sahara said, "are us. We're a family living with the fear of splitting apart."

"Sahara, do you want to tell Amar something more about that?"

Sahara knotted a lock of hair. "It's great you've come back to therapy, but we're still living two lives, you at the office, and me at the group. And we've never dealt with the biggest issue from the time I became pregnant." Sahara's stomach tightened. But she was ready for this. "I'm afraid of you, Amar. I expect you to blow up any time. I have to tiptoe around, watch what I say, do everything to take care of the King or he'll chop my head off."

"That's the big issue, my temper? May I remind you that all I wanted was to postpone having kids, and you *defied* me, made your choice and left me out of it. That's not the big issue?"

Sahara was surprised at how fast his anger peaked. "This is what I'm talking about. Look how angry you are! How can I talk to you?"

"But you piss me off! You're still leaving me out of things, telling the group whatever you want, at my expense. You're building a wall between us with your damn qaraq!"

"You're the one building a wall. With your anger. I'm afraid for the baby's safety. You still may want to destroy him for all I know."

"That's it!" Amar swiped his hand violently. "You want to break up this family because you're afraid, go ahead. But don't ever accuse me of not wanting this child again." Amar was up on his feet. "This is insulting. I shouldn't have come. Great job, Doc." He stormed out of the office.

41

This is about all I'm good for these days, Naji, Sahara thought, stroking her enlarged belly. A baby-making machine. It's enough for me to deal with stories popping up and to stay healthy for you, baby. And calm: your Dad and I won't confront each other. It's okay.

It was mid-August, and Sahara sat on the patio, enjoying the mist of fountain spray. She needed the quiet, the simplicity. She let herself feel drowsy and heavy.

" 'One day his elder brother said to him...' "

Sahara became instantly alert through the heat. Did she hear a voice?

"...'I've decided to go on a hunting expedition.' "

Words from the Nights? Who was saying them? Was she dreaming?

The voice started again. A greeting. A reassurance. The start of a story. She recognized the village where she had lived as the thirteen-year-old Sondre, hiding out in a secluded room. She listened in amazement.

The Tale of the Boy's Intrusion into the Secluded Room

Once there was a child named Nils who had lost his mother and father during a terrible and long-fought war. His home was destroyed and he wandered the streets of his small town for hours. Only five years old, Nils did everything he could to avoid the terrifying soldiers and find shelter and food. He discovered the town's hiding places, secretive back alleys, and underground cellars.

On his third day of hiding, the lonely boy came across the bakery and stuffed his pockets. Sneaking out the back door of the bakery, he found an alley where there were several doorways to houses. One door led down some stairs to a hallway. At the end, Nils entered a marvelous blue room. Blue was his favorite color, and so without thinking he gathered up a blue shawl, globe, and ostrich feather and arranged them together in a row.

An adolescent girl jumped up behind him and placed her hand over his mouth. She had recognized the boy, and he recognized her as Sondre. Sondre scolded him for sneaking into her room, and worse, for leading the soldiers to her lair. The boy bit her hand and then cried that no soldiers had followed him. She slapped his face and cursed his intrusion again, demanding that he stop crying and quiet himself.

Nils begged her to let him stay. Reluctantly Sondre let him remain, knowing his life was in peril. She would have preferred to enjoy the peace and quiet by herself, hiding out from the world with a little bread and water. Sondre loved the cozy warmth she felt from her private island, wondered how such a feeling could be so deep and physical within, marveled that it might be the onset of her womanhood, and fantasized

270

about a lover coming to her room, and the two of them enjoying their corner of the universe together. It all seemed natural and inevitable, as if it had already happened.

Sondre's fantasy was destroyed by this new wart on the skin of her contentment. For two days the boy whimpered for his parents. When she explained that their bread would last if they took small bites, Nils ate three times as much as she. At night she ordered him to stay in his corner of the room, but each morning she awoke with the warm body of the boy curled up next to her. Worst of all, he spent his day rearranging things. She scolded him about it but he would not stop, so she decided the activity would quiet him. He created a line around the room with all of the blue objects: a shelf containing a robin's egg, a stuffed duck; the blue divan covered with the azure shawl; a corner niche piled with blue shells, vases, jewelry.

Their food ran out and it was necessary to retrieve more. Sondre insisted that the five-year-old get their food, since he had intruded on her and eaten most of it. When the boy cowered at the prospect of being caught by the soldiers, Sondre made it a game: could Nils play hide-and-seek with the soldiers, without them knowing it? Could he pretend that he was on a treasure hunt for precious gold in the form of bread? Could he sneak back to the room without making a sound?

The boy was delighted at the games Sondre suggested and took to combing the streets for food every day. Nils discovered hidden caches of food in abandoned homes, shops, and even the storehouses of the soldiers. He found secret shortcuts so if he was spotted he could get back without discovery. It was more than fun for him; he proudly delighted in his big boy resourcefulness in foraging for their livelihood.

Sondre was not only delighted with the endless source of food, but also with the hours of free time for herself, peaceful hours in quiet rest and delicious fantasy. They reached a comfortable agreement. Sondre cuddled the boy at night and Nils provided food; Sondre gained her private hours and Nils arranged the blue room as he saw fit.

Sondre took to thinking of Nils as her baby brother, even her child, within the same fantasy she had of sharing a lover in the room and bearing her lover's child. She began to worry more about Nils' trips into town, sometimes feeling remorse that she had ever forced him into it. The child was more and more daring, especially now that he reached his sixth birthday. He began spying on the troops, to keep an ear out for incursions into their neighborhood. He knew that things were getting worse for the soldiers: lack of stores, frustration at being holed up in a town that saw no action. He had heard musket shots and seen sword duels for no reason at all. The officers played terrible games with their men, promising extra rations for anyone who found a lurking townsperson. One day he watched soldiers strip an old man, spread goose grease all over him, and parade him through the streets before executing him. Nils rushed back to tell Sondre.

Sondre held the boy close to her for hours, comforting his shivering body. No doubt they would do the same to anyone they caught now, including a six-year-old boy. The next time they needed food, Sondre volunteered to take to the streets. Nils would have none of it. He needed her comfort, but he could still take care of things. Moved, she begged his forgiveness for treating him cruelly at first and scolding him so much. She felt a deep need to atone for her treatment of him.

Nils forgave her with the nonchalant shrug of a child. He was already planning his new strategy to get by the soldiers. He told Sondre not to worry, gave her a small kiss on the cheek, and walked to the shelf containing blue animals and knickknacks. With utmost seriousness he chose a blue elephant figure, and tucked it into his pocket for good luck. Then he bounded out the door in search of food.

Sondre had the terrible premonition that she would never see him again alive.

ق

When the voice finished telling the story, Sahara asked question after question. But the voice was silent. In disbelief, she tried to make sense of things. The story was about her lifetime as Sondre, but Nils was a soul with whom she had a deep connection. And still did! The voice of that soul had greeted her, had told the tale inside her mind, had spoken from *inside* her. That was it!

The voice belonged to the baby. It was Naji.

42

"From the womb?" Zack questioned. "Please, my poor little brain is stretched enough."

"Why?" Dr. Machiyoko responded. "Since we are souls who live many lives, we think a soul might speak after a lifetime. Why not before the next?"

"It's true, Naji is in the interlife, a soul waiting to be born," Elvi said. "A child in utero communicating as an adult soul is entirely possible – but very unusual."

"No kidding," Zack said. "My condition is still unchanged: my brain hurts."

At this week's meeting, Bax had declined to do an early life recall, so Sahara had shared the baby's story. Despite Zack's doubts, the group marveled at the miracle.

"Naji joins the qaraq!" Porcy exclaimed. "You didn't tell Amar, did you?"

"That would be fine," Zack said, "if you and baby want to be institutionalized."

Sahara informed the group that since the failed therapy session Amar was full of smoldering rage, just as he had been after she chose to keep the baby. They were keeping their distance, so she had not told him about Naji. Some insisted it remain a secret, while others advocated including Amar, since Naji was his child, too.

"Let's let Sahara make her own decision," Elvi said. "I'd like us to look at Naji's story. Since he shared this tale with his mother, the Sondre-Nils situation can be seen as a mother-child relationship. You two might have a long history of being parent and child."

"I wonder if Sharzad had children in Persia," Sahara said. "In the Scheherazade tale, she has three children with the King, though that's an ending that may not be authentic."

"Here's another lifetime connection," Dr. Machiyoko said. "Remember that the Goddess Sahnra had a moment with the thief where she felt like she was holding a child in her arms. In Naji's recall, Sondre accuses the child of invading her space, of stealing her peace, like when Sahnra accused the thief."

"The Red Isle tales are mythic," Zack said, "a pack of lies, but mythic lies, very old. Sahnra must have preceded Sondre. Since Sondre felt a deep guilt at her treatment of Nils, maybe it's her unconscious memory, or karma, from her harsh treatment of the thief."

"Especially if the thief had her child's soul." Sahara felt uncomfortable about her treatment of the thief. Something terrible had happened, she had blocked it out, and Amar had been on her case to look at it.

The therapist saw Sahara's distress. "We don't even know when Sondre and Nils lived. I'd like to explore this time further, to see if I had a lifetime back then."

Dr. Machiyoko was shy to tell her recalls in group. Sahara was touched that she put herself out there for the sake of clarifying issues concerning Naji. Although the therapist could hypnotize herself, she asked Elvi, also a trained hypnotist, to guide her back to the wartime era. Soon she was in a place where war raged all about her. The group listened as she told her story in a hoarse, world-weary voice, an octave below her normal range.

The Tale of the Clinging Boy and the Blue Elephant

You cannot afford him anymore. He hangs on to you just as you hang on to the army, sucking up the little juice there is. Things get worse. As they do he gets worse, his pleading, his begging, and you have less and less to give.

The war is everywhere now. It assails every town, seeps into every argument, and bleeds into love affairs. The loved one's face is like a rose, a poet once said, but now the rose has eyelashes like thorns, which wage war against the lover's pining heart.

The war has become too expensive. Now that every nation and every belief are battling each other, the stakes have become too high. To win means having the deadliest weapons, the most brilliant military advisors, and the largest army. And that means more stomachs to feed, more boots to shod. The Lords have limited funds, but the more they have the less willing they are to share with the King, so they become new enemies, form new alliances, and perpetuate the war. What waste! But the real price of war, the real waste is that there is no victory, only battered towns, ruined buildings, and burned crops.

The continual devastation has brought a halt to farming, trading, and normal commerce in the towns. People are begging, looting, surviving however they can. The treasuries are depleted so the armies plunder to survive. It's a marriage made in hell: people scour the countryside for pickings as large groups of hungry warriors huddle together. The people have become camp followers: they do any menial task, especially the women, to be thrown scraps from the troops. At least they receive protection from staying close to the army. Until they run into a battle.

You were doing well with this marriage. People needed a go-between to ask for things, to gather up the available resources. And the soldiers needed a common voice to speak their needs. They could not stoop to request a shave, a stolen bottle of wine, a warm body. You provided an invaluable service. You profited from the expense of war. The more desperate the need, the more valuable you became.

The advantage of camp followers is that their hanging on guarantees you repeat customers. But they are also pests you cannot get rid of, beleaguered unfortunates who feel their misfortune earns them the right to anything you have. And then there are the strange bedfellows, like the boy. So many children lost in the war, so many who have lost their families. How can you turn them away, especially one with such a sad, beautiful face? He hung on to you, and you could not let go of him. You gave him free passage.

On the good days you felt like royalty, granting favors, controlling the price of goods in your itinerant treasury. On bad days, you wondered how you had fallen so low. Once the daughter of a wealthy shopkeeper in an affluent town, you had dreams of being a Princess, of rising above your station on your family's wealth. How foolish. Yours was the kind of town the war went after first. Now you think back to your past, the Princess who lost everything except how to buy and sell.

You persevered. You fought as hard as the soldiers, building up a business. You who wouldn't stand for the whines of beggars. Pay up whatever you have. Work it off. This is war, not charity. But you took in the boy, who not only clung to you, but also did everything you asked. He went off for days at a time, foraged, scavenged, and brought back things to pay his way. Useless things, bits of glass, portraits in broken frames of grandmothers, missing keys, worthless books.

And his prized possession, the one thing he gave you as if you were a real Princess, as if this was a treasure worthy of royalty: the blue elephant, no more than a hand high, dug out from some abandoned parlor. Good luck it will bring you, he said, clutching your arm in the rain. It is a thing of magic, you will never die with the elephant by your side.

He has such a great need for you to survive. He clings so hard that sometimes you wonder if his will for you to live is greater than his own will to live. Why are you so attracted to his clinging? He eats your wares, your livelihood, and all he can do is bring back discarded knickknacks that you won't be able to sell. A blue elephant!

You cannot afford him anymore.

ق

"It must be Nils!" Sahara exclaimed.

"He has the blue elephant," Porcy said. "He must have brought it from the room."

"But what happened to Sondre?" Sahara asked.

"It was wartime," Zack said, grimly. "Anything could have happened."

"At least Nils ended up in caring hands." Dr. Machiyoko was still groggy. Her memory of the recall was patchy. "Did we figure out when the war took place?"

"Oops," Zack said, "we just let you babble on about war-time economics."

"I'll do some research," Verle offered. "I've got a few ideas."

"Know what else we're missing?" Porcy commented. "No sign of Amar. If he *were* in the qaraq, wouldn't he be the father of this child? Somehow connected to Sondre?"

"Good question," Zack said, turning to Sahara. "Does this mean you'll be telling Amar about Naji?"

43

Zack and Elvi went on vacations in mid-August, so the group took a break until the end of the month. Sahara still did not tell Amar about the recall from the baby. Dr. Machiyoko's memory had involved a child as well, perhaps the very same child in Naji's story, so she merged the two tales and told her husband it was the therapist's recall. Sahara was anxious to find out if he had a lifetime back then. She suggested she hypnotize him.

"I've seen Elvi do it a couple times," she said. "It's just guided meditation, I've done that before. And you responded to hypnosis with Dr. Machiyoko."

"She knows what she's doing. What if I flip out or something?"

"Don't be a baby, you're not going to flip out. It'll be a light trance."

"What's so important about this war? Can't you wait till your group?"

A little truth would be motivational. "Some of the group thinks you should be in this story. Since you haven't 'showed up,' they doubt your place in the group's history."

"Are you serious? What about Porcy? Have she 'showed up'? This is bullshit."

"I agree, it's ridiculous. But I know you feel left out because you don't spontaneously recall lifetimes. Here's your chance: I'm sure you're part of the story."

"You're appealing to my competitive edge, aren't you? Score that trade!"

"I'm appealing to your innate power. I believe in you. I want you to be part of this."

"All right. Let's do this thing."

Amar stretched out on the couch in the living room. Sahara guided him through a relaxation exercise, then had him focus on the moments in the story. To her relief, Amar found himself in the town! Many times the images he saw were blurred, but he trusted Sahara's questions and articulated what came into his head, whether he saw it vividly or not.

The Tale of the Deserting Soldier

"I am Sondre," Sahara said quietly. "The boy Nils has gone out for food. I am afraid for him, since earlier that night he saw soldiers torturing a townsperson."

– Yes, I know. I am coming to you.

Sahara's stomach tightened. Suddenly she remembered that night. Hours after Nils had left the room Sondre heard someone walking down the hallway, a heavy, purposeful step – not Nils. The owner of the house? A soldier come to ravage her? She had rehearsed this moment a thousand times in her head. She crawled under the divan, torn between her own terror and concern for Nils.

– I enter your room but see no one inside.

"Who are you? What do you want?"

– I have Nils.

As the intruder spoke Sondre recognized a foreign accent.

– Sondre, please. I need your help."

He called her by name! If Nils needed her help... Sondre crawled out from the divan and faced the intruder. Her worst fear came true: it was a soldier! He held Nils' limp body in his arms. There was blood on the boy's clothes.

– Do not be afraid. I will not harm you.

"What happened?"

– He is dead. The war has gone on too long. I tried to stop them. I rescued him from their cruelties, but not from death. I am sorry.

"How did you find the room?"

– Nils told me. I took him to a safe place to recover. He told me of his parents, this special room, of you. He loved you very much."

Sondre was uncomfortable hearing this since she felt responsible for Nils' death.

– He wanted to see you again, but was afraid to give you away. I had to wait till the soldiers were asleep. I rushed him here, but it was too late.

"What happens now?"

– Is there a cemetery? It will be dawn soon. You must tell me where to go.

Sondre gave directions to the curious, kind soldier. She watched him carry Nils out the door, an innocent victim being taken away from a storm. Then, foolishly, inexplicably, she did not flee, but waited for the soldier to return.

"Did you come back to the room?"

– Yes. I return to the beautiful girl with the wonderful reddish-blond hair. She stands in the center of the charming room full of blue objects.

Although he did not look at her, Sahara saw the intensity of Amar's gaze. Inside Amar's mind, the soldier was piercing Sondre with his eyes. Then, without any further prompting, Amar continued the story from his, the soldier's, perspective.

"You are not afraid," I say.

"You are a soldier," Sondre answers. "If you want to kill me, you will."

"I am done with killing. And cruelty. I only wish ... I don't know the word in your tongue ... desert."

Sondre giggles. "You only wish ... to go to the desert?"

I smile at her tease. Do I tease back? "I only wish ... a little dessert."

"I know a good bakery."

We burst into loud laughter. She claps her hand over his mouth. Her hand feels good on my face. I touch my hand to hers and gently lower it. "I am not used to hiding."

"Or speaking my language. You want to *desert* the army? To run away?"

"The officers are insane. They'll do anything, even to their own men. I was already insubordinate enough for them to kill me. Now with helping the boy, I can't go back."

She touches my elbow. "Thank you. For what you did for Nils." She releases her hand. "What will you do?"

I look into her eyes. What will I do? I have journeyed through madness and violence, which I now realize was not in vain. I was on a quest, a perilous mission, and the ragged aftermath of my journey has led me to *her*. I lead her to sit on the divan.

"I will stay here with you. I will stop fighting and fight for your love. I will not let you be a ship passing me in the night. I will wait out the war with you, even if it continues another

283

three decades. I will stay in this perfect room, perfect because you are here."

She looks back at me, and her face expresses a hundred different feelings: she is awestruck, she is hopeful, she is feeling the same as I am, she is incredulous that we could be feeling the same thing, she is skeptical, she is angry at her doubt, she is questioning my face, she is admiring my face, she is happy, she is delirious, she is speechless, she is full of things to say, she is full of guilty pleasures, she is unbelieving at her good fortune, she is reminded of her great misfortunes, she is sad at all the pain in her past, she is tugged back and forth between the memory of pain and the new hope replacing it, she is overwhelmed by all of her emotions, she is unable to contain her feelings.

At that moment, I say, quietly, "I love you."

Tears burst from her eyes. I enfold her in my arms. With every tear she sheds I smile for what I have confessed to her, for the warmth I feel holding her now, for the days ahead we can share. My love for her feels like it was always that way, and will always be.

I have found my soul mate.

Besides hunting for food and wood through the winter, I am on the lookout for news of the war's progress, or should I say degeneration. As the months continue, events become more complicated, but the endgame is near. The Empire is everywhere, and the French army I deserted scatters in all directions, making new allies, bizarre alliances with southern, Mediterranean forces, Swedes from the north, even the Turks, normally the thorn in the eastern sides of Europe. The Empire is like a bear in a gaming pit, much stronger than any of us small dogs of nations, but in alliance, a large enough number of dogs can bring down the largest, most ferocious of bears. But we are sick to death of it all.

So Sondre and I hide out together in our lifetime in a room, making love on the divan, sleeping in each other's arms through the day, staring at the funny array of blue knickknacks Nils created in his short life. He feels like our lost child, though he was child to neither of us. Strange how events create odd families, unforeseen marriages. Sondre and I do not share holy matrimony, and yet we are the most sacred of couples. Our room is no house, but it is our home, our world, our universe. The blue elephant I retrieved from Nils is our sun, every picture hanging on the walls a constellation, every piece of furniture a galaxy.

What little I know of astronomy and philosophy I learned from a fellow Englishman, who fought alongside me in my first days of campaigning. He spoke to me constantly of radical ways of thinking. Some of this came from English schooling, but many of the ideas simply came to him, as if they had been buried in the soil of his memory, simply waiting to sprout. He spoke of the vastness of the universe, its outer boundaries next to other universes. Speaking of the cycles everywhere in Nature, he compared the rising and setting of the Sun, the creation and destruction of the Cosmos, and the ebb and flow of our sexual energies. How my mind spun! How my groin ached!

The idea that impressed me the most came from an English poem. It matches our situation so perfectly I am convinced Sondre and I are its chosen spokespersons. The idea suggests a way of action, or perhaps inaction, that is the most humanly appropriate response to this insane war. If the war is ever over, I wish to let everyone know about this Idea. I would dedicate my work to the immortal soul of Nils in thanks for bringing me to the room, for joining me with Sondre. To me Nils was the embodiment of the Idea, and his blue elephant the symbol of the bliss brought to the soul when it embraces the Idea.

Sondre laughs her head off when I speak like this. She tosses the poor little elephant on the floor and embraces me. We make our own bliss.

ق

Sahara was in tears by the end of the story. It was such a beautiful expression of the deep love she had for her mate and child. She was in such a tender place that when she brought Amar out of trance she was shocked by his reaction to the tale.

"I said all that? I don't believe it. I understand that I don't remember everything under hypnosis and you have to remind me, but I think you've made this up."

Sahara felt slapped in the face. "Recalls don't just get handed to you on a silver plate. You don't always get lodged in the suite in the palace overlooking the garden. You have to come upon it yourself, do a little hunting, a little cutting and pasting."

"I marvel at the lengths you will go to convince yourself that knitting these tales together gives you license to believe anything about them. It's a past life. An iceberg has a soul. I was once married to my neighbor's mother. Soon you'll tell me you get recalls from our unborn child."

The baby kicked. Hard.

Sahara gasped. Her nervous guilt at lying to Amar about Naji's tale had gotten to her. The heat, the discomfort, the tensions, everything closed in on her. Weeks of sparring with her husband, apologizing for the beliefs dear to her, listening to his abusive doubts compounded inside her. Naji had kicked her into action.

"Are you my husband or what?"

"Excuse me?"

"Do you support me or not? Do you have faith in what I'm doing? Forget my graduate work, I gave that up months ago.

286

Do you have the remotest belief in recalls, in the group, in my interest in it? Or are you going to continue to bugger me with your doubts?"

"What do you want from me?"

"You just had a memory of a past life. A past life, for God's sake! That's a miracle, don't you think? Don't you? We could celebrate this recall with the group, which I believe you are a part of fundamentally. We could tell them your story, which all but proves our roles as soul mates. Do you have a jot of faith in the constancy of our love? Can you believe anywhere in a corner of your heart that our love may have lasted over time?"

Sahara pushed Amar off the couch. "I need to lie down."

The force of Sahara's tirade stunned Amar. Her plea for his belief in their love was making him guilty; it had only been days since he had made a pass at Ooma. On that day he had vowed he would pay more attention to Sahara's wishes. He had gone back into therapy with her, but he was still not convinced about past lives.

Sahara cut through his silence. "Do you have the slightest interest in what the Idea is, the thing you became obsessed about in your past life?"

"Of course I do. Don't mock me. What's the poem? Who's the poet? What's the Idea got to do with holing up in a room for your life? I care about all of that."

"Good. Any idea what the Idea is? Does it ring a bell?"

"No. But I'd like to find out. That what you want to hear?"

"I want to hear that you'll come to the meeting next Tuesday."

"If that's what you want, of course."

Don't do it, Mom! a voice called to Sahara.

Sahara thought she was hearing things. She ignored the voice.

"I want to hear you tell the qaraq about our lifetimes of love."

You're asking for trouble, Mom! Stop!

Am I crazy? How can you talk?

"You're right, Sahr," Amar said. "I should come. It's our therapy. It's our history."

Make him change his mind, Mom. You'll regret it!

Sahara put her head in her hands. Amar would have a field day if he knew she was hearing voices. You don't recall past lives, you're just delusional. She looked up from her hands. Amar's face was completely sincere. She directed her thoughts at the life in her belly. Stay out of this. Then she reached for Amar's hands.

"Great. I'll do some research on the poet, on the wars in Europe."

"We'll figure out what the Idea is," Amar said, squeezing her hands.

I know what it is! the voice said. *I'll tell you! Listen, I'll whisper it to you. I don't want him to hear it.*

Quiet, Sahara thought at her belly, not now.

Later.

44

Sahara was extremely nervous as she and Amar climbed the stairs to Verle's attic the following Tuesday. For weeks now she had had trouble sleeping, never finding a comfortable position for her body in bed. Naji was talking to her at any time, day or night. What he said was unpredictable, a word here, a long speech there, but the upshot was that Sahara was exhausted. She had not told anyone in the group that Amar was coming and was trepidatious about their reactions. Finally, Naji had given her information about the Idea: once Amar shared his tale, how would she continue without revealing Naji as the source?

She fought to remain calm.

As they approached the top of the stairs, Sahara gave her husband a tentative smile. She had twisted his arm to take a day off work and he ended up cranky as a result. But she knew his mood had more to do with nerves about the meeting.

Everyone was there when they entered the room, silencing the friendly chatter. Sahara introduced her husband to Elvi and Verle, and quickly reminded Bax and Amar that they had met at the New Year's Eve party. When the courteousness of the introductions wore off, the group returned to silence.

Thank God for Zack. "So, little brother, you're giving in to this hooey?"

Amar smiled. "I heard it was BYOPL. Bring Your Own Past Life. I've got mine."

"Wow, me too. I'll tell you mine if you tell me yours."

And so the joking of the two old friends broke the ice, much to Sahara's relief. Elvi invited Amar to share his story right away. When he was done, Verle was the first speak.

"A lot of what this soldier said jibes with my research about long drawn-out wars. Europe had a bunch of them: the Hundred Years War, closer to the Middle Ages, the Eighty Years War in the 16th Century, and the Thirty Years War early afterward."

Sahara said, "There was talk of the war lasting thirty years, or longer."

"A lot of these wars bled into one another, so to speak," Verle continued. "The Eighty Years War set up conflicts for the Thirty Years War. Point was that the fight was on for the borders of modern Europe, the rebalancing of power between the rich nobles and the Kings. That took a few centuries, so there's your endless war in the soldier's story."

"What empire was he talking about?" Amar asked.

"Suspect that's the Hapsburgs. The Thirty Years War was mostly about crushing the vise grip they had on Europe. The Hapsburg Empire was in Austria, but they also squeezed Europe from the other side in Spain."

"I had a Dutch lifetime when the Spanish were messing with the Netherlands," Zack said. "Probably Spanish Hapsburgs just before the Thirty Years War. Now this'll be controversial, so

know that it's based on a real event I read about after my
recall. It takes place in a Dutch seaside area called The Zyp."

"How in hell do you know that?" Amar demanded, with
only a bit of humor. Sahara detected a bit of jealousy that her
husband's old friend was so fluent in remembering his past.
She also noticed a tension in the group.

"For the info, from the Internet. For the recall, from a
birthmark."

"Like the Tlingit," Elvi said, as if she were appreciating a
fine wine.

"Is that code?" Amar asked.

"The Tlingit's a tribe who bear birthmarks relevant to a
past life. If a man's killed by a knife in the back, in the next
life he's born with a mark where he was stabbed."

"I have a birthmark right here." Zack pointed dead center
on his sternum. "The other day, when I was thinking about
these latest recalls I felt the strangest tingle there. It was like
my whole front wanted to pull apart. So I focused on it, using
my superpowers just like Aunt Elvi showed us, and a splendid
little tale unfolded in my brain."

"So the game is guess-who-the-fuck-are-you?" Amar said.

The group tightened another notch. Elvi said, "Amar, when
Sahara and Bax joined the group, I asked them to observe the
first time. It's unusual you shared a recall, quite precocious
really." Somehow Elvi knew Amar's sore spot of inferiority,
and she nurtured him in the most sincere way. "Sharing a
recall can take its toll. Just sit back and listen."

Masterfully done, Sahara thought, I should take lessons.
Amar listened intently, but his chair was pulled back a bit from
the circle, as if to keep the group at a distance.

"My turn?" Zack said, and Elvi nodded.

The Tale of The Zyp

How many generations have you served these people, protected them from the cruel sea, and kept their farmlands safe from disaster? In return, how often have they repaired you, patched your walls, and filled the holes that permeate your strong surface? So what are they doing up here on the wall, with their hammers and poles, poking and prodding, opening up the very holes they have patched for generations?

Your purpose is to stand firm and keep out the sea with your walls. You cannot let these miscreants break you down. But look: it is Hans, the finest mason in the county; and the burgomaster of the local town, an important man; and I recognize the fine horsemen from the estate up the coast. These are good people, loyal to the land and their nation. Have they lost their minds? They will kill The Zyp, destroy their farms and food supplies.

What a nightmare for you, to fight against the very people you have protected. You have loved these people, envied their mobility while you stood still, watched their children run, their carts roll back and forth on the fields. You have only rested at low tide, with your back to the sea, chest proudly out to the land.

Once again the sea builds up against you and you arch your back, pushing against the tides. These madmen are here with their tools, opening up more and more ways for the water to get through. You must stop them with guile, with unexpected craft. Here: a chip of stone is about to break off where Hans hammered it. You aim, and the shard flies off in the direction you send it. Hans is hit and falls from the wall. Again a rock shelf comes loose and you throw it at the burgomaster who comes crashing down.

More people come, more insanity. A whole village has shown up to bring you down. Which is worse, the pressure from the sea at your back, or the digs and stabs you suffer in your chest? The children join in the act now, kicking with their wooden shoes.

You can take no more! Fighting is useless! Water pours in until your entire wall cracks. You have been holding it together, day after day, tide after tide, holding on to your strength, your fortitude, your responsibilities. You have never once given in to the temptation of going with the natural flow of the tides, the ebb and flow of the moon, the dark, natural pressures that build up inside you, that want you to burst forth, to explode like a star dying in the sky above, like the lusty men and women of the town bursting forth their liquid love, like the universe caving in upon itself only to explode into a new creation. You have suppressed the deep, collective memory of these forces within you, fought the natural cycles, fought the tides, fought Nature.

No longer.

The water breaks through you now, the people scatter in all directions. For once you will mate with the sea, you will explode forth and go with the natural flow. If insanity rules the countryside, a Feast of Fools gone wild, then you will celebrate darkly with the people you served. Your heart breaks in two for them, a sea of blood, an ocean of tears rushes through the chest cavity of your walls. Your lower regions burst. Your entire structure gives in.

And the fields flood and the sea enters the forbidden territory of the farms. And your walls break into a thousand pieces, ripping your soul from the physical edifice. It rises above the sea and the fields and the farms. You look down at the land you loved one last time and see a terrible and wonderful sight. Spread for miles over the fields is a vast enemy army that drives toward the villagers, but the sea washes over them, scattering and drowning them. The enemy is vanquished due to the destructive actions of the people, the sacrificial act of destroying you and their farms.

You mourn your fate as you drift away, but you are released. You understand that your final purpose in death was to save your destroyers. Your soul releases many lifetimes of envy, anxiety, and insecurity. Secure in your accomplishment, you move on, happily anticipating a new journey for your soul.

ق

"You were a dike!" Porcy guessed.

"Now devolved into a gay man in Jersey with a ceramics collection," Zack said with a wink.

"You set me up for that one, honey."

"So you were a stone wall with a soul," Verle said, seriously. "But it's hard to believe an enormous inanimate object has a soul."

"Verle, how dare you question that a Dutch dike could have a soul," Amar said facetiously. "We buy anything here, right? Because we have faith. Damn the skeptics!"

"Amar, please," Sahara said.

"What about the Idea, Sahr? You did research into poets. Enlighten us."

Sahara squirmed. She couldn't avoid her new recall about the Idea any longer. "I found the poem that contains the Idea. It's by John Donne, the English poet."

"But he's a contemporary of Shakespeare," Zack said. "Shakespeare died before the Thirty Years War."

"Donne died in 1631, in the middle of the war. Left behind two hundred poems. He liked to wed images of pleasures of the flesh with images of infinite spirituality."

"Wasn't he thrown in jail for seducing a teen-ager?" Zack asked.

"He married her later, became an Anglican clergyman. Flesh and spirit."

"So you've had another recall from the 1600's that clarifies the Idea?" Elvi asked.

"Kind of." Somehow she would have to leave Naji out of this. "Let me tell you."

45

The Tale of the Secluded Room and The Idea

Once there was a lonely, distressed soul caught between lifetimes. It was poor Nils, barely six years old, ripped from the world by a horrendous war. The war had been going on for so long that the ectoplasmic stratosphere above Europe was a superhighway for attached souls, those suffering beings who cannot let go of some great sadness or horror from their lifetime. Drifting with them, Nils was haunted by the gruesome image of an old man, tortured and naked, paraded around the town by vicious enemy officers. The memory of the beautiful, cozy, blue room was not enough to calm his soul. So Nils searched for some clue, some key, some idea that would release him from his misery.

In one of his poems, John Donne describes two lovers, enclosed in a room with the sun outside their window, distanced from the rest of the world by the intensity of their passion. The room becomes the entire universe for the couple, the sun shining on them the same as the sun shining down on the world, the East and West Indies both lying beside them in bed, the lovers becoming all states and all princes in the world.

Donne's poems were published only after his death, in the 1630's, in the midst of the war. The time was ripe for an idea like the room-as-a-universe, a hideaway from pain.

The idea inside the poem became an Idea: just as the room becomes independent from the world by becoming the world itself, so the Idea detached itself from the poem, gained independence as a separate interpretation, and grew into a philosophy of life. The Idea was to live separately from the terrible world, by creating a world of one's own, through love, through isolation, through survival in its simplest form. The Idea was to escape the world and its terrible war, to inhabit the smallest, safest, simplest place, to inhibit the range of activity and be content with eating, sleeping, and sex. The Idea was related to the oneness of natural cycles: if an orgasm can be the explosion of a star, then a room can be a universe.

As an Idea grows, It can be embodied, can take on properties of a Life, can be inhabited and given the will of a Soul. As Nils floated over Europe and looked down upon the suffering, he spied the Idea fulminating, crossing the Channel to France, and he recognized its allure. He swooped down and pulled himself right into the Idea, just as a workman pulls on his overalls for the day's travail.

And the soul of Nils, now the Idea, headed out to plant the Idea into all the attached souls over Europe and all the suffering souls in the war, to reorganize people's thinking so that their world could become a tight, safe place within themselves or their rooms.

Once the soul of Nils, embodying the Idea, saw that word was spreading, he was ready to move on. Without the will of a spunky young kid to drive it further, the Idea sank into obscurity until the early 1900's, when Donne's poetry was rediscovered.

ق

"That's not one for the history books," Zack commented when Sahara finished.

"More personal, you think?" Porcy said. "Like some folks prayed for the King's health and happiness and victory over his enemies, and others prayed to get out of town."

"My interest is with Sondre and the soldier," Dr. Machiyoko said. "That's Sahara and Amar's souls, discovering the Idea in their secluded room of endless love. Another example of the positive spirit the two of you have shared."

"L'chaim to both of you, but I have a burning question," Zack said. "This is Nils' lifetime, right, after he dies and is reborn as an Idea. Another big stretch for me, but here's the thing. Nils is six when he dies. The soldier said that when he met Sondre the war was soon to end. Thirty Years War ends 1648, so Nils dies in the mid to late 1640's. But this new story suggests that the poem existed around the 1620's, the Idea came over to the continent in the 1630's, spreading to the soldier before he came to Nils' town."

Amar followed Zack's reasoning. "How could Nils become the Idea if it was around before he died, possibly before he was even born?"

"The soldier already knew of the Idea before he even met Nils. Sorry to be the perennial skeptic, but can we cross being reincarnated as an Idea off the list? The time thing has bugged me ever since Dr. Machiyoko's story about Nils. How does a six-year-old die in his town and end up a camp follower in another part of the war?"

Sahara tensed.

"My recall was not necessarily about Nils. It could have been another child," the therapist said. "But Naji's recall was definitely about Nils."

Sahara cringed.

"Naji's recall?" Amar asked. "What are you talking about?"

"Your baby," Dr. Machiyoko said. "Sahara told us a recall she heard from –" She stopped, seeing the fear in Sahara's face.

"You heard a recall from the *baby*?" Amar said to Sahara. "He's aware of past lives?"

"Naji is still connected to the interlife, the world between worlds," Elvi explained calmly. "He's more in touch with past lives than any of us."

"Naji told you a story? And you told the group?" Amar was clearly angry now.

"I told you much of the story," Sahara explained feebly, "mixed with Dr. Machiyoko's. I just didn't tell you I heard it from Naji. I didn't think you would believe it. You're so skeptical."

"You trusted your beloved qaraq. But not me."

Porcy said sharply, "There's no reason to trash us."

Amar barked at Porcy. "I just want some truth! Did Nils live with the camp followers or with Sondre?"

"Nils found Sondre in the room," Zack explained. "She gave him hell at first, for intruding on her peace, on the Idea, I guess, which he hadn't become yet."

Verle made things worse. "Sondre was so tough on Nils she made him brave the soldiers to get food. Made her horrible guilty later, when the soldiers killed him."

"Naji was Nils – and you treated him that way?" Amar asked Sahara.

Dr. Machiyoko saw where things were going. "She grew to love the boy, despaired of her act, saw Nils as her child with the soldier, with you."

"That helps a lot," Amar said to Sahara, "knowing you'll love your child, after he dies. What gives with you in the past? It's like whatever you did to the thief, which you won't tell me."

"Because I don't *know*!" Sahara said, raising her voice. It was the issue she most feared. "You're a fine one to talk. We haven't even scratched the surface of your violence."

"How dare you! Not here!"

"EXCUSE ME!"

The room fell silent. Everyone looked over at Bax.

"Yes, Bax. What is it?" Elvi asked.

"I'm ready," he said, so quietly the group leaned in to hear him. "Regress me."

46

Baxter Tenderheel had kept silent for the past few weeks of meetings. He was not comfortable with these people, starting with the fact that they were all older than he was. But he promised Porcy he would come, and hoped he might quit his fears in the process.

Then there was Sahara Fleming, the woman he had seen several times on his trip across country. Why was he drawn to her? It was time to figure things out. When her husband threatened her, Bax knew he had to do something to stop it.

"This is a welcome opportunity," Elvi said, pulling the meeting back together. "We learned a lot about these recalls in the 1600's. We know how Sondre and the soldier found their love." She turned to Sahara and Amar. "That's important for the two of you to take in. The other things – how Naji's communicating, the odd timeline of his two lives, what Sahara did or did not tell you, Amar – these things are complicated. Let them rest for now."

Amar pulled his seat back again, his anger slightly subsiding with Elvi's calm voice. Sahara thanked Bax silently for his interruption; it reminded her of how he had jumped in to rescue Porcy from a mugger.

"So Bax," Elvi continued, "you're ready to look at the source of your fear? I'd like to ask questions about your work with Porcy. Then, we'll work backwards."

"Will this feel weird?"

Elvi smiled warmly. "You'll be nice and relaxed. You'll only recall what you're ready to deal with. And share. Ready?"

Bax unconsciously brushed his nose with a finger. "Sure."

Elvi put Bax into a light trance, than gently asked about the Tarot, I Ching, and palm readings he had done with Porcy. Bax answered slowly and thoughtfully.

The Tale of the Five Women in the Celtic Cross

Elvi asked, "When Porcy read your palm, what was your life line like?"

– Long. Real long life.

"Did you see death in the Tarot?"

– Death card. Mr. Skull on his horse.

"Did this mean you would die?" Bax paused. "What did the card mean?"

– That death was in my thoughts.

"What else did you see in the cards?"

– A little family. Under a rainbow.

"Was this your family?"

– No. Ran away from them. New family. In the future.

"Anything else in your future?"

– Lots of new beginnings. Judgment Day. Release.

"Releasing your fears? Fantastic. Do you understand what these fears are?"

– No. From my past. Can't see.

"Don't search for it. Just let it come to you. Take a deep breath."

Bax thought he saw a woman, maybe a Princess? Unhappy, isolating herself, a hermit. Was she standing in a tower, looking down to the ground below? Would she jump? Bax knew it was not him, but who was it? He lowered his head.

Elvi perceived that Bax's past was not open to him. Since something terrible was driving those fears, the answers might not come in a day. She tried another tact.

"In the cards you saw a family in your future and Judgment, your release from fears. Once you're free of them, what happens? Did the cards give you any clue?"

– Depends on the women.

"The women?"

– Five women. The other five cards. The Queens. The Empress. One at the bottom of the spread. Four in a row at the end.

"Who's the one at the bottom?"

– Queen of Pentacles. Porcy. My foundation. Where the money comes from. I saved her. She saved me. Released some fears. Almost a year now.

"So this is a good card.'"

– The best. What would I do without her?

Elvi saw a way forward. "What about the four women in a row? Tell us about one. How does she determine what happens after you release your fears?"

– Miss Cachay, Queen of Wands, finds jobs. Wants to help.

Porcy said, "That's Cachay Goodkin, Zack's momma. We go back a way. We thought Bax might get some help from her because she works with Social Services."

Bax looked up at the attic rafters, focused out in space.

– Something before.

"Before?" Elvi asked, hoping for a past life clue.

– On the road. Chicago. Cachay there, too. Gave me hand-outs. But on my case.

"Did you see her again?"

– With Porcy. Tried to help me. Didn't like her. Don't need her. Don't want her.

Elvi raised a hand to quiet Porcy. "Why did you avoid her?"

– Wants to straighten me. Get me construction work. Too many accidents. Holes.

"Thought you had given up your fears here. Why the safety issues?"

– Old dog. New tricks.

"Okay. Tell us about the third woman."

– Queen of cups. The lone Princess. Seen her twice, too. At Rock-It CD store: Punk, heavy metal. Both looking for Nirvana.

"The group, right?"

Bax smiled.

– Yeah. Cute. Great eyes. Black canyons. Made me want to stay in Glenclaire.

"The second time you saw her?"

– New Year's. Nice party. Nice house. Searching for someone.

"The girl from Rock-It?"

– Someone else. Saw her here, there, no contact. Frustrated. Pent up. Found Rock-It girl. Alone. Long, thick, black braid.

"Oh, Christ. That's Ooma," Amar interrupted.

– We went for it. Let her braid out. Made out. Real short skirt. Fingered her. Wet in a second. She was getting close. Indian dude came in. The end.

"I'm supposed to just sit here and listen to this?" Amar said.

Elvi shot a look at Amar as she continued. "Bax, you've released many fears through your ... social interaction. That's good. What about the fourth woman?"

– The High Priestess. Dr. Machiyoko.

The therapist smiled a girlish smile.

"How does she determine what happens after you release your fears?" Elvi asked.

– A guide. Tries to help me sort myself out. But I end up confused as hell.

"Bax! Baby!" Porcy could not contain herself. "I'm the money woman, you ignored Cachay, you fingered little Ooma. Now you're playing Dr. M. What are you doing?"

Elvi gestured to Porcy, quieting her, but acknowledging her questions. "Okay, let's take a moment. Bax, who are these women to you?"

Bax looked down.

– Don't know yet.

"What do we mean?"

– Don't know!

"Who are they?" Elvi insisted

– I just – I need them all. All of you. I feel safe. Free to say anything. Do anything.

He stopped, looked up, and opened his mouth. But it was Porcy who spoke.

"Family."

Porcy, Dr. Machiyoko, and Sahara broke into grins and stared in anticipation at Bax.

– Yeah. Family. What I've been searching for. All these smiles. All those fears done now. Found a new family. A real family.

"Excellent, Bax, excellent," Elvi said. "It's all very new to you, but vital that you see it. Good. Let's finish up. Who is the fifth woman in your new family?"

– The Empress. The outcome. Amazing. Sahara Fleming.
"Oh Lord," Sahara said. "Can we take a break?"

Elvi indicated for Sahara to be silent. "What is intriguing about her?"

– Mystery woman. Seeing her for years. Out of reach. And she's hot. Gave me something to search for.

"We know this," Zack said, exaggerating boredom. "San Francisco, Chicago, etc."

Amar pulled his chair into the circle. "You saw Bax before?" he asked Sahara.

"No, no, Bax saw me," Sahara said. "Like a vision – he's already told the group."

"But you didn't tell me, how interesting."

"Bax," Elvi said, "was it Sahara you were searching for at the party?"

– It was *her* house. Had no idea. Shock. Red hair popping up. But no contact. Didn't give up after party. Found reasons to come by from Porcy. Real estate check-ins. Took walks in the neighborhood. Saw her walking her cat. Hid in the bushes.

Elvi sat back and looked at the group. "Okay, qaraq, Bax agreed to this, and it means getting to the truth. Keep your hats on. Bax, I want you to speak to Sahara."

Amar stood up and began pacing outside the circle.

Elvi continued to focus on Bax. "Your mystery woman is no longer a mystery. She's right here. What do you want to say to her?"

Bax paused, lowered his head, and was silent.

"Is it sex? Love? Just to look at her?"

Bax looked up.

– I just want to see, to be with her. Find out who she is. Find out who I am.

As if he weren't in trance, Bax looked over at Sahara, who met his stare.

– You are the reason I came to the group.

ق

"That's just great!" Amar said, pacing faster and faster. "First I'm told to shut up because I don't believe someone can have a past life as a Dutch dike. Then I'm humiliated because my wife's told you all that my unborn son's been speaking to her, but she hasn't bothered to tell me." He stopped pacing and faced Bax. "And now I have to listen to this dickhead salivating over my wife!"

"Please, Amar," Elvi said. "Let me bring him out of trance."

As Elvi gave Bax commands to awake, Sahara turned on her husband.

"Leave him alone. The whole point is to help him release some terrible fear, and you're ready to stomp on him."

"So you'd fuck him if it helped release his fears, is that it?"

Sahara was barely suppressing a rage. " I put up with you hanging with Ooma for a couple of lousy recalls. Stop throwing blame around and abusing your welcome here."

"I hear this cowboy is hot for you, I'm not allowed to say anything? I'm abusive?" Amar walked over to a wall and leaned against it, too furious to look at Sahara.

Sahara looked around at the group. Bax was barely out of trance and the other members looked fearful of the shouting match going on. But no one was stopping her.

It was time.

"Yes, Amar. You have abused me. With your disbelief, your threats, your anger." This was harder than her passion had led her to believe. "Would you all like another story? Another exercise in an earlier lifetime within a lifetime?

"Here we go: The Tale of the Demon and the Pregnant Wife."

47

The Tale of the Demon and the Pregnant Wife

I had thought Amar Rash was my ideal love, brought to me through mutual love of Persian tales, Sufi poems, world traveling. Then we moved to New York and New Jersey: a new man emerged, needing me for something else: a modern housewife with dinner on the table. He prevented me – the role prevented me – I was prevented from my work. But maybe it was temporary, I would figure it out.

Then I was with child, in need, vulnerable. He transformed into a demon, a bottled-up genie of anger, a volcano of silence. I lived in tension, in emotional red alert. My body changed, my chemistry bubbled, and my head played strange tricks. The tricks became bad dreams, waking visions, odd thoughts. I was remembering things I'd never lived, fantasizing desires I'd never wanted. I learned that the visions were past lives.

What was this last one? I see myself hug Amar, but as I do, he disappears, I blink and we are hugging again and he whirls around, I blink again and he –

Let's take a moment and consider the recalls about Amar and me. Are we really soul mates? Is it an ideal love? Is it worth all the bullshit?

I had a couple of really old lifetimes, one gaining con-sciousness as a landmass and another in some Heaven evolv-ing toward the angels. Amar is nowhere around (unless he was the Copulating Angel I mounted the Heavens with, but I doubt it at the moment).

He catches up to me later in a couple mythic lifetimes. We are brother and sister divinities of the Red Isle, fighting over sacred relics in the sky above the Sahara (my personal creation). Then we become the North and South winds and we're still duk-ing it out in the air, stuck in a recurring cycle of violence. The point: the first times we know we lived together, hubby and I are wrapped up in violence and animosity. I get the hell out.

We can trace our next lives historically, starting with 4th Century Sassanid Persia. We're warming up to our bit as a couple in this story, but so far Amar is a murderous pawn of an insane Queen. If we're talking model for Scheherazade, I'll be successful in taming my killer. More violence, but is it our first shot at love?

Then we jump to 1600 and beyond in Europe. I'm married to Cachay (excuse me? Zack's mother?) in France, and then fall into the arms of soldier Amar during the Thirty Years War and counting. I don't seem particularly happy with Cachay as my husband, so I go for it with Amar, even though we're on opposite sides of the war raging around us.

To wit: still can't shake that violence, but we're starting to bring on the love.

Then there's this beautiful lifetime in The Suburb, mod-ern, realistic, but full of bizarre details. The Suburb? Still, it completes a progression: we are madly in love, things are peaceful at last. Earlier in this present day life we go through beautiful serendipities to find one another. Shouldn't our marriage be a blissful culmination of this evolution?

Back to reality. Amar and I had our last big fight about my insistence on having the baby. He said he was completely baffled by my stubbornness. He became enraged at his inability to sway me. Life was going so well for us, he had given me so much, and he just wanted to wait for a better time. We fought for hours, cycling from reason to rage, moral high ground to personal low ground.

Finally Amar seemed to capitulate. He went into the kitchen to fix himself something. He was in there for a long time, so I got up and went to see how he was doing. He was leaning on his hands against the kitchen counter, head lowered. I thought he was crying. I wanted to comfort him. I came up behind him and put my hands on his shoulders.

As soon as I touched him, he exploded. He whirled around. He yelled at me with a terrifying voice. He grabbed me by the shoulders and slammed me against the kitchen wall. His hands reached out, as if about to strangle me. I pulled my head as far back as I could to avoid him. He realized my terror and froze for a few seconds.

He stopped as quickly as he started. He yelled "I could kill you!" and rushed out of the room. Only then did I notice my hands covering my belly, protecting the baby inside.

Weighing the good with the bad, here's my question: is there always violence in this relationship despite love, or is there always love here despite the violence? Or are the two, violence and love, Amar and Sahara, made for each other? Or are they just plain incompatible?

ق

Sahara threw herself back in her chair, exhausted. It had taken months to confess that one horrible act of violence, the bedrock of their hostility toward each other. She should have told Dr. Machiyoko at the very beginning. Now the whole group knew.

Porcy was in shock. Dr. Machiyoko leaned forward, furrowing her brow as if to will her brain into a solution. Elvi, Zack, and Verle sat alert, but not speaking. Bax was on the edge of his chair, focused on Amar.

Amar stepped toward Sahara. "Let's go." He extended his hand. Sahara remained still. His extended hand began to shake. "Let's GO!" Amar swiped his hand violently toward the doorway. When he took another step toward Sahara, Bax jumped out of his chair. Sahara jumped up in a protective response. She circled away from Amar's reach, but moved toward the door.

Amar addressed the group. "Thank you. It's been highly informative. I won't be returning for another meeting. Besides the fact that I think past lives are a crock of *shit*, they are very, very dangerous and destructive. Sahara will not be returning either. And I expect all of you to stay the hell away from her. She needs to have this baby in peace."

Amar turned and walked to the doorway. He reached out to take Sahara by the arm, then thought better of it. He motioned toward the stairs and she walked out the door.

She did not look back at the group.

END OF PART TWO

PART THREE

48

Sleep is hard enough with an eighth month bellyful. No position comfortable, especially after hours confined to bed. Bed arrest. And troubled thoughts, fears ...

... darkness, through the amber, nothing beyond but dark. Nothing but waiting, but also trying to peer into the dark. To see something: another soul, waiting, willing to live ...

... decaying, waiting to die, to vanish from the Earth. Ahead, nothingness. Dark worse than death. Pure absence. Will I be aware of it? That's terrifying.

Fear settles into pure panic. Fear of fear. The long look into the endless dark. But if I am aware of it, then time goes on endlessly. There is no way to *imagine* pure nothingness, because what I am imagining will still be there, as something. I look, not into endless nothing, but the pure endless infinity of Time. Adrift on the neverendingness of being.

The immortality of the soul. This is truly the most terrifying.

Awake with a jolt! Violent but shallow breath.

Can't sleep like this, Sahara thought. Too many souls, too many lifetimes in my head. Need rest. Trapped between anxious wakefulness and uncalm sleep. Just lie here. Stare at the ceiling. The textures in the paint. The patterns. Rough-hewn. Mindful of something, top of another room, an earth room, a cave. Lying in my cave.

Sleepy again. The ceiling patterns move. The cave swirls. Drifting between waking and sleeping, the place of open time, of travel in time. It's happening again, traveling back. Let it happen, keep me away from the awful dark.

The Tale of the False Borzu

Shapes flickered on the cave ceiling, thrown about by the burning, smoking stick, the shadows, the curves and hollows of the cave surface. It was cold. A good cold, the numb cold that usually fills my bones, the comfort numb I wrap myself in every day.

We are the Borzi, the people of the cold, those who overcome winter. We have needed to become like the cold, to freeze out the pain in our muscles, in our empty bellies. And so I lay here in the cave, looking up at the ceiling, awaiting the Great One's arrival.

The Great One. I laughed out loud, thinking of Srpa's report of her meeting with the Great One, the silly man in furs, prancing around her, dropping his seed too soon, missing his mark. Another time we crouched outside a cave during the visitation, and heard cries and screams from inside. This was our Great One, returning through the ages to visit us?

316

We had to go through with it, thanks to Ourm. She claimed to be visited by Borzu himself, the Great One, the great hunter who saved our people from hunger and cold. Her union with the Great One made her belly full, her living proof. She convinced the elders of her claims by reenacting the union with the Great One for them (probably with them). When they demanded further proof, she brought other women to the elders, called upon the Great One to come to them and seed them with his power. Ourm convinced the elders to practice the visitation of the Great One upon all the women of the clan.

The clan has lost much of its desire to hunt and seek shelter and has become lost in this practice. It has been a terror for some of us, bringing us tears and pain. I want Ourm's blood for this. She has destroyed the real power of Borzu, his strength, the power he gives to us, to our men as they hunt, to the clan as they prepare for the winters.

I heard a motion further back in the cave.

Some of us do not believe it is really Borzu. Some have been left, abandoned, without a visitation; others have coupled, and, approached by mates afterward, smelled the same smell on them as the Great One, knew their mate had come to them as the Great One. Our own men, dancing about, masked as the False Great One! I laughed at this thought.

A voice hissed at me from the depths of the cave. A giant shadow loomed on the wall opposite the fire stick. I pulled my furs about me and crawled to a fold in the wall.

I heard the voice again, this time from another direction. A loud bark exploded in my ear. I turned and saw a huge beast: a man, but as tall as two men, with the most frightful face. I ran to the other side of the cave, but the beast lashed out at me, grabbed my furs and pulled me back harder than any man has before. The huge figure tore at the furs, pulling some off, and hauled me down to the cave floor on my back.

I had not expected such a powerful form, let alone a demon like this. I had not expected anyone! In my terror, I tried to think of friends who had been visited by fools. I tried to laugh: I imagined a child laughing and only saw her sobbing. I saw in my mind another, not of our tribe, laughing, weeping. Then my whole body shook with sobs.

The demon grabbed my hair in fistfuls, shook me, and then lifted my head, letting out a low, dreadful noise that pierced right through me.

"Booooooooorrrrrrrrrzzzzzzzzuuuuu!"

The Great One! The great hunter had visited Ourm, and now it was my turn. Borzu wanted me! I was ecstatic, ready for Borzu to take me. But the moment was fleeting. Still holding my hair, he picked my torso off the ground and flipped me around with a violent twist. Pain shot through my spine. He pushed my face into the earth and thrust himself painfully into me from behind. I screamed into the dirt, but no sound came....

ق

Sahara focused her blurred vision and looked toward the voice speaking to her.

"Glory be to God! Color has returned to your face. I thought I was losing you. You'll be fine in a minute."

Sitting across from Sahara in the bedroom was a woman she had never seen before.

49

"I'm Cachay Goodkin. Zack's mother."

Sahara recognized the name but not the face. The woman was several shades darker than light-skinned Zack, and had a much more formal and stern presence than her son.

"I rang the bell, but you didn't answer," Cachay said. "The door was open so I came in to drop off some food. You should lock up if you're going to be alone. I had the run of the place and found you passed out in here."

Sahara nodded understanding but was still very weak.

"Zack should have told me sooner that Amar was holding you hostage."

"You know my husband?" Sahara asked.

"For years," Cachay said, her tone admonishing Sahara for not knowing this fact. "Used to work in his grandfather's jewel shop when Zack and Amar were kids."

"I remember now. Zack used to baby sit Amar."

"Correct." A gold star from the teacher. "He's still acting like a baby, keeping you under house arrest, scaring everyone in that ridiculous group. I'll have a talk with him."

"Mrs. Goodkin, I don't trust my husband's reaction if you talk to him. I just need calm. The baby's due in a few weeks."

"You need to get the blood flowing, young lady. Where's your robe?"

"Please, Mrs. Goodkin –"

The woman looked as if she had been hit by a child's spit-wad. "It's Cachay. Listen to me, Sahara Fleming. I am going into your kitchen to make us some tea. Then we are going into your living room to rest on the couch and have a nice conversation. You'll feel better if you join me."

There was no arguing with this woman. By the time Sahara had put herself together, Cachay had poured tea and was leafing through one of the books on the coffee table.

"*The Thousand Nights and One Night. Volume Seven,*" she read aloud. "Richard Burton. The actor?"

"No, an English translator of the Arabian Nights. And a well-known explorer – as famous as the star of *Cleopatra* in his day."

"You read the other six volumes?" Cachay inquired.

"There are ten of them, and yes, twice."

"What about this? 'Marvels and Tales: Journal of Fairy-Tale Studies.' "

Sahara planted herself on the couch. "It's a scholarly journal, all about history and analysis of things like Brothers Grimm, Mother Goose, the Nights."

"I'm impressed, little Miss Scholar. But your fancy journal's overdue at the library."

"What's today?"

"Oh my Lord, she's lost track of time, being cooped up in here. It's the ninth of September. To be exact, today is 9/9/99. How about that!" The intrusive woman picked up another volume and an uncharacteristic look of wonder appeared on her face.

320

The Tale of Henry Whitelock Torrens

"Torrens, H. W. *Selection from the writings, prose, and poetical.* He lived in India, right? During the first Afghan War."

Sahara picked up her cup of tea. "You know about Anglo-Indian history? Is that how you know Torrens?" The only people Sahara knew who had heard of him were Nights scholars. Torrens had begun an English translation, but only finished the first fifty Nights.

Cachay gazed at the book as if it glowed in her hands. "I know he was too busy with the damn war. No time for scholarship, his true love."

Sahara felt a chill up her spine. How did Cachay put her finger on the truth? Torrens was an English aristocrat raised in India in the 19th Century, well educated, able to read Greek, Arabic, Bengali, an amateur scholar. He held several positions in the Asia Society in Calcutta, did translations for them. But he was one of the British men managing Indian cities, running military operations, and seeking out intelligence reports: an ancestor of James Bond. He would have had to juggle his scholarship with his political duties.

Clutching the book, Cachay continued her thoughts. "They were worried about Afghanistan. Too close for comfort to the Hindu Kush. The Russians had already tried to go in there, and failed. Just like in our times. But the operations didn't stop Torrens from being involved in a new version of the Nights in Calcutta." Nonchalantly, she sipped her tea. "He put his stamp of approval on it before he went off to conquer Afghanistan."

"It's called Calcutta 2," Sahara said, dumbfounded by Cachay's knowledge. Calcutta 2 was one of the later Arabic editions that may have falsely added stories to expand the manuscript. Europe was mad for the Nights, and for a Westerner "The Thousand and One Nights" meant there should be that many tales. Just as Europeans wanted more and more tales from exotic lands, the British wanted more of the lands themselves. Calcutta 2 was a kind of literary imperialism.

Sahara thought she would test Cachay. "There is doubt about the origin of the manuscript used for Calcutta 2. It's possible it was authentic but there's a lot of mystery behind it. The German critic Schlegel actually criticized its expansiveness. He said that the more voluminous a collection of Nights stories, the worse it was. Calcutta 2 was the worst."

Cachay bristled. "Torrens wrote a letter back to that German. He defended the edition by claiming how good the new and improved stories were."

"Cachay, how can you possibly know about that letter? Only Nights researchers would come across it. Have you read it?"

"Of course I haven't read it," Cachay said, bluntly. "I don't know how I know."

Sahara remembered that Zack had slipped past life accounts into her mailbox. "Is this one of Zack's tricks?"

Cachay laughed loudly. "No! He's home worrying about you. Angry with Amar for not letting him see you. I brought food, not mischief."

"Sorry. I appreciate your concern. Tell Zack not to worry." Sahara sat up a bit. "But I'm intrigued. What about the book? You had a strong reaction to it."

"Yes, I feel something as I hold it. A sadness, maybe."

"Why are you sad? Can you visualize anything?"

"Are you doing that mumbo-jumbo Zack tells me about?"

"Maybe. Humor me. Close your eyes and tell me the first thing that pops into your head."

Cachay did so, still holding the book. "The heat. It was India, right? I see Torrens in some gorgeous mansion in the hills, hiding out from the sun, sick of the heat."

Sahara probed. "Why is he hiding out?"

"He wanted it all, the translation, the positions of authority, the successful Afghan campaign, the welfare of the Empire in India. Torrens loved India, he was born and raised there. But it all went wrong. The greedier he was for it, the more it unraveled. Like Schlegel: the more stories, the worse. Other people published translations, whole translations, before he did. In England."

"Yes, Edward Lane, the first complete Nights in English."

"The sun and heat was a cruel reminder of Afghanistan, too. Torrens convinced his superior officers the campaign was correct. But the operation backfired and turned into a fiasco. Some of the men he shared his love of the Nights with were murdered. One man in particular, who negotiated with the chieftains."

"That was Macnaghten. His name is on the published edition of Calcutta 2."

"His head ended up on a pole. Torrens would not forgive himself."

"But it was war. Macnaghten made his choice."

A hint of pain appeared on Cachay's face. "It was something else. A loved one. Torrens' first wife. She had died a few years before everything happened. Torrens felt it was his responsibility, bringing her to a place like India. But he found a new life: he remarried, the Calcutta manuscript appeared, he started his translation, and he got involved in the campaign. And then he lost it all, like he had never left behind his wife's death."

Sahara let the silence resonate. She thought of a story in the Nights about a man named Ghanim. He comes to Baghdad and sets up shop as a merchant. A well-respected merchant dies and Ghanim feels he must attend the funeral out of duty. After many hours he wants to leave the funeral and makes his excuses. But he gets lost, wanders into another cemetery, and ends up locked in a tomb. Henry Whitelock Torrens was like Ghanim, escaping one tomb only to be trapped in another.

Cachay opened the book to a portrait of Torrens. "My God, look at this creature. What a fop! This isn't a man who planned a bloodthirsty coup against Afghan warlords."

"He didn't. He had a different proposal, more temperate, which the generals ignored. Later he got the brunt of blame for the campaign failure."

"Poor soul." Cachay closed the book and placed it on the coffee table.

ق

"I never knew about his first wife," Sahara said. "In the book there's a biography, but it only talks about the wives in the last paragraph, doesn't deal with them as people."

"Things haven't changed much, have they Miss House Arrest?"

"Very funny. But seriously, this is uncanny. How can you know things that even I don't? You obviously have strong memories of your past lives."

"What in Heaven's name are you talking about?"

"There's no other explanation. You must have been Henry Whitelock Torrens."

324

50

"One sign of a past life is an unexpected knowledge of something," Sahara said. "If you had lived as Torrens, or his second wife, say, it could explain why you have this information."

"Nonsense, you said almost everything. You're the expert. I just filled in, using my imagination." Cachay cleared the tea things and went into the kitchen. Sahara was baffled by her dismissiveness, but then again, she didn't seem the type to go in for mysticism. Sahara remembered that she and Cachay had a loveless marriage back in France. Chuckling to herself, it seemed believable, though Cachay wouldn't believe a word of it.

When Cachay returned from the kitchen, she was ready to rush out the door. "Don't rest too much. You should get out of the house for some fresh air."

And with that, she shut the front door and was gone. Sahara was relieved after she left. The last thing she needed was another battle with a skeptic.

Cachay Goodkin was not Sahara's only secret visitor during the final days of her pregnancy. It would have taken more than Amar's threat to keep Porcy away from the house. Not about to break her habit of stopping by while Amar was at work, Porcy became bolder in her visits as Sahara's due date approached. One day at dusk Sahara answered the doorbell to find Porcy standing there with a large paper bag.

"What are you doing here? Amar could be home any minute!"

"When suppertime arrives, the servants bring home the trays of rare delicacies. Or at least Mexican food, my fave." Porcy walked past Sahara to set the bag down on a table. "I called Ooma: he's working late and he'll be on the 9:29."

"Did he know you called?"

"I'm not that crazy, sweetheart. You two hungry?" She patted Sahara's huge belly.

"Starved. You got news, too?"

"You know me, girl. News and enchiladas. I'll get some plates."

The group had suspended meetings after Amar's explosion, but had reconvened in mid-September. Porcy had supplied Sahara with new recalls and gossip. Sitting down to eat, Porcy revealed that at the last meeting there had been a recall about Bax.

Sahara tensed at the expectation in Porcy's eyes. Bax had practically come on to Sahara in front of her husband, and she could not deal with her own attraction to the tall, introverted young man. It was an absurdity that did not fit her life with Amar and the baby.

With a mouthful of rice and beans, Porcy said, "I had the recall at Cliffside Hospital."

"You had the recall? In the hospital?"

"I wanted a peek at your birthing room. Big mistake. I just smelled that old, familiar hospital smell, that winning combo of ammonia, blood, urine, and laundered sheets, and my mind spun back to my childhood hospital stays."

"I don't get it. I thought this was about Bax."

"It is, but it started with a memory of one of my childhood deliriums. So cupcake, you have to hear about me as a crazy kid to get to the juicy bits about Bax."

Sahara felt relief that this resilient, fascinating woman had come to visit. Guiltily, she was happy to hear more about Bax. She nodded assent and Porcy began her memory.

The Tale of the Lost Soul

Our society doesn't really take care of those of us living inside visions. As soon as we become dangerous, it's off to the loony bin. In this light, we could say that I have had two lives. In the real one I never knew my mother and father, my foster mother died when I was twenty, and I was in and out of mental institutions. The other life was a fantasy: visions, inner voices, and alternate worlds. When I was ten I climbed onto my foster mom's roof because I was convinced I was a giant plant growing to the sky. A neighbor broke my fall when I lost my balance. Something in a previous life must have shattered me so much that I could not connect to reality in this life. I was lost, calling to spirit beings for help.

From the safety of my sanity today, I truly believe that I traveled to other worlds and dimensions and realities. I know that I also conjured up some places out of my imagination. It took until my thirties to distinguish between reality and fantasy because for me it was about distinguishing between everyday reality, fantastical 'real' worlds, and my personal fantasies. There was much to work out before I could focus on the everyday world.

Between each lifetime we pass through one Heaven or another, a waiting area, a process, a meeting with a spirit guide. All of them can be called interlives.

In one of my more nasty fantasies I had trapped myself amid a group of demons with iron tentacles, probably triggered by hospital workers clutching me. When I wished that they would vanish, they vanished. I had such a feeling of power that I wished to see the demons and there they were, pulling and torturing me again. I wished them away again – successfully – and then wished for a comfortable bed – successfully – and then wished for an open field with a blue sky – successfully! I thought: what do I really want?

I lay in my field, gazing up at the sky (probably strapped down on a gurney by orderlies), and considering each possibility: Hot Fudge Sundae, tender dark-haired lover, moonlit night, three-story house, black-and-white tabby kitten, trip to Bermuda. Soon I stopped thinking up the next wish and the parade of desires continued its journey across the sky. Familiar faces appeared, old friends, an inner circle of confidants (I was most likely surrounded by a gaggle of caseworkers assessing me). My dearest wish in the world was to be free of madness and out in the world of men and women.

It struck me that this wish reflected the deepest yearning in my soul. I cared about others, even though I was prevented from doing so in my present condition. My desires tended toward human bonds, companionship, the crush of the mob. I thought: we are what we wish; I can make this heartfelt wish unfold. And so I wished I was back in the interlife, near to other dear souls like myself.

In the interlife we have a soul name, a designation for the being that lives through all the different incarnations we experience.

I noticed that the field and the sky had disappeared and in the distance I saw a silver-white light approaching. It was so familiar that at first several things crossed my mind: a futuristic passageway in a spaceship, the walls of an ancient stadium in a remote galaxy, the album cover of an electronic band from the late Sixties. I became engulfed in the silver-white glare, which transported me to another plane of existence.

I recognized that I had come back to the interlife. It was a beehive of activity. As I floated through, I passed office cubicles where workers stared at screens depicting various actions on Earth. I saw side rooms where groups of elders sat in conference, weighing the virtues of mortal prayers. I nearly collided with runners, rushing inscrolled messages from cubicles to elders to a vast switchboard area controlling the deployment of wishes delivered through coincidences, windfalls, and happenstance.

The maze of working spaces thinned and I drifted down long hallways, where occasionally I met a lost soul sitting against the wall. I spoke to some and learned that these poor things had lost a parent, a sibling, a loved one, or a child. The halls became longer and darker the further I went. At last I encountered a lone soul seated in virtual darkness.

I recognized the lost soul: it was Bal.

In the interlife, my soul name is Po; you, Sahara, are known as Sha. In this lifetime we know Baxter Tenderheel as Bax; in the interlife he is Bal.

Bal barely recognized me, and was surprised when I gave him a warm embrace. I held him for a long time, in acknowledgment of his despair, the last lost soul in the farthest corner of this most obscure area where wishes go to live or die.

I gazed into Bal's sunken eyes, pleading to him without words to tell me his ordeal.

"I have nowhere to go," he said, without breath. "They will not fulfill my wish."

When I asked him to explain he said, "I have lived too many lives. In each life none of my hopes are met, and I often meet an untimely death. Within a century I have died in the battle of a remote war, been killed by accident as a young girl, and faced murder and abuse. How can I continue the endless cycle of life and death if all I see is death? I wish never to be reborn, but my wish has been denied."

Was I sadder for Bal's negative feelings or for the rejection of his plea? I held him again, looked with comfort into his eyes, and listened to more of his gruesome lifetimes. I had to convince him not to give up on the living world.

I do not know how I managed to turn Bal around. But I do know that my encounter with him turned me around. As close as I can piece it together, that vision of meeting Bal in the interlife occurred shortly before the period of my hospitalization when I began to understand everyday reality and wish for a lifetime among the living.

ق

"This is a key to Bax's fear of death," Sahara said. "You can't remember what helped him overcome his despair and be reborn?"

"Wish I did. Elvi tried to send me back to this place for more info, but no dice. And Bax can't recall anything about that time either. But even if he can't remember the traumatic lives, I remembered something to help him, so maybe others – "

"Yes, our lives are all intertwined," Sahara said. "We can all help."

"So how 'bout it, babe? When're you coming back to the group? We miss you."

"You think I don't miss the group? It's my qaraq. But I have to sit tight until the baby's born. It's too dangerous."

"Just come back when you can. We need you." Porcy cleared the table. As she went to the kitchen she turned to Sahara and said:

"Bax needs you."

51

The Tale of the Unborn (beginning)

Push! Get out of here! I struggled to break free of the body, to escape the sac. The ridiculous, sticky goop was seeping in everywhere. The resin engulfed the body so there was no motion possible. I managed to break free from the disaster, squeezing myself onto the bark. I oozed through the sap to where it was less thick, sticking to a safe area of bark. An antennae's length away, the body ceased writhing and gave in to the resin choking it.

Safety was no consolation if I was stuck here forever. I had to transport myself, but I was a long way up. Could I squirm some more, channel some motility from my friends the sperms? There's a leaf: if I could reach it, hop on, it would eventually fall into the water.

Gah! Not again, this time a huge mound of sap bearing down, pushing me into a crack in the bark. It's trapping me in its net, cornering me with no escape route. I'll be here forever, an egg waiting to be born, endlessly before the start of a life, a child who won't grow up, whose growth is halted, shrunken, eclipsed. Forever waiting to be a baby.

What is it, baby? Are you all right?
I am fine, momma. Don't worry.
You were troubled. Waiting to be born? Are you impatient to be out in the world?
I am content in here. Close to my memories. Entertaining us with a bedtime story.
I don't understand any of this.
You will. I will finish the story later.
Will you still talk to me after you're born?
I don't know.
I can't wait to see you, my darling.
I'll come out when I'm ready. I'll be ready when I come out. Do not worry.

Sahara felt nervous about her encounter with Naji. Was she losing her mind? If she was unstable now, what would labor be like? But Naji's voice had been so comforting, so full of love. As with recalls, she had no control over when the baby contacted her. She was unnerved about Amar discovering her mental activities. That evening at dinner she decided to test the waters.

"Amar, are you still against me having my own recalls?"

"We have an agreement. No nonsense before the birth of our child. End of story."

That was that. Until after dinner, in the living room, when he brought up the subject.

"So you're still having recalls? Can't you repress them?"

"Can you repress your dreams?"

"Never tried. But you're not sharing them with your little buddies, right?"

She hated this condescending. "No, I'm not sharing them with my little buddies."

"I'd hate to think Bax was hiding in the bushes waiting to hear your latest recall."

She avoided this response, since her latest recall had occurred when she was thinking about Bax. "You tire me out," she said and went upstairs to bed.

Amar followed her upstairs. "All right, I give up. What's your recall about?"

Sahara felt triumphal relief that he was still interested in the stories. She told him her memory of waiting in the cave, doubting the visits by Borzu, and being brutally attacked.

"That's gruesome," he responded after hearing the tale. "This was you? For sure?"

"Oh, yes. I can still feel it in my bones."

"You didn't find out who this demon was?"

"In another recall." It pained Sahara to think a lovely fantasy about the boy from Colorado triggered another recall of a violent sexual encounter. She wouldn't mention Bax. "My day is a lot of drifting in and out of sleep, weird positions to ease spasms, and Naji kicking me. A combination of pain and spinal twists and my body is yanked back to a hard cave or an act of violence."

"You've got my attention. What happened after Borzu visited you?"

The Tale of the God-Urge

The Borzi have gone mad with their God-Urge. Everyone becomes Borzu, puts on a mask and joins the dance. Flames of fire spread to every man. They think they are demons, great hunters, Gods; even Elder Circle claims rutting most important, more than the hunt, food.

My tribe despises the Borzi. We do not believe in Winter, the Borzi blessing. We hate the cold, their comfort. Their Ancient One, Borzu, their Great One, they say was the greatest of hunters, left hundreds of kills for the tribe. Hunted the Drilke, mythical beast that feeds an entire tribe. Protected tribe from threat of Winter.

But things are different now with the God-Urge. Hunters from the Three Valleys come to take part, get a taste of Borzi flesh. Not welcome, so we must slip in, unseen, unnoticed. Best at night, little fear of discovery. Masks and low fires. Last time I went into one of their caves, found a waiting female, ready for the taking. Took her, face in the ground.

Next chance I got, I came back for more.

Nighttime. Stole a mask from behind the bush, waited till end of opening rite, grabbed a stick, joined fire circle, picked up whipping movement with stick, blended in. Shouts, grunts, hollers, as we each became Borzu, doused with the spirit.

There were three fire circles. One for elders, one for children, one for everyone else, where I danced. A lone woman entered my circle, raised her arms, and cried out. Many called back: "Ourm, Ourm!" Some believe the God Borzu had first visited her. Ourm screamed in ecstasy, bared her breasts, and leaped on one of the masked Borzus of her choosing.

Ourm and mate disappeared into the fire shadows. Females took to the center of the circle, some as heated as the men, some thrust in against their will. No more tricking them that one God visited them. Now there were many. Even we from the Three Valleys, not of the Borzi. Things were out of control. The chaos enflamed me, roused the God-Urge.

And then she was thrown into the center. My mate from the cave. I recognized her red hair shining in the flames. I wanted her. The God-Urge acted as if it were only meant for her. I whooped with delight and desire, ran into the center, knocked down others who went after her. As I grabbed her hair, my fist struck the last rival who challenged me.

I am bigger than most of the Borzi, perhaps the biggest that night. I carried my prize to a thicket of bush away from the fires, tossed her back on the ground, stood over her. She gasped, not in fear, but in recognition of my enormous size. I was the Borzu of the cave, the Great One who had visited her! She quickly backed away on her elbows, shook her head violently as she looked up at me. There was no thrall on her face, no anticipation of coupling again with the God-Urge.

She leapt to her feet, slapped my chest, and gestured toward the fire circles, toward the caves, toward her tribe. She repeated the gesture a number of times, in accusation. The gestures said: You are not one of them, you are not of the Borzi. You are not Borzu!

She began shrieking, calling out. No one heard her cries in the din of chanting and shouting. Through the bush I caught a glimpse of Ourm, astride a hunter from my valley; the sight of her bearing down hard on one of my tribe inflated my need.

The woman from the cave reached out and ripped the mask off my face. Astonished and angered, I pulled her to me. She struggled against me, but I was too large for her, hounded me with more gestures. She shoved the mask up to my face, answered my thrusts with mock thrusts of her own, and threw her arms wildly toward Ourm and the others.

You claim to be Borzu and yet you force me with your pathetic thrusts, she accused. You are worse than the others. I despise my tribe now, rutting from sun to moon, under Ourm's craven spell, despoiling the name of Borzu the Great Hunter. But you are false, you are the farthest thing from a God, you are the dirt on the floor of that cave!

Her anger incensed me and I attacked her more fiercely. The harder I pierced her the harder she pierced me with her eyes. When I poured myself into her, she continued to stare but her eyes went blank, as if she had turned to stone. She clutched my arms with a shockingly tight grip, digging her fingernails into my flesh. I had never seen such fury in a female's face. In my tribe, when I had my first girls? Or somewhere else, where I had learned to fear the scorn of a wounded mate?

With my thoughts wandering, my accuser pushed me off balance and I toppled onto the ground. She spat in my face and when I instinctively brought up my hand, she kicked clods of dirt and stone at me. I lay there in my shame as she ran off.

I wanted her more than ever. Satisfied for the night, shamed for the night. Knew I could never have her again. But I had had her. Picked up the mask. Stared at the carved face of Borzu. I detest you. I will never play the hero again. Hate Winter. Hate shame. Hate her. She had the problem. With her tribe. She was the outsider.

I saw Ourm once more. Shrieking, full of the God. I looked down at the mask. What did it all matter? I put it on and dove into the bush. Straight toward Ourm's screams of joy.

ق

"This was clearly not your lifetime," Amar said when Sahara finished the story. "You're the victim, but it's through the eyes of the false Borzu. Who do you think it was?"

Sahara was not ready to give her opinion, knowing it would stir up trouble. "You really think I was the victim. I held my own, didn't I?"

"You did get to him at the end."

"You think he was changed? He just continued fucking his brains out."

337

"That was the way back then. They were living in caves – it was prehistoric."

"That justifies rape?"

"It puts things in context," Amar said. "They were close to being animals."

"Do animals rape? Or do they mate?"

"Give the poor caveman a break. His whole tribe sanctioned this behavior. There are hundreds of studies about primitive cultures having spirit worship where the person takes on the character of the God and it leads to ecstasy or mutilation or great sex."

"You call rape great sex?"

Amar was quiet. He could not argue this point. It had been a month since Sahara had confessed his act of violence to the group, but it still hung over them. Finally he spoke.

"Who do you think did this to you?"

Sahara could not evade it any longer. "Amar, as you said, this was not my lifetime. There are only two people other than myself whose past lives I have recalled."

"You think I raped you."

She felt her husband tense next to her. "I've had recalls about you."

"But these may not be recalls, they may be products of your own psyche. Yes, I did violence to you, and you haven't – we haven't – resolved it."

"You're saying I'm fantasizing you as a Neanderthal to resolve the violence?"

"Okay, I'll take your stance: our souls have been repeating these awful patterns. It still doesn't make sense. In all the tales I'm a powerful creature, confident, direct. This guy is sneaking around in a mask, taking advantage of a chaotic situation. That's not my soul."

"Who else could it be? You were even justifying his behavior, taking his side."

Amar had a revelation. "What about Bax? The guy stalked you. In your own bushes. He's a big guy, like the caveman. It's perfect."

"Just because Bax is attracted to me doesn't give you the right to call him a rapist!"

"Jesus, that does it!" Amar leaped out of the bed, headed for the door, turned back. "I won't lie there and be falsely accused of raping my wife. We just can't do this anymore. We had an agreement: no more past life crap until the baby's born. And you know what? I say no more after he's born, during his childhood, as long as he's in this house. You have a problem with violence? Getting rid of the past lives will do it. No more stories."

He left the room and went downstairs to sleep on the sofa.

52

The Tale of the Unborn (continued)

Why did I hesitate? Right now I have to get over to that leaf or I won't make it. Already it's harder to move. I'm such a child sometimes. I can't even get started, I'm too deep in this crack. The sap is hardening, it will continue to do so with night, with the cold, with time. Will I live through it? Will I be in a perpetual state of frozen lifelessness? I'll never move. I feel a wave of panic. The sap crushes in on my soul. I want to scream.

Focus on my new little world here. Find a comfort in this tiny orange home, a world without blue sky. Focus on the future, looming grand ahead. The world is waiting for my entrance. The royal family waiting for the birth of an heir. I am the source of a new life, I must survive. I must prolong this life-before-life as long as possible, as long as it takes until birth.

Naji? What's wrong?
Nothing, mama. I'm fine. Just more of my bedtime story.
What story? Are you sure you're okay? What is this life-before-life? The interlife?

No.

Life in the womb? You're telling me about your life now?

No. I was in a tree. Stuck.

You were in a tree. I don't understand, baby.

You will. I will finish the story later. It's almost time. I'll see you soon.

Sahara had not been to therapy for several weeks. Given everything that had happened with Amar and Naji recently she was anxious about her session. But her fears disappeared as soon as she saw Dr. Machiyoko's smiling presence.

"You look great, Sahara. Huge, but great. How are you doing?"

Where should she start? "The baby's fine. He's been chatting with me."

The therapist's eyes twinkled. "So precocious. How has that been for you?"

"It's wonderful. His voice is so warm and soothing. Should I be worried?"

"That you're hearing voices? Some mothers have unusually strong bonds with their babies in vitro. If you're deluded, the whole group is. We believe he's telling you recalls."

"Oh my God, how stupid! It's a past life! He called it a bedtime story."

After Sahara told Naji's tale, the therapist moved from the stool at the foot of the couch back to the gray armchair. "You didn't think it was a recall?"

"There's stuff in it about waiting to be born. I thought Naji was getting impatient."

"But he isn't?"

"He seems perfectly happy inside me."

"Maybe you're impatient for the birth to arrive," the therapist suggested.

"Sure, and scared. But there's a link between his story and being in the womb."

"Maybe he's comparing the ease he feels now with the problem in his past life."

Sahara considered. "He was trapped then, perhaps as an embryo, so that makes some sense. He's covered in sap, and panicked about being trapped for all eternity."

"Sounds like an emotional reaction, not a literal state. But why the sap?"

"That seemed real. He said I would understand when he finished the story."

Dr. Machiyoko twisted one leg around the other. "How do you feel about his tale?"

"You mean, do I feel trapped in sap because of my marriage? Very clever, Doc."

"So how are things with Amar? How are you doing?"

Sahara recounted recent events, the two tales set among the Borzi, and her fight with Amar over them.

Dr. Machiyoko responded: "You're sure this huge caveman was Amar?"

"I'm not sure of any of it. I just believe it must have been Amar."

"I'm just asking because for all his disbelief, Amar has never denied that a recall referred to him. He's never refused to see a connection between a tale and his life today."

"No, only blown up at me because of it. I suppose you're right. God, you're so fair and objective about him I could slap you."

"Why do you think you need to see him as a caveman?"

"You want me to state the obvious?"

"Yes. I want you to state the obvious."

The answer was still difficult for Sahara to speak. "Because he threatened me." She felt a familiar tightening in her throat and stomach. "Because he was violent."

The therapist leaned forward. "He pushed you against a wall and almost strangled you. Sahara, I must ask you this. It would be better if Amar were here, but it's still necessary. Has he done things to you at other times?"

Sahara was relieved at the question. "No!" She smiled tensely. "Not in this life. Though I'm afraid he might. His anger is frightening, and I always see him holding it in."

"Have you felt the need to leave him?"

"For weeks after the incident in the kitchen I thought about it But I didn't know where to go. I have no family close, and I wouldn't want to be alone."

"What about the qaraq?" Dr. Machiyoko asked. "We all care about your safety."

"I didn't know about the qaraq until later. But who would I stay with? Zack, Amar's old friend, who's right next-door? Verle, in that attic? Porcy, with Bax there? The idea is to ensure my safety, not encourage Amar to strangle me."

"Sahara, I want you to know that if you're ever in danger, you must contact me. And if you need, you can always stay with me." Sahara was surprised by how much she was touched by Dr. Machiyoko's offer. The therapist observed her patient's emotional state from talking about the lingering threat of Amar's violence. "How are you doing?"

It was the third time she had asked the question. Sahara felt annoyed by it. "This is going to sound wrong, anti-feminist, deluded, whatever. I'm still holding out for the soul mate idea. I've been through a lot with this man, this soul. I'm working through centuries of stuff. It's my ray of hope when I despair about the marriage."

"I understand. But there's a group with a complicated history. We must have gone through all sorts of relationships with each other. Could someone else be your soul mate?"

"You mean Bax?"

"I don't know. He may be feeling that way. It could be Verle for all we know. All I'm saying is that it's frightening to give so much because of an idea that might be false."

"That doesn't frighten me," Sahara said, defiantly. "I feel in my gut that Amar is the one, even with such a tormented relationship."

Dr. Machiyoko re-crossed her legs. "What frightens you, then?"

Sahara felt a surge of anger at the therapist. "What do you want? Are you back to the violence? What do you want me to say? I'm scared of Amar because he tried to kill me. There! Are you happy now? Because it doesn't do much for me. Frankly, I've been hanging in there with Amar. I'm not that afraid of him hurting me at this point."

"Because he's your soul mate? Because you've been going at it for so long?"

Suddenly Sahara's anger released into something else. Underneath was a deep-seated fear. She thought of the lives she had recalled that were centuries old, eras old, as old as the planet. It was too breathtakingly vast. Then Naji's panic in his story came back to her: the terror of being sealed alive in amber sap forever. It *was* like her marriage!

"What is it, Sahara?" the therapist asked quietly. "What are you feeling?"

This time Sahara was not upset by the probing question. She let it hit her full force. She looked at Dr. Machiyoko, a friend who had offered her shelter, and poured out her soul.

"What if Amar and I are wrapped in this torment for more centuries, eras, eons? What if we're stuck in this kind of relationship for the rest of eternity?"

She wept inconsolably.

53

The Tale of the Unborn (continued)

Caught in the amber. The cruelest color. Translucent enough to see shapes and movement, viscous enough to block any understanding of that movement. Teasing amber, maddening amber. No wonder the blue of the world looked so good later on, the blue of the sky I fell from, through the leaves and into the blue of the pond. Bluish green water, baby blue sky. A piercing fondness for blue.

Anything but amber, the fossilized resin of pine trees, trapping insects, babies, embryos, and eggs. A lone female egg trapped for years, waiting for some heroic male to free it, to sex it, to bring it back to life. The male doesn't come, will never come. And I am fertile. I am brimming with life. I am dying for life. Let me be born!

Do you like my story, momma? I'm sorry it made you sad.
I love it, sweetie. It was good for me to cry. Are you finished?

No, I haven't been born in the story yet.
This is you in the story? A past life?
A lifetime.
The sap, the amber turning to fossil. It seems like a very long time ago.
Can you guess what I am, momma?
That's very hard. A dinosaur?
Silly momma, that's too big!
An egg?
That's it!
But the egg grows into something, doesn't it?
You'll see. But not right now.
Why not, baby?
Because it's time!

It was just before dawn when Sahara felt the first contractions. Amar helped her remain calm and carefully got things ready. But Sahara implored him that Naji was not waiting. They had chosen the hospital in Livingston, even though it was a bit further away, but by the time Amar started the car the contractions were already coming steadily. As the sun pinkened the horizon, Amar raced to nearby Glenclaire Hospital Emergency Room.

Sahara was calm, fully expecting an easy birth. Intelligent for months inside of her, this magical child would control his arrival, chose the time, scoot down the birth canal. Things started off like those births she had read about: the African woman leaving the trail to have her child in the bush, the mother in the taxi delivering her own son, the squaw squatting down in the field during harvest.

Then the delivery took a turn for the worse. The pains, contractions, and commands to push seemed harsh and never-ending after the light quickness in which things had begun.

She could not breathe, yet she had to breathe. Any mystical thoughts of her son slipping into the world were drowned out by the physical relentlessness forcing itself on her.

Still, it was only three and a half hours later that Naji Rash was born.

All was well with the baby, but because of the daunting jolt on her emotions, Sahara was not completely aware when they handed Naji to her. She had trouble believing that the voice inside her head had transformed into this tiny, fragile, fleshy thing. Would he speak to her, now that he was no longer inside of her? Hormones flooded through her body and brain. Something inside of her collapsed. Throughout the day she traveled in and out of sleep, in and out of the reality, and visions overtook her.

The Tale of the Mi'raj of One Thousand and One

Once upon a time there was a little blue egg, as pretty a blue egg as your grandmother had ever seen, and it was only a matter of time before the pretty blue egg split into two and grew into a fine young baby named Nadrash. Nadrash's mother loved him and held him and cried when she thought back to the little blue egg he had once been, but Nadrash shushed his mother and told her that if she cried about Nadrash no longer being a pretty blue egg, then she would have to cry about his other lifetimes being over.

She would have to cry that he was no longer a prankish little tike named Rashid, who stole a time machine and went racing around the spacetime continuum, out of control. She would sob at him not being a young brave in the pre-colonial Bay Area, who could, for merit or discredit, wrap his supernaturally long penis around his waistline seven times. She would weep at him as a thief caught red-handed on the Red Isle, who faced a terrible punishment. She would bawl at the ruler of a land whose boast was the astonishing silver-white gaming arena known as Radium Stadium.

She would whimper at a vision in front of her, a flaming numeral One.

A door opened and an old man walked through. He was kindly and gentle and smiled the smile of a hundred benign viziers. His silver-white hair flashed as he crossed the room. Was he the mastermind of the Stadium? He sat down on a chair and placed his wrinkled hands in his lap as if they were precious artifacts to be kept safe. He looked knowingly into the mother's eyes, although she could not truly see him.

She was staring through the open gateway of her vision, now two flaming number Ones, imposing as pillars. She searched into the space between the numerals, came upon her egg-child's dazed and unruly history, and gazed into his future. She witnessed his saunter down the birth canal, bright blue days engaged in rolling over for the first time, holding a bottle in one hand, walking, talking, and growing up to be a real boy.

As the young mother walked through the woods of Nadrash's past and future lifetimes, the trees thickened and the path darkened as she considered his significance. With his hundred lifetimes, the babe was older than the old man with the silver-white hair. Nadrash had passed through the interlife, was as aware of the process of Time and rebirth as the wisest living human being. This infant had brushed up against the everlasting world.

On the path through the dark woods she met a middle-aged woman bearing a crown made of straw. The woman passed the mother silently, as if she was slipping out of a room, then disappeared down the forest path and through a door.

Another woman appeared on the path, her head surrounded by bouquets of flowers. In the flowers the mother saw an intertwining, tangled connection between the woman, the old man, the middle-aged woman, and herself, as if the jumble of stems meshed their hundreds of lifetimes together. She looked into the woman's warm and friendly eyes, and stared in wonder as the two eyes turned into burning circles, matching the brilliant flame of the numerals. The circles transformed into numbers, ciphers, into two luminescent Zeroes, as shiny as the dark, full of nothing, hollow and vast as everything.

The Zeroes retreated into the distance as the two Ones reappeared, vastly separated as if arriving from faraway eastern and western train stations. They closed in toward each other, creating a force that pulled the two Zeroes back from the horizon. The mother felt the effort of the numbers tugging at each other as an intense muscular ache in her core. She moved back and forth between the aching physical reality of the vision and its ephemerality, between the solidity of the Ones and the nothingness of the Zeroes, between the smallness of the One and the powerful, philosophical depth of the Zero.

The numerals contracted into each other, the two Ones flanking the two Zeroes. They lined up, no longer separate, simply One, Zero, Zero, One, the countable emblem of the uncountable. As the numbers formed this integer of Infinity, the mother sensed that the people she had encountered had never left, that she were in all the places she had ever been, that all the lives of her newborn babe were still spinning around her. She saw the eyes and arms and bodies of the people in her life reflected in the numerical shapes. The corpus of the qaraq appeared, and in the same way that the number symbolized endlessness, the bodies symbolized the innumerable cross-relations of their lifetimes. So many lives, even in a finite form such as hundreds, so myriad and populous.

But the mother knew in the depths of her soul that the lives were not finite. As the numerals burned as bright as a shiny blue egg, she saw that the soul is destined to be reborn over and over again, physical flesh crumbling to ephemeral spirit only to reaffirm itself as some new glob of matter in some new world. The number was the physicalization of the mirage, the Mi'raj of the One Thousand and First Heaven, the neverending cycle of life after life, pain after pain, death after death, the Maya of worldly existence.

And the mother realized that just as her blue egg had manifest as a beautiful male child, she herself would never die. Rebirth had her trapped. There was no way out.

ق

Sahara gasped.

"My God!" Dr. Machiyoko started, "you okay?"

Sahara peered through sticky, watery eyes. She looked around the hospital room, half expecting to be somewhere else. On the window sill sat was a huge bouquet of flowers and a golden Bundt cake. It was nighttime: in the glow of streetlights outside the window Sahara faintly saw a grove of trees.

"What is that?" Sahara pointed to the sill.

"A cake. Cachay brought it. Zack was too scared to come himself. Afraid Amar might send him to the emergency room." Dr. Machiyoko smiled, hoping to lighten Sahara's dark face.

"I'm in the hospital?" Sahara felt stupid asking.

350

"Yes." Dr. Machiyoko was reassured that Sahara was getting her bearings. "We all took turns sneaking past Amar to see you. Verle came first. Porcy brought the flowers."

Sahara tried to remember what she had just been through, something about the group, endless past lives, some central image that was just outside her awareness. She sat up. "Where's Naji? Is he all right?"

"Great. Beautiful. Got your big blue eyes. He's in the nursery."

"Where's Amar?"

"He's been around all day. Seems to have accepted my presence, as a member of the medical profession. Welcomed another opinion."

"Why? What's wrong?"

"You've been out all day. You were admitted this morning and it's been almost twelve hours. How are you feeling?"

"Drained, but all right now. I had some kind of weird vision, obviously a long one."

"I suspected as much, but we've kept a close eye on you. I'm glad you're coming around. Let me see about getting your baby in here. I'll tell Amar you're up."

"You're an angel, Doc."

"There's a water pitcher on the table. Try to drink a bit."

When Diana left Sahara tried to take stock of things. The surroundings reminded her of associations from her fantasy, like the 'straw crown' Bundt cake, the street-lit grove of trees as the darkening forest, or Porcy as the woman with the flowers. She was still disoriented about the time, which made sense given her experience of neverending Time.

She saw her chart hanging from her bed and leaned over to retrieve it. She looked at the top of the first page to find the date. It was the first day of October:

10 / 01.

351

The flaming numbers rushed back into her memory. That had been the central image of her vision! A symbol of eternity, of the Infinite. How bizarre that Sahara had spent hours watching that number and all of its meanings, and never once connected it to *The Thousand and One Nights*. The realization that she of all people had received that vision eased her mind a bit. A Thousand and One was in her consciousness as a Nights scholar. Perhaps it was more of an imaginative hallucination on her part than a true call from some devastating, eternal force.

Then she read on the chart the time of Naji's birth.

10:01 A.M.

That was a bit too weird. She wondered if she had been aware of the date and time before she began her hallucination.

Amar walked in the door. A nurse followed him, holding the baby.

"Thank God!" Amar rushed over to the bedside. "I was so worried. How are you?"

It felt so good to squeeze her husband's hand. Whatever had been wrong between them felt very far away. "I'm all right. Sorry I gave you a scare."

"You gave me a beautiful boy. That's what counts."

Amar looked back at the nurse, who brought Naji to the bed. Amar stayed next to Sahara as she took the baby. To everyone's delight, Naji reached up with his hands, found his face, and tried to rub his eyes.

"You happy to see your mom?" Amar cooed.

"It's okay now, baby," Sahara said, half to Amar, half to Naji.

Hi, momma! You okay now? I missed you!

Sahara caught her breath at the sound of Naji's voice in her head. Had anyone else heard? Of course not.

You're fine, momma. Aren't you glad to see me?

I am, baby, I am, Sahara thought. You are so beautiful. I'm so happy to see you at last.

The nurse went to the bed table to pick up the container of water. Sahara saw that there was a digital clock behind where the water pitcher had been. As she looked at the clock for the first time, she saw the number click over:

10:01.

54

In one of the early translations of *The Thousand and One Nights* In the Eighteenth Century, a previously unseen epilogue to the Scheherazade story appeared. In it, Scheherazade brings forward the three babes born to her during the thousand-day period, and beseeches Shahryar to release her from the death sentence for the sake of the children. The king consents, reassuring Scheherazade that he had intended to spare her for some time. In effect, the children save their mother's life.

In an echo of the mythical past, Naji's appearance in the Rash household created a truce between Sahara and Amar. The new parents felt blessed with the physical beauty of their child. Naji had a caramel complexion, his father's deep-set dark eyes, his mother's strong nose and luscious oval mouth, and an unusually thick head of dark hair with henna tones, a perfect combination of his parents' ancestries.

For the first time in months Amar came home from work early so he could spend time in adoration of his son. Sahara cooed and played with the baby endlessly during the day, her neglected scholarship completely forgotten. How easily a squirming newborn eradicates my awareness of the immortality of the soul, she thought. Naji did not pester his mother by planting words in her head.

The members of the qaraq continued to visit, especially Dr. Machiyoko, who set herself up as the hospital's liaison during postpartum. Amar accepted her presence in the house and tolerated Porcy or Zack's visits, understanding their crush on his child. When he was not around, the qaraq members entreated Sahara to rejoin their meetings. Momentum had run down for the group; last week's meeting had been canceled. Sahara worried that solving the group's problem would destroy her peace with Amar.

October marks the transition from lawn mowing to leaf raking season in the suburbs. Baxter Tenderheel was hard at work cleaning up yards for Porcy's real estate clients, a gesture she hoped they would remember when they sold their houses. Bax liked the work since it paid his room and board at Porcy's home. She made all the arrangements, and there was no long-term commitment.

One afternoon while Bax was working at a mansion in the Glenclaire hills, his rake hit an odd bump in the well-manicured lawn. Discovering more bumps as he cleared the leaves, Bax saw that there was a network of molehills. He got down on his hands and knees to inspect the dirt mounds and an unexpected inner calm overtook him.

Ever since Porcy recalled her meeting with him in the interlife, Bax had obsessed about what had brought him to such despair. As his hands touched the earth he sensed with great excitement that he was being taken back to that interlife, to a time after Po, Porcy's soul name, had convinced him to try a new incarnation. He saw his soul in the interlife, researching choices. Plunging his hands into the soft molehill, Bax let the memory enter him.

The Wombat's Tale

Nothing strenuous. If it's to be, then let it be safe. Let me hide out somewhere. From danger, from society. In exile, yes, I've done that before. In some hole in the ground.

A burrower! Perfect choice. A nocturnal animal. Safer in dark. Easy hunting. Something lazy, like a three-toed sloth. No, idea of hanging upside-down freaks me out. Another nocturnal marsupial? Here's one: vombatus ursinus.

Pointed ears. Shuffles along on short, fat legs. Looks like a three-foot-long bear. That's the ursinus part. Not as cute as a koala or panda, but still mighty adorable. And look here. Solitary life. Short mating season. Underground life style. Lots of escape tunnels. Eats plants and seeds. I don't have to hunt!

Wait a minute. Wombats exterminated as pests in Australia by the 1800's. Uh-oh. Fur so coarse doormats are made from it. Ouch. But now they live in Tasmania. There are protective regulations for wombats.

Always wanted to see Tasmania. The wombat it is!

And so Bal, Bax's soul, incarnated to Tasmania as a wombat in 1977. However, Tasmania did not put the wombat protections into law until 1978. Still, his life started well.

Warm. Dry. Next to the milk. Face right up against Momba. Didn't have to turn. World outside. Snuggled in closer. Had everything I needed. Safe. Paradise. Never want to leave.

Momba kicked me out of the pouch when my claws got too sharp. I discovered digging. What a thrill! First tunnel tucked nicely under an old log. Pompa showed me how to open up a den at the end. Cozy warm. Like Momba without the milk.

Second tunnel came back up out of the den. Hit the surface beyond the log. Surprise! Dug back down again. Big curving burrow this time. Aimed for the den. Couldn't find it. Back up. Back down. More and more tunnels.

Finally hit the den! Back out, connected more tunnels to it. Curving burrows, rootstock blind alleys, escape hatches. Q-turns. All roads lead home.

My first burrow system. Shiny disc in sky was bright and round when I started. Got small for a while. Now big again. Took me that long. Not bad for first time out. Took my time, too. Slept all day. Foraged in the grass for supper. Then to work.

It's a good life.

On the lawn, Bax squeezed his fingers in the earth. A childlike grin crossed his face, rare for the quiet young man. Then, his hands dug deeper into the molehill. He clawed the ground anxiously as the memory unfolded.

Nighttime. Still proud of my new burrow. Ready to explore. Find a new patch of grass. Shiny disc still bright. Easy to see. Where I'm headed. Where I've come from.

Out of nowhere. Huge flying creature. Talons. Wings. Pulling, yanking. My legs picked off. Coarse fur ripped apart for a fleshy feed. Barely still alive. Bird had his fill. Discarded me from the air. If wounds didn't kill me, the fall did.

My soul rose above the shredded carcass. My pain was gone, but not my anguish. How many more lives would I waste? So much for an easy respite from annihilation.

The scorching sun baked my remains. Several varieties of ants and beetles gnawed at my cadaver. That evening, shortly after suppertime, three boys delivered my corpse a hundred thousand blows with an old cricket bat.

357

Could not look upon the carrion any longer. Let my soul rise. Drift. No interlife. No new choice of lifetime. And then: by default. Plunged down. Outside Greeling, Colorado.

1978: Bax Tenderheel is born.

ق

When Porcy drove by the mansion to pick up Bax she found him quivering on the lawn. He was covered in dirt and ripped up sod, a two-foot deep hole in front of him. He had the look of a frightened child on his powerful, sculpted face. Seeing his trauma, she asked him no questions at first. Thankful she had remembered her new cell phone, she made a quick call and then helped Bax sit up. He was cold as ice and his breath came in shallow spurts. She comforted and warmed him in her arms.

When Porcy tried to get Bax to talk, his hands tightened, his head tucked down into his chest, and his arms covered parts of his body in protection. When he tried to speak it was in fragments, punctuated by his trembling.

Finally, a car pulled into the long driveway. "What took you?" Porcy cried out.

"I had to take the baby, get him ready," Sahara began. "Why didn't you call 911?"

"Gut instinct. He's not dying. He's just scared. He won't talk to me. You're his 911."

"What am I supposed to do?"

"If I knew I'd do it myself, honey. It's something to do with that interlife. When I talked him into being reborn into this life. I'm gonna regret that."

Sahara knelt down next to Bax. "Is that right?"

Without looking up, Bax answered, "Not this life. The one before this one."

"That's it, baby, tell Sahara. I'll go watch Naji." Porcy let go of Bax and Sahara instinctively sat down and let Bax hunch over and put his head in her lap.

"What happened? What scared you? Talk about it, it'll release your fear."

"Too much pain!"

Sahara wanted to stroke his head but she stopped herself. "I'm sorry it's so painful. When I gave birth to Naji, that was painful enough. Then I spent hours in an intense vision, a terrifying, relentless cycle of pain and pleasure. I know what despair feels like, wanting to get out of it for good. I'll understand. I'm one of your magical women. Tell me."

Trembling, on the verge of tears, Bax slowly recounted his story. As he spoke, Porcy returned to listen, bringing the baby and a carrier pouch. When Bax finished his shocking tale the women remained silent. Bax rose from Sahara's lap and mindlessly shoved dirt into the hole in the lawn. Sahara put on the chest carrier and Porcy gently placed the baby into it.

"Leave it, sweetie," Porcy said to Bax. "I'll tell them you declared war on the moles."

Bax stopped and turned on his knees to the women. In his line of sight was Naji, snuggled against Sahara in the marsupial-like pouch. The sight confused and yet pleased the young man.

"That your baby?"

"Yes, Bax," Sahara said, "This is Naji. Would you like to see his face?"

Bax nodded. Sahara knelt beside him, positioning herself so Bax could see the baby nuzzling against her breast.

"Wow," Bax said, leaning in to her, "a baby wombat." For the first time he smiled. He smelled the pleasant mixture of Sahara and the baby. "He's a beaut."

Sahara took pleasure in the moment. It felt good to be near the handsome youth, but safe with the baby between them.

She contemplated Bax's genuine wonder at the infant. Five minutes ago he had reported the most gruesome of deaths. Now this fragile being, who a few decades ago, a few drops of time in the scheme of things, had rejected all of life, this resilient exile sat beside her in awe of her newborn babe.

55

That week Amar went out of town on a business trip. He brought Ooma to sort through the mountain of documents needed for the meetings. They used his hotel room as a headquarters: there were files and copies piled everywhere. Ooma had a duplicate key to the room in case she had to retrieve a document during the meetings.

On the first night, after Amar went to bed, he became aware of someone entering his room. He lay still for a minute, thinking it was a dream. Then he carefully turned to face the intruder. In the dim light through the hotel window, he saw Ooma standing by the bed.

"What are you doing here?" The young woman did not answer. Her dark eyes glistened as she looked at him. "You shouldn't be here. What's going on?"

Ooma opened her mouth but did not utter a sound. Because of her warm, physical presence, Amar had not noticed her distress before. Thinking of his wife and child at home, he spoke in a formal tone. "Ooma, I beg you to explain your troubles."

She opened her mouth again. "Bad dream."

Ooma was so capable at the office that Amar was surprised to discover this frightened, childlike side to her. "Is that it?"

"More than a bad dream. Huge, awesome, confusing." Amar saw her shaking. He jumped out of bed, threw on his robe, and fetched a blanket. Wrapping her in it, he led them to the couch. Ooma kept a corner of the blanket close to her mouth as she spoke. "There were incredibly real things ... I want to remember ... it's hard. Oh my God!" She reached out and touched his arm. "It was a past life." She drew the blanket to her mouth.

"You've got to be kidding," Amar said, half exasperated, half laughing. He thought: here I am away from my wife, a beautiful girl in my bedroom, and she tells me she's had a recall. I might as well be home.

Ooma was struck hard by her boss' comment. "I'm sorry! I'm not intentionally trying to drive you nuts. I can't help it." She sucked on the blanket. "Can I get a hug?" Not waiting for a response, she dug her head into his shoulder, an animal burrowing into its den.

Amar put his arms around her tentatively. "Sorry I snapped. Tell me your dream."

Ooma pushed away from him. "Really? I thought you were sick of them."

"No, actually. It's just ... complicated. Tell me."

The Tale of the Elephant in Baghdad

It's all blurry and confused now but of course it's a dream so one thing leads to another and maybe I'm remembering it exactly as it played out. The last thing I remember seeing before I fell asleep was the clock by the bed which said 12:01

and I remember thinking 'Midnight' but then somewhere in the dream I heard "There is no such thing as Midnight" but I didn't know what it meant or maybe I did but I don't remember now.

There was an elephant.

I think I was the elephant but, like, excuse me, why am I an elephant?! but at the time I didn't feel that way I just was and every once in a while I bent down and scooped up some food with my trunk and, you know, that voice in the back of your mind when you're dreaming, that voice said you're an elephant look at your trunk how cute but then the voice only lasted as long as it would take for the food to get to my mouth and I started chewing and new thoughts entered my head, as the elephant

an all-seeing, all-knowing, very friendly elephant who was the talk of Baghdad that year having been brought all the way from Hind with my mother, grandmother, great-aunt Ploorkejh and three male cousins, seven of us in all. At least they kept some of the family together since I was only a baby not even eight years old, the time when the young ones first walk away from their mothers but Ruling Mother was not with us just my mother who said that Ruling Mother had passed on as much as she could though who would use knowledge of our watering holes all the way here in the desert. My cousins were to fight in the Caliph's army alongside the other captives or so I heard when I pretended to be taking the longest drink in history from the one watering hole in sight but really I was listening to my cousins squawk away about their future military exploits. I had very good hearing back then even by elephant standards my mother used to say because she told me her uncle Snhork could stand at the edge of one village and hear a baby sleeping in the next village and everyone knows that elephants hear some of the lowest sounds in the world so my mother said if ever I was in trouble to kind of rumble into the ground and then listen for help from the low sounds rumbling back out of the earth. Thank Ganeh I never had to try it

and thank Ganeh we made it all the way here what a trudge poor grandmother barely able to stand the whips and prods and open air sun no wonder Ruling Mother told mother everything she must have known grandmother might not make it how sad but how wise of Ruling Mother. Everyone was mad about being yanked from the jungle and the rest of the family the thirteen others were made to work and barely given enough to eat but I didn't mind and they say oh Hommy you're just a baby you don't understand the cruelty but I like our mahouts they play with me and slip me treats and spray me when I'm not looking to scare me but I love that and the children all love me here because I'm so friendly and they pet me and laugh and try to ride me but mother won't let them. Why not! the soldiers are riding Crauwgh and Narugh and Sshourhn and she cries but doesn't stop them

and I'm happy here for another reason something about the place but that isn't it exactly because when I think about the place I have bad memories blurry memories like in a dream. Something bad happened I was a bad girl even though I didn't want to be but then when I stop thinking about the place I'm happy again

I kept hearing the elephant's thoughts in the dream and all the things the elephant was hearing the cousins the calls from Mom the low camel farts in the Baghdad market but then there was yet another voice in my head that seemed to come from a distance not like Snhork listening to the next village but from on high and the voice put images into the elephant's head that came to me in the dream

images of the marketplace the back alleys doorways to rooms where secret things were happening and a plate with thirteen dates on it and seven long sips of mint tea and ten or eleven persons huddled over parchment sheets arguing fiercely then laughing nodding and all the time telling stories new and old endings of stories with the shutters kept closed the voices hushed and it is my task to keep the proceedings a secret

not that I want the stories to be secret by no means the stories come from the streets from the storytellers the stories belong to everyone and our project is only a secret to those who would set rules upon them rules that have nothing to do with stories or people. I keep our project underground so the stories can stay where they belong but also appear more beautiful than ever which is why we stay in the darkened rooms arguing about which story belongs next to which and what the curvature of the whole should be

and it is grand work and the eleven people work late by lamplight and complete the first set of thirteen and in seven years the other thirteen and one for good measure but the number to celebrate was to be Three Hundred and Seventy-Nine glorious year of completion but my task failed and those for whom we kept underground found us out so I sank into dark despair and never saw Three Hundred and Seventy Nine

and yet it was still a time to glorify said another voice the voice from on high which comforted me we have made a great work it said and there have been many bumps in the road along the way of completing this most unique of books and our very souls that went into the stories have suffered and given out suffering as if we had traveled through each of the Seven Hells each with eleven hundred mountains each filled with thirteen thousand devils and though we took great pains to experience and create and collect and order the book even so we should praise ourselves for this great work for it will live beyond all of us

and I was comforted by the voice and felt a great relief as if I had been in a prison cell and the door was flung open and I glimpsed down a long corridor into a vast space or stretch of time and I could hear from an enormous distance the sound of troops slowly advancing and I could see my cousins in battle regalia but it wasn't my cousins it was elephants from an ancient time from the Persians who fought Aleksandar and the Ruling Mothers always share their knowledge down through the families so elephants never forget anything and I remembered I had been in Baghdad before not as an elephant but working on a great book and I knew that those who worked with me on the book would still be in Baghdad when I returned as Homma the elephant and that it would be a relief to be near them again a relief to not have to understand what was happening to the precious book now that it was in the hands of the courtiers those whom I had failed to exclude and a relief that the book had been completed despite all our pains

and then the dream turned dark and I saw evil deeds that had nothing to with an elephant or a book but I still felt connected to them I was perpetrating them I saw naked bodies piled on top of each other and I felt myself atop the bodies and I felt the same surge of freedom rush through me as before the feeling that I could see down vast hallways of time and could live for as many lives as I wished because There was no such thing as Midnight and then there was blood and severed heads and I tried to hang on to the wonderful feeling of immortality but I was pulled down by depravity and the lovely bodies vanished but then there was a face in front of mine and I felt seven delicious kisses but with each my soul plummeted further down in despair and for all my efforts to maintain my pleasure and my freedom and my power I could only feel evil and I became known as an evil Queen and I tried to salvage my bad name through the book but in the story I was a depraved antagonist and I wished for my own death and yet I kept returning to work on the book and I learned to relish the task of keeping it underground especially since

I cringed at the evil Queen's presence in the book but in the end I failed even that

then the relief the thank Ganeh relief the seventh kiss relief the sweetest bliss among the sourest the cold comfort of the book's greatness despite its painful source the all-seeing looking toward the source the fascination of seeking who I am the great secret of my soul and it is time to let the secret come up from underground to share the secret that There is no such thing as Midnight there is no end to Time there is only the seven heavens of the eleven universes of the thirteen angels each of whom can take you beyond to their own seven heavens of their own eleven universes of their own thirteen angels each of whom can take you beyond to their own seven heavens

and I see all of this I see beyond my evil and suffering I see beyond the book and at the end of the dream I know the elephant knows the evil Queen knows all of us know the book is more than a massive project completed by Three Hundred and Seventy-Nine but will stretch forward into the vast future just as it stretches back into the vast memory of the Eleph'ans those who never forget the histories the Aleph'iant those of the largest hippocampus who remember back before the oldest worlds and the All-knowing Alephoscidiant who never forget the source of All Occurrence, the secret of Immortality:

However vast the time scale, there is always one more vast.

ق

Ooma pulled the blanket tighter around her. "That's when I woke up, barely able to breathe, my head bursting as if my brain were expanding beyond my skull."

Amar looked at the beautiful young girl. So many things she had shared felt familiar. They talked deep into the night about the many connections and confusions in Ooma's vision.

She surmised that the evil Queen was Uzmeth, her Persian incarnation, and he assumed the book created in Baghdad was a version of the Arabian Nights. Uzmeth's depraved history became source material for the Queen who cuckolds the King in the Scheherazade story. This helped Ooma understand why in the dream she was depressed and tried to keep the book a secret: her bad reputation had become legendary.

They wondered about the group compiling the book. Amar was confused about the recurring numbers, especially 379, too early a date for the creation of the Nights. They questioned the elephant Homma's link to the compilers of the Nights, the higher voice speaking throughout, and the bizarre names at the end, elephant-like beings who could see endless Time.

Ooma was struck by a revelation. "I've forgotten that this is about my past lives. If I lived as Homma and other beings in the dream, that explains how the elephant has all of this knowledge about Uzmeth and the creators of the Nights in her head, why she feels a comfort at arriving in Baghdad. Her soul lived through all those experiences."

"That's a simple enough answer, but there's still confusions. Who's Aleksandar?"

"Every Persian kid knows that. It's Persian for Alexander the Great. Who's Ganeh?"

"That's easy: Ganesha, the elephant God of the Hindus. What are the seven kisses?"

Ooma had an inkling about the seven kisses, related to when she and Bax had kissed at Amar's New Year's Eve party and she had an out-of-body experience. Trying to understand that experience was one of the reasons she was drawn to the group's work. But she wasn't bringing that night up to her boss. She had a new thought.

Amar saw Ooma contemplating for a minute and enjoyed gazing at her caramel skin. Finally, she smiled at him, a dark veil of anxiety lifting from her face.

"I told you once that as a girl I was this good Muslim child. I loved having faith and believing in spiritual things. I think Uzmeth wanted immortality, some kind of spiritual bliss, but the bad stuff became connected to her search for a higher ground. She reincarnated as a compiler of stories and tried to work out her legacy unsuccessfully. So she returned, or rather I returned, since I'm identifying with the spiritual quest here, as the all-seeing Homma, who cut through all the lust and violence, transcended the cruelty of the world through her childlike nature, and tapped into a vision of immortality, the very thing Uzmeth wanted. I believe the dream was about my interconnected past lives."

Amar yawned. "I guess I can't know for sure. I don't have these visions."

Ooma was newly energized by her realizations. "I had a friend who hypnotized herself. She said it was easy. Let me hypnotize you!" She threw off the blanket.

"It's late. We have a lot on our plate tomorrow. Let's call it a night."

Ooma was crestfallen. "Boss, I can't go back to my room. It's too creepy."

Amar hesitated. "I understand." He took the blanket from her. "I'll sleep on the couch. You take the bed. Good night, Ooma."

Ooma walked to the bed, took off her robe, and pulled back the covers. Then, running back to the couch, she grabbed Amar and pulled him into bed with her.

56

When November arrived, Sahara made several decisions. Bax's emergency recall convinced her to rejoin the group. While Amar was away she felt relaxed about this choice, but on his return she became fearful about sneaking off to a meeting at night. Since the members of the group all had flexible schedules, they agreed to meet during the day while Amar was at work. For the sake of the baby, she requested they meet at her house.

When the group arrived, Sahara fretted about the subterfuge: every water glass ring, rug stain, or out of place pillow screamed out treachery. She begged them to be careful. "Amar's been especially sweet since the trip – but I don't trust it."

Elvi suggested, "Maybe we can rotate the meetings to different places."

"Good, 'cause I'm never coming here again," Zack teased. "Sahara's about to have a heart attack, and I'm afraid to pee."

"Then it's settled," Verle said, "Next meeting's at Zack's."

"Bring your mother," Porcy said. "She can help cook and clean."

"My house?" Zack said heavily. "My mother?"

"You'll all have to volunteer if we rotate," Elvi said. "Let's move on. We need to help Bax deal with these horrible fears."

"I know you went through a traumatic event, Bax," Dr. Machiyoko began, "but I have another perspective. There's an old folk saying, 'You can't cheat Death.' It's exactly what you tried as a wombat. You chose what you thought was an easy life."

"He wasn't trying to trick Death," Sahara said. "He was avoiding another painful demise."

"I just want Bax to think about how he's looking at death in this life. Are you still hiding from it, or are you ready to face it? It's a huge question for you."

"Yes, ma'am," Bax said. "It is."

Bax's humility in the face of the therapist's challenging statement relieved a tension in the room, which Zack expressed. "This is okay, calling someone out on a past life action?"

"It's tricky, but potentially very valuable," Elvi said. "I suggest everyone think about it, and for now we'll take it case by case. Bax, may we continue along these lines?"

"Sure, ma'am. Not like I haven't been thinking about it."

"Excellent," Dr. Machiyoko said. "Here's my question. When psychiatrists use past life regression to heal patients, they often take them to the end of that particular past life, beyond the moment of death, and ask what lesson was learned. Did you learn anything?"

"Not much. I still wanted out of living. Hated it."

"As the old man of the group," Verle said, "I learned a while ago that there's a difference between being mad as hell at life and being ready to move on from it. I've wanted to chuck it plenty of times. Lately I feel that whenever I go is fine. Excepting I'd miss present company, of course."

"You're talking about the difference between rejecting something out of fear and renouncing it," Sahara said, "the

Hindu idea of transcending the cycle of life and death. That's what my vision in the hospital was about."

"You still owe us that recall," Zack said.

"Not now." Elvi wanted to help Bax move forward. "Do you see a lesson here?"

"I was pissed off at Death. And I spat on Life," Bax said. "So Life and Death spat back. Instant karma, right? So I'm still stuck with my fears."

"Yes, we've found an immediate cause for them, but we still don't know what brought you so low when Porcy met you in the interlife."

"Yeah, there's got to be more bad deaths hiding behind the wombat," Zack said.

"I thought you didn't believe in all this stuff," Sahara said, "and now you're ready to be Bax's big reincarnation hunter."

"Jury's still out. But Bax's recall was more convincing as a non-human lifetime."

"As another Doubting Thomas, I have to agree," Verle said. "It was simple and sparse, like I'd expect an animal to be. I could accept some more non-human stories."

"Bax, we need to look for more trauma in your past," Elvi said. "Are you up for it?"

"I guess." Bax sniffed. "It'll hurt again?"

Elvi explained carefully, "I'm going to bring you back to a time when you felt enormous strength. We're going to explore the opposite feeling from fear and weakness."

"Can I do that sometime?" Zack said. "I could use the lift."

"Hush, boy," Verle said, "or you'll be hosting every meeting."

As she put him into trance, Elvi gave Bax the image of his higher self, a spirit guide who was protecting him from further harm. She had him rise up to his guide and be carried to a past time where he was strong and free. The group soon marveled at his description.

The Tale of the Boukh and the Sacred Instrument

Huge bird. Talons like baskets. Hold several boulders. Several humans. Huge wings. Size of fields. Blot out the sun. Cross an ocean in little time.

Hunting for treasures. Fourth gift for Queen Kharanto. Spy oceans and jungles for her. Faraway islands. Look for shine. Listen for shimmer sound. See musical instruments glint under trees. Whole village playing together. I swoop down. Screams. Have my pick. A beautiful one for Queen Kharanto. She will claim as her own. Her own invention. What care I for human ways? My duty to her. My oath.

On sixth return to the Red Isle eleven archers wait for me. Defeat them. I am strong. But never have I had to fight. The Queen ordered them! Corner her after fight. She backs away. Terrified. Stares as if at ghost. Cries out: the Infant Prince! Grasps necklace at her throat. Beads scattered on parapet.

I feel betrayed. Was loyal, tried to be good. Gave up flock for her. Why be good? Wanted to hide. Found a quiet shore. Head in the sand. Body cool in waters. Slept. Recovered strength. Human sailors came to shore. Climbed on me. Thought I was island! My whole life is islands! Flew far from any island. To a new desert. Helped God fight Goddess. Rescue Instrument.

"Sahnra and Ambanari!" Sahara exclaimed. "Bax was the roukh in Amar's desert sky battle."

"Porcy," Elvi asked, "does Bax know about any of the Red Isle stories?"

"No, he came into the qaraq after that. I've never told him."

"So there's no cryptoamnesia here," Sahara said. "None of this information was suggested by us, so where else would it come from but a past life."

Bax continued.

Flew out of desert with Instrument. Vast now. Sea of sand. Came to river. Still desert, but water too. Huge shelters. Big enough for roukh. Shaped like pyramids. Buried Instrument. Nighttime. Dark and safe. Then returned every ten years. Protected Instrument for centuries. Roukh had different time. Lived for many human lifetimes. Long after Queen of Betrayal dead.

Then disaster. Dug up pyramid cache one time. Nothing. Where was Instrument? Who would steal such a thing? Again: why do good for world, if world only returns betrayal and theft? Would not let evils of world weigh me down. Became stronger. Had been too passive. Had abandoned my self. Flew everywhere looking for sacred Instrument. Whole world. More time passed. Went back to where I had first seen it. Jungle island.

Found it in same village! Swooped down again. So happy. It was time to bring back what was lost. Time to forgive the Red Isle. So long ago. Surely a new Queen will receive me. My gift. Open arms. Fly to Red Isle with Instrument. Racing. Vision blurred. Where is palace? Unfamiliar shoreline. Lonely huts. An arrow! Out of nowhere. Through the chest. Another. They still hunt me. Why? Three arrows to the heart! My strength goes. Too much pain. I fall. Drop the Instrument. It falls to shore.

I plunge into ocean. Float like an island for a short time. Barely see the Instrument stuck in sand. Young girl running toward it. May it destroy you. And your wretched Queen. Your wretched, red island. I sink. My red blood stains the waves. Loyalty is folly. Last sight. Red hills in high distance. Helping others folly. Red waves bob. Blur my vision. Action folly. No more. Under. Folly. Done.

ق

Elvi brought Bax back around as Dr. Machiyoko whispered, "Queen D'aulai. I was that girl who found the Instrument, took over the Red Isle, and destroyed it."

"Now we know how the Instrument returned," Verle said. "It's astounding. You've almost all had lives on this red island."

"We still don't know what corruption led to the thefts of the instruments. It was before Queen D'aulai and well after Oumkratania. Maybe it was this Kharanto."

Elvi gave Bax some water. "I thought this lifetime would show you strength to face your fears. But it backfired."

"You got him killed again," Porcy said.

"But the roukh was strong. And devoted," the therapist said. "You're a big, bold, amazing soul, Bax. And we got closer to your fear of death."

"What a brutal path you're on," Sahara said. She felt a rush of empathy. Bax smiled at her, and Sahara saw him in a new light, a mature soul who had suffered great losses.

"Shall we take a break?" Elvi asked. "I think Bax could use one."

As the group rose from their chairs, Sahara thought that she should check on Naji, bring out some more drinks, splash some water on her face. She stood up, deciding what to do first.

She went to Bax and gave him a warm hug.

57

The qaraq lounged comfortably around Sahara's house during the break. She chatted softly with Bax in the kitchen, then went to check on the napping baby. Porcy and Elvi talked about their favorite spiritual books, Zack checked his cell phone for messages, and Verle showed Dr. Machiyoko a collection of leaves he had brought from the churchyard. Delighted by the leaves, she begged one from the grandfatherly man like a child pleading for a toy. When the meeting resumed, she gazed at the patterns of the leaf veins.

At Elvi's request Sahara told the group about her intense and abstract vision in the hospital. She emphasized the manifestation of the number 1001, its significance as a symbol for endless reincarnations, and the frightening prospect of immortality. Since the members usually were busy making the myriad connections between their past lives, they rarely stopped to contemplate the vast and awe-inspiring reality behind it all. Porcy asked if Naji had spoken to Sahara during her hospital revelations. Sahara shared the fragments of Naji's tale about the egg trapped in amber.

As she spoke Dr. Machiyoko continued to inspect the leaf. Zack noticed her rapt focus, the unusual expression on her face. Her head tilted at odd angles.

"Doc, what's up?" Zack asked. The group looked toward the therapist. She opened her mouth several times before she could speak.

"Naji's story. Something in the veins of the leaf. Patterns, like the tree, the bark, the resin. It's important to all of us."

"The woman's psychic just looking at a damn leaf," Porcy said, enviously.

"Tell us what you're seeing," Elvi said.

The Tale of the Compound Eye

Not sure what I'm seeing. It's like you're not there, you, the world, you the veins of leaves, the textures of tree bark, the branches of ferns, the predators scurrying in the forest. But there are hundreds of you. Is it the same you? Yes! The same leaf, refracted in many, many images, all rotated around themselves. Here's a flock of flying things, or one thing flying, multiplied by its many reflections.

What am I? Which of the reflected images out there is not you but me? Am I whatever it is that is making the images, refracting you in this world? What is this world? A world of trees and ferns, flying beings, jungle beasts.

For a moment I see another world, of creatures lined up in vast rows. Watching. Boulders and fighters. Watching with me. Do I sit in one of the rows, or is it me multiplied?

Hey! The view shifted radically, like someone grabbing my head and yanking it back to look at the sky. More flying creatures? A cloud of dust? Whorls blind my vision.

Now the view swings down. Swamp? Riverbank? Many legs, one, two, three –

No more legs. Back to ferns, back to sky, back to swamp. Sun shines down, with clarifying brightness. The view is not only a beautiful kaleidoscopic lens but also a constantly shifting perspective. Confusing, murky, thrilling, obscuring, dazzling, spinning.

– three, four, five legs? They feel like they are under me, a strong, exciting, new feeling of legs under me, gripping, climbing, clinging. I feel a strong attraction to the legs. They are my legs! Not yours, mine. But what am I? I am not you, so beautifully quintupled and clouded over. I am the eye of this vision, the center of these reflections. I want to bask in these wonderful visions of the world.

I love my legs, love the feeling of landing on my feet. Then popping into the air, through the swamp. When I land back on my feet, it gets dim, fewer eye-echoes, more clouds. Then still. Nighttime. Just watch the legs on the bank, so dim, like one eye closing.

ق

Dr. Machiyoko slowly opened her eyes and squinted at the light. "That was something. Like I could see 360 degrees around me all at once. Where was I?"

"A swamp region, but you weren't aware of a time period," Elvi said "What kind of creature has such dazzling vision?" the therapist wondered.

"A bug," Verle said.

The therapist's movement stopped. "A bug?"

"Compound eyes. You've all seen it. Insects see multiple images at once."

378

"But her view kept shifting up, down, sideways. Is that the same?" Sahara asked.

"I did feel like I could see everywhere, except towards my left side."

Sahara sized up the therapist. "With every vision you described, the very act of seeing lit up your face with enormous pleasure."

Dr. Machiyoko squirmed in her chair. "Really? Did I –"

"Doctor, you said this was important to the group," Elvi said. "Do you know why?"

The therapist leaned forward in thought. "I received the images when Sahara was talking about Naji and the egg. I must have linked them to my recall and thought the whole group might be connected to it."

"Did anyone else feel connected to the egg tale or the insect tale?" Elvi asked.

"Why are you looking at me?" Zack asked Elvi.

"You were the first to notice Dr. Machiyoko's strange behavior."

The therapist peered at Zack. "What aren't you telling us?"

"It's probably nothing. Maybe we should move on."

"Zackie..." Porcy growled.

"All right, all right. I felt something while the Doc was talking. And now that we've discussed her recall, I know what it was." In a stage whisper, he said, "I was a bug, too."

58

"You were in that world, too?" Dr. Machiyoko said to Zack. "What is it?"

"Search me," Zack said. "I was watching you do those twitchy things before you even started your recall, and I got a quickie déjà that I had flitted around like that once."

"We should hypnotize the boy, find out more," Verle suggested.

"Why don't we call it a night?" Zack said. "Isn't that Naji crying? Meeting adjourned."

Elvi chuckled. "Zack, no one is going to force you to be hypnotized. But it would be nice to get more information about Diana's recall."

"I've never been regressed," Zack said. "Repressed, yes, regressed, no."

"I did it," Bax said, "and I was scared shitless."

"You can do this," Sahara said. "I insist."

Zack closed his eyes and took a deep breath. "Okay, Elve. Do me."

The Tale of the Winged Insect

It's like a weird drug, you're made out of veins and they're all lit up. The rest of your body is transparent, catching light, catching wind. Hold on! A million miles an hour, that's what it feels like, on your skin, and veins, vibrating so fast you can't tell they're vibrating.

(Hang in there, Zack thought. I'm shaking like a leaf. Just go with it.)

What a feeling – speed, lightness, light – a roller coaster feeling, up, down, down, jammed over there, up, back. You've got it now, on top of it, going for the ride.

(Oh my God, this is turning me on! How embarrassing. I'm getting hard. Are they looking?)

What a ride! Spread your wings, feel that sun, the only way to know where up is. So many turns, dives, spins, turns. Keep it pumping pumping. Something's holding you together, telling you where to go, keeping an eye out, or a hundred eyes, able to steer in any direction in a heartbeat, in a flutter, a hundred flutters every heartbeat. So fast, so free, like a prisoner being released into the arms of a lover!

(I can't stand it! I'm so hot. Don't touch it! Can they tell? Do you care anymore?)

Can't get enough of this. Don't look back, or watch your back, let them do what they want behind you. The right hand doesn't know what the right hand's doing. Things whipping by you in flashes. Flashes that have raced by before. Can't nod off for a second. Don't let go. What is letting go? Does it mean give up or go for it? Let fly!

(I'm going to let fly! It feels too good. I can't help myself. Too hard, too soon, too hot, too easy. I've got to get a boyfriend.)

381

Come down! What a trip, what a high. Higher! Down! Coming down. Time to rest. To stop. Only for a little while. Want to be back up – right away!

(Done. The shaking is going away. I didn't know these recalls could be so intense. Is the wet spot visible?)

ق

"That's it? You're done with me?" Zack grabbed his journal and placed it over his lap. "Just need to jot down a few notes."

"Where were you?" Dr. Machiyoko asked, unsure if anything had been clarified.

Zack made a show of finishing a sentence in the journal before he answered. "I didn't see much, so I'm not sure where the place was. Everything was fast, shifting like in your recall. It was about the speed, the physical sensation, not the visual."

"What was the physical sensation?" Elvi asked.

Zack was embarrassed by the question, but he covered it up by a show of intense contemplation. "It was like a motor, a whirring, a fluttering, a beating of ... wings. Wings, that's it! Since I felt connected to the Doc's bug, I must have been a flying insect."

"The constant shifting of perspective and ups and downs are common to both recalls," Elvi said. "That certainly could indicate flight, changing directions in midair."

"But Zack didn't have the multiple vision I had," Dr. Machiyoko asked.

"And you remembered a stillness," Zack joined in, "but I was constantly flying."

"You were free, Zackie," Porcy exclaimed. "Letting go is freedom. You've let go of so much this life: Paris, your music career, traveling constantly, which is flight itself."

382

"In any event," Elvi said, "we have a flying insect on our hands. I welcome anyone to explore their connection to these lifetimes on their own. We should stop."

"You're right! Amar could be on the next train," Sahara said. "Everyone out!" As the group cleaned up impeccably, Elvi went to Bax to make sure he was all right. Porcy offered Verle help getting back to the church. Zack slipped into the bathroom.

As the members left, Sahara asked Dr. Machiyoko to stay a minute. Her therapy session was the next day and she wanted to raise an issue in advance. Amar had been asking her questions about the Nights and various numbers, which she described to the therapist. Sahara was unsure how to handle her husband: if she avoided these conversations she lost out on positive contact with him; if she got wrapped up in his queries she might divulge something about a recent meeting or recall – forbidden fruit.

What should she do?

383

59

The next day Dr. Machiyoko was on her third large cappuccino when Sahara arrived for her session. She had circles under her eyes and kept stifling yawns.

"Sorry. Been up all night working on your number problem. You're going to be surprised."

"About what to say to Amar?" Sahara asked.

"No. You may not find that as significant as what I've discovered."

"But isn't it odd that Amar has been asking about sevens, elevens, and thirteens since he got back from his trip with Ooma?"

"Perhaps," the therapist said. "But didn't you say you were less concerned about Amar's reactions than about your relationship with him over vast amounts of time?"

"Yes, but what does –"

"Then let go of your fear of him." Dr. Machiyoko's tiredness made her impatient with Sahara's anxiety. "I've always encouraged you to share things with him. That's key in healing the relationship. So what if a bit of a recall slips out?"

"I don't want to jeopardize the group by –"

"We'll deal with that if we have to. We're the qaraq!" Dr. Machiyoko took a long sip of her coffee. "Now, I can't wait to tell about my research last night. I started with a couple numerology books and looked up fun facts about sevens, elevens, and thirteens."

"You mean like seven and thirteen are about good and bad luck?"

"That kind of thing, but also Kabbalistic processes. Here's the work I did on the other recurring number, 379." Diana showed Sahara a piece of paper with various figures on it. "In Kabbalah you add up all the digits of a number. So I added up the digits of 379:"

$$379 - 3 + 7 + 9 = 19$$

"The sum is nineteen. But you want to reduce the sum to a single number, so I added the digits in nineteen together:"

$$19 - 1 + 9 = 10$$

"The number ten still has two digits, so I added them together:"

$$10 - 1 + 0 = 1$$

"What's the significance of the single number at the end?" Sahara asked. "What does it mean that 379 can be reduced to the number one?"

"Lots of meanings," the therapist answered. "Power, ambition, obvious ones like unity, uniqueness. But nothing set off sparks for me. How about you?"

"No. I still think 379 is a historical date. Amar says the numbers are connected to the creation of the Nights, which nobody really knows anything about. 379 A.D. in Persia was in the middle of a weak period of Sassanid rule. A perfect time for our friends Uzmeth, Ardryashir, and Shah Zabar to be wreaking havoc inside the Empire."

"But they were the historical precursors of the Scheherazade characters, so they couldn't have created the Nights?" Dr. Machiyoko said. "What about 379 B.C.?"

"There were story cycles being developed in India back then, which are some of the oldest sources for *The Thousand and One Nights.* But Amar specifically asked me about the creation of the Nights as a book, meaning a written version of the story collection. The ancient Indian stories spread to Persia and Arabia by oral transmission. The date eludes me."

"And the numerological meanings eluded me. But in a good way," Dr. Machiyoko said. "I was up till three in the morning poring over this stuff. I kept reading and reading, and looking at numbers, until I got sucked into this strange, mystical mindset. As I stared at the words and figures, it was as if my own voice, but with some unrecognizable foreign dialect, was speaking to someone. The voice brought me into a new world.

The Tale of the Four Encoded Versions

I find your latest document deeply disturbing, Ccycch, if only in its limited viewpoint. I will not sweeten my words to you, since clearly you feel that I, your subordinate, Mmymch, Kr., am unimportant in the scheme of things. But you have no idea what the scheme of things encompasses. Yes, you are my elder, and I should respect you, despite your reputation as a conniving gossip. But DUHG's bio-circuitry has been updated:

the system can now hunt down items from the last eight universes! What miniscule meaning does elder status have in the face of such magnitude? And what meaning does respect have in light of your recent scandal with the underage assistant?

I embrace the work of the Inventor. The network created by DUHG's search capacity is a miracle. Sometimes I think I am the only one culling the mountain of mythflow left by the Inventor from the previous cosmos. I am not (as you whisper behind my back) dependent on her, sweeping up her tale pieces. I no longer care which administrator you're fondling, Ccycch, I won't be victim of your conspiracies. I embrace all our resources at Aleksanjra Datatheke, every timeload from DUHG, every application of the Alphorythm.

And I embrace my deepest responsibility: to encode every hidden structure in the data until I have the biggest picture. Then I will be like a munificent royal, sitting atop her private spectator's box, taking in her people and their sport in the Stadium. I take in the innumerable compilations and structural connections of the myths. Just as the Stadium is a metacode for all the work done on the myths, so the Versions of the myths are a metacode for the limitlessness of the soul's creativity.

Therefore, Ccycch, your limitations are painfully obvious, your mandates outdated, your structural analyses two universes old. If the Encoding Project is to be fully realized, if a unified, integrated Version of the mythflow collections is to be created, a massive reorganization of the Project must occur. If you don't do it, I will take it off your hands the way you took him off mine.

Here's where you should start, if you aren't too busy with my ex. During the last universe DUHG found an ancient version of the texts, The Rabyon Nhiih. We already had a different text, deriving from more recent times, known only as

Version 4-X2. It is now clear that the two texts are related. The Rabyon Nhiih, an Ur form of the Version 3 collections, can be called Version 2 (Version 1 being a mythical 'original' version).

It has been understood for a long time that all Versions utilize a continuous frame tale to contain their stories. The more recent discovery that the frame tale of The Rabyon Nhiih, the story of Sheruzat and her King, turns up in nuclear bits throughout Version 4-X2's frame tale is truly astonishing. Following that lead, researchers are finding bits of The Rabyon Nhiih stories in Version 4-X2's tales.

To give an example, in the fifty-ninth chapter of Version 4-X2 appears this reference: seven islands, each with a mountain, each mountain having eleven trees growing on its slopes, and each tree with thirteen heads hanging from its branches. A gruesome image, but easily tracked down in The Rabyon Nhiih, although there is only one island of seven with trees and heads, and no mention of eleven or thirteen (sly old DUHG obviously slipped in The Alphorythm in the 4-X2 version).

This structural interface between the Versions is fascinating, and yet you have squelched the research efforts to explore it time and time again. You have rejected half of my grants, claiming that 'the methodologies of Mmymch, Kr. are heretically unorthodox.' Heretically? Does that old-fashioned word go along with those leather costumes I found in your locker? Is that how you stole him away? If he likes that sort of thing, good riddance!

There are excellent projects going on at lower research levels, which have been waiting to be funded or flagged ahead by you for months. Much work has been done on the soul-characters of Version 4-X2 and their identifying traits. But what about this idea of their glimpses into past lives? How does a set of one hundred and eleven glimpses repeat itself? Exactly?

Randomly? Palindromically? New research shows that the stories of Version 4-X2 consist of pairs of lifetimes, enchained in a karmic rotation scheme that obeys its own Alphorythm. But what about the latest theory, that the karmic pairs are ordered in a design akin to Rabyon fabric or crosslog puzzles?

Finally, Ccycch, you and I are among the few people aware of the latest find: a text that may actually be the Version 1 collection, which was translated into numerical code and passed along through time and space in the universes. Wherever it 'landed' the code influenced the development of that world's cultural progress. Thus numbers preceded and influenced symbologies, mythologies and literatures of many cultures.

Astounding, all astounding! Will you do anything to encourage these brilliant ideas, Ccycch? Of course not, you will discourage and even block most of the research. Why do I hurl these criticisms at you without fear of retribution? Is it the blindness of jealous vengeance? No, I have shared all this with our superiors (including the embezzling). Your tenure as Director of Research is over. They have agreed to your removal by end of day.

Happy landings!

ق

"So either I was hallucinating from sleep deprivation, or this is extraordinary."

"Both, I think," Sahara said. "But it's too bizarre and dense to be just a fantasy."

"Where do you think it comes from?"

"It's not from any past time we know about. And yet this DUHG thing is digging up stuff from the past with some highly evolved information technology."

"Like a super-computer beyond our dreams? Is this a vision of the future?"

"My God," Sahara said very quietly, "you've had a precognition of a future lifetime."

"Told you I was psychic. Damn!" The two sat in silence, letting the idea sink in.

Finally Sahara spoke. "You know what else is amazing? This Rabyon Nhiih, is a collection of stories broken up into chunks, called Nhiih. Ring a bell?"

"The Nights? The Nhiih are the Nights?"

"And Rabyon is Arabian, as in Arabian Nights, and the mention of Rabyon fabric 'structure' could be an Arabian carpet, which has a complex formal design."

"The frame tale of The Rabyon Nhiih is the story of Sheruzat – Scheherazade."

"You got it, Doc. It's the remnants of the Nights as seen from deep in the future. You foresaw a future civilization doing some serious cultural-anthropological study of it. But how could the Nights survive so long, bridge the creation of new universes?"

Dr. Machiyoko yawned. "I just poured this thing out. You expect me to understand it, too? I was searching for numbers."

"There was that Alphorythm which related to seven, eleven, and thirteen."

"Right! In the story with the seven islands. Do you recognize it from the Nights?"

"The heads on trees sound familiar." Sahara thought a moment. "Yes, it's from 'Hassan of Basra,' the part of his quest where he visits the islands of Wac."

Dr. Machiyoko tried out the name. "The islands of Wac. That's for sure. The whole thing's crazy, down to the jealous rivalry between the two researchers."

"And the past lives! There were structures about karma!"

"Was that cryptoamnesia?" Dr. Machiyoko wondered. "But how would I have gotten all those structures in my brain? A hundred and eleven glimpses – what is that? None of it explains how the numbers relate to the creation of the Nights." Dr. Machiyoko let out a tired sigh. "I failed in my quest. I could have spouted out times tables about the future for all the good it did. Seven times eleven equals seventy-seven stories! Seven times thirteen equals ninety-one déjà vus! Ta da! The key to the universe!"

In spite of the therapist's slaphappy outburst, Sahara got very serious. Furrowing her brow, she worked out a problem. "Seven times eleven times thirteen. Do the math."

Dr. Machiyoko scribbled on her desk blotter. "Oh my God."

Sahara looked at the therapist in wonder. "The key to the universe, apparently."

Dr. Machiyoko said the answer aloud:

"A thousand and one."

60

—◦/◦/◦—

After weeks of silence, Naji shared a new lifetime with his mother.

The Tale of Sahnra and the Instrument Trader

There once was a clever fellow named Zananzi, who traveled up and down the eastern coast of Africa, selling wares and items of interest. One year a set of wondrous musical instruments came into his possession, from the Red Isle, the large landmass that lay across the water from where his tribe lived. Among the bronze instruments was a beautiful xylophone with a shimmering tone, which had been worshipped by the islanders simply as the Instrument. Zananzi had an artisan study the designs and create replicas that he could trade. He could not afford everything to be made of bronze, so the replicas were carved from wood. The sound was not shimmering, but nonetheless pleasant and attractive to the ear. Zananzi brought along the Instrument and other bronze originals to entice his traders.

Zananzi loved traveling from beach to beach under the blue sky and near the blue waters of the sea. Each new village marveled at the instruments and soon Zananzi ran out of his goods. He returned home, surprised his family and friends with his good fortune, and made three more successful expeditions.

Zananzi had heard of trade routes to the northern part of the continent, and beyond the sea to foreign desert lands, so he arranged for a caravan to take his goods across the savannah toward Egypt. Along the way, Zananzi saw poor and struggling villages and grassland drying up from the desperate cultivation of it. In Egypt Zananzi bargained with Arab traders and exchanged his wooden instruments for fine goods.

One Arab merchant invited Zananzi to sail to his home in Tyre, where they enjoyed the harbors, the gardens, and the women of that culture. He promised himself to a beautiful daughter of the merchant, but asked to return to his homeland to bring back the largest collection of instruments yet. As a token of good faith, he gave his bride-to-be one of the bronze xylophones, although he made sure to keep the original Instrument in his own possession.

Zananzi was excited by his entry into the world of Asia Minor. He retraced his steps back to his homeland, prepared his large shipment, and promised family and friends that he would return with his new bride. After trading the heavier items along the coast, Zananzi moved inland to take stock of his merchandise and the precious bronze originals, and prepared the caravan for the trip across the arid grasslands.

The night before departure, Zananzi heard a strange rustling sound outside his tent, as if the wind itself was speaking.

When he got up to secure the rustling tent flap, a gust of wind opened the tent wide. To his amazement, a woman in a white robe stood outside the tent. The wind whirled around her, blowing the veils around her face.

She spoke in fury. "I am Sahnra, seventh incarnation of the Goddess of the Red Isle. I have searched for you, and have had to journey to this forsaken place to find you."

Zananzi's throat clenched in fear at the sound of the Goddess. He knelt low to the ground with the tent flap still whipping around him. "What possible cause could bring your great Being in search of this humble, undeserving trader?"

"I have come with a terrible vengeance to wreak upon your head."

"Please, Goddess, which of my unspeakable transgressions has affronted you?"

"You make a convincing show of modesty, but it does not speak well that you are oblivious to your crime. Have you not had in your possession, to your great advantage this many years, the sacred Instrument of my worshippers?"

Zananzi relaxed slightly and sat back on his haunches. "If you are saying, merciful Goddess, that your worshippers created this Instrument, then I am a common criminal. But this Instrument was fashioned neither on the Red Isle nor on the shores of my own people, the Zanj. The Instrument has an ancient luster that dates back to our common ancestors from a faraway jungle island across the sea. I assumed you knew of its great antiquity, since you are all-Seeing and all-Knowing."

Zananzi was treading on fragile ground now. Sahnra was well aware of the origin of the Instrument. She had already put up with one haughty thief who informed her of the deceptive beliefs of the Red Islanders. She acknowledged that this man showed infinitely more respect. Perhaps her harsh treatment of that earlier thief had become known to the Zanj, the people of the mainland, and had softened this wretch's soul.

Despite Zananzi's deference, Sahnra was not pleased. "How dare you pretend to the Truth, to the true origins of things, and use them to justify your wealth and success. All you have done is pollute the sacred purpose of the Instrument by making cheap imitations and spreading them far and wide."

As she spoke the wind caused the tent flaps to swat the trader in the face. "Please, Goddess, if you will not spare me, think of all the innocents under my care in the caravan."

Sahnra was through sparring with him. Deep inside her soul was a dried up core, shriveled from past catastrophe. The Goddess raised her arms high overhead to release the burning rawness of her spirit. The desert sand spun around them. The tent flaps corkscrewed around Zananzi's torso, held him firmly in place, and lifted him off the ground. Hot funnels blew throughout the caravan tents. Animals and equipment wheeled up into the air. The bronze instruments joined the Goddess' new form as a windstorm.

Sahnra thought of the generations of desperate farmers who had overworked the lands. Monstrous cyclones pulled up every last blade of grass, spreading their destruction northward toward the Nile, laying down an arid barrier between the southern and northern ends of the continent. She thought of her dried soul. The winds ground everything into a fine sand that covered all of North Africa and became known as the Sahra, the Great Desert.

Sahnra lifted her beloved, endangered bronze artifacts still spinning in the sky and gently settled them on the desert floor, burrowing them into the sand for protection. As for the little trader, a self-deluded innocent who had shown her respect, Sahnra felt a deep remorse that she had treated the poor soul so harshly. The last twister spat forth Zananzi, exhausted, shocked, and naked to the blistering sun, and the wind gently set him down miles from the Instrument and much closer to the shoreline.

Zananzi crawled as fast as his weakened body allowed, unsure in which direction the coast lay. He welcomed night-fall, but realized it was still daytime, and that the sun had been blotted out by some object overhead. It was an enormous bird, scouting the desert for some prey below. Was Zananzi really looking at the gargantuan roukh of legend? For an instant Zananzi panicked, fearing to be picked apart by this hungry monster. But the forceful sandstorm blew the bird off its course and it disappeared.

A bank of clouds moved in unnaturally fast and seemed to counteract the winds. Zananzi thought he perceived in the shape of the clouds the enormous head of a man, shouting at the sandstorm assailing him. Was Zananzi witnessing a mythic fight between the Goddess and some divinity in the form of a cloud?

Then an even more unbelievable sight appeared. A full-grown elephant came flying across the sky, head-ing directly for the Goddess' sandstorm. The roukh had returned to defend the cloud-God-head, bearing a half-dozen elephants in his claws. Sahnra and the roukh hurled the elephants back and forth at each other like children playing kill-ball. Zananzi mused on how his lowly form observed the mighty forces battle it out from a safe dis-tance. He had the odd feeling that he had done a similar thing before.

Then he thought: all of North Africa has to pay the price for the Goddess' anger, and now the Gods are using these peace-ful beasts for ammunition! And I was punished for desecrat-ing a xylophone! He was furious at the Goddess' treatment of him, Africa, elephants! He would survive this peril; that would be his revenge upon her! Zananzi turned away from the stormy skies, and continued crawling out of the Sahra.

ق

Amar sat down quietly across from his wife and son in the nursery. "Sahr," he whispered. Could she be napping, her eyes open? He spoke louder, "Where are you?"

Sahara shifted her head. "Desert," she said, barely audible.

Amar clapped his hands and Sahara awoke, facing her husband. Instinctively, she caressed Naji's head, satisfied herself that he was safely asleep. "You're home early." She rose from the glider and placed the sleeping baby in his cradle.

"Nice surprise, huh?" he said with sarcastic bite.

Still groggy from the trance, Sahara sat back down in the glider. She did not want to do this now. It hurt to think straight.

"Were you doing that trance thing with Naji? How could you endanger our child?"

"Dr. Machiyoko says it's natural. The baby's an open vessel to the interlife world, having just been there. It's not harmful."

"What about your promise? You deceived me. It's like sleeping with another man."

Sahara could not return his intense stare. He was more right than he realized. She had been thinking about Bax, his lifetime as the huge roukh, the desert battle. It had led to Naji's story as the African trader, but it had started with her fascination with Bax.

Sahara knew she had to tell some of the truth. "Amar, I can't just stop it. The baby spoke to me. It's not like I sit home doing recalls with him every day. This was the first time since he was born, I swear. And it worked, Amar, it's amazing! I

397

don't want to hide these things, I want to share so much, about Naji, about you and me!"

Sahara's passionate sincerity tugged at Amar. He softened but he could not relent, not yet. "I have to trust you as a mother that you mean no harm to the baby. And I believe you can't control this connection. But it's still a betrayal."

Sahara thought of the group and all the stories she had not told him. She thought of Cachay's uncanny probing into the Nights, of all the women killed by King Shahryar, of his Queen who deceived him so terribly. Sahara felt like every one of those women, the deceivers, the victims, the redeemer Scheherazade. Could she redeem this situation?

"Amar, if I tell you what I learned from Naji, will you stay calm?"

The promise of a new tale tempted Amar. He thought of the recall Ooma had shared with him, his own deceit. He cradled his face in his hands. "Can't I just come home from work to a nice meal and a peck on the cheek like the rest of the schmucks on the train?"

Sahara rose from the glider and kissed him. "Come into the kitchen and hear Naji's tale while I make that nice meal."

When Sahara was done telling the story, dinner was on the table and the baby was awake, fed, and lying quietly near the dining room. Amar took in the new tale. "So you think this is the horrible action you did to Naji as Sahnra?"

"You don't think so?" Sahara said. "Sahnra destroyed his caravan of goods, left him for dead in a desert. She ravaged an entire ecosystem!"

"The Sahara desert, your namesake, where you were born. I'm either supposed to think: A) Wow! It's so karmic! This traumatic interaction between mother and child to this day defines your nature, your very name; or B) Isn't it a bit too cutesy for Sahara to be creating the Sahara, isn't that

398

a perfect example of known facts weaving a subconscious story?"

"You think it's all in my imagination?"

"God forbid I should come out and just state that, for fear you'd turn into a tornado and sack our home before dessert. Ecosystem aside, what you did to Zananzi wasn't unspeakable. You spared his life. You acknowledged that he was more polite than the first thief, the one on the beach. I think you spared Zananzi because you had already done the unspeakable. I think you're letting yourself off the hook about the first thief." Amar triumphantly scooped a forkful of rice into his mouth.

"Maybe you're right," Sahara admitted. "Maybe I'm blocking the thief out."

"And it's taken mindmelding with the culprit himself," Amar gestured over to the gurgling baby, "to shove the truth back in your face."

"Ooo, he said the truth, Naji, hear that? Daddy's coming around! Is it so hard to believe, you and me up in the sky, mythically knocking the wind out of each other, tossing elephants like flying plates, fighting over something brought on by our child? Familiar?"

"Yeah, especially the elephants."

"Excuse me?" Sahara held her fork in midair.

Amar had slipped. He had relaxed about his recall with Ooma. He tried to cover. "That date I mentioned? Were there elephants in Baghdad then?"

"Baghdad? Not one of the usual elephant hangouts." She saw Amar avoid her gaze. "This is from a recall, isn't it?" Sahara probed. "Want to tell me something?"

Amar continued to eat, not looking at her.

"You're ready to kill me for sneaking a recall in my own home, and you're off with – " Sahara gasped in revelation

– "with Ooma, right? Who else? On the trip! Okay, I won't be jealous. I won't insert your cock in the microwave. Don't listen to Mommy, Naji. No, the information, even from Ooma, is more important to me. But when you withhold information, on top of forbidding my own recalls ..." Sahara exhaled. "You want to call it even?"

Amar looked up from his plate. He was delighted with the compromise. He made a show of thinking it through with difficulty, then said, "It's only fair."

"Fine," Sahara said, and went to get dessert. "So, out with it."

Amar recounted the tale of the origin of the Nights, but confessed nothing about Ooma's visit to his bedroom. Sahara was disturbed by the correspondences between Ooma's dream and her own vision in the hospital. There too numbers had haunted Sahara; there too Sahara had seen into the endlessness of Time, just as Homma the elephant had. Sahara had told Amar nothing of this, and she was too worn down to broach it now.

"We're not doing so bad, are we?" she said. "We vaporized each other across the skies of Africa, wiped out whole agrarian societies. And here we are – troubled and argumentative, no doubt – but duking it out in comfort over butterscotch mousse."

He loved his wife's moments of perspective. "By God, my misfortune is nothing compared to Ambanari's, to your brother's past life." He looked over at the gurgling Naji. "Or compared to this one's terrible demise as the thief."

They had earned a moment of peace by their mutual confessions. With great feeling for her husband, Sahara said, "Thank you for staying open, because the past lives are keeping us together."

And possibly breaking us up for good, Sahara thought.

61

The Tale of the Unborn (continued)

Would I want to grow up in a world like this? Look at the pathetic bug trapped over there. Is this the great adult life I could have if I wasn't stuck myself? And yet to be free, to swim, to fly... Let me out of here! I do want a life, a birth, and a childhood. I don't want to be wet behind the ears forever. I'll never sprout wings without a metamorphosing adulthood.

I've been inside this thing for so long I can't remember. Lately it's been breaking apart. Dripping. Now I'm one of the drips. I'm dripping, I'm falling from high above, from the tree. I hit many leaves and branches, which break my fall. Down I go until I gently plop into the water. I am tiny, practically invisible. I float for days, weeks, bits of the drippy goop around me washing away. Then I hit something else sticky, a globule, a cluster, a raft of eggs. I am home. I latch on, float with my family in the blissful water.

Naji? We're back to the egg story?
It's almost over.
Are you all right? I'm sorry about your father.
It's okay, Momma. It's hard for Poppa. It's hard to under-
stand the lifetimes.
Naji, how can a baby be so wise?
Not for long, Momma. Not for long.

Following Porcy's advice, Zack asked his mother to host
the next qaraq meeting at his house. Not wanting to get
entangled in her aggressive control of things, he conven-
iently scheduled a buying trip for himself. Cachay confronted
Zack about leaving her alone with the bizarre group and
insisted he give her some idea of the proceedings. When
he described some of the recent recalls she became very
interested in the Red Isle, relieved that she could participate
in some way. Unsure what she meant but satisfied that his
mother would help out, Zack went on his trip and the meeting took place.

On his return Zack attended the next meeting, which took
place at Dr. Machiyoko's office. As he came in, he told the
group, "My mother won't talk to me about last week. What happened? What'd you do to her? Did you videotape it for me?"

"Woulda helped, 'cause now we gotta catch you up," Verle
said. And with that, the group described the previous week's
meeting to Zack.

The meeting began with Sahara recounting the harrowing
encounter between Zananzi and Sahnra in the desert. She had
told Zack the tale before he left on his trip, and in turn he had
told his mother. As Cachay brought trays of cheese and fruit
from the kitchen, she interrupted Sahara several times to correct her. On finishing, Sahara expressed regret.

"I wiped out an entire way of life for the people of North Africa, just to take a musical instrument from my child's soul." She looked at Naji, sleeping on Zack's numerous throw pillows. "Imagine when he's shaking a rattle – I might kill him."

"Don't judge yourself," Dr. Machiyoko said. "You've never suffered anything as terrible as that in this life."

"It's all nonsense," Cachay said. "The Sahara formed over thousands of years."

The group tensed. "How do you know this, woman?" Verle asked Cachay.

"I studied the economies of developing countries in business school. Got real interested in Africa, so I learned all I could. The Red Isle is obviously Madagascar."

"Obviously?" the old man said. "We've been chewing on that one for months!"

"With elephants being tossed around you're either in Africa or India," she expounded. "Egypt and the Sahara settle that argument. Bottom line? The 'Red Island' is the nickname for Madagascar, fourth largest island in the world."

Testing her, Verle asked, "Why's it called the Red Island?"

"Color of the soil, from volcanic earth in the central mountains. You all got another problem with your story. Xylophones are all over Africa, like the Chopi in Mozambique, right across the water from the island. But there's no xylophone culture on Madagascar."

As Cachay went back into the kitchen, Sahara said, "Your son's story ended with Zancq escaping to Africa with the *last* xylophone from the Red Isle. That could explain it."

"We still don't understand the corruption that Zananzi was fighting against," Elvi said.

"Was it just Queen Oumkratania wanting glory for herself?" Porcy asked. "She passed off the Instrument as her own creation, but it came from somewhere else."

"Cultures steal from each other all the time," Verle said. "Bet it's more complicated."

The group got quiet, momentarily stumped. Cachay returned with tea and began pouring out mugs. "It was all Queen Kharanto's fault." The group looked at her quizzically. "When Zack told me about your Red Isle, I remembered I'd kept a journal when I was studying African nations. I dug it out and found some awful strange entries, all about this Queen Kharanto. Don't know why I wrote them, and never wanted to share them before."

"This is the perfect time," Elvi said. "It must be why you're here today."

Cachay finished pouring and brought the journal to the group. "Tea is served."

The Tale of the Corrupt Queen

Journal, Chicago. Oct 12.

Strange daydream. A huge palace on a cliffside of an island, overlooking a harbor and a town. In the fortress, the Queen spent all of her time in the Keep, afraid to go outdoors, even to cross the courtyard and enter the sanctuary, for fear of assassination. She was furious that the power established by her noble ancestor had been undermined. Now the people worshiped the Gong Ageng and its priestess caste, and looked upon any Queen as mere figurehead. All day and all night the Queen was haunted by the chants and bells rising from the sanctuary because she could not override the Gong's power over the monarchy.

She would have to embrace the Instrument.

She had her counselors 'make the discovery' of an ancient text that revealed all Queens as holy descendants of the original

Goddess. Since the current Goddess of the Instrument was called Kharanto, the Queen changed her name and proclaimed that she, Queen Kharanto, was divine overseer of the priestesses and the Gong Ageng.

Happily walking the short distance between the Keep and sanctuary, Queen Kharanto reveled that she had just created a legacy beyond her lifetime. She had assumed the power and glory of her beloved ancestor Oumkratania.

Nov. 15. New palace info.

Queen Kharanto needed to create a great new work to solidify her legacy as Goddess-Inventor. She organized a system that pushed the priestesses to invent new creations for the queendom. The tightness of the work schedule kept the priestess caste too busy to challenge the Queen's new powers.

One day Queen Kharanto stood on the lookout parapet with its 360-degree view of the eastern shoreline of the island, the nearby cliffs, and the inland plateau. The lookout stretched along the length of the Keep, since it was designed to house a platoon of archers. As the Queen admired the unique red soil of the central lands, a massive black shape neared in the sky: a flock of the enormous birds migrating north to the Red Isle. To her surprise, one of the gigantic creatures alighted on the lookout, wings spanning half its length.

"I salute you, great Queen," the roukh began, startling Queen Kharanto with the sound of its majestic voice. "Be not afraid. My kind has been allies of your people since Queen Oumkratania. Are you her fair sister?"

"I am her descendant, seven generations hence."

"That is a fleeting moment to us roukhs, who live hundreds of years. Your name?"

"I am Queen Kharanto, Goddess-Queen, preserver of the great Gong Ageng."

"My father brought that noble Instrument from over the sea to Oumkratania."

"Where did your father get the great Gong?"

"There is a series of great islands to the east, even vaster than your domain, which contain a great many treasures." The roukh continued to describe countless wonders to the Queen. The loyal creature was impressionable, and in no time the Queen had secured a promise to bring her back a new Instrument as worthy and powerful as the great Gong.

After the roukh returned with the flock, Queen Kharanto presented two new Instruments to her people. They were considerably smaller than the Gong Ageng, but soon the worshippers wanted only to hear the Twin Sounds. Unlike the undifferentiated noise of the single Gong stroke, the new double bronze kettles actually made musical rhythms and phrases. The Gong was retired as a sacred relic. Knowing nothing of the roukh's gift, only that magical creatures visited their divine Queen, the Red Isle inhabitants worshipped Queen Kharanto as a great Creator. The priestesses became her servants, no longer entrusted with the protection of the Instrument sanctuary. The security of the sanctuary and the Queen-Goddess was now the duty of highly disciplined guards, whose fierceness still did not dispel Kharanto's lingering anxiety about leaving the fortress grounds.

The steadfast roukh returned to the island many times, always bearing in its claws a new, unusual musical instrument from the distant islands. Queen Kharanto acquired various bells, kettles, smaller gongs, and xylophones. She hoarded these, not wanting to dilute the power of the new twin instruments. There would come a time when she, or one of her descendants, would need a unique 'invention' to add to the sacred Instrumentarium.

She had secured the future for the Queens of the Red Isle.

"So Queen Oumkratania started the treachery, but Kharanto continued using the roukh to trick her realm into submitting to the false Queen-Goddesses," Sahara said.

"Bax, my lad," Verle inquired, "in your memory as the roukh, did you envision these great islands where you got the instruments?"

"When I flew I saw many shapes below. Where I landed was like an octopus."

"Sulawesi! An island with tentacle-like peninsulas. I thought it might be Indonesia."

"This makes sense," Dr. Machiyoko said. "The Indonesians have the gamelan, an orchestra made of bronze xylophones, pots, and gongs. I saw a gamelan in Berkeley. The musicians sat across from each other and played amazing rhythms, like in Zack's tale."

"The supreme spiritual instrument of Indonesia is the Gong Ageng, just like on the Red Isle," Verle said. "Its sound symbolizes cosmic time changes."

"So I flew the instruments all the way from Indonesia to Africa?" Bax wondered.

"Across the Indian Ocean. Cachay, when was the Sahara desert finished?"

Cachay pondered as she poured second cups of tea. "Around 1500 B.C."

"So if that's when Sahnra was around, Kharanto and Oumkratania lived centuries before, in the Bronze Age, when the Indonesians started making their instruments. Some anthropologists say that at that time Indonesian traders boated all the way to Africa."

Sahara said, "Zananzi told Sahnra that the instruments came from far away islands."

"It's uncanny," Verle said. "There are things common only to Indonesia and southeast Africa, like yams and vanilla plants."

"And instruments, in the past," Elvi said. "Please continue your story, Cachay."

New Years. Another Queen fantasy.

Queen Kharanto trained the new priestesses, oversaw the best new voices, and enjoyed the chants that previously had driven her mad. One evening the Queen was struck by the sweetest sound coming from one of her acolytes in the sanctuary. So taken was she by the singing that she ordered a guard to fetch the girl and bring her to the lookout. It was a beautiful spring twilight, and the Queen wished to hear the song with the reddening sky surrounding her. She would enjoy her empire to the fullest.

On the parapet, she was surprised to find a tall, confident girl with poise and grace beyond her years. The girl looked the Queen directly in the eyes, a bold move for any servant. "I am Khajy, your grace." The Queen noticed the girl did not call her Goddess.

"Khajy!" The Queen whispered in the girl's ear, "Since I favor you, I will tell you a secret. My original name, before I became Queen-Goddess, was Khajy."

"I know," the girl said. Before the Queen could express her surprise, the girl stepped back and asked, "Would you hear the song?"

Queen Kharanto felt unable to resist. She leaned against the parapet, her back to the sea, and enjoyed the first strains of the chant. The power of the beautiful music swirled against the backdrop of the flaming sunset, which further reddened the inland plateau. As the girl's voice rose in volume, the sky became increasingly ominous. The acolyte's voice lowered to a huskier tone, and clouds moved in from the ocean behind the Queen. The singer began embellishing her melody with spinning melismas and rising and falling scales, and storms spread throughout the sky, cyclones whirled on the ocean's horizon.

The girl's height and strength burgeoned to its full dimension. The music hit a crescendo, matching the storms' force, driving through Queen Kharanto's veins. Completely subject to the music, the fearful Queen knew she stood before the true Goddess.

The Goddess whispered in the Queen's ear. "Now I will tell you a secret. My original name, before it was stolen by a Queen and I was reduced to disguising myself in my own sanctuary – my true name is Kharanto."

Trapped, the Queen pleaded, "What do you wish of me? I am your servant."

"I know," the true Kharanto said. "Listen and take in my potential to destroy you and your unfortunate island. I permit you to continue your charade, for I will not see the worshippers of the Instrument confused and disbelieving. But do not debase the sacred rites or weaken my faithful priestesses any further. Although I am not invulnerable, my incarnations will plague the Queens of the Red Isle and expose their corruption. One final warning: beware the roukh, for with him, the queendom will fall." With this pronouncement, the Goddess raised her arm and all the clouds, twisters, and storms disappeared. The Queen once more faced a young acolyte, who finished her sweet chant, gave one last direct look, and walked down to the sanctuary.

March 15. Back to the Red Isle!

After Kharanto's warning, the Queen stayed in her Keep for months. The priestesses issued an edict that the name Kharanto would revert to the Holy Goddess, and the Queen would be renamed Khajy. Queen Khajy raged at the news, but restrained herself out of fear of reprisal. Still in control of her guard, she carefully organized the archer division to watch for the roukh on the lookout day and night. When the roukh finally appeared, ten archers discovered that even their flaming arrows did not penetrate the bird's coarse skin. Queen Khajy witnessed the eleventh archer string his great bow with a deadly sword. The roukh hurled him over the parapet. At that moment the Queen felt she had seen the defeat of an eleventh challenger countless times before. Other strange visions brought her off guard and the roukh cornered her.

The roukh flung his latest gift across the lookout. "Why do you wish me dead?"

The Queen trembled. "Forgive me, mighty one. A terrible prophecy from Goddess Kharanto equated your return with the destruction of the Red Isle."

"Then I will leave and never return. The roukhs have never wished your island harm. But you have betrayed us. No longer are the roukhs in alliance with the Queens of the Red Isle. I will serve only the Gods and Goddesses of this land, for clearly it is they who control the feeble mind of its Queen."

"Wisely spoken, noble beast," came the deep, smooth voice of the Goddess Kharanto. "But my prophecy stands, even if you fly half way around the world from this doomed place. You have work yet to do for my descendants. We praise your loyalty and wish you good speed!" The roukh flew away, sad to have broken with the Queens.

Years later, a great-great-grand-daughter of Khajy had the bold insolence to attack the current Goddess with a sacrificial knife, the one weapon able to destroy the deity. She murdered the Goddess in front of the great Instrument, then slaughtered all who witnessed the savage deed. She rebuilt the priestess caste to serve her corrupt court. There were other Queens and other Goddesses, and other struggles. The Queens kept their vigilant watch for the roukh for generations, until at last he returned to destroy the queendom.

ق

"No!" Bax exclaimed. "The roukh forgave the Queens and returned with a peace offering. The Instrument, the xylophone from Indonesia."

Sahara empathized. "The roukh always did the right thing. And they shot him down, after generations of lying in wait."

"It really is sad, isn't it?" Dr. Machiyoko said. "A corrupt state was trying to protect itself from ruin by shooting down an animal on its way to help them. In doing so, the xylophone came into my hands, as Queen D'aulai, and I brought down the government with it."

"Their defensive action caused their downfall," Elvi said.

"Exactly," Sahara said, "and with it, the fulfillment of Kharanto's prophecy."

"Your extraordinary tale filled in a lot of gaps," Verle acknowledged, with a smile at Cachay. "You have a connection with our past lives."

"Nonsense. It's just something I made up when I was bored with business school." Cachay cleared some cups and went into the kitchen, glad to separate herself from the group.

62

In Dr. Machiyoko's office, at the current qaraq meeting, Zack commented on the previous week. "So my mother blew off the whole past life thing. No wonder she didn't talk to me."

"Like son, like mother," Porcy said. "You've had your doubts."

"At least I'm still here, sopping up the reincarnation juices."

"But you weren't there last week," Porcy scolded.

"And we've got lots of work today," Elvi said. "Let's finish catching Zack up."

The next agenda item for last week's meeting was Sahara retelling Ooma's recall about the all-seeing elephant. The qaraq was intrigued by another group like themselves, responsible for creating a version of *The Thousand and One Nights*. But what truly fired them up was Amar having hidden the recall. Weary of the issue, Sahara asked Elvi to move the meeting forward and told her she had brought new information about the flying insect.

While getting her first massage since Naji was born, Sahara had gone into trance. She had all the sensations of flying, but when she willed herself to an earlier part of the lifetime, she froze. Something constrained her, like being in a dress that is too tight. If she moved forward in the lifetime she was free of the constraint and able to fly. But even then the images of flying were sporadic and uncomfortable. She did not prefer flying to whatever had come before. She missed her life before the binding time but could not see it.

Dr. Machiyoko offered to regress her back to that time. The therapist gently guided Sahara back to the earliest time in the insect's life. Sahara described it for the group.

The Tale of the Swimming Insect

I'm in water! Swimming! Crazy swimming! Like the flying, but more fun. Darting this way, then that, then back. And skimming, just teasing the top of the water, barely touching it I'm so light. This is who I am. Not that beast with the heavy armor who can only hang onto a stick as if for dear life. Not that flitty airhead who flies around all day, sucking up vermin. No, these are my happy days, my youth.

I have friends, many of them, and we chase each other all day. Great chases, for we can all turn and dart in any direction. Impossible to catch, impossible to predict. I love this teasing play. I love the feel of the cool water on my belly and the warm sun on my back. I never want this to end.

I'm getting slower. I had such a sleek body. I was that body, that's what focused my attention the most. Beautiful shiny sections linked together and ending in a forked tail. I used to whip that tail around, even though it was short. But now I can't turn as fast, I can't whip around the water. There's a pressure on my back, near my head. It's like I'm carrying a heavy weight there, like a shell. It grows outward. I'm worried I can't swim anymore. I'll sink. I have to get out of the water. But I love the water! I'm not ready for this.

I clamor on top of a rock, my legs barely supporting the weight, although they are bunched up under that part of my body. I grab a log with red bark, hold on, and rest. I'm so tired and it's so difficult to move. I won't walk. I've never liked walking. I'll only cling and climb. God, I hate this thing on me! I'll just lie here until the sun bakes it off.

Dr. Machiyoko intervened. "Sahara, let's check in at that later point in your life, when you can fly. You've gotten rid of this shell and now you've got wings. Go there."

I'm teasing and turning again, now in the air. It's wonderful, but now the chasing is more aggressive. There's a new heat in the air, of pleasure and danger. Not from predators, but from the mates. We mate now that we fly. I have already mated. A terrible thing. Caught in the chase, pinned down, another body over me, pressing into me, wings flapping in individual bursts.

Then I filled up with eggs. My babies. Where would I take them? What would I do? I flew and flew and was drawn to the water. Of course! My little ones can have all the easy and fresh silliness I enjoyed. They would be safe in the water, before their wings come. I laid them in my favorite spot in the pond. I did not need to worry about their safety, though, for my mate came to guard them. And to guard me. No one else was touching me, no one else would have me.

And now the children swim happily through the rippling pools, and I am left to fly out my days, which will end soon. The best years of my life were as a water child, and the greatest amount of time. Once I became a winged creature it was not a new life but rather the beginning of a short end to this one: fly, mate, lay, die. So I sit on my red log near the pond and watch my little ones play. It feels strange to be a spectator. Were there others who watched while I swam and romped? It seems there must have been, it seems logical somehow, but I never saw anyone.

I worry for my offspring. Like me, they frolic all day. Will they withstand the trauma of the best joys of their life coming to an end? I cannot bring myself to see them turn into hardened shells. I can think no more about it. I will die first. And I do.

"Keep going, beyond, to the interlife," Dr. Machiyoko said.

I float up and away, to a familiar place, very familiar. It's a place I've seen recently, in this life, an afterlife place. It's the levels of Heaven I saw in a recall! I'm floating up through the levels, through the darker, lower levels, past the water level, the land level. I want to go from the dark to the light, from the gardens to the air level above. But I burn up, I fall. I fall into my life as an insect. That was my interlife before becoming the bug! I passed through water and land and air as an insect, too, but was most comfortable in the water. My time with the angel had brought me lightness, so I could play freely in the water, I could bring myself to fly as I must. But it was still a hard transition.

"What about the interlife after the insect life? What did you learn?"

I knew I was still struggling between the light and the dark. As an insect, I was a pioneer, my new lightness allowed me to adventure, risk dangers, try new things. But I did not want to leave my childhood playfulness. I felt that great weight on my back.

That weight, the thing holding me back. That's a dark, difficult side to things that I still struggle with now. I find the

415

lightness in my soul, the optimism, and it gets tainted. I find a fascinating career, meet a gorgeous man, and he ends up shackling me, preventing me from pursuing my work. I settle down in a lovely home, with a beautiful baby, and he brings tension, deception, and violence into the house.

"What is the lesson, Sahara? What will you do with the weight on your back? How will you find your way through the darkness, back to the light?" Sahara thought deeply before answering. Finally, still in trance, she spoke:

I will never let this happen again. I will break free. I will fly freely at last.

ق

When Dr. Machiyoko brought Sahara out of trance the group was silent. Sahara was clear and conscious immediately, her last statements fresh in her mind. She thanked the therapist for leading her to the real heart of that lifetime.

Back in the therapist's office, Zack asked, "So I'm caught up? Because no one's asked about my week." He looked at Sahara. "You of all people should want to know."

Sahara got up to check on the baby. "Why me?"

"Because I saved your ass. I saved all your asses." Zack sat up in his chair, like he was ready to teach class. "Last Tuesday, during your meeting, I was not out of town on a trip. Yes, I was avoiding all of you. Actually my mother. I was in the city on business, downtown, so at lunchtime I had this instinct to visit Amar at the World Trade Center. More true confessions: I've been scared to see him for weeks, but that day I had a bad feeling about him. It led me right to the Twin Towers.

"Thank God I went. I found Amar ready to leave the office and go home. He said something about a fight with Sahara,

416

some secret recalls, and all of us keeping in touch with her. He was on his way to see what was going on during the day. Gasp you should, but luckily I was there. Why drive yourself nuts with suspicion, I told him, when we can have a nice long lunch and catch up. We buddied up enough that he didn't get home until dinner and the group soldiered on, safe from discovery. In short, I saved the qaraq's ass."

"On behalf of the group, let me offer our sincere gratitude," Elvi said.

"You're welcome. Would you like to hear what Amar and I talked about while you were all tracking down bugs? By God, if I were you, I wouldn't be satisfied until I heard about the other recall Amar and Ooma shared together."

And so Zack told the group about his lunch with Amar.

63

After the second martini Amar's tongue loosened. I've known him since he was a baby, but I've never seen him do the morbid drunk thing. He bemoaned the failure of his grand plans since moving to New Jersey. The reconciliation between his father and grandfather was at an impasse. His marriage was falling apart, his child some strange supernatural being. He made a killing in the market, but come the millennium the whole thing may tank. He just wanted to seal the deal on all these things – family, marriage, career – but instead he was a terror to his wife. His need to have everything neatly resolved had led to a messy disaster. On and on he went and on and on I tried to bolster him. Can you get help I asked? Tried that, didn't work, he answered. Can you talk it out with Sahara? Constantly, it seems, he said. Is there anyone else you can turn to?

That's when he confessed his times with Ooma.

If any hanky-panky's going on between them, he didn't let on. What has been going on is a mini-qaraq, a trance for two. Up until last week it was only Ooma who had had recalls; Amar shared his despondency that he never received his own.

She insisted on hypnotizing him. She prodded him at work every day to let them try it. Finally, she talked him into it. Not just the hypnosis, but leaving work to go to her house.

Ooma tried a million things to relax Amar, but he was the worse subject in the history of hypnosis. He was wound tighter than a weightlifter on steroids. When simple suggestions and relaxation exercises failed, she tried the shiny object thing, the ticking metronome, even counting sheep. Finally, she got up and stood behind him, rubbed his shoulders ever so gently, and whispered Arabic prayers, Praise be to Allah who has eased your tribulations, that sort of thing.

Ooma speaking a foreign tongue did the trick. Amar's mind wandered, and wandered, and wandered, until his mind was thinking only of wandering, was dwelling on wandering, was reacting so strongly to the endlessly and purposelessly wandering that he entered a far off, unknown realm. These thoughts and memories poured out of him.

The Tale of the Settling of the South Pole

The Continental Drift craze is highly overrated: see the world, get a new perspective, turn your life around. Excuse me, but enough wandering already. The campaign to justify free-floating landmasses is getting old. This ridiculous lack of decision about our position keeps us drifting endlessly. And it's endlessly frustrating to me when someone cannot make up their mind; when an entire planet cannot get it together, I lose all patience. First of all, anywhere on the planet is pretty damned nice: warm, breezy, and plentiful. To hear tales of the old Snowball Earths makes me content to set my roots down anywhere. I've no tolerance for those who blame the 'forces

419

underneath.' If there are some supposed plates shifting under the Earth's crust, that's no excuse for avoiding our responsibility, our duty to form this planet's motherlands. The plates only control you if you let them. Stop the procrastination. Hunker down and make a choice.

Another thing. Why in God's name is there not just one South Pole? Isn't it hard enough that something so crucial to a planet's identity is invisible? Is it really necessary to have a Geographic Pole as well as a Magnetic Pole, not to mention the Geomagnetic Pole? And let's not forget the elusive Instantaneous South Pole and the South Pole of Balance, a bogus concept if I ever heard one.

These indecisive terms are not only foolish and embarrassing to any self-respecting member of the planet, but also downright befuddling when it comes to finding your way around down south. Granted, the planet wobbles a bit on its axis, so the imaginary line serving as the axis shifts around. That's the Instantaneous Pole, you know: here one instant, there the next. But I have no forgiveness for this South Pole of Balance thing, the 'theoretical' center point of the 'imaginary' axis wobbling around the 'invisible' South Pole. What a lie! To add insult to perjury, the South Pole of Balance has been moving six inches toward Australia every year! What the hell does it want in Australia?

I remember a time before Australia even existed, before all these fancy-schmancy Poles. There was one South Pole and that was that. Sure, we were blissfully ignorant. We didn't know that nine hundred miles away there was another South Pole, the Geomantic Pole, the source for the Earth's magnetic field, which you only feel in outer space. But how find your way around the South Pole in outer space? We didn't need such idiocies.

Back then, when everything else headed south to hook up with Gondwana and form Pangaea, I thought it was just more

420

shilly-shallying. We had been drifting south for quite a while, each new latitude with a more gorgeous climate. Then the whole gigantic landmass turns clockwise! My end, the furthest east, was becoming the southernmost, the bottom of the mass. Was this a slap in the face? Do they think that shoving me to the bottom of the heap will shut me up? No, the bottom of the world is a special place in my book. All this does is fuel my yearning to settle down. What a great spot to end our journey: The South Pole!

I feel a tingling. I am so delighted I mistake it for excitement. But it is no fleeting mood swing. Everyone feels it, at least down here. High atop a mountain a hunk of iron sends out a curious signal. The shoreline quivers with a new radiance, pulling in more than tides, sensing a different set of waves around it.

Deep underground an enormous sediment of coal glows with a galvanized fervor. As we get closer to the South the coal glows brighter. Rays burst forth from its pitch-black dominion, or are the rays arriving from the outside? From the Pole? The rays flow through the coal, jet out beyond the shores, swirl over the mountaintops, and billow out in beautiful curvilinear patterns.

We cease drifting. We sail along the arcs of these magical lines. We do an about-face, change direction, change polarity, in order to make a decisive move. The coal reaches a fever pitch of liaison with the rays and hurls us forward toward the Pole, pushes us to the end of the planet. We are charged with a magnetic connection, magnetized by the Pole. The Earth's polarity lures us in.

I embrace this forward motion. I adore this great natural phenomenon. I have purpose, destination. Push me, shores! Pull me, veins of ore! The South Pole seduces me and I fly into its arms. I am home!

With this thrill comes another feeling, a love for this land. No other part of Gondwana has the same meaning for me anymore. Let the waffling drifters have their territories; I am for this piece of the planet, this magnetized, polar-bound chunk. I am a loyalist, a partisan. I feel the jangle of the Magnetic Pole on me. I plant my flag in the dirt of the Geographic Pole. Who cares if the know-it-alls say the one pole shifts by miles every year while the other lies atop an unreachable peak. Damn the theorists! Place it wherever they like, name it whatever they will, I have decided: I am for the South Pole.

No one will move me from here. No mythical subterranean force will yank me from this spot, this end-of-the-earth location. I feel invincible. I want to teach everyone the great strength of my position, and help them find their home. In my past there were those who might have wished I fall from this position of power, but I throw aside such fears. I want closure, finality, ending. If the flaccid Gondwanans want to continue their wandering, they'll have me to contend with. I'll give them a continental tug-of-war they will never forget.

I revel in the Pole's warm, sensuous environment. This land will never dry up, break apart, or freeze over. I have found my resting place. I will be happy here forever.

ق

Amar finished his diatribe with a sharp swipe of his hand. Ooma put her hands back on his shoulders and brought him out of trance. And that was that: it was time for dinner.

By the time Amar finished telling me about his hypnotic fling with Ooma we were on our fourth martini. Thinking over the recall, Amar lamented making the same mistakes over and over again. He had placed his faith in a warm, cozy home, but we all know it was destined to break apart and freeze over.

422

And now once again he had placed his bet on a warm, cozy home, but his marriage was falling apart and entering an Ice Age! If I had known then that the Poles did not freeze over until millions of years after Gondwanaland split apart, I could have comforted him. I didn't check it out until later.

As soon as I knew the qaraq's meeting was over, I sobered up Amar and got us on the PATH train to Hoboken. After transferring to the Glenclaire train, Amar started piecing together where his recall fit into others he had heard. Sahara had recalled a story about a very early supercontinent. Dr. Machiyoko had remembered a lifetime on the southern landmass of Gondwana, while still warm, which was breaking apart from the planet's latest supercontinent of Pangaea. Amar's recall came between this early formation and later breakup of landmasses, perhaps during the formation of Pangaea. After these stories came Verle and Ooma's memories of the last piece of land breaking off from an icebound Antarctica to form the island of Atlantis.

This order seemed a dependable chronology for the supercontinent lifetimes. Amar had sobered up figuring it out. Clear-headed, despite an oncoming headache, Amar thanked me for listening to his sob story and went into his house.

At the meeting in Dr. Machiyoko's office, Porcy interrupted Zack's narrative. "What about my recall? Oops, sorry, babe. Are you done?" Zack nodded. "Sahara, remember my story of being a plant that got squashed into a coal deposit, which lit up with energy? I must have been the coal in Amar's story."

"Your coal deposit was magnetized and pulled his landmass toward the Pole," Verle said, "moving him into his new place on the planet."

"Just like my moving Amar into his new house," Porcy said. "Except I wasn't magnetically attracted this time. It was repulsion at first sight."

"That's what I call karma," Zack said.

"Exactly right," Elvi agreed. "We just discovered karmic twins: a pair of lives entwined in the past – Porcy and Amar's polar magnetic lifetimes – that are resolved in a future pair of lives – their 'lifetimes within a life' about finding the right house."

"So you're saying I was able to get past my dislike of that man and sell him a house," Porcy said, "because in the past I charged him up, and moved him?"

"You told me that when you closed the deal, you met Amar's family, found out he and Zack grew up together, and changed your entire view of him," Sahara said.

"Yes, I got a lesson in the complexity of people."

"So in the past when you moved Amar, he benefited by the settling of the drifting continent. In the present when you moved Amar, you benefited from an insight into human nature. That's good karma."

"Except!" Bax blurted out. "Amar's still an asshole, messing around with Ooma."

"Thanks for reminding me." Sahara tugged at several strands of her hair. "I'm trying to decide which is worse: my sneaking off to the qaraq or his triple deceit: going to Ooma's house, letting her hypnotize him, and sharing recalls behind my back."

"I vote for the triple deceit," Porcy said. "He's getting away with murder."

Sahara sighed. "But I can't confront him about Ooma because he'll ask how I know. I can't bust Zack, or tell him I heard it in a meeting I'm not supposed to be at."

"Frustrating," Dr. Machiyoko said.

"Maddening," Porcy said.

"Messed up," Bax said.

"Hopeless," Sahara said.

"So," Zack said, "are we caught up?"

64

—◦◦◦—

"There was one more recall at the last meeting," Elvi said.

"Oh yes, a doozy!" Verle said. "I was complaining about the recalls of insects, landmasses, and the like. Memory can't preserve such old, non-human experiences!"

"The old skeptic thing," Zack yawned. "I got over that with the wombat."

"Verle was going on about how the old lives still needed examining, and I jumped in," Dr. Machiyoko said. "You think that's old? You think that's weird? And I conveyed a recall that was so strange I had put it out of my mind for many years."

The Tale of the Lovers' Spat between Two Atomic Particles

I was lying out in the sun one afternoon, one of those perfect blue sky days where the light is translucent. I was on my back, gazing upward, and I saw these odd little squiggles of light curlicueing in front of my eyes. Maybe it was a trick of the light, maybe I was seeing little membranous things in my cornea. If I focused properly I could witness the circling dance of these tiny, sperm-shaped doodads moving randomly in the air.

This sight mesmerized me, and it occurred to me that I was actually seeing particles on the atomic level. Regardless of the preposterousness of this notion, I was convinced of it, so convinced that I felt like I was one of those nuclear particles dancing around. Then I heard this bizarre conversation in my head, between two of the atomic particles!

"You said you wanted to do this! Come on, Za. Let's go!"

"I'm not going over there. It's not right."

"You're such a weak force. You won't even jump quantum levels with me. You never want to do anything."

"I'm doing my best, Du! It's really tight in here. I can barely move."

"Of course you can. You just need a little poke."

"No! Please don't do that. Too close, you'll smash something."

"Fine." Du started to dart away.

"Again?" Za said. "Next thing you'll be hopping the next isotope that comes along."

"You're no fun! Let's grab some mass."

"I thought you wanted to be close," Za said. "The 'most intimate space in the cosmos'."

"I know what I said. But you split a neutrino every time I quiver up to you."

"Your energy's all over the place. You might blast me to some other dimension!"

"Really, Za. You're overreacting. You're impossible!"

If you were spinning around this atom with our unfortunate couple, of course you wouldn't be hearing this banter. You would not hear words, or see Du slap her hand to her forehead in frustration, or see Za clutch a pillow to his chest. You might see Du as a free electron, zooming in on her lover, taking a spin around him, giving him a bump or two, then spinning off in another vector, to another orbital, another atom. You might sense Za as another electron, desperately trying to hold onto a regular path around the nucleus, or as part of the nucleus, squirming, holding tight to the center. You would not be surprised to find Za at one moment as a muon, fading away after too short a half-life for his taste, but then reappearing as a tau-particle, then a bottom quark. His anxieties are getting the better of him, you might say, he's making himself unstable. You might see Du try to help him by clinging tightly to him with every magnetic charge she can muster. But then she spins off again, then cozies up to Za, then splits herself in two. Za changes into three particles at once, shoots off some gamma rays in Du's general direction, and sinks back into the nucleus.

You might see all or none of this. 'Might' is the operative word of the Uncertainty Principle, after all. And if their argument could be translated into words, it would continue:

"You're driving me crazy," Za might say, contracting his mass into a tighter ball. "You're either all over me, or nowhere to be found."

"I thought you were attracted to me," Du might respond. "Why did you come here?"

"Why did you ask me to come? You obviously have your own agenda."

"The only reason you want me here is to hold your hand. To help you be big and brave enough to be a simple little particle."

"I hate it here," Za would say. "You tricked me into coming with your tale of some made-up pleasure world. I'd give anything to go back."

"So why not get out of here?"
"You'll come with me?"
"No way."
"Du, I'm begging you."
"You repulse me."
"Please!"
"Just go!"

And with that you might see a seemingly reckless colli-sion between two random particles, changing the configura-tion of an atom, sending out new energy into the cosmos. And one particle might be sent packing off with the energy, leav-ing the other behind. The other particle might happily orbit around her home, stick herself onto a new friend, and hop from lover to lover in the nuclear darkness, all the while fore-seeing a space where lover's quarrels could be expansive, not confined to puny, atomic space, but set in a vast, public arena where thousands could cheer a battle to the finish between two embroiled mates.

Far-fetched? Unbelievable? Or just uncertain? Certainly, given Uncertainty, Za and Du might never have existed at all, or not as quarreling, fantasizing lovers. Or Za, sailing out into the cosmos, might be just beginning his lifetime in the world of deep, inner space.

ق

"Wow!" Zack said.
"Pretty far out," Dr. Machiyoko said.
"I don't believe it."
"It's unbelievable that a soul might incarnate as atomic matter," Verle agreed.
"It really pisses me off!"

428

"We already discussed this to death last meeting," Porcy said. "Let's move on."

"It's not the unbelievability," Zack said. "I feel furious. What Du did to this Za particle was horrible. Knocking him out into space, wasn't that it? Do you find that amusing, Doc?"

"What's going on?" Dr. Machiyoko asked. "You're turning red."

"My skin is burning, dammit! I'm out of control mad. Fire is flaming in my heart."

"Just keep breathing, Zack," the therapist said.

"You keep breathing, betrayer! Elvi, what is happening to me? I'm possessed."

The facilitator got Zack to calm himself, then said, "You're responding to Dr. Machiyoko's recall from the depth of your soul. Very likely you were Za, furious at Du."

"And I've been harboring a grudge against her for fifty life-times probably. She's my therapist, for God's sake! We'll have to meet for an extra twenty years now."

"Do you want more information about this?" Elvi asked. "I could regress you."

"Hell, no! I don't ever want to see that –. Sorry, sorry. Sorry, Doc. It's Za talking."

"It's all right," Dr. Machiyoko said, patting Zack's knee. "At least we're caught up."

"Praise the Lord and pass the whiskey," he said.

"Get some air, everyone," Elvi said. "That was quite a ride. And we haven't even started today's recalls."

65

During the break, Zack made a feeble attempt at reconciliation with Dr. Machiyoko. Sahara fed the half-awake baby so he would settle back to sleep for the rest of the meeting. Elvi stepped outside for a cigarette. Verle thought through some new research he had done. Porcy and Bax remained seated, deep in whispered conversation. When Elvi reconvened the meeting, Porcy explained that recently she and Bax had conducted a séance to search for more of his frightening past lives.

"We didn't find any new ones, but we each recalled a lifetime that connects to my plant/coal lifetime and Amar's South Pole story."

Elvi asked who wanted to go first, and Bax began his story.

The Tale of the Clumsy Pollen Catcher

I'm a plant. In a swamp. Little creatures scurrying. In and out of water. Simpler life. Simpler plants. Ferns. Mosses. Quillworts the size of trees. Everywhere. Like weeds. The planet overrun. So vulgar with their spores. Sex in the mud. Wait till wet.

I'm a new plant. No spore fucking. Something brand new and risky. Seeds. Fruit. Pollen. Detached sex. Borne on the wind. Never feel a thing. Let fly my pollen and hope for the best. Who knows where the sperm goes? Tricky timing. Tricky wind business. Catch those pollen just right. Catch as catch can.

Right next to me. A new stem shot up. What a pretty thing. Mine for the asking. Before, I'd have to guess. Who caught my little guys? Now I'll know. Girl next door.

She grew up fast. Half way up me in one season. She was ripening. That's a tease. Couldn't wait to plant some goodies in her garden. Shot my wad all over. Keep it together. Not like those disgusting club mosses. Keep your roots on.

Wait for a hefty breeze. Seeds, leaves, twigs everywhere. Tinkling of seedpods in the air. Odd. Where have I heard that sound? Bells? Heavenly music. Mesmerizing.

Snapped out of my ecstasy. Wind licked the grains right off me. Just in time to see the little buggers fly. Right over to my sweetheart. Open up and take me. Catch 'em, babe! There's one! Grab it! Oops. Okay here's more. You got 'em. No! Damn! Okay here you go. Open up wide. Now! Now! Okay, now! Holy zygote!

Further down the lane I spied little me's popping up all summer. But nothing from the sweet little thing next door. Beginner's bad luck. New thing this cross-pollination. Harder than the mud fuck, much. Heard some get help from insects. Disgusting notion. Stinger stuck in you. Please and no thank you!

Better luck next cycle. Fresh breeze. She's more gorgeous than ever. Wanted to reach out and grab her. No touching. Common. Leave that to the ferns. It's time for fruit. Had more pollen than ever. Just seeing her wave made me drop my stuff.

A little critter picked up seed. All over his spine. Hey! Mail boy! Scoot that over to my honey. He did it! There you are, love. She bent down for the grains. That's it, lift them up, down the hatch. Don't drop them! Butterbranches. Okay, have some more. Nice breeze, and ... perfect shot. Right down the pipe. Ah! Bounced out! How'd that happen? How'd you do that? What is wrong with –. Steady, steady. There's plenty more ...

Each time she bungled it. Dropped the grains. Batted them away with an accidental brush. Next season even worse. Finally caught some. Pretty style sucking them in. Make that seed! But she so unnerved about it. Shook like a leaf. A thousand seeds. All died.

Horror. No more the comic klutz. She had a real problem. I felt sick. Should I help? Lean in on a breeze, rustle a little. Empathize. Might be worse, darlin. What a fool! Better just stay away. Shoving pollen in her face every day. Call an insect? Never. Got my pride. Sure she does, too. Probably not much left though. Stop it, you're awful. One grain at a time? Would save on wasted ones. Gentle breeze, no line drives. Here, love, catch sort of thing. What if she did and killed the seed again? Repeat horror. Who could live through that again? She'd decompose on sight.

Nothing to be done. Send my grains the other way next season. When she's not looking. Hate to rub it in. Such a dear. Wave to her every morning. Knew that I cared. What a blight! Rather be a fern than anything! Hunker down in the mud. Grope around till we find each other. What bliss to be in the ground. Down and dirty. Go at it to our roots.

If I can't reach out and touch her. If I can't seed her to fruition. I will squeeze her by the roots. Grab her by the bottom. Shake her to her foundation. Sneak in the back door. Hide under her covers. Tunnel into her prison. Excavate her

432

treasure. Plunder her quarry. Unearth her. Hit rock bottom. Soil myself for her. Dirty my hands. Penetrate her core. Enter her. Probe her. Her crux. Her essence. Kernel. Soul.

ق

"Okay, we get it," Zack said. "Stop already."

"Hold up, Zack," Elvi responded. "Maybe there's more."

"There is," Porcy said. "Bax honey, those roots, not yours, but the other plant's. Were they shallow or deep?"

"Shallow," he said quickly.

"And could you reach her roots? Was it difficult?"

"It was very hard to push through the earth."

"Was that all?" Porcy considered her next words. "Did she help?"

Bax sunk his head. "She tried, but she kept getting in the way. One root reached out to me, another pushed me away. Accidentally. She was so clumsy."

"Yep, that's me all over." Porcy leaned back and laughed. "I was the other plant."

433

66

"Since when are you clumsy, Porcy?" Sahara asked.

"Oh Lord, I'm the clumsiest! Maybe it's because of past lives."

"I'm curious about this root grab you did," Sahara said, gazing at Bax. "It wasn't sex, that's the pollen thing. I just wonder how it felt." Bax returned her stare.

"Squishy, yet tough, strong," Porcy answered. "My recall picked up where Bax's ended. That's was I felt during our séance. I was sweating, and I got that squishy feeling you get between your toes, like liquid gel. I focused on that sensation, expanded it, until I felt that my feet were rooted in swampland, my thoughts full of the very ancient, very young planet. New life was springing up everywhere. It should have been an exhilarating time.

"But I was dissatisfied, unhappy with the life around me. I felt stuck, trapped. I was used to much more progress in life. But now I was planted in the earth, but not deep. I felt uncomfortable being both stuck and unstable at the same time. I hated my life. Hated all the life around me."

"No wonder you had trouble with cross-pollination," Dr. Machiyoko said.

"My heart wasn't into it. But Bax saved me. He kept after me, showed me the way. It was like a secret door to the garden swung open, and there it was."

"The garden?" the therapist asked.

"The planet," Porcy answered, "the whole planet. Let me go back to where Bax tried to grab my roots. You'll see."

The Tale of the Enamored Boots

We tried three times to intertwine our roots. Each attempt took longer than the last, the last occurring over many centuries. How we stayed alive that whole time is a mystery. Ferns and selaginellas were living up to a thousand years back then. But us puny little seed-bearers, we were the new kids, the runts. We got power and food from each other, nourished by our joined rootstocks.

The first time I felt his touch I did not know what was happening. It was like a rush of water through my roots. My neighbor waved his branches at me. It was like a little smile. I felt a gentle tug on my root: it was him! I tried to pull away. He'd been spewing little grains on me for years, and now this. But I did not have much control over my roots. I had barely planted them in the dirt. He met my resistance with another tug, and another, and before I realized it he had wrapped his devious root around mine.

Pulling against him was in vain, though his grip was not hard or painful. I tried relaxing my hold and slipping through his root fingers. As soon as I tried this, there was a new grasp on another root. He was coming at me from all directions! When a third underground tendril twined its way around me, the tingling energy I had felt shot up a notch or two. It felt good!

435

My despondency melted away and a new desire fed me. I began growing my own roots toward his, at first slowly, dependent on climate and moisture. When I was able to navigate more freely through the earth, I sensed where his root clung to mine, where he might go next. I sensed the logic of his actions, the vectors in which he directed his roots, the patterns of his thoughts. I felt exhilarated that I was so attuned to my neighbor. All seemed so familiar to me, as if we had seen this played out long ago above ground.

I was premature in my happiness. I sent a root across the mud, knocking an alien root out of the way. A new root grabbed mine from behind, but I brushed it away. Another root held on quietly and calmly. It had been him all along. I had stood in the way of my own pleasure. I kept getting in the way, moving away from where I should be. It was extremely hard for me to stop undoing myself, but the calm grip of his roots helped. He would clasp several of my roots at once and pull me deeper underground until I felt like I had real roots, thick, sinewy, deeply hidden roots that no one could see but my protector. Over the years we made more and more connections, until our root systems were totally interwoven.

But I was not destined to find bliss in this world, or come by it as a passive receiver. Once we settled into a quiet life of clinching and curling, disaster struck. We entered a time of great seismic activity. With the first upheaval of the earth, large rocks pushed up from below, straining our bonds. Layers of dirt and sediment shifted all around us, twisting our already tightly wound foundation. Many of my neighbor's mighty arms broke, leaving me holding a dead, dysfunctional rootlet. Every root was threatened. All was chaos.

We did not surrender. For the second time we wrapped ourselves in each other. I was not about to give up the one thing that made this life bearable. Let my branches burn, let my stem decay, I would not abandon my roots. My beloved's strength was unmatched, inspired, gargantuan, but it was not enough. I had to unleash my instincts, numbed by previous passivity, and fight as hard as he did. I used my off-centered clumsiness to feel at home in the chaotic upheavals. Often I found one of his roots lifeless from a previous tremor, and with my new strength pulled it to safety and revived him.

But there was no conquering the ferocity of the convulsions. After decades of tumult, our roots completely separated. A large hill pushed up between us, violating our intimate space. We grew on either side of the protuberance, I in my own private valley, and he on the lower slope on the other side of the mound. I did not lose heart. I had a new fighting spirit.

For the third time I searched him out. I sent roots in all directions for I had no idea where he might be, perhaps in an entirely different place. He might even be dead, but I believed I would not feel hope if that were true. I hit rock walls, other strange plants, and ever increasing bodies of water. I burrowed through the hill, down under the hill, around the hill. I dug as deep as possible so I couldn't trip myself up. It was not a clumsy effort. For the first time, I felt pride in myself.

It took many more years, decades, maybe even centuries, but one cloudy afternoon my deepest and farthest root ran into something familiar and welcoming. I had found him! Sucking up every nutrient from the wetter and wetter soil, we accelerated our root growth so that our interlacing was rapid and sturdy. Other tentacles rushed to the area like giddy lovers. We grafted our rootstocks together in a lasting bond; pollination was a thing of the past, a dead issue. More and more moisture flooded our love field, helping to expand our root system, our legacy. The third time was a charm: our stems stood a great distance apart, each unseen by the other, but our roots – our footing, marrow, bedrock, substratum, crux, center and soul – lived happily ever after.

For the first time, I loved this planet and everything on it.

"I get it!" Zack shouted. "Bax brought you back to life, made you feel better about yourself and being in the world. For his karmic reward, when he was ready to chuck it all in an interlife, you got him back on his little wombat feet; and when he was wandering around this life half scared to death, you brought him home, gave him a cup of tea and a Tarot reading, and made him feel better about himself and being in the world."

"Excellent, Zack," Elvi said. "You're coming along nicely."

"I thought karma was immediate," Verle said," so that in the next life you reap what you sowed in the previous life. These karmic twin lives are probably millions of years apart. Why the delay?"

"Karma is not neat and tidy," Elvi answered. "It's more like the twisting, searching roots in Porcelain's story. Yes, there are usually some repercussions from one lifetime to the very next one. For this reason, Porcy's helping Bax on his feet in the interlife was quickly and simply rewarded by Bax saving her from the street robbery. But true resolution of a karmic relationship can take many, many lifetimes, especially if there's deep causes. Porcy was discontent with being on this planet: that problem runs deep; Bax's rescue back then was a long-term investment, and it's come due now."

The qaraq was silent, fascinated and shocked by Elvi's rare outpouring of knowledge. At last Porcy broke the silence. "I wasn't done, ya know..."

The water that nourished and invaded our soil continued to rise over the centuries until it had covered the top of our hill and beyond. The depth and extent of our roots kept us going, long after the oxygen ran out, oxygen that would have ravaged all of us, decomposed us and all the plant life around. We were miraculously preserved in the mud, under the swamps, a life after death that was a life after life. Our merged roots became indistinguishable from the compacted loam. The commingling of stalks, stems, roots and muck from all over was a pure extension of what I had reveled in with my first love.

But the pressure was on. Water, rock, and plant residue bore down on us. The force was maddening. Still, no hardening, concentrating, integrating or disintegrating could bother me. Eons passed. We turned into a darker, denser, shinier form of matter than plant life. We were unfazed. We let go of the plant kingdom for the mineral world. We had become inky, onyx deposits of coal.

ق

"Eh, voilà, mes amis, from a klutzy plant, to a determined root seeker, to a chunk of coal with magnetic charms, and finally to the South Pole." With a flourish of her hands, Porcy concluded, "We are back full circle to Amar's recall, and we connect more dots in our far-fetched, but increasingly believable chain of escapades. Non?"

"The karmic links do add a new light to these old lifetimes," Dr. Machiyoko said.

"Like they happened yesterday," Zack said, "or at least the day before."

"Helps me buy into the tales about spores and fossilized bug drippings," Verle admitted. "And gives me courage to bring up a new theory about that swimming and flying insect. I believe it was a prehistoric creature, from before the dinosaurs."

439

67

As the meeting continued, Sahara heard Naji whimper. When she went to check on the baby, he whispered in her mind.

The Tale of the Unborn (conclusion)

I wrap myself in the gel passed among my sister eggs as we float along in the water. The sticky substance keeps us together. A bonding elixir that gives me life after millions of years trapped in amber. Then my sisters absorb the goo inside of themselves, and so do I. It grows, or something grows, and we separate from each other.

The elixir that saved me before is now my undoing. It is the elixir of fertility, the epoxy of reproduction, sperm preserves. I am to be a mommy. A new bug grows in my ancient egg sac and bursts its seams, destroying my safe water vessel as it becomes body and tail and eye. A complete nymph.

ق

As Sahara quieted the baby, Verle addressed the group. "I found several insects that produce water-born children of the sort Sahara recalled. I think ours is a dragonfly."

"I love dragonflies!" Porcy said. "I hope I was one. Their wings are so beautiful."

"All shiny and shimmery," Bax agreed. "They're so delicate."

"Just like me," Zack said. "Verle, how the hell do you know this?"

"In Dr. Machiyoko's recall, the insect was still, not flying, when it was cloudy or dim or nighttime. Dragonflies only fly when the sun is out."

"When I felt like a pair of wings," Zack said, "there was heat beating down on them."

"Dragonflies have two pairs of wings, a front and back pair," Verle said. "The wings don't form until after childhood, when a hard shell called the chitin armor develops over the dragonfly's body and then breaks off."

"Like a butterfly emerging from a cocoon," Elvi said. "So the swimming insect that Sahara remembered was from before the chitin armor and wings formed?"

"In childhood." Sahara rejoined the group. "I was a happy dragonfly in the water."

"It's called the nymph stage," Verle said.

"An ironic name," Dr. Machiyoko said. "Sahara was a child, a free spirit, a pioneer as a nymph; but when sexually active as an adult, she wanted to hide herself."

"It's more than ironic," Sahara said. "Naji just told me more of his story. The egg was fertilized, then a swimming creature was born in the water. He called it a nymph."

"Naji was a baby dragonfly!" Porcy said. "Or the egg that made the baby."

"Dang! There's even more connections," Verle said. "Sahara's dragonfly nymph-child had crazy movement patterns and a lot of stopping and starting. Just like in Dr. Machiyoko and Zack's recalls, when they were flying. All of you must have been dragonflies, and I wonder if everyone in the qaraq was a dragonfly." Verle turned to Elvi with a big smile wrinkling his face. "Would you regress us to find out?"

"A group hypnosis?" Zack pressed his fists against his temples. "It's getting late. Sinus headache."

According to Elvi, a good headache can promote a deeper trance. The qaraq agreed to a group regression and Elvi described the meditative process. She induced the group into a hypnotic state and gave them the suggestion to travel to a dragonfly lifetime.

The Tale of the Chitin Armor

At first Zack received an image of an aquatic being, swimming and squirming through tight cavities in another being's body that squeezed the life out of its victims. Horrified by this apparition, he knew it was not of the dragonfly's world. Shifting his focus to the insect, Zack felt aware of his dragonfly lifetime at the point when the chitin armor began to form.

You are so excited to be sprouting wings. As you grow into little buds, at the scapulae, you feel the armor's closeness. You are under the strong, loving arms of his embrace. You pinch the back to feel close to the body, too. You return the embrace.

Zack's headache came in and out of his consciousness, playing tricks with his perceptions. His memory shifted to another awareness, a different perception of a dragonfly, but at the same point when the armor developed.

442

I want to feel that something good is happening, that the armor is a warm blanket wrapped around a shivering child. There is an intimacy between my nymph body and the armor shell. It cuddles me, nuzzles me, shields me, so I cozy up to it, embrace it.

But I feel like I'm being hidden from the world, smothered, or descending into a black hole. The armor continues to grow and tighten, encasing me and the budding wings like a stifling lover. The wings want to break through and be free. I want to flee the relationship.

Zack's pain returned and again his recall shifted to a new point of view, this one complete with snippets of dialogue, as if from one of the recall scripts Zack wrote.

Besides the sprouting wings, nymph-body, and armor-shell, there is a larger presence, an overseer. "How dare you call me overlord, chitin, I protect you!" A fearful presence, fearful of the tension bearing down on the nymph, of the wings about to burst forth, of the fierce armor engulfing everything. "You brute! When will you stop?"

The overriding climate of fear cracks the chitin armor with the violence of ice in a sudden spring thaw. Pieces of the shell fall from the nymph-body and off the red-bark log where it has perched. The last pieces of the armor weigh down the wings, but one flitter of the nymph would free the soul to fly. The overseer holds it back. "Do not move! Stay!"

Once again Zack's perspective shifted. He felt the annoyance of the armor shell with the overseer's grip on things.

I challenge you! You think you lord it over us, but as just punishment, now you must truly rule, and it will be chaos that you rule, if rule you can. Try to guide them when I am gone. Hold on now!

With the last flick of my shell onto the ground, the creature, nymph no more, soars into the air with a breathtaking bound, wings vibrating wildly, dangerously, desperately. I share that burst of energy with the dragonfly, the exhilaration, the thrill of first takeoff. I am glad it is finally over and I can be done with the struggle.

Stunned by the moment of flight, Zack sees that what started as an indiscriminate mesh of body and armor and wing-stub has ended in four distinct entities. The outrageous wings span the sky, spreading to nearly a yard wide. The nymph body does not accept its adult state. The fearful overseer steers in the air for dear life. Overreacting, the remaining shell crumples into pieces, mingling with strips of red bark from the log perch.

Finally, Zack returned to the first point of view, his own awareness of the dragonfly.

You were wrong. The closeness you felt with the nymph and the chitin armor has vanished. It was close when your wings were only stubs next to the nymph's skin, encased in a bit of armor near the top of the spine. But as you grew, your wing tips got further and further away from the spine, abandoned nymph and childhood, and left the shell broken on the ground, alone and discarded.

ق

When Elvi brought the group out of its collective hypnosis, Zack insisted on telling his recall first, wanting some reward for transcending his headache. The group responded to the shifting points of view in his recall with confusion, curiosity, and occasional familiarity.

They turned to Elvi for clarification. "Verle had the right instinct. Everyone in the group has some connection to this world, but it is a highly unusual connection." She looked around Dr. Machiyoko's office at each person in the group.

"I believe you were all part of the same dragonfly."

444

68

Elvira Young's background remained a mystery to the group. She never discussed her personal history or even other places where she guided souls through the waters of their past lives. It was only at moments like this, when she exposed a bizarre truth with utter confidence, that the qaraq got a hint of her vast experience in the secrets of reincarnation.

"A group of souls often meets up in a common time or place, even within the same family," Elvi explained. "Sometimes an entire population that has suffered a large-scale trauma rejoins in a later life. Much more rarely does a group of souls find themselves in the same body. I've seen this phenomenon only a few times before."

"So you're saying we were body parts," Zack said. "Like on the black market."

"Except alive and all within the same active body."

Suddenly Zack had a hundred questions. "We were all part of the same dragonfly? Who was which part? What was I? Should we name it? How about Ginger?"

"Your first recall was definitely about the wings," Dr. Machiyoko said. "But you just told us the wings were a yard wide. Can dragonfly wings be that big?"

"The wingspan confirms that our collective dragonfly, Ginger, was from prehistoric times," Verle said. "Meganeura monyi, from the Carboniferous Period. Three hundred million years ago. A dinosaur of a dragonfly, but well before dinosaurs."

"So why was I recalling the nymph and the armor if I was the wings?" Zack asked. "Why was I appointed Viceroy in charge of recalls in everyone's absence?"

"The wings form close to the body, so you were aware of the nymph," Elvi said.

Sahara followed up. "I was the nymph, and since the armor was wound tight around me, it was also mixed into your awareness."

Zack nodded understanding. "Some relationship there! The armor squeezing hard on your poor little nymph body, Sahara. You're like: What a brute! Get me outa here! And he's like: Fine, I'll split. And he does, literally."

"Sounds like my marriage," Sahara said.

There was a resounding silence in the room.

"Maybe Amar was the armor," Porcy mused. "The names even sound alike."

The afternoon was starting to wear on Sahara. If it was her husband wrapped around her intimately, then she was relieved when the stifling presence broke off from her into a crumbled shell. She was going through the same thing now, three hundred million years later! Were they that set in their ways?

Zack spoke. "So I was Ginger's wings, the body was Sahara, the chitin armor was Amar. What were you, Doc?"

"The eyes, or at least one of them," Dr. Machiyoko answered. "I had those multiple images in my recall, which Verle thought was the compound eye of an insect. But I want to know who and what this overseer thing was?"

"An oversoul," Elvi explained. "When a group of souls shares one body, there's still a soul belonging to the whole being. And one of you would have been that oversoul."

446

"Whoever it was," the therapist said, "was domineering, trying to control everyone."

"Sounds like my mother," Zack joked.

There was another resounding silence in the room.

"Wait a minute, you think my mother was the soul of this bug?" Zack was troubled by the implications of Cachay being connected to the collective lifetime. Could she be a member of the qaraq? "Are we really buying all this? Verle, buddy, help me out here."

"Sorry, my friend, I'm buying it," Verle said. "There's even a clue we haven't mentioned yet. Sahara remembered clinging to a log with red bark when her nymph stage was ending. Zack also remembered taking off from a log with red bark, and Amar's shell fell off the same log. Same bug?"

"This pond area could have been full of red bark logs," Zack said. "Or every dragonfly and her sister could have learned to fly off the same Community Flying Log."

"I think you're in denial because of your mother being the oversoul," Porcy chided. "Speaking of which, the armor challenged the oversoul at the time of first flight. But what kind of challenge is falling to pieces next to your opponent? Sounds like quitting."

"Don't think of the armor as quitting but letting go, releasing the oversoul into the next stage of life," Elvi said. "I'll explain it in a parable. For once I get to tell a story."

The Tale of the Servant's Revenge

Imagine the servant of a spiteful Princess who hates men, refuses all suitors, and drives her father, the King, mad with frustration. Whenever the servant mentions a lover, the Princess

447

cuffs him across the face, once hitting him with a brass candlestick, knocking out all his teeth. The servant despises the Princess.

One night the King, who is looking for some important papers, calls the servant from his sleep. He thinks he has left them in the Princess' rooms and orders the servant to fetch them. Normally the Princess' bedchamber is open, but the servant finds the door locked. After procuring a key the servant is shocked to spy a sleeping lover wrapped around the Princess in her bed. The shock turns to delight. Snatching up the missing papers from the floor, the servant returns to the King and reports the Princess' illicit rendezvous, a slap in the face to her father. The King storms into his daughter's bedroom, orders the lover to be thrown into the dungeon, and chides his hypocritical daughter as she stands exposed in front of him, ashamed, bereft of her love.

"The tale of Ardeshir from *The Thousand and One Nights*," Sahara exclaimed. "Elvi, you're full of surprises today! I'm impressed. What's it got to do with anything?"

Let's call the chitin armor-shell Amar for the sake of argument. Amar was in the same situation as the servant in the story. The servant didn't try to cover up the Princess' affair, but withdrew to inform the King. Same with Amar the armor: tired of the oversoul 'Princess Cachay's' authority over him, he withdrew his shell as a way to expose her to a harsh circumstance. By releasing the dragonfly to fly and mate, Amar forced Cachay the oversoul to bare her sexuality in public, to enter the mating game. He challenged her to spread her wings, to mate, to bear children.

How delicious it is that Cachay's present day child, Zack, embodied the wings that took her into this challenging flight.

448

Just as Naji can enlighten his mother about the interlife because he is closer to it in time, so Zack as the wings could enliven Cachay the oversoul's awareness and experience of the world. It is as if the parent is a tiny ant that has crawled into a gigantic hand, the hand of a human who bears the soul of the child, who at this time has a much larger view of things.

ق

"Hold on!" Porcy interrupted. "I'm sick of hearing about Zack as the wings. I am positive I was also the wings."

"I told you there are front and back pairs of wings on a dragonfly," Verle said. "You were each a pair, I suspect."

"I was the back wings," Porcy said, hoisting herself up in her chair. "I'm sure of it."

"Fine, I was the front wings," Zack said. "But you didn't know what you were doing."

Verle intervened. "In my recall there was a lot of this tension between the different parts of the dragonfly. I think the challenge to the oversoul was greater than we think. Flying was bad enough. Mating when the nymph-body was reluctant was worse. Given that the parts of this dragonfly were such separate entities, each with a soul, there must have been a special edge to these challenges. The oversoul had a civil war on her hands."

449

"My recall will shed light on this battle of the body parts," Porcy said.

The Tale of the Dragonfly's Four Wings

We should have been a pristine, glittering spectacle of harmonious flight. That's the way it had always been. When no one else had wings, we bugs were the pioneers, the first to fly. Among the winged ones, we dragonflies were the most precious: wings of blue-green iridescence with a flexible coating that allowed figure-eight patterns in our wingstroke.

We had the extra, wider pair of back wings, first unfolding on a log of red bark. The most beautiful wings in insectdom. Burst out of that armor and ready to fly. We knew how it had always been done, in perfect harmony, the front wings coming down for a stroke, we in the back matching them, stroke for stroke, up, down, rise, fall. A streamlined efficiency that led our body straight ahead or straight back for food, or a drink of dew, or a suitable mate. The double pair of wings was a bejeweled celebration of the union of front and back.

The winged glory was not to be. The wings in front of our pair took off not in the normal sense of flight but in an obsessive overreaching to the sky. Giddy to be airborne, high on speed, my crazed partners raced around the air like greedy demons. How were we supposed to keep up? Were we expected to read the others' mind, not a familiar idea to a creature without much of a mind? We tried to flap to the same beat, but all we achieved was a clumsy attempt at synchrony, clumsy flight patterns, and clumsy dives.

A new sensation caught hold of us in the back: fury! How dare they challenge us so! Four can play that game. Our pair stopped fluttering. The body pulled up abruptly. We flapped the left wing, then the right. The poor creature darted this way, then that. We played rhythm games with the front wings, which broke out of their obsessiveness and noticed our rebellious strokes. They flapped down, we stroked up; they stroked up, we flapped down. This maneuver gave more power to the dragonfly. We shot ahead, like a sunray popping through a tree branch. Every maddened movement our front partners put forth, we countered with a move of our own, causing delightful twists in direction.

It's true what we've heard: no matter how aggravating something is, over time it will influence your very soul. So it was with us: the unpredictable twists and turns, which we created with our contentious struggle, became our reality, our joy, and our reason to live.

Was it really a war? No. Wars are battles to the death. Our heated flight patterns, the shifty changes in directions, the contentious counterstrokes: all this was a battle to the life.

ق

451

"That explains everything," Zack said, "as clear as a light in the middle of the night."

"What are you talking about?" Porcy said quickly.

"To you I'm the bad guy back then, flapping around like crazy, making you perform all those shifts in direction. So what do you do? In this lifetime you make me shift my direction, give up Paris, give up travel. You clip my wings!. You make me end up in Jersey, with my mother, the oversoul."

"But there was purpose in your returning here: my gathering the qaraq together. Back then, as the dragonfly, all that shifting was just loco."

"I agree," Dr. Machiyoko said. "In my recall the other week as the eyes of the dragonfly, I could see in every direction except to the left side of Ginger's body. Now I understand why. I was her right eye. In the regression we just did, I saw things from the perspective of the left eye, which was a completely different soul. A soul that despised me."

70

"What makes you say it despised you?" Elvi asked.

"Some of the views I had from the right eye perspective switched back and forth," the therapist said. "I'd see something to the right then switch to the left abruptly. Crazy."

Porcy said, "So the two eyes were in conflict, just like the wings?"

Diana hesitated. "Not exactly..."

"Was it like a war," Porcy asked, "or were they just working each other? Were the eyes trying to keep track of where the wings were taking them? Was it like when the brakes are gone and you're running down a mountain? Was that it, baby?"

There were too many questions. A thousand images flashed through the therapist's brain. Perhaps twenty-five thousand images, for inside each dragonfly eye there are twenty-five thousand tiny eyes that latch on to the target the dragonfly desires. The memory took hold of Dr. Machiyoko again. Inside her mind she became lost in this host of desires.

The Tale of the Battle between the Right and Left Eye

What a pair of wings on that one you gotta check this out don't you want to be under that one slurping away on your shiny stuff? Take us over there spread me out on that leaf see the veins popping out on those wings the veins popping out on that leaf. Zoom in on those cells of love.

Where are you going get away from there back down here zoom over here what are you looking at no no no can't believe it. You're hungry? Ucch what a sight all those worms crawling on that branch too many worms don't your eyes hurt every rib on every undulating section of disgusting flesh do we have to look at this? Why are you always wanting to eat always casting those eyes about for stupid little morsels?

Back over here you get some sucking love over here forget those poor little maggots we ate two minutes ago you need some love. Oh look at that yes this is why you shed your skin get down on that log there's two of them oh maybe we can get a double thing going don't they look fine those gorgeous dragon hunks waving their wings at us. Look at those drops all over them what is that dew or pond water or rain or just hunk sweat from thinking about us oh yes hundreds of drops making me wet get down in the pond and swim right in me. Dive dive dive!

Not to the right! I can't see over there where you going and don't tell me it's dinner time. No, not pond water scum now you're thirsty damn you could have drunk your fill off the backs of those winged brothers get your tail back over there.

You don't want a mate do you you're living back in your childhood swimming around in the pond happy as a little nymph. You gotta grow up now stop avoiding the facts of life get out there and do it you can't hide in your shell anymore. That shell is long gone lying in pieces by the red log ready to love from the moment we took off spreading those wings it's time to fly it's time to zoom in on the truth and stop looking the other way.

Sharp left that's the way swerve over to that branch no over this way I saw a cute tail swinging by that rock not over there no more leaves you've got to be stuffed yes back over here turn left up down nice move yes this is the way to fly. I'm feeling it now couldn't get it at first too scary but starting to get the drop curve of it where is this wing taking us where is that wing taking us no one seems to know what they're doing. Just want to fly to bust out find some tail but you are in my way you are interfering in the grand plan.

Are you going to remain a virgin your whole life will you pass some kind of test prove something protect your honor? Look at all the boys out there let's go over to that one can't you see how beautiful he is look at the thousands of little parts to him blue green flickering sunlight bouncing off his outstretching wings look look look. Every thousandth of a loving hunk makes me swim with glee fly with pleasure you drive me crazy pulling the focus zooming in on some morsel of bark ucch how can we eat that stuff. You gotta move with me we are a bundle of grace no not the fronds to the right yes the group of guys flapping in the breeze to the left of that algae not the reeds they taste awful why don't you come around to my side look look look that's the one he sees us he's coming over here don't you dare turn keep your eye on the prize not your virgin prize the real prize the reason we're flying the reason we're living the reason we're going take these thousands of tiny eyes of ours and zoom in on love and drop thousands of eggs down in that luscious water. Look look look look look look look!

Immersed in the fragmented view of another soul, Dr. Machiyoko recalled the right and left eyes as fleeting images. This strange experience split her focus within the dragonfly world, and also loosened her mind to receive images from other memories. She felt herself detaching from her body and moving about inside a double of her brain. She dove down under the waters of a brilliant multicolored world, then flew up into the black sea of space, then landed in a twin palace bustling with twenty slave girls!

She tried to settle back into her dragonfly recall. She returned to her awareness of the lascivious insistence of the left eye to focus its thousands of sub-eyes on a mate. As the soul of the right eye, Dr. Machiyoko felt forced to witness a sexual encounter she did not wish to see or have. She failed to subvert her twenty-five thousand gazes.

Suddenly she flipped into another memory. The wet, swampy pondland of the Carboniferous Period reminded her of another sexual encounter from her present lifetime. She had witnessed a man carrying a young woman across a flooded field, and then watched from a safe distance as the couple made love. It was a memory she was not prepared to explore further, or share with the group.

ق

When Dr. Machiyoko came back to awareness, Elvi acknowledged the toll that the long meeting was having. Before adjourning, the group happily agreed to take a week off for Thanksgiving and then meet back, in Verle's attic, their original home.

71

Verlin Walker had never been in the Glenclaire Fresh Foods. As a bachelor Verle did not frequent supermarkets, especially exotic, expensive ones. He had been asked by the church to shop for the Thanksgiving feast. As he entered this garden of earthly delights, a long grocery list in his hand, Verle was afraid.

You can do this, he thought. You're a fine specimen for your age. You can still string two thoughts together, climb a six-foot ladder to change a light bulb, and use that new-fangled Internet. His confidence diminished as he looked down at the list. Organic pumpkin puree? Chanterelles? Ponzu sauce? He saw a young African-American woman pricing cans, thought to ask her for help, then thought better of it. I don't need no stinking help!

Try as he might, Verle could not get the hang of the store's layout. He pushed his shopping cart from aisle to aisle, retracing his steps dozens of times. As a mantra, he kept congratulating himself on his contribution to the last qaraq meeting. Becoming vexed at each elusive item on the list, his dragonfly research crossed his mind. The dragonfly had three sets of ganglia, nerve cords that controlled the eyes, mouth, and spine. Feel like I only have one ganglion in this infernal market. Where do they keep the okra?

And then it all converged on his brain at once: the crowded aisles of strange ingredients, his murky recall from the meeting about warring insect eyes and wings, the image of ganglia firing off messages to control things. Verle clutched his shopping cart for support as his memory traveled back to his dragonfly lifetime.

The Tale of the Budding Brain

The oversoul was worried. The dragonfly was so at odds with itself that it might never find a mate, let alone produce the one hundred thousand eggs necessary to preserve its lineage. The oversoul itched to command but did not trust any of her subjects. They were half-crazed, dashing about in random patterns. Who could she turn to?

The nerve center of the dragonfly had a mind of its own, too, but a good instinct, a fair attitude, and a discerning sensibility. The three ganglia parsed out commands as equitably as possible, given the circumstances. For every lusty action, a self-nourishing act followed; for every turn toward the right, the opposite movement occurred. The oversoul prayed that the nerve center could transcend its instinctual nature and solve the problem by thinking. What this bug needed was a brain.

With a pressing need to organize its messages, the nerve center set out with a scheme: for every nerve impulse to feed, it sent out two impulses to the wings to swerve or explore, and three impulses sent elsewhere to mate. In this way, hunger would have less priority than flight or lust, but would not be neglected. Within the hour the nerve center had lost track of which ganglion had fired last, or how long ago since a signal from the mouth had happened. The struggling ganglia attempted a second organizational scheme: three mating signals in a row, then three food signals, then three flight path signals, all followed by four mating, three food, two flight signals, then five, three, one, then six, three, zero... After an hour of this, the weary ganglia admitted all was lost. Its nerves were shot.

In the heat of the midday sun, the nerve center let go of control and went for the ride. As it followed the organism's chaotic rhythms and bipolar actions, it perceived a beautifully irregular pattern. Launching into action, the developing intelligence tweaked a few firings in the gangliar puzzle and the wings shifted into coordination: as the front wings stroked up the back wings stroked down. Their conflicting activities meshed into a rhythmic compatibility.

The alternating wing patterns removed all possibility of direct flight paths, common to all other insects at the time. What else in the chaotic workings of the dragonfly could fit the new wing pattern? The two eyes and their thousands of collected images! There was the key to allowing the dragonfly to freely shift direction and know where to go. Hover. Move. Hover. Move. The wings brought the insect to a new point, the eyes scouted for a second to determine a path and then the wings shifted in the wind, carried off somewhere else, and hovered again for a moment, eyes scouting, then a new direction, hover, scout, shift.

To all of us who watch a dragonfly flutter about, or a bumblebee or hummingbird, this rhythm of hovering and darting off in a new direction in three-second cycles is quite familiar. Back then this motion was radically new; no one had ever seen such a complex, innovative, and beautifully angular dance of exploration and desire. Other dragonflies and damselflies yearned to mimic it, moths and mosquitoes picked it up in no time, and even small land creatures with high metabolisms scurried to and fro in the same rhythm.

The oversoul had bargained on using the fair and discerning nerve center to do its work, work for which the oversoul's domineering authority was inappropriate. The bargain was won: the ganglia had evolved into a thinking brain and saved the organism. The budding brain liked the taste of this Progress and loved the process of making a delightful puzzle out of a hopeless complication.

And so the dragonfly's 'battle to the life' was over. Weeks later her eggs hatched into the next generation of nymphs scurrying across the pond. The wings of the matured insect, working together with the eyes and the body, flew down to the red bark log. The pieces of its chitin armor still lay in the red-stained earth next to the log. The dragonfly nestled down among the remnants, and laid itself to rest.

"Excuse me, sir, are you all right? Can I help you?"

Verle snapped out of his reverie. The young woman stood by his cart. His previous shopping panic had been replaced by his pride as an evolving brain.

"No thank you, young lady," he said, picking up the list. "It's nothing I can't handle."

72

"I'm so happy to see your funky digs again, old man." Zack smiled as he entered Verle's attic space for the first meeting in December. When the group agreed to continue meeting at the church indefinitely, Zack said, "That whole rotation thing was a pain in the ass. I was sure Amar would bust into my house and break a few precious vases."

"Amar's like a brother to you," Porcy said. "Worry about Sahara. How is Amar?"

"We just celebrated our first holiday with both Amar's father and grandfather. He's been full of good cheer and generosity. He's been coming home early to be with Naji and me. Ooma's on loan to another colleague who has to finish the Y2K preparation before the New Year." Sahara shared her despondency about the many lifetimes in which she and Amar had repeated the same issues. Could millions of years of struggle be ending? Could they change things around in this life, given this gift of awareness of their souls' journey?

Elvi supported Sahara's hope by offering everyone in the group the spirit of thanksgiving for their amazing accomplishments. When she asked for any new information about their dragonfly quest, Verle recounted the story he had received in the grocery store.

"I had a feeling of great exhilaration and peace when it was over," he said. "I felt especially proud of having figured out the brain's puzzle by myself."

"I know you're touchy about this," Sahara said, "but I thought you joined the qaraq to work with others again and not do everything solo. Is there a karmic lesson here?"

Verle remembered refusing help from the woman in Fresh Fields. "No doubt about it. In that case, I yield the floor for the last recall from the group regression. Bax?"

"I wasn't a dragonfly," Bax said, to everyone's surprise. "I was some kind of four-legged animal that came along later."

"A tetrapod, from the late Carboniferous?" Verle asked. "Cute little critters."

"Maybe, sir," Bax said. "Anyway, I died, turned to fossil. I think my fossil fused with Ginger the dragonfly's fossil. Took millions of years, like Naji's egg waiting to be born. In fact, when my corpse fused with the dragonfly, I heard things that the dragonfly's soul remembered from before its birth. From the embryo that was trapped in amber."

"You're saying you heard things from Naji, millions and millions of years later?" Sahara asked. "The fossilized egg chatted with the fossilized corpse?"

Bax nodded.

Zack said. "Prove it."

"Here goes nothing. It starts when I'm still alive."

The Tale of the Vanishing Fossil

Cave. My home. Rock formations surrounding. Old forms from the past. Embedded in rock. Some very familiar. Another cave? Ice mountains? Patterns in rock. Glyphs. Shells. Clustered shapes. I scramble up rock shapes. Footholds. Hiding places. Favorite perch. Knew it well. Red tinged rock with feathery arc lines.

Thunderstorm one night. Lightning hit against rock. Next morning bits everywhere. Favorite perch fallen. Red rock broke away. Afraid to touch it. Unfamiliar family of rocks. New shapes. Two arcs. Like wings. One broken. The other whole. Beautiful. Wing connected to a core, like a body. Something else fused with body. Like a bit of shell. Armor. Dragged wings - body - shell - rock into cave. Loved the wing. The whole one. I curled up in its curve and hugged wing tip. Like a pillow. Comfort at night.

But life is hard. Kill or be killed. Must eat more than I kill. Need more food. Weak. New beasts attack me. Wounded, crawled to cave. Hid away, wrapped in wing. Little life left, little comfort left. Died in her arms.

Remained in shell-wing long after death. Storms buried entry in rock. Hidden away. Much time. Flesh gone. My soul remained. Bones to stone. Fused with wing, shell, whole fossil. Many parts wrapped in each other. I hugged the wing. My fossil, my soul.

Then, a great moment occurred. Soul of winged creature stirred. I plugged into images of its life. Amber cage. Swim, wet, happy. Struggle, new kind of flight. Death near red log. Cave engulfs red log, parts of creature. Wings become red tinged arcs in cave rock. Then my time, my death, our fossil.

Much time passed. Cave ceiling dripped limestone onto limestone fossil. It washed away connections, unfused joints. Smashed wing first to disintegrate. Then shell, bottom half of body. Only top half, wing, my skeleton left. Must save them. At least wing. Felt closer, like mate in life. Like she who gave me life.

Impulse to wrap into wing harder than ever. Tighten the mesh of her limestone. Took enormous effort of will. Heroic. Will to survive. She who gave me will to live. Let me never die! Tried so hard. More I hung on more I lost. Too much pressure. I pushed too hard. My strength destroyed the remains. Wing was vanishing, my bones limestone dust. Bit by bit powdered the floor cave. Cave collapsed. Wing and I an outdoor spectacle. Small crawlers came and sniffed last bits of wing. Then she vanished.

Could not hold on any longer. Speck of lime left. A speck still noticed by a meandering anklyosaur. Pecked by a passing pterodactyl. Kicked by a hairy toe. They will remember. Then they will die. Pterodactyl tells a child, child remembers. Then dies. No speck remains. No trace. No memory. Vanished.

Future scientists have something to dig. But this fossil came before. Before a small child found his first trilobite in Southern Ohio. Before a rack of bones could be museumed into a dinosaur. Long before. A fossil gone before the existence of fossils we have found.

Vanished.

ق

"I must have been the beautiful wing that you loved, right Baxie?" Porcy winked.

"I think you two were seed plants, then coal headed for the South Pole, and then a dragonfly wing and its fossil friend," Verle said. "It follows Earth's chronology."

"I love it, Verle," Porcy said. "Bax and I, in our classic, Platonic way, could barely touch as plants. Appropriately, we couldn't be close as dragonfly body parts. Our next karmic step was to join together in death as fossils."

Zack made a thick lip of sadness. "So I was the broken wing. Story of my death."

"It's so weird you should have memories of Naji's egg life, Bax," Sahara said. "As the egg, Naji prolonged life before his birth for millions of years, and as the fossil you prolonged life after your death for millions of years."

"Now that's karma, Bax," Porcy said. "You hung on to each bit of our fused fossil till the bitter end. But recently you lost the will to live, let go of any shred of connection to life."

"How is that karma?" Sahara asked. "Wasn't preserving this fossil a good thing, a heroic act? Why then would he be punished with a crippling loss of will?"

"Maybe he was holding us back," Verle offered. "You all who were fossilized were prevented from becoming dinosaurs for millions of years."

"You think his karmic lesson was to learn not to be such a big hero, to move on?"

Bax replied. "I lost my will to live when I got fed up with bad lives. Bad deaths. I had too many short lives. Maybe that was my karma for the fossil life lasting eons."

Sahara squatted down next to Bax and took his hand. "It's all right now, Bax. We're all going through something. An old life of yours was twisted around the soul of my newborn. Your fears kept bumping into me as you traveled around the country."

465

"And all of us were crammed into Ginger," Zack said. "Crazy."

"But too intricate to be chalked up to cryptoamnesia," Dr. Machiyoko said.

"Don't you find it all uncanny and incredible?" Porcy asked.

"And awe-inspiring?" Bax squeezed Sahara's hand.

A line from Scheherazade leaped into Sahara's mind: they stripped off their clothes and in front of everyone... Shocked, she pulled away her hand from Bax.

"On that note, let's call it a day," Elvi said. "We'll return to the church next week."

But Sahara was not sure she was returning at all.

466

73

Later that week Sahara Fleming had a dark night of the soul.

She had not fallen asleep all night. Sleep deprivation from feeding baby Naji had pushed her into that state of weariness where sleep is as inevitable as it is impossible. She had lain in bed in a half-awake state for hours, going over her deepest troubles.

She had never quite recovered from the vision in the hospital, of endless Time and endless rebirths, the ominous numerals 1001 facing her like a gargantuan gateway to the Infinite. The numbers had been reinforced by both Ooma's and Diana's visions of the deep extremes of Time, one in the past, the other in the future. And now the interwoven dragonfly recalls of the last weeks seemed to prove the depth of the group's history. The qaraq's relationships seemed endless.

As she drifted in and out of consciousness, Sahara had a fantasy of a group meeting. Along with the current members, Ooma was also present. Was the meeting in Sahara's imagination, or was it a precognition of a meeting in the future? At the meeting, the group discussed the idea of parallel existences, how after shifts in reality, such as a crisis or a silence at the end of a piece of music, a soul can start existing in an alternate reality which occurs simultaneously with the previous reality.

Anything and everything might trigger a parallel life-reality to come into being, Sahara thought. Staring into Sherry the cat's eyes the other day, she had had a déjà vu of staring into some other creature's eyes long ago. Now she wondered if in that instant she had shifted into a parallel existence. Did such things occur on a daily basis?

Disturbed by these thoughts, Sahara tried to sleep again. She drifted into a new vision.

The Tale of the Two Paths

In my search for a transcendent place of existence, I found myself walking on a path through dense forest. The path was difficult and obstructed at every turn by fallen logs, creepers, and puddles of mud. As I walked, crawled, and climbed, I knew I was traversing my own soul, with its countless lifetimes and their hazards.

Eventually the path left the woods and came out onto open scenery of rounded hills and verdant valleys as far as I could see. I knew where I was: the promised land of transcendence, for I was finished with my trudge through the dense forest of lifetimes. I breathed in the cool, fragrant air and resumed my walk with a newly energized stride.

No sooner had I rounded the first bend in the hilly terrain than I came upon a fork in the path. I had not expected any such decision to be thrust upon me, for I was convinced that I had reached the end of my journey. To the right the path led up a hill and to the left it wound down into a valley. I paused to rest and think. I had finally been granted what I deserved, so my heart cried out to take the higher path.

I ascended the hill, convinced that what I wished to attain was located at its summit. I arrived out of breath but exhilarated, and fell down on the ground to rest. As I lay on my back I felt myself become one with the hill, with the sky, with the lands stretching out in all directions below me. My mind was free, as if the passing clouds drifted in and out of my head. My feeling of oneness transformed into a feeling of wholeness, that I encompassed the world. Various people and places and memories and events entered my consciousness, and I felt that I encompassed them, too. I was completely inside myself, convinced that I contained the entire world inside me, that I was the sleeping giant on the hill who had dreamed the entire universe inside her head, that nothing outside of me existed, that life was merely an illusion that I had invented from my inner being.

ق

My God, that can't be true, what self-indulgence, Sahara thought. How could she believe she alone was the Creator? No, it must be a warning of the two paths to transcendence, one is false, not even a parallel possibility. What a nightmare!

Other images went through Sahara's head as she lay there in the dark, a dark not unlike the inside of the sleeping giant's mind, dreaming the universe. There were images from the Nights: demons arguing over a beauty contest, roukhs carrying off humans, lovers swooning at each other's fragrance, unable to rest until they had satisfied their passions, and a mysterious woman making signs from a balcony: index finger to her lips, index and middle finger pressed against her bosom, then pointing downward.

469

Signs. What did they mean? Everything seems to be a sign pointing toward something. What about those numbers, seven, eleven, and ... that number 379, a date supposedly referring to the creation of the Nights, but which made no sense.

Later in her nighttime deliriums Sahara returned to the fantasy of the group meeting, but this time she was absent, and Amar and a grown-up Naji were there. The group continued their talk of parallel existences, imagining endless, tiny, parallel variations of one lifetime, multiplied by all the lifetimes in the qaraq. Sahara tossed in her half-sleep at the thought.

Then Elvi told the group that Sahara had found a practice using parallel lifetimes to escape the cycle of death and rebirth. After this revelation the vision became cloudy. In the dark, Sahara struggled to understand. What was this practice? Did it save her or kill her? Did she find transcendence? From the evidence of the vision where she trod up the wrong path to a self-indulgent moment of solipsism, she was not going to make it.

Sahara lay awake, fidgeting with her hair, waiting for Naji to stir. How could she continue this agony, haunted by such soul-ripping questions, while caring for her baby? She curbed her anxiety and made one last attempt to sleep before Naji woke up. A half hour later, she entered into a state of true restfulness, and her mind found a blessed respite from her questioning and searching.

The Tale of the Two Paths

Eventually the path left the woods and came out onto open scenery of rounded hills and verdant valleys as far as I could see. I knew where I was: the promised land of transcendence, for I was finished with my trudge through the dense forest of lifetimes. I breathed in the cool, fragrant air and resumed my walk with a newly energized stride.

No sooner had I rounded the first bend in the hilly terrain than I came upon a fork in the path. I had not expected any such decision to be thrust upon me, for I was convinced that I had reached the end of my journey. To the right the path led a hill and to the left wound down into a valley. I paused to rest and think. I let my mind relax and I did not worry or push the decision.

After a short while I rose from my place alongside the path, and felt drawn down into the valley. Ahead of me on the path were flowing streams of fresh water, comforting groves of shade trees, grasses and wildflowers everywhere.

I knew not where this delightful stroll would take me, nor was I truly concerned. I simply kept walking, but ever more slowly. Each breath I took of the magical air seemed to slow my pace. I filled my lungs until I felt that I was made of the air itself. I stopped every few steps to take a deep breath, and paused at the bottom of each exhalation. With each pause I became aware of a condition even beyond the lightness in the valley.

I stopped seven more times, breathed eleven more times. After the eleventh exhale, I let out even more air, making a twelfth exhalation, and finally released every bit of air for a thirteenth exhalation. Then a vacuum of space opened up before me and I stepped through, disappearing into the bliss of nonexistence.

ق

As Sahara got out of bed to comfort the crying baby, she felt a great burden lift off her shoulders. She had not fallen

471

asleep during her last hour in bed, but now felt an incredible feeling of comfort from her brief taste of the renunciation of the world.

Once she fussed over Naji and Naji fussed over her, Sahara's thoughts reverted back to questions and worries. Was that a real vision, a precognition of her ability to escape the cycle of death and rebirth? Which of the two paths was she going to take if indeed these were visions of the future? Was she really cut out for such a leap of the soul? As she held Naji to her breast, Sahara was full of awe and pride that she had received a message of transcendent power. She would retain these images for a long time.

However, none of the questions she had just considered were the pertinent issues of her current situation. She was still putting together pieces of her own past life puzzle, marveling at the complex interrelation between her recalls and the others, and accepting the challenge of the vastness of the qaraq's history. The real issue was how to deal with everything in front of her right now, not at some mythical future time. Her meltdown during the night convinced her that the past life work was overwhelming her.

Naji finished nursing and Sahara remained rocking him in the glider. After a few minutes of this silent, calm activity, she came to a decision. She would start a purification process, focus on mothering her child, and quit the group. She felt exhilarated by the choice, gave Naji a warm kiss, and got up to put him in his cradle.

As part of her purification, she would honor the good faith that currently flowed between her and Amar. Without inciting him by revealing the group meetings, she would discuss the more intense images she had been holding back: tonight's vision of enlightenment, the string of appearances of the number 1001 and its relation to the Infinite, and the strange hints at hidden structures connecting the Nights with everything, like that bizarre date 379 – another code for the Infinite? Some lost event in Arabic history?

Suddenly Sahara stood up from the cradle. Of course! She ran downstairs to the den, grabbed several books off the shelf, and furiously began flipping through their pages.

Amar found his wife in the den later that morning. "Baby keep you up?"

Sahara gratefully received a cup of tea from her husband. Pointing to her head, she said, "This baby kept me up. But I have good news. I've figured out what the date 379 means." Sahara closed the book she had been reading and led her husband over to the 'Arabian niche,' the L-shaped sitting area where the couple cozied up on plush pillows. "When Ooma told you about that time in Baghdad, did she describe anything about the city, who was Caliph, for instance?"

"No, just that there was a Caliph. What have you found out?"

Sahara was in a talkative mood, despite her exhaustion. She described her experiences in the night, as well as explaining how her vision in the hospital fit with Ooma's elephant lifetime, how the number 1001 was wrapped up with the notion of the Infinite."

"Slow down," Amar said. "Why are you and Ooma both thinking about these numbers?"

"Dr. Machiyoko foresaw work in the future related to the Nights and the numbers showed up there, too." Sahara explained that the immense scope of the Nights, the hundreds of stories that included history, mythology, romance, and current events, was a parallel to the countless lifetimes a soul passes through. Any numbers or images that recur in the memories of their interconnected community support the link between endless stories, endless lives, endless Time.

Amar listened intensely. "But what about the number 379?"

"It's so simple I could shoot myself," Sahara said. "It's a date, right? About the writing down of a version of the Nights. In Baghdad. So why doesn't 379 A.D. or 379 B.C. make any sense? Because in Islamic Baghdad they have no business with A.D. or B.C. They date things from the Prophet's flight from Mecca, the Hejira, which occurred in our 622 A.D. So it's 379 A.H. After the Hejira. And I call myself an Arabic scholar!"

"So you ran down here to look up 379 A.H. in your books. Any luck?"

"A version of the Nights might have come from 379, but there's little record from then."

"Except for one thing," Amar said. "The Hejira dates from 622 A.D., you said? And 379 A.H. would be 379 years after that. Do the math."

Sahara thought a moment and then inhaled sharply. "Oh my God. It's 1001 A.D."

"Some version of *The Thousand and One Nights* was created in One Thousand and One," Amar said. "That's what Ooma's story is about."

"Amar, this stuff is freaking me out. When I was in the hospital with Naji it was 10/01. The first time I looked at a clock it was 10:01 P.M. Diana and Ooma had recalls with sevens, elevens, and thirteens multiplied together to make 1001. I saw an ominous 1001 figure in my vision. And the making of the Nights by some group like us occurred in 1001 A.D."

Amar reached to enfold her in his arms. "It's okay, love. A lot of these 1001 sightings may have been suggested by hearing other people's recalls."

"It's more than power of suggestion. Something's going on. And a new millennium is about to happen. The year 2000, with all the Y2K fears of the globe shutting down when midnight strikes. I'm scared, Amar, I'm actually scared by all of this." Amar stroked her hair and she let herself sink into him, away from her distress. "This heavy-duty, cosmic stuff is too much for me right now. I just want to be at home with Naji and cuddle with you at night."

"We need to lighten up this house, the way we used to," Amar said. "Let's throw another New Year's party. I've got new clients to entertain, and we'll invite those poor souls who I banished from the house. Let's show Porcy and Zack and everyone that we're not buying into this hokum. We're celebrating our life and our child. What do you say?"

Anxiously, Sahara asked, "You really want to invite people from the group?"

"Let's be generous of spirit. Let them see I'm not such a monster. We can enjoy them in a new context. It's a great idea. We'll be King and Queen for the night."

Sahara did not wish to stir up any new suspicions from Amar, so she threw herself into the planning for the party. In the weeks leading up to it Amar was so full of love and generosity that Sahara found it quite easy to maintain her separation from the group. Her spirit was lighter and she enjoyed the baby's playfulness more than ever. Did Naji understand that his mother was abstaining from her inner search? Was he staying out of her mind and enjoying his life as a carefree infant?

As the month progressed Amar's new benevolence and ebullience spilled over into the bedroom. It had been months since they had made love, and even though her body was still tender, she welcomed the intense contact with her mate.

On the day of the party, Amar was in a particularly sensual mood, but Sahara was anxious about having the group members in her home. Everyone was coming except Elvi and Verle, who had obligations at the church. As late afternoon approached Sahara was dropping utensils, constantly wiping her hands on her apron, and fidgeting with her hair.

Amar stopped by the kitchen to calm her down. "If you have to fiddle, why not play with something useful?" He untied her apron, took the cheese grater out of her hand, and backed her against the counter. She admonished him to be careful of the deviled eggs.

The doorbell rang. Sahara pulled away from Amar and ran to answer it. It was Ooma and Chris, another Glenclaire State student whom she had been dating recently. Sahara led them into the kitchen. "Thanks for helping out," Amar said, patting the young man on the back and, without embracing Ooma, quickly heading to the living room.

Ooma kept silent as Sahara gave them a host of instructions and left Chris to organize utensils and Ooma to clean the insides of the Cornish hens. Sahara went upstairs to check on Naji. She had a couple hours left, which she spent on meaningless details. As she greeted the first guests, she realized that she had nothing to do but enjoy the party.

Porcy and Bax were the first qaraq members to arrive. Sahara felt very nervous about Bax being in her home. When she saw him, another image from Scheherazade flashed in her mind: the black lover who climbed a tree to leave the harem after an orgy.

477

"You poor thing, you're all wound up," Porcy asked, as Chris took their coats. "Baxie, fetch us some libations, please. Sahara, I've been waiting to see you all week. You've missed some great things. There's more news about the Red Isle, and –"

"Ssssh! Porcy, please be careful. Amar still knows nothing about the qaraq."

"It's the new millennium. Time he came around."

Bax came back with hot mugs. "Wassail. Ooma made it strong." Bax seemed like he had gotten a new toy for Christmas. Sahara felt a ridiculous shiver of jealousy.

Porcy said, "Go on, Baxie, go play with your friend in the kitchen. But not like last year. That boy Chris knows where the carving knives are."

After a parade of Amar's clients trudged in from the cold, Dr. Machiyoko arrived, sporting a mini-dress. "Happy New Year!" Behind her, Zack came in with his mother, Cachay. As Chris took their coats, Zack peered into Sahara's mug at the wassail.

"Have this young man deliver mine personally."

"Don't be crude, Zachary," his mother scolded. Sahara and the therapist exchanged a look and mouthed 'Zachary' to each other. Cachay turned to Sahara. "Thank you for having us. I know I wasn't exactly invited, but I see I need to keep an eye on my son."

Sahara and Porcy went outside to the heated patio, where the fountain was still flowing. Sahara was happy to be in her favorite spot, and the wassail lifted her mood considerably. As they sat at a corner table, Sahara entreated Porcy to speak quietly.

"When we came up the stairs for the last meeting Verle was playing that shimmery gamelan music from Indonesia," Porcy said. "Said it had triggered something in him. So Elvi regressed him and it opened up the whole Madagascar thing again. Remember Zananzi, Naji's trader life? How he was on his way to Tyre, to marry the daughter of a sea trader, having given her a xylophone? Tyre was in Phoenicia, and in Verle's past life there was a trader named Ugrit from Phoenicia. Ugrit inherited an instrument with mysterious powers and origins."

"So Ugrit the trader was a descendant of Zananzi's fiancé," Sahara said. "Was Verle Ugrit?"

"No, but Ugrit was very protective of her."

"Her?"

"Verle was the instrument, a xylophone named Vaalat. Listen."

The Tale of the Shipwrecked Xalafon

Ugrit proudly displayed the Instrument at market or to foreign traders. He told everyone about this Instrument, how unique it was, how fortunate they were to do business with him because of the luck and prosperity that contact with this sacred relic would bring them. He played up the Instrument so much that his colleagues and customers believed he was descended from religious power figures from distant lands.

Ugrit came to belief his own myths. Because his family had passed down many fears about playing the Instrument, he devoutly refused to demonstrate its musical qualities. He refused business to customers who insisted on stroking or hitting the bars of the Instrument. Fearing some jealous trader might make off with his precious artifact, he displayed a long curved knife to prevent any tampering with the Instrument.

Ugrit named the Instrument Vaalat, in homage to the Goddesses of Phoenicia, the Baalat. He curled up next to his bronze favorite as he slept, stroking it and speaking as to a female lover he would cherish and protect to his dying day.

"Vaalat, Vaalat, my heart is heavy. I cannot rid my mind of a terrible foreboding. My thoughts drift like the sea to strange, dark images. Somewhere in my past I suffered a great defeat, though the memories flooding me are not of Phoenicia or any place I have visited. In one image I sip a warm liquid from a cup on a chain about my neck. The liquid soothes me, since I have done great harm to someone who cared deeply for me." Ugrit stroked the bars of the Instrument. "I dread that harm will come to us, Vaalat."

Ugrit's fears came true during an expedition down the African coast. His ship crashed into rocks during a violent storm. Crew and passengers scrambled ashore, returned to the shattered ship when the storm abated, unloaded goods and brought them to the nearest market. But Ugrit was washed farther south, separated from his goods and Vaalat.

Vaalat found herself in the hands of a Phoenician trader who had always been a rival of Ugrit's. This merciless trader considered casting the Instrument onto the rocks to spite Ugrit, then thought of the coin he might earn and took Vaalat to a busy fishing port.

At the open market there, a local griot named Kibondo tested Vaalat's quality as a xalafon. In the last two centuries mallet instruments had enthralled the African populous and Kibondo was excited to find such a rare example. He stroked Vaalat's bronze bars and lifted her up to peer at her resonators, discovering a strange symbol underneath. He reached into his bag, drew out two wooden mallets, and hit Vaalat. Ugrit had never permitted anyone to touch her, let alone strike her!

Kibondo struck again and Vaalat became aware of a sound, not the brutish noise when one being strikes another, but a clearly pitched sound. Kibondo struck once more and Vaalat felt a desire rise up inside her. He struck again and again, the strokes now a rhythm beating up and down her spine. Never had Vaalat heard anything like it! Vaalat felt tremors all through her body, tickling, shivering, cascading her being with vibration. Pleased with the sound, Kibondo haggled for the xalafon and took Vaalat away from Ugrit's rival.

And so Vaalat became fully cognizant of her existence. Music was her birthright. She may have been some kind of ritual object deep in the past, but surely her power back then was through this sound. The legacy that Ugrit bragged about, the royal Queens and Goddesses who had sought out glory through their sacred objects, surely their glory and longevity was little compared to the mastery and beauty of the playing of the Instrument, the intricacy of the interlocking mallet rhythms, and the pleasuring of people. It was now more important for Vaalat to be special in how well she connected to others, not how sacred, glorious, and superior she was to them.

Vaalat's soul rose up within her and was reborn.

"Very beautiful," Sahara said, genuinely moved. "I love it."

"I don't." Sahara and Porcy turned to see Amar standing over their table.

75

Amar offered Porcy a mug of wassail. "We really don't want to be wrapped up in that past life nonsense, do we?" Sahara could see the tension in her husband's jaw, despite his jovial tone. "It's New Year's."

"I better check on the guests." Sahara started back into the house.

"Sahara," Amar called, a slight touch of demand in his voice. "don't go far."

"Oh, please," Porcy said, facing up to Amar, "you put your lovely wife under house arrest, so there's a lot of news to catch up on. It *is* New Year's, so lighten up."

Porcy grabbed Sahara by the arm and marched out the terrace doors. In the kitchen, Sahara was glad to see Ooma still sweating over the counter. Bax worked next to her. Porcy opened the refrigerator, pulled out a tray of appetizers, and set it down on the breakfast table. Sahara sat with Porcy in the nook. She kept her voice low.

"Is there more story? Please hurry, Amar might walk in here any second."

"Relax. Did you wonder what happened to Ugrit after the shipwreck? Verle had one more memory fragment from this lifetime, one particular performance, where Kibondo played Vaalat in an ensemble of seven musicians. What was fuzzy was the fact that Ugrit was there, maybe trying to retrieve the Instrument from Kibondo, maybe arguing with him before the performance, but he stood near Vaalat the whole time."

The Tale of the Shipwrecked Xalafon, conclusion

The musicians played separately, each outdoing the other with their skill. Then they began to form small groups: a plaintive duet between Vaalat's xalafon and the streams of sound from a seventeen-string kurdan; a fiery trio for the two kunga drummers and the rhythmic harpist; a quartet for Vaalat, the kurdan, one of the kungas, and a fellow on double ram's horn. Finally, these six musicians joined forces for an exhilarating climax.

Two other figures stood in the playing area with the musicians: a percussionist who sat alone on the side, and Ugrit, clutching the curved knife at his side.

Vaalat was glad when Kibondo began the final piece off with a fast, repeating rhythmic figure that invited the players to fit in over it. The harpist locked in a second repeated pattern and Vaalat sank into the wonderful flow happening between them. The kungas increased the energy with their driving rhythmic bounce, the kurdan sang out a lilting melody over the busy accompaniment, and the ram's horn glued it all together with long, sustained tones. This was glory! Vaalat thought.

Ugrit was silent and still, listening intently but deep within himself. When it was Kibondo's turn to solo he played like a true master. Vaalat made a conscious effort to pull himself off the earth, to allow as little resistance to the resonation of the sound. The tempo increased. The villagers rose to their feet in rapture.

Ugrit snapped out of his reverie. Near him, the lone percussionist pulled a new Instrument out of his sack, a large gong, rare among Africans. The sight of it drew a gasp from the already excited crowd. Ugrit reacted to the sight of the gong with panic and fear, recognizing something at its appearance. The other musicians became aware of the odd percussionist holding the gong in one hand and a large mallet in the other. It was the signal to drive the music to climax, and Kibondo hammered furiously into Vaalat.

Ugrit turned from the gong to Vaalat and back several times, barely able to contain his distress. The music swelled, the kungas brought home a final rhythm, and everyone, on the stroke of the gong, was ready to lay into their instruments with a resounding attack.

At exactly the same time Ugrit pulled his curved blade from its sheath and raised it high above his head.

The mallet struck the gong. The knife pierced through Ugrit's own flesh. The flooding sound of the gong drowned out Ugrit's scream.

ق

Sahara stood up, knocking her chair backwards onto a stack of cheese trays.

"Looks like her year to get drunk," Ooma said to Porcy. "Some water? Aspirin? Rehab?"

Porcy grabbed a Perrier, quickly guided Sahara to the back stairs at the rear of the house. "Drink this, baby. Breathe. Good, you're still with us. What's going on with you?"

484

Sahara sat on a stair and put her head between her knees to breathe. "The Gong ... Ageng ... curved knife ... the thief ... told me ... I ... killed ..."

At that moment a distressed Bax showed up. "She okay?"

"Do us a favor," Porcy said, "fetch Dr. M."

"Right!" Bax turned on his heels, glad to have a mission.

Sahara sat up slowly and tried a sip of water before speaking. "End of Verle's tale. Same image as my recall of the first thief on the beach. The one with me and Naji." She took another sip. "I remember it all now."

The Tale of Sahnra and the Thief, conclusion

"Goddess! Stop! I will tell you everything!"

"If you wish peace, show me one difficult truth from your tale."

"Very well, Goddess. It will expose a layer of dark rot among your people. You are only among them now because your predecessor was vilely destroyed. Behold."

I curled my hair around his head and looked into his memory. Clearly as the feel of sand on my skin I saw the great Instrument hanging proudly in its shrine. An incredibly tall man approached it, carrying an enormous mallet. Next to him stood a beautiful figure whom I recognized as the previous Goddess. As the man prepared himself, a dark female figure emerged behind the Goddess. She held a curved blade above the Goddess, ready to strike. The memory was completely vivid and real to me. I knew it was the truth.

As the man struck the Instrument with the mallet, the blade pierced the Goddess. The flooding Sound of the sacred Vessel drowned out her scream of shock and horror.

485

The entire moment ripped through me.

Just then Bax brought Dr. Machiyoko to the back of the house. The therapist checked Sahara's pulse and breathing, and when she deemed that the woman was not in danger, she encouraged her to continue the story.

A wave threw a foam of seawater onto the beach where we lay, clutching each other. The cold wet jarred me from the image of the Gong and the murder. I eased my grip on the thief, loosening several strands of my reddish coils from around his neck.

"Goddess, how do you look inside my soul like that?" he asked.

"Never mind, thief. Who are you? How do you know these things? This horrible assassination came to pass before you were born."

"Before you were born, Sahnra. I call myself Zanaj. I am one of the Zanj people on the mainland. Our name comes from the Zabaj people, from the distant island we all came from originally, before our boats took us across the sea, before some of us broke away to live on the Red Isle. I am called Zanaj in honor of those first people, before evil set in."

"You will tell me of this evil now. And curb your disdain."

"Shall I sugar you with sweet words, like a bedtime tale? Very well."

Once upon a time there was a beautiful Queen named Oumkratania. She had everything in the world, but it was not enough for her. She wanted something beyond the pleasures of her palace and the obedience of her people. She ordered her chief Minister to find something amazing and new that would make everyone on the Red Isle marvel. And so the Minister looked far and wide, for failure would mean his death.

A noble roukh, friend to the Red Isle, found the Minister weeping in despair. The roukh comforted the Minister and told him to wait for a week and a day until he returned. The enormous bird flew with all his might to the distant island from where he knew our people had come. He knew of wondrous musical instruments there from the Zabaj community. The roukh chose the most magical Instrument of all, the mighty Gong Ageng, and he flew with it in all haste back to the Minister, who delighted in it, and presented it to the Queen, who also delighted in it.

But Oumkratania was only after long-lasting fame. She slew the Minister and claimed she herself had invented the Gong. The people marveled, and the priestesses adopted the Gong into their worship. The Gong became a symbol of the everlasting, of cosmic Time. When Oumkratania died, other Queens coveted the same glory and struggled with the priestesses for control of the Instrument's power.

Around this time, Cachay came upon the small group huddled near Sahara on the stairs. Expecting to hear party chatter, she was surprised to recognize the Red Isle world.

"Perfect timing. We're up to your part in the story," Porcy said. "Evil Queen time."

Cachay bristled, but did not leave. Sahara continued Zanaj's tale to the Goddess.

Queen Khajy began the struggle between the Queens and priestesses, Zanaj continued, and the Goddesses attempted to keep the peace and preserve the Instrument's sanctity. Most recently, a Queen destroyed the Goddess with the sacrificial knife. She commands her people with malevolent will, hiding the truth, and her priestesses have either fallen in with her corrupt beliefs or been murdered. Deceit festers throughout the queendom.

"I tried my best," Zanaj said, "but the tale does not end sweetly."

"You have not told me how you know so much about the queendom," I said. "You are hiding something." I coiled a strand of hair tighter around the thief.

"I am from a family of spies who vowed to reclaim the Gong and other instruments from our motherland. We revere the ancient blacksmith Panji, who gave us tools to forge bronze. In his name we have forged a way back to the Instrument by uncovering the truth."

"Did this reverence teach you spying and thievery? I do not believe or trust you."

"I know the location of the sacred knife."

"You bluff, miscreant."

"It is hidden underneath the Gong platform, retrievable by a secret latch on the right side, where the mallet hangs. My family also knows that the knife has a magic power and that the Goddess is vulnerable to its sting only at a precise stroke of the Gong Ageng."

I instinctively knotted a strand of hair. This was more than a mere thief, but someone who carried with him dangerous knowledge. I spoke carefully.

"You have convinced me, Zanaj, of the verity of all you say." I relaxed my grip on him. He did not attempt to escape. "Where will you bring the Instruments?"

"My family awaits me. If I could leave this island I would rejoin them on the shore."

"Why should I trust your people with the Instruments?"

Zanaj smiled for the first time. "I offer you our good faith. My family has known the secret of the knife for generations, but we have never put it to use. We respect the Goddesses of the Red Island for their protection of the Instrument."

I released my grip on him. "I will aid you. Gather the sacred vessels."

"Mind if I join the party?" Zack was the next person to discover the group.

"Just make sure she has enough air," Dr. Machiyoko said. "Go on, Sahara."

Zanaj slowly stood, stretching his muscles from the pain I had inflicted. He retrieved the stolen Instruments from the sand. I wrapped my hair around him and the Instruments. I let a number of strands blow free in the wind, allowing them to pick up the power of the pre-dawn air. The golden-red locks fluttered, then whipped, then whirly-gigged in the air until we lifted off the ground and flew toward the mainland shore.

I held Zanaj slightly above the waters, reminding him of his fragile connection to life while in my hands. The feeling of holding a child in my arms returned. He was a threat to every Goddess; why would I want to embrace him? I fought down the soft sensation.

All this time, Zanaj guided me to the location where his family was waiting. "There, where the water dashes into that large cave. See? Those five people are my family."

I headed toward the group of people, now waving and shouting. We alighted on the beach. I held the Instruments off to the side, safely out of reach of the waves.

"Thank you, Sahnra. You have liberated your sacred Instruments."

I pushed Zanaj forward on the sand in front of me. His family came running to him, ecstatic with glee at the sight of him and the Instruments.

"It is a great day, Goddess!" Zanaj said, turning back to me. "Now you must help us bring down the Queen-usurpers."

"And then what?" I demanded. "Usurp the usurpers?" My words froze him to the spot. As his family reached him, they saw the fury in my eyes. I stepped toward all of them, my hair whipping wildly in the wind. "If you overthrow this Queen, new rulers will establish your own corrupt ways: spying, stealing, defying deities even when they have you in a stranglehold! Do you think I would permit your group of criminals to pass down their dangerous secret? And risk my own vulnerability? Fools!"

I had the thief and his gang in my trap. My hair lashed out at each of them. The weaklings screamed. Zanaj ran to me and implored me not to kill his family. Once again, my heart melted; a strand of hair softened around his shoulders. By his sacrifice, I would not rectify the wrongs of those in power. The Queen and Court had overstepped their territory. Through his courage, Zanaj had opened my eyes to the truth. Still, he too was a danger.

The strands of my hair grabbed his head tightly, snapped it around to face his family. I whirled my sun-red locks and drew the hapless family members toward Zanaj and me. I forced him to witness my spinning hair slice his family into ribbons of blood and flesh.

The sight of the carnage was too powerful for him. Zanaj's eyes glazed over. A dozen strands of hair spiraled through his body. In his final moment, Zanaj saw that the truth does not achieve results. Then he was no more than blood upon the sand.

ق

After a silence from the group on the stairs, Zack said, "What a downer."

"Don't be so melodramatic, Zachary," his mother said. "It made me feel much better. I may have been a despicable Queen, but I was from a long line of despicable Queens. They claimed their glory from the so-called originality of the Gong Ageng, but its originality was an illusion. There was nothing new under the sun."

"Anything that appears new always has a predecessor," Dr. Machiyoko said. "Now we know that Indonesian travelers settled on the coast of Africa and then Madagascar."

"We still don't know who stole the Instrument from the Pyramids," Bax said.

"We've got the rest of the story," the therapist said. "After the Queens started their myth, Zanaj failed to take the Instrument back to the mainland. He was reborn as Zananzi the trader and thwarted by the Goddess in the desert. The roukh hid the Instrument at the Pyramids, found it in Indonesia, and returned it to Madagascar during D'aulai's reign of terror."

"When the trader Zancq took an instrument and spread it across Africa," Zack said.

"And according to Verle, as late as 1000 B.C. another trader named Ugrit relived the myth of the Instrument," Porcy said. He witnessed the great artistic value of the Instrument, saw that it was superior to greed for glory, and killed himself. A neat moral and end of story."

"Look how much the qaraq has figured out, especially after Sahara returned to the meetings," Dr. Machiyoko said. "I know we'll find that missing piece of the story."

"What an ordeal you've had, Sahara," Porcy empathized. "This is what you've been dreading, finding out what terrible act you did to the thief. No wonder you blocked it out."

491

"That thief had the soul of Naji. I did that to my baby."
Sahara rose to her feet. "I should go check and make sure he's
all right."

"He's fine."

Sahara froze. The group looked up the stairs in the direction of the voice. It was Amar. "Go check on him yourself,"
he said, "not because it's about time someone did, but because
you had a recall where you discovered you were capable of
violence to him."

Backing off the stairs, Sahara mumbled, "How long have
you been listening?"

"Long enough to hear that there's an informal meeting going
on of the blessed and forbidden qaraq." His voice was calm,
but no less menacing. "It's bad enough you're whispering
your goddamn stories in the corners of my party. Bad enough
I hear that you returned to the meetings behind my back."
Slowly and deliberately, he started down the stairs toward the
group. "Bad enough you share a story I have asked for many
times, that I suspected you were hiding: what you did to the
thief. Bad enough that I should hear it last."

Amar's voice rose as he got closer to Sahara. "But how
dare you put me through hell because of my anger, my violence, when you yourself, down in your soul, are capable of
the most horrific violence imaginable." He was at the foot of
the stairs now, punctuating his words with sharp blows against
the banister and the wall. "Why should I bother curbing my
anger!" He closed in toward his wife.

Bax stepped between Sahara and the fuming Amar. "Stop.
Don't hurt her."

"Oh, her big hero."

"Amar Rash! What do you think you're doing?" Cachay
stopped the altercation between Amar and Bax with her com-
manding voice. "I didn't entrust Zack to look after you all

those years ago just to see you grow up into a bellowing beast. Next you'll have mounted her and enjoyed her in front of your guests. Apologize this instant!"

"Stay out of this," Amar said, his voice already softened.

"Oh hell, Amar, I don't want your damn apology." Sahara voice was hoarse. "Go play with your Wall Street buddies and leave me alone." She bolted up the stairs.

Naji was asleep in the nursery, but after Sahara told the sitter she could have a break, she picked up her love bundle and brought him into the bedroom. After holding the baby close to her for a few minutes, she placed him gently in his basket.

Dr. Machiyoko poked her head into the bedroom. "How are you feeling?"

"I'm all right, thanks to Cachay." They laughed at Zack's staunch mother scolding Amar. "I'm going to lie down for a bit."

"Good. It's less than an hour till midnight. I'll leave you alone."

Sahara lay on the bed, her eyelids extremely heavy. She lost track of time and only vaguely heard someone enter the room. A body lay down next to her on the bed and gently touched her shoulder.

"You okay?"

In her drowsy state, Sahara turned to see who spoke. It was Bax.

493

76

"What are you doing here, Bax?" Sahara said. "Where's Ooma?"

"We're on break. Everything's under control. I was worried about you."

Sahara knew she should get up from the bed, rejoin the party, and get away from Bax.

"You've been important to me," he said. "Porcy's been great, but you're different." Bax moved his hand along the bedspread. "You look real nice."

"Thank you, Bax." Sahara tried to think of something to say, to acknowledge Bax's sincerity, without crossing a line. "You're the one person in the group who's actually been helped by the past life work. You've become stronger through it. God knows, the recalls have wrecked everything and everyone I've touched."

He reached out and touched Sahara's leg. It was meant as a gesture of sympathy, but Sahara felt desire shoot up and down her lower body. "Thanks for standing up for me," she said.

"It's good for me. Helps me overcome my fears." Bax caressed Sahara's leg and hips. Sahara wanted to extract herself but feelings rose inside her. She remembered the charged fantasies about Bax that had triggered her recall of the rape in the Borzi world. Bax moved closer to her. She could not trust her intensifying feelings. She placed one hand on Bax's face to stop him from getting closer, put the other hand on her hip to stop Bax stroking her.

"What the hell! What the bloody hell!"

Sahara jumped up from the bed, almost backing into Naji's basket. Amar stood in the doorway. "Past lives at our party! A group meeting on the back stairs! And now this!"

Bax got up cautiously from the bed, not sure where to go. "Mr. Rash. Sir..."

"Don't try," Sahara said. "Just get out of here."

Amar pushed Bax aside to get to the bed, and threw the covers back. "Why not stay and fuck her soul out, Bax?"

"Amar, please, not so loud." She had to get him away from Naji. She headed out the door and down to the living room. Amar followed her.

"Perfect! If you're going to fuck during the party, you might as well do it in front of the guests. Sahara quickly sent the sitter upstairs. Amar entered the living room, shouting.

"Honored guests! Attention, please!" There was instant silence in the room. "Have you all met my lovely wife, Sahara Fleming – the whore?" Bax crept into the living room and stood next to Porcy. "And her lovely consort, the fox in the harem-house."

Porcy said, "What are you doing? Are you drunk?"

"Yeah," cried Charlie Rosenfeld, one of Amar's colleagues. "It's almost midnight."

"No such thing as midnight, Charlie," Amar said, "Not this year, not any year. I just found my wife in bed with this young stud, and I'm mad as hell, and I don't want to spoil the party, but the party has been spoiled, and anyone who wishes to be unspoiled should bugger off and go find their own midnight, because there's no such thing here, just endless endless blackness."

Sahara was shocked her husband was so out of control in a situation that would impact his career. "Amar, our guests. Please."

"Excuse me, Miss Scheherazade, bastion of morality." He swiped his arm along a row of glasses and flung them to the floor. "And I'm the bad guy, a side of myself I've only recently discovered, thanks to my wife, my big brother Zack, and his group." Guests from the office cautiously fled to the front door, where a frantic Chris went to find their coats. "I'm the murderer of virgins, the rapist caveman fucking my way through a sacred orgy! Or fucking my way through the office with Ooma Qadir. My own wife thinks this, right before she beds down next to the baby!" Amar knocked over a vase and upturned a tray on a table. The rest of the guests got up to leave.

Only the members of the qaraq stayed. Amar ran to the kitchen. "Ooma! Get the hell out here and prove my innocence. I am guilty only of what you people do: dig up a few stories." Ooma, wiping off hours of kitchen grease and grime with a towel, stepped gingerly into the living room. "Ooma, have I done anything to compromise you?" Amar glared around the room at the group. "Tell the Court."

"We've gotten into past lives after hours sometimes. That's it."

"Do you remember the last recall? Tell the group about the place where my wife says I raped her, disguised as the tribal God Borzu."

This new development surprised Sahara. How were Amar and Ooma involved in the Borzi world?

Ooma looked around the room, like the little girl performing Persian poetry for her parents' guests. She could do this. She looked at her watch. Fifteen minutes to midnight.

"And Ooma," Amar said, "tell it from my perspective."

The Tale of the True Borzu

It is my third drilke of the day. The dying animal lay on the ground. I will have time for more. The sun does little to the cold and wind. I have been careful with spear and arrow, let the wind help guide the shafts.

The men warn me not to take too many drilke. Many suns ago I took one and left it so I could chase another. When I returned the cold had taken it from me, no one could cut it open, blades were broken, the ice held it to the earth so we could not drag it back. Brga was not pleased and this made me feel the fire inside. The next hunting time I still felt the fire. I threw the spear at a drilke close to Brga.

"Cut it now if you wish," I shouted at Brga. "I will still hunt. Brga scolded me, warned me to cut my own. My rage shivered up to my shoulders like the wind at night. I pulled my spear from the drilke and shook the blood at Brga's face. "I give you! Do you not take?" Brga stepped toward me but I held the spear to his chin. Finally he bent down to the drilke. You cannot refuse such a gift. I wiped the spear on his fur and walked away.

I hunt now with my men. Some stay to cut the meat. Some scout. Only a few hunt with me. We take so many that we need only a few hunters. All know I will take the most. I throw the strongest spear, aim the straightest arrow, find the best of the herd.

497

I cannot stop to cut, to drag the carcass, remove the horns. I do not care for these things. When I think of this work I feel the fire, the rage. Yes, my men must eat, our women, our children must eat. The drilke keep us alive. But I live only for the hunt.

The hunt enflames me. Like the day Brga lit the fire inside me. As I search in the wood and crack a twig, the fire sparks. As I brush against thorns or feel a branch snap at my face, the fire flares. Then, as I see a buck standing quietly, the fire blazes. My arms burn to throw, to shoot. To kill. I cannot hear or feel anything but the rush of flame through my head. I know then that I do not kill for need but to release the flames so hot they blind, turn to blaze to light to sun to heat to good to me.

After, when my eyes see again, I don't know why there is blood on my hands. Then I remember that I killed the beast. And the fire returns: why is the drilke dead, no good for hunting anymore? And I release the fire again, I hunt to feel the fire and its light.

I have followers now, some by fear, like Brga, but many who know there will be many drilke to eat, to hunt, to feel gladness at the taking. They call me Borzu now, after the spirit of the cold wind that throws the spear. They think I am the spirit of the frozen wind.

It is always cold here but coldest in winter and last winter the coldest in the old men's memory. All looked to me as the wind bore down and asked what should be done, Borzu, what to offer the wind, how to live with the ice? All the talk made the fire burn in me: I am not Borzu. I shouted at my men to save the drilke for the winter. Some learned how to use the ice to keep the meat good. I shouted at others to keep the people quiet. These men made rules for sharing the food, to keep us alive in the winter. Borzu, stop the cold, keep your winds away. I cannot do this, I will not do this, the ice fire shouts. And the men set up fires, find deeper caves, and use the furs to keep out the worst cold.

I do nothing but release the fire and the men do all the rest. The people hear me shout and see me send the men away and then the men do good things for them. They tell stories of Borzu sending men away and great things happening. The stories are told so often I feel I have heard them my whole life.

In the springtime other men and women and children see how we have lived well through the hardest winter, how the Borzi thrive. And we are joined. I command many now, as many as suns before the next winter. There are more and more to feed, to help, to protect. I continue only to hunt, to take the drilke, to feel the fire release at men, at the hunt, at my women. There are many of them and many children by them.

I hunt, I command, I shout, I breed. Where first he enraged me, I now welcome the cold spirit Borzu into our land. I lead the Borzi, the warriors of the North wind, the winter people. I am Borzu.

ق

Dr. Machiyoko spoke up. "Sahara, I remember your recall about the Borzu impersonator in the cave. Amar, if you were the original Borzu, the hunter who became a myth to the Borzi, then you couldn't have been that fake Borzu in a mask."

"There was another recall," Sahara said, "from the perspective of the rapist. He was an outsider who had snuck into the Borzi's secret rites. I thought this recall was Amar's."

"But it wasn't Amar's lifetime," the therapist said.

The qaraq followed Sahara's gaze to Bax. Bax kicked the chair next to him.

"It was my lifetime! I recognized it when you told us. I didn't say anything because I already was an outsider in the group. Always the fucking outsider!" Without looking at anyone, Bax stormed out of the front door into the cold winter air. Porcy headed after him.

"Aren't you going, too?" Amar said to Sahara. "I know you get us mixed up, the proud hunter and mythic leader, and the devious, weak-willed rapist. I can see how that's confusing. But maybe you prefer to blame me for everything."

Sahara headed for the stairs, then turned back. "I'm sorry, Amar."

Amar plopped down in one of the living room chairs and said, "The rest of you, go on. BEGONE!" At Amar's booming command, Chris ran out the door. The baby sitter came downstairs and left. Zack and Cachay approached Amar but he waved them away. Dr. Machiyoko joined them on their way out.

Ooma remained with Amar. She poured each of them a glass of Champagne, then raised her flute in a toast. "Nice one, boss. Here's to finding new clients in the New Year."

Amar downed his glass. "They'll be back. There's a recession coming. Is it New Year's yet?"

Ooma looked at her watch. "As this old elephant said: 'There is no such thing as midnight.' It was ten minutes ago, when you were banishing your guests."

Amar reached for the Champagne. "It's not like I had anyone to kiss." Ooma took the bottle away from him and went into the kitchen. Amar sulked quietly until Sahara came down the stairs, Naji in her arms, a travel bag over her shoulder.

"Where are you going?" Amar asked.

"Someplace safe," Sahara said, heading for the coat closet.

"Oh for Christ's sake!" He slammed his glass down. "Where are you going?"

500

"I'll let you know when I figure it out. Maybe." She wanted to get out of there as fast as possible. Before she changed her mind.

"There *is* no such thing as midnight," he said. "No New Year, no celebration, no end of the old year, no end to anything, just nonstop pain."

"Yes, lifetime after lifetime," Sahara said. "I should have been warned by that first recall of you as the killer Ardryashir. 'Get out now, run, flee.' Better late then never."

As Sahara opened the front door to leave, Ooma came from the kitchen with a broom and dustpan. Avoiding Sahara's gaze, she began sweeping up the broken glass.

"Ooma, I'm sorry if I thought the worst of you," Sahara said. Ooma nodded, without looking up from her sweeping. Sahara was about to say more, but thought better of it.

She walked out of the house and closed the door behind her.

Ooma looked up to see Amar's reaction. He sat motionless.

"Okay, boss, on your feet. We've got a big mess to clean up."

77

Of all the people in the qaraq, including anyone who had remembered a past life, all but Verle and Porcy lived in houses. Verle's attic room at the church had space enough to hold meetings, but the sparse furnishings could not provide for a guest. Porcy's humble apartment had a foldout couch, which was being used by Bax. Of the houses, Ooma lived with her parents and younger sister, Amar was without his family that New Year's Day, Zack lived too close to Amar, and Cachay lived in the Glenclaire hills, but Sahara had never seen her house. No one knew where Elvi lived but everyone assumed the mysterious woman did not live in Glenclaire.

Dr. Machiyoko's house was the only logical place to go, Sahara thought as she stood out in the cold in front of her house. She was about to fetch more things for Naji when the door to Zack's house flew open. He stood in the threshold, Dr. Machiyoko behind him. Sahara rushed up to the house and embraced them.

"We saw you come outside with the baby," Zack said. "Couldn't leave you alone with Mr. Hothead and his pet squirrel."

Diana grabbed the travel bag off of Sahara's aching shoulder. "You ready to come home with me?"

"Di, how did you –?"

"Psychic, remember?"

"Let's go before he comes out to give Ooma a ride home."

"Take the Mercedes, leave him the Camry," Zack said.

As Sahara pulled out of her driveway, Zack ran up to her car. "I've got the spare key to your house. If you need anything..."

"Thanks, I really appreciate what both of you are doing. Sorry it's so messed up."

Zack backed away from the car. "It's all part of the story."

When Sahara moved in with Dr. Machiyoko, the two women were like roommates, cooing over the baby, eating out often, and staying up all hours to discuss what Sahara should do with her life. Whether out of fury or confusion, Amar kept silent after the disastrous party, neither tracking down Sahara to confront her, nor cutting her off from their bank accounts. She cherished the silence between them. To Sahara, the New Year's catastrophe was a clear sign that she must embrace her independence. Her primary focus was to renew her studies, find work, and provide for her child.

Other members of the qaraq visited to check up on Sahara. Verle surprised them one Tuesday night; neither woman had seen him since before Christmas. The qaraq meetings had been canceled in January while Elvi was out of town, and Verle was feeling bereft at the emptiness in his room. The women spent more time comforting the old man than talking over Sahara's plight.

Porcy and Bax came over the day after the party to make sure there were no hard feelings about the false Borzu revelation. Bax brought Sahara a bouquet of roses, as if in apology after a thousand centuries. But she knew that to respect her new independence, she should not get involved. She was relieved when he did not visit her during the month.

Both Zack and his mother came regularly to deliver food, bring things from the house, and help with the baby. Neither Sahara nor the therapist warmed to Cachay and her crusty manner; nonetheless Sahara was careful to express her appreciation of the help. When Zack discovered that Dr. Machiyoko shared a love of Asian art, the avid collector began bringing over small relics and prints to decorate the therapist's spare home. The budding closeness was odd to both of them. It was even stranger when Zack shared a vision he had received, of a lifetime that cast new light on the bond between them.

The Tale of Zizagh and Dizalegh

You were a very private woman named Dizalegh, and I was a confident researcher named Zizagh, who had hired you for a project sorting out a cache of journals and interrelated documents. Over the years, the dazzling complexity of the material had inspired others to graft their own structures onto the collection, but completion of the project had defied everyone.

You were an extraordinary assistant, Dizalegh, absorbing all the stories and ideas in the collection, able to sort through them in your head whenever a reference was needed. When I lost you, I was unable to work, not just because I could not concentrate or because every word of the journals reminded me of you. I could not read through my tears.

Long ago the actual texts had been transferred to an electronic medium, and more recently the texts were read by the new hands-free reading lens technology. A text is now in the shape of a pair of contact lenses: simply pop the reading lenses in your eyes and the book appears in your vision. Unless your eyes are drenched with tears, like mine.

I wish I had one of the decades-old volumes in my hands, with pages pressed from synthetic woods, or one of the original Twenty-First Century journals with its fiber and elephant dung sheaves, now tucked away under filterglass in the Library of Constance, for then I could watch my tears splash upon the culprit pages that held us together. I could hold our beloved text in my arms, as if embracing you, and remember your love of the project.

You fell in love with it all, not just the ethereal histories of tales that stretched back into time, or the chaos of oral transmissions, undated journal entries, and past life strings; you also had a romance, as I did, with the idea that it was all connected, that the fictional and the real-life, the past recalls and the future visions were all part of a Big Story, an Urtext that had evolved through ages. We itched to anthologize. We pushed to find a form that could encompass it all, preserving past work, layering on new ideas. You fell in love with our mission. Now, through my tear-stained eyes, I see that you also fell in love with me.

It was unfortunate about Liligh.

I was blind to the consequences of my desire for Liligh. It seemed like a perfectly natural, mutual attraction. Liligh was beautiful, strong, and creative. I loved her sculpture, the wild freeness of her work in stone. Liligh and I had a deep, loving bond. I may have been in my late fifties and twice her age, but I still had two-thirds of my life ahead of me.

Of course every partnership has its pet peeves. I hated sleeping with her in her studio, with all that chalk dust in the air, and the chisels and hammers and knives lying around. And Liligh never could see my work as a truly creative endeavor. She teased me about being a copyist, echoing others' words to make my own life complete. Unlike you, Liligh could not see the project as a wondrous entity, greater than the sum of its collected parts. She laughed when I showed her the structures you and I were constructing.

Perhaps, Dizalegh, it was your involvement in the project that made Liligh denigrate my work. Every time she met me at work and saw you there, it was guaranteed that Liligh would argue with me for the rest of the night about the superficiality of my career. It infuriated me, and I would defend your role in the work passionately. After all, we had been working together for twenty years!

One day, you discovered that for many of the stories, the teller explained what had triggered the recalling of the past life. These triggers, or glimpses into other time periods, came in many diverse ways, from hypnosis to visual textures in soapy water, birthmarks, out-of-body travel. We decided to list them all. Superimposing them onto the collection of tales, we created a cyclical structure from our list of one hundred and eleven glimpses.

"A hundred and eleven ways to have a déjà vu!" Sahara said.

"The qaraq has already experienced dozens of them," Zack said. "Don't you recognize hypnosis, my birthmark, or the soapy water from your supercontinent recall?"

"You think these triggers from our recalls suggest that Zizagh is researching a collection of our qaraq's lifetime stories?" Dr. Machiyoko asked.

"See what happens when I buy into the group's work?" Zack said. "I have an ego-driven fantasy of a magnum opus preserving our lifetimes. It's either the biggest case of cryptoamnesia yet or else it's a vision of a tome created about us in the future."

Dr. Machiyoko was not quite ready for this thought. "Why do you think I'm Dizalegh?"

"Dizalegh was a quiet, private soul, with a surprising, smoldering emotional core," he said. "Recognize anyone?"

The therapist was only half-convinced. "But we're such an odd match."

"Look at Amar and me," Sahara sighed. "If we're supposed to be the archetypal soul mates, we're sure blowing it."

"You're just evolving into some new form of soul mates," Dr. Machiyoko said.

"Yeah, that old 'kill a few hundred wives so the real one can step up to the plate' was getting stale," Zack joked.

"All I see is a stale pattern of high drama," Sahara said. "In your story, you two are finding an original path to love."

"The wheel turns," the therapist said. "One life you guys are breaking apart so you can come back stronger; another life Zack and I find a new niche for ourselves."

"Only to encounter our own high drama," Zack said. "Shall I continue?"

On the day we finished constructing the cycle of one hundred eleven glimpses, we were joyous. We reached out and touched each other's hand in innocent enthusiasm. At that moment Liligh showed up for dinner, already upset that I was working late. That night we fought as bitterly as ever. I had brought a pair of reading lenses with the work Dizalegh and I had just finished and Liligh was furiously jealous. She hurled hunks of stone and stray hammers across the studio/bedroom. I subdued her and we fell into a heated passion on the bed. Thinking we had resolved things, I put on the lenses to read.

As I lay there, Liligh continued to minister her charms on me. Fully aroused, I took off the reading lenses and put them on the bed. Then I saw Liligh reach for a stonecutting knife. She grabbed my swollen manhood in one hand and raised the knife in the other. With all her might she plunged the knife into the bed next to me, shattering the reading lenses. She stabbed at them a dozen times, then threw me out of the studio.

You had been smoldering with private rage against Liligh, for her insults to me, the endless fighting, the maddening distractions she imposed on the project. Furious at Liligh's final affront, you visited her studio and, with the same stonecutting knife, attacked her sculpture. When she tried to stop you, you chiseled away at her body, her hands, and her eyes, leaving her mutilated and blind.

All along I mistook your feelings, Dizalegh, for love of the souls whose lifetimes we cherished as if they were family. Once we read a tale of a couple whose love was only understood when they were reborn in a distant future lifetime. Had we lived this before? The mystical feelings bonded us closer and closer together, but I did not see your love burning bright until your fierce act of vengeance. Even worse, I did not recognize my own love for you, eclipsed by Liligh's youthful hold over me.

And now it is too late. When you returned we wept together for the gruesome unveiling of your love for me. We wept over my foolish epiphany that I was equally in love for you. And we wept that the authorities would take you away from me forever. I continued to cry for months afterward. Once I regained the illusion of stability, I was allowed to visit you in prison, since I needed your knowledge to complete my work. But I am inconsolable: our love will never be fully realized, our work never fully completed.

ق

"How incredibly sad," Dr. Machiyoko said. "You think you got it bad, Sahara? This is our future!"

"I'm not sure it's a precognition," Zack said. "I've never had one before."

"The story had those reading lenses, not books," Sahara said. "But the reading lens technology suggests the future. So does the reference to originals from the 21st Century."

"If you're to become the expert on glimpses into other times," Dr. Machiyoko said, "you should think about what triggered the story. Maybe it will clarify if it was a precog."

"I saw an image of an open book in front of me," Zack said. "I wasn't reading the book, it just hovered in the background as I heard the words in my head. The book felt symbolic to me, like it represented a whole lineage of story cycles like the Arabian Nights, but pointed ahead to this collection of lifetimes with a complex structure. It encompassed and surpassed the Nights."

Dr. Machiyoko suddenly sat up straight. "I bet your collection develops into the encoded Versions I envisioned. They're both a mix of the Nights and past life stories. My precog even mentioned one hundred and eleven glimpses! You saw the future, Zack!" The therapist's smile disappeared. "That means I'm going to jail."

"Who knows what will really happen," Sahara said. "There's still so much we don't know. We've remembered a slew of lifetimes, concocted tons of links between them, but there's still a thousand and one missing connections. It's hopelessly complicated."

"Hope is on the way!" Zack pulled out an enormous piece of paper from his bag. "Who else could find a delightful puzzle in this hopeless complication? Our very own dragonfly brain, Verle." Zack cleared aside coffee mugs from the dining table and unfurled a color-coded chart. "Verle reconstructed all the recalls the qaraq has had. The obvious pattern is that we've remembered lifetimes in recurring worlds, like Persia and Madagascar. How to organize the other worlds? Verle lifted some butcher paper and magic markers from the church's Sunday school and went to work on the problem. Look what he found!"

Zack finished unfolding Verle's giant chart with a flourish. Sahara and Diana marveled at a step-pyramid figure, with the number of the qaraq's lifetimes listed next to the worlds.

10 - Dragonfly
9 - The Red Isle
8 - Gondwanaland/pre-Stone Age
7 - Persia/Mideast
6 - 30 Years War/Donne Idea
5 - Borzu + North-South Winds
4 - Story collection or Interlife tales
3 - China, The Seven Palaces
2 - 1500s France or Suburb
1 - Tree or Atom tale
Plus: 15 - 'lives within present lifetime' stories

As Sahara and Dr. Machiyoko took a minute to absorb the chart Zack said, "We've told seventy-seven tales so far; that's the numbers seven and eleven multiplied again. It's all so special I could cry. I think collecting the qaraq's lifetimes into some sort of anthology is an amazing idea."

"Knowing there's some grand creation ahead gives me courage to deal with whatever drama is coming at us in the future," the therapist said.

"It gives me courage to face the endless lifetimes in my visions," Sahara said.

"I love it!" Zack said. "First of all, we all have to start keeping journals. I'll be happy to collect the qaraq's writings and put them together somehow."

"A self-fulfilling prophecy," Sahara said. "Now that I'm a free woman, I'll help out."

Dr. Machiyoko pointed to the chart. "Think about this. We know the dragonfly world had ten stories because there were ten of us who were the body parts. There were only nine lifetimes for the Red Isle because Porcy didn't recall one. But maybe she had a lifetime there. Maybe we're missing a couple stories for the eight-life world and so on."

"So Verle's chart is a road map to help us recall the next pieces of the puzzle. For example," Zack said, "there must be more elephant lives. And plenty involving *The Thousand and One Nights*. And the interlife. Anything is possible."

"No," Sahara said. "Everything is possible."

END OF PART THREE

THE END

APPENDICES

513

CHRONOLOGICAL ORDER OF LIFETIMES
(as far as the qaraq understands it)

The Tale of the Supercontinent   Formation of Earth, billions of years ago

The Tale of the Unborn   Carboniferous Period,

The Tale of the Clumsy Pollen Catcher   360 million years ago

The Tale of the Enamored Roots

The Tale of the Bituminous Coal Deposit

The Tale of the Settling of the South Pole

The Tale of the Ascension to the Fourth Level of Heaven

The Tale of the Swimming Insect   Permian Period, 286 MYA

The Tale of the Chitin Armor

The Tale of the Servant's Revenge

517

The Tale of the Corrupt Queen
The Tale of Queen D'aulai's
False Reign
The Tale of the Demise of the
Red Isle
The Tale of the Shipwrecked
Xalafon

Height of Phoenician trading, 1000 BCE

The Tale of the Two Winds

(next incarnations of Sahnra
and Ambanari?)

The Tale of the Escape Wind

The Tale of Uzmeth's First
Orgy
The Tale of Uzmeth and
Dinzadeh
The Tale of the Nighttime
Stalker
The Tale of Shah Zabar and
the Mystery Killer
The Tale of Sharzad and
Dinzadeh in the Alcove
Ardryashir's Tale
The Tale of the Elephant in
Baghdad

Sassanid Empire, 224-651 AD

Bahram IV, reigned 388-399
AD

379?

The Tale of the Seven Chinese
Palaces
The Tale of the Corruption of
the Seven Palaces
The Tale of Oolon's Revenge
in the Seven Palaces

(which Dynasty?)

The Tale of the Marriage of   Richelieu, 1585-1642
Silvie Saintonge
The Locksmith's Tale

The Tale of The Zyp   30 Years War, 1618-1648
The Tale of the Wartime
Hideout
The Tale of the Clinging Boy
and the Blue Elephant
The Tale of the Boy's Intrusion
into the Secluded Room
The Tale of the Deserting
Soldier
The Tale of the Secluded   John Donne, d. 1631
Room and The Idea

The Tale of Henry Whitelock   1806-1852
Torrens
The Tale of the Doomed Tree   Newark Railroad, 1856

The Tale of the Ugliest Bride   Verlin Walker, b. 1906
in New Orleans
The Tale of the Romance in   Diana Machiyoko, b. 1960
the Japanese Tea Garden
The Tale of the Three-Year   Sahara Fleming, b. 1970
Migration Pattern
The Tale of the Lost Soul
The Tale of the Wombat   Wombat Protection Laws,
                                  1978
The Tale of the Journey to the   Baxter Tenderheel,
East   b. 1978
The Tale of the Faithful Young   Ooma Qadir, b. 1981
Moslem and her Secret Book

The Message of Verlin Walker	Verle starts church job, 1990
The Tale of the Prodigal Son's Return from Paris	Porcy's reading of Zack, 1993
The Tale of Common Ground	Sahara meets Amar, 1996
The Tale of the Demon and the Pregnant Wife	Sahara/Amar move to NY, 1997
The Tale of Ardra and Solomon Rash	
The Tale of the Glenclaire Realtor	
The Tale of the Vision in the Attic	Porcy forms group, 1998
The Tale of the Five Women in the Celtic Cross	
The Tale of the Mi'raj of One Thousand and One	Naji Rash, b. 1999
The Tale of the Two Paths	(Future lifetimes?)
The Tale of Zizagh and Dizalegh	
The Tale of the Four Encoded Versions	

Unknown Chronology

The Tale of the Lovers' Spat
Between Two Atomic Particles
The Tale of Shaell and Arand's
Ultimate Happiness
The Tale of the Thirty-Seventh
Birtheve Surprise

INCARNATIONS
[brackets indicate this individual's story has yet to be
recalled]

Sahara (soul name: Sha)
    Vaalbara, primal landmass
    Interlife, third level of Heaven
    Dragonfly, nymph-body
    Borzi woman
    Sahnra, Goddess of the Red Isle
    The South Wind
    Sharzad, daughter of Sassanid vizier
    Silvie Saintonge, wife of French locksmith
    Sondre, refugee in 30 Years War
    Sahara Fleming, childhood migrations
    Sahara, Near Eastern Studies grad student, lover of Amar Rash
    Sahara, housewife
    Sahara, in a parallel lifetime
    Shaell Offmore, housewife, The Suburb

Amar
    Gondwanan at settling of South Pole
    Dragonfly, Chitin Armor

522

Borzu the Hunter
Ambanari, God of the Red Isle
The North Wind (Boreus)
Ardryashir, slave to Uzmeth
Deserting soldier, 30 Years War
Amar Rash, son of Solomon, grandson of Ardra
Arand Offmore, husband, The Suburb

Dr. Machiyoko
Dragonfly, Right Eye
D'n-Gwn, Gondwanan chosen by Licgh Nuo
D'aulai, Queen of the Red Isle
Dinzadeh, slave of Uzmeth
Deng She, seventh Chinese wife
Army camp follower, 30 Years War
Diana Machiyoko, first generation Japanese-American
[Dizalegh, future story collector]
Mmymch, Kr., future Versions researcher
Du, atomic particle

Zack
Dragonfly, Front Wings
Interlife, attached soul near Atlantis
Zancq, son of priestess of the Red Isle
Shah Zabar, Sassanid Prince
Dike, The Zyp, Low Countries
Doomed Tree, 19th Century Glenclaire
Zachary Goodkin, artifact collector and trader
Zizagh, future story collector
[Za, atomic particle]

Verle
Dragonfly, Brain
Sea Bird, end of Gondwanaland

Vaalat, xalaphon, antique Instrument of the Red Isle
Mr. V., victim of Ugly Curse
Verlin Walker, caretaker, Glenclaire Unitarian Church

Cachay
Dragonfly, Oversoul
Khajy, Queen of the Red Isle
Guilaum, French locksmith
Henry Whitelock Torrens, Anglo-Indian official and scholar

Naji
Dragonfly, Egg
Zanaj, the thief on the beach
Zananzi, African trader
Nils, six-year-old boy in 30 Years War
The Idea, Donne's room-as-the-universe
Naji Rash, enlightened fetus

Ooma
Ice Mountain, end of Gondwanaland
Dragonfly, Left Eye
Oumkratania, Queen of the Red Isle
Uzmeth, 140-year-old Sassanid Queen
Homma, elephant in medieval Baghdad
Oolon, Chinese aristocrat
Ooma Qadir, Iranian-American daughter

Bax (Bal)
Seed-bearing plant, Carboniferous Period
Animal Fossil, fused with Dragonfly fossil
Rival tribe member, disguised as Borzu
Roukh, ally of the Queens of the Red Isle
Ba'ash, slave and favorite of Uzmeth

Xa, Chinese Lord of the Seven Palaces
Interlife, Bal in despair
A Tasmanian wombat
Baxter Tenderheel, Coloradan runaway
Bax, handyman in Glenclaire

Porcy (Po)
Clumsy seed-bearing plant, Carboniferous Period
Plant fossilized into a vein of coal
Dragonfly, Back Wings
Porcelain Honeywell, Glenclaire realtor
Porcy, gatherer of people for past life work

Unknown
Dragonfly, Left Eye
[Ugrit, Phoenician trader]

ACKNOWLEDGEMENTS

My deepest gratitude goes to my wife Sarah St. Onge, for her affirming first read of the first draft, an act of true love, and to my editor Barry Jay Kaplan, who did everything in his power to teach me clarity and concision in the face of density and complexity. Much thanks to those along the way who helped me cross over from the sweet meadows of music to the choppy waters of book publishing: Barry Kaplan, Deborah Brevoort, Arielle Ekstut and David Henry Sterry, Eric von Lustbader, Peregrine Whittlesey, Stephen Zimmer, and the folks at CreateSpace. My spirit has received great daily support from the students and faculty at LaGuardia HS Dance Dept., especially its literati, Cedric Tolley and Carla Levy. I am indebted to Michelle Brock, for my first past life regression in this life. Finally, much love to my soul family, Sarah and Gabe, who have co-habited with the book for years on end.

My research sins are multifold, including sins of omission, lack of depth, and gratuitous inclusion, not for the sake of the story but my own fascination. I take sole responsibility, but would prefer to blame the following:

The Thousand and One Nights: Robert Irwin (his inestimable *The Arabian Nights Companion*), Muhsin Mahdi (his incomparable study, *The Thousand and One Nights*), Tahera Qutbuddin, Nadia Abbott, Eva Sallis, and the many fine translators, adaptors, and editors of the great story collection, Antoine Galland, Richard Burton, Edward Laine, John Payne, J.C. Mardrus, Powys Mathers, Husain Haddawy, Joseph Campbell, Jack Zipes.

Reincarnation, the Interlife, and Past Life Regression: Dr. Brian Weiss, Edgar Cayce, Michael Newton, Roy Steinman, Ursula Markham, Samantha Doane-Bates, Helen Greaves, Joseph Head and S.L. Cranston, David Hammerman and Lisa Lenard, Michael Hathaway, *The Tibetan Book of the Dead*, *The Egyptian Book of the Dead*, Sophy Burnham, Mary Roach, Wendy Doniger (*Karma and Rebirth in Classical Indian Traditions*), Carol and Philip Zalecki (*The Book of Heaven*).

Inspiring Literature: Ferdowski's *Shahnameh*, *The Thousand and One Nights*, and a few of its followers, Boccaccio, Calvino, Borges, Mahfouz, Rushdie, Robert Irwin; for Structural Genius, Joyce, Woolf, Faulkner, Yehoshua, Ryunosuke Akutagawa (*Rashomon*), Milorad Pavic, Jan Potocki (*Saragossa Manuscript*), Charles Palliser (*The Quincunx*); for Invention of Worlds, J.R.R. Tolkien, Frank Herbert, Terry Brooks, David Wingrove (The *Chung Kuo* series); for pioneering Karma Lit (along with myself), Anya Seton (*Green Darkness*), Joan Grant, David Mitchell (*Cloud Atlas*), Anne Brashares (*My Name is Memory*), M.J. Rose (*The Reincarnationist*); for other Unique Visions, Audrey Niffenegger (*The Time Traveler's Wife*), Katherine Neville (*The Eight*), and Jan Caldwell and Dustin Thomason (*The Rule of Four*).

Science: Stephen Hawking, James Gleick, Brian Greene (*The Fabric of the Cosmos*), Max Tegmark, Fred Alan Wolf, John Mcphee, Ted Nield (*Supercontinent*).

Exhibitions: Metropolitan Museum's Islamic Art Wing (and the visiting Louvre exhibit), Asia Society (Art of Sasanian Iran), Alhambra Museum in Granada, Spain.

History and Myth: John Teeple (*Timelines of World History*), Brigitte and Gilles Delluc (*Discovering Lascaux*), James Frazer (*The Golden Bough*), Henrietta Bernstein (*Cabalah Primer*), Robert Nevill Dick-Read ("The Phantom Voyagers," on the Indonesia-Madagascar connection), Stefan Härtel (Sasan), Iraj Bashiri (*Art of Sassanian Iran*), Gavin Menzies (*1421,* on the Chinese discovery of America), the Visitor's Center and L'Abbaye in Saintes, France, Glen Ridge Historical Society, Kenneth McLeish (*Myth*), and many sweet visits to Wikipedia.

Made in the USA
Charleston, SC
23 January 2014